Mouches Volantes

Eye Floaters
as
Shining Structure of Consciousness

Floco Tausin

Translated from German by Andreas Zantop

Leuchtstruktur Verlag

ISBN 978-3033003378

Copyright © 2009 Leuchtstruktur Verlag, Bern, Switzerland

Printed by
Lightning Source Inc., La Vergne, TN, USA
Lightning Source UK Ltd., Milton Keynes, UK

Contact and further information:
www.eye-floaters.info

Contents

Preface 7

Introduction 9

1

A Recalcitrant Secretaire 17

The Perfect Restoration 22

Dissolving the Small World in the Picture 30

Seeing the Picture as a Whole 37

The Attractive Force of Matter 44

Acquiring a Taste for It 53

The Afterimage of the Secretaire 66

2

Afterimages 78

Circular Figures with Double Membrane 89

Wanting to Know 101

The Inner Pressure and the Flow of Energy 118

Developing the Emotional Body 134

Dancing out of Mind 155

3

Mouches Volantes 175

The Emmental Cooking Pot 196

The Layers of Consciousness 214

Listening to the Rushing Sound 237

The Shining of the Basic Structure 262

4

The Right Side of Consciousness

The Bridge with the Double Arch 288

Iris the Seer 305

4

The Left Side of Consciousness

On the Bridge 329

The Navel 349

Preface

In ophthalmology, *mouches volantes* are free-floating particles in the eye's vitreous which impair the eyesight of the person affected. The common English term for these is »eye floaters«.

Such opacities of the vitreous can have different causes; in most cases they are age-related rather than pathological. In bright light conditions, the shadows of these particles are projected onto the light-sensitive retina and thus become visible to the viewer as small rings, dots and strands which appear to »fly« through the visual field, following the eyes' motions. Eye floaters are widespread, in itself harmless and not effectively treatable with our current medical means.

This explanation of *mouches volantes* makes sense to us, even if we are not ophthalmologists, because it refers to our everyday realm of experience accessible with our intellectual mind.

When the *eye floaters* attracted my attention for the first time, however, it happened in an environment that was quite different from that in which our everyday experiences take place. In this way, I was confronted with a totally different interpretation of these dots and strands floating before my eyes.

At this point in time, I had already learned the art of focused consciousness development from a person who lives in the remote solitude of the Emmental region in Switzerland. This man who calls himself Nestor, as well as my experiences in the vicinity of the headwaters of the Emme River, triggered a development within me which caused me to radically change my life habits and views of the world. In the course of this alternative way of living, my visual perception eventually changed as well: I began to see, and get to know, exactly these dots and strands. Ever since, the *eye floaters* are my object of study and concentration.

In a world dominated by materialism and rationality it is totally understandable that this phenomenon is interpreted as »particles in the eye«. Nestor counters these paradigms with his own uncommon experiences – experiences resulting from seeing the *mouches volantes*. *Seeing* in this case does not mean the ordinary sensual perception but an immediate realization beyond all rational thought, brought about by ecstasy techniques and resulting in an insight into a deep consciousness of the origin of what we call, and take for granted as, »our world«. In this sense, the act of seeing is directly related to the *mouches volantes*.

In this environment I tried to figure out whether there is more to the phenomenon of *mouches volantes* then just »particles in the eye« – in other words, whether it is possible to prove the main assertions in the teachings of the seer Nestor to be true: namely, that the *eye floaters* are the initial parts of a shining *basic structure* formed by our consciousness which organizes our everyday perception of objects in our field of vision, making them appear sensible; and that the mystical entering into one sphere of this structure will enable us human beings to maintain our consciousness beyond the point of physical death.

The discrepancy between »particles in the eye« and »shining structure of consciousness« is considerable so that both explanations can exist side by side, at best, in our rational thinking but not in our feeling and acting. This is important because the act of seeing, which is supposed to bring about insights into the phenomenon of *mouches volantes*, is not just an intellectual exercise;

rather, it requires an appropriate way of living. This novel is based on a true story and will give insights into the worldview and practice of that mystical way of living in which the notion of »particles in the eye« is, at best, a distraction from seeing, from directly seeing the shining structure of consciousness.

Introduction

The search for an old, no longer used piece of furniture which I intended to restore and sell led me to the upper midlands of the Bern region in Switzerland, that hilly landscape which connects the lowland with the Alps.

There, in the most remote part of the Emmental, near the headwaters of the Emme River, I hoped to find such a piece of furniture, no matter if it were a small cupboard, a chest of drawers or a little table, like they often stand around unused in the attics and sheds of the scattered farms.

As I drove up the valley on that Sunday, to the small remote village at the foot of the Hohgant mountain where I wanted to stop over and begin my search, the first thing I realized was that the land on both banks of the Emme River was unequally developed and populated. On the right side of the Emme, still »young« at this particular point, was the village, and the hillside had been cleared to make space for single farms and pasture farming.

The sloping hillside on the other, the left side, however, was virtually uninhabited. Instead, large areas of woods indicated extensive forestry use; only sporadically, bright green spots with a timber structure in the center stood out from the dark green surroundings.

In the village itself there wasn't much to find: a bus stop, a hairdresser, a small shop, a sawmill, a school with a gym and a few farmhouses – all close together.

One could literally smell that everyone around here knew everyone else. And when I met a villager of the elder generation on the street, I was immediately involved in a casual chat about all the world and his wife, after which I knew: in comparison to the lowland, the winter arrived here earlier, brought along more snow and lasted longer; and in the summer, *Höiete*, the Swiss term for haying, took place only twice. The people up here were not as spoiled as those on the broad valley floors who were able to harvest hay three or even four times a year.

Some of the older inhabitants seemed to cherish the peace in this remote valley. The majority of residents, however, actively participated in the ongoing club life of the village, of which all the trophies, medals, carvings, tin cups, photos of proudly posing yodelers and choristers in the glass cabinets of the only pub in the village gave testimony. In the evening, I visited this pub and asked the guests on what farms I might be able to find a suitable piece of furniture which would conform to my ideas. This I did after I had canvassed the widely scattered farms in the vicinity of the village all day long, only to meet cautious reluctance and distrust. Either the people had no time or no piece of furniture they were willing to let go of, or they had neither one of these.

The only visitors at this early evening time were sitting at a round table in the corner – four older gentlemen who had come together to play cards and exchange news. Contact was quickly established, my request swiftly explained. The gentlemen were glad to help me with their knowledge, but at first they only named farms I had already visited. This went on for quite a while until one of them came up with the idea that I should try my luck on the other side of the Emme. All four of them started laughing so that I had to inquire how serious they were with this particular tip.

»Out there on the other side are only woods and stones and marshy meadows,« one of them said with a loud voice, dismissing my ideas and aspirations.

»And goblins,« his neighbor joked, a man who was called »Hänsu« by everyone.

The man who gave me the tip explained that there are indeed a few houses on the other side. »There are five properties,« he knew and took a big puff from his fat cigar. »But the people living there rarely show up. Those are townspeople who only spend a few weekends out here in the summer.«

Another man whose face was visibly reddened vigorously threw down one of his playing cards and disagreed with the first man: according to him, he had seen these people in the village during the deepest winter months as well. He also knew that one of them was an artist who used to exhibit, every now and then, paintings and sculptures in this pub and others in the region.

»Anyway, they own the entire land over there,« the man added who so far had said nothing. »But they don't do anything with the land. They just leave it fallow.« He seemed uncertain with his words and, while speaking, looked over to the man with the reddened face. The latter took the bait and got all worked up about the fact that these people would not even clean their woods – which in turn caused all the other gentlemen to join in and rant about the disrespect and laziness of those people on the other side.

»Guess they're staring into the blue all day,« Hänsu called out, to the amusement of everyone present. In any case: at the end of this short discussion they all agreed on the fact that it was a *cheibe Züüg*, a *nuisance* with tourists of that kind, and Hänsu, reminded by the others that it was his turn, ordered four more glasses of beer.

The next day I decided to drive over onto the other side of the Emme and to try my luck there. Perhaps I was encouraged by Hänsu's remark that the people on the other side might leave their furniture in the same unused state as their land – which he didn't mean serious of course. I crossed the Emme, and for a while I drove on a narrow, untarred road through thick fir woods. Eventually, the way led me to a smaller farmhouse which looked visibly different from the farms on the right side of the Emme: no open doors and gates were to be seen, no equipment was standing around, no orderly heaped-up dunghill could be smelt, no geraniums were gracing the windows – the property yielded an unusually empty and vacated impression. Instead, a large window pane, obviously built in some time after the house had been erected, extended nearly across the entire façade of the house facing the valley.

I knocked on the door. No one opened. I peeked through the tinted window pane, but all I could see was a closet and a bed next to a tiled stove. Then I opened the door to the stable and looked around. There was no cattle inside, just a few bales of straw and a workbench with all kinds of tools covered with dust on it. A strangely familiar smell entered my nose – an aromatic scent like perfume.

The moment I wanted to leave the stable, my eyes were caught by something dark which was concealed behind the bales of straw – the contours of an object which I couldn't identify from the distance.

Seized by an insatiable curiosity, I moved the bales towards the side and revealed something which struck me at first glance: it was actually an old piece of furniture in need of restoration. But it was so unusual that I had a difficult time to determine what exactly it was that I had there before me.

The striking feature of this piece of furniture was that its upper part consisted of three steps with rounded edges. It reminded me of a stepped pyramid resting on four legs: from the bottom up, length and width of each step were shortened, whereas the height, in turn, increased; the uppermost part was the highest. Way over on the left side, a large sphere was prominently projecting out of the wood, giving this piece of furniture a striking asymmetry. Its back side was flat – a step pyramid longitudinally cut in half.

So, according to its form it was most likely a secretaire: one could sit down in front of it and use the lowest part as writing surface. But there were no small doors or cabinets, no shelves for books in the upper parts, and the piece of furniture didn't keep its width upwards, either. Instead, in each of the three parts of the secretaire two drawers were built in side by side – so it could have been a kind of commode as well. The strange thing, though, was that the handles of five drawers were missing. There were no signs, either, that these drawers ever had a handle attached to them in the past. Only the drawer way down on the right side had such a handle, but it couldn't be pulled out. Same with the other drawers: they couldn't be opened. My guess was that they simply jammed because they were warped due to old age.

The secretaire was made of massive oak. And, aside from the delicate inlays and legs adorned with elaborate carvings which obviously were added later, it was made of one single piece of wood – the trunk of a gigantic oak tree. This was extremely rare, and I knew that this rarity could be sold at a high price. There was hardly any practical use to this piece of furniture, though: a commode with six drawers which became smaller and smaller on the way up, with only one drawer designed to be opened, did not really imply the intention to optimally utilize available stowing space. No, this piece of furniture was solely an object of art.

The thick layers of dust and cobwebs indicated that the secretaire had been standing in this corner for quite a while. Put aside and then forgotten. But, as far as I could judge, it was still in a fairly good condition: here and there, some holes and scratches were visible; a few pieces of those prominent carvings on the two right side legs were broken off, the inlays were damaged in a few spots, the only drawer handle was rusty and had to be replaced. The whole thing was about a one-week job, perhaps ten days, I estimated.

When I glided over the secretaire with my hands, I revealed the name of the former owner and a date under the dust and dirt covering the lowest right hand drawer, written in dark-yellow German type letters and surrounded by lavishly elaborate flower ornaments:

Mari Egli 1888

My heart started pounding. I was convinced that I had made the discovery of the century with this extraordinary piece of art. Absorbed in my thoughts, I walked towards the stable door, and only then did I see the man in the door frame which I suddenly stood right in front of. I was startled and cringed which in turn made the man laugh. In my embarrassing confusion I started to stutter out excuses for my intrusion.

The man, however, didn't seem to be interested in my explanations. Instead, he noticed that this particular piece of furniture might have a certain appeal to me. I confirmed this and hastened to enumerate the amenities of that beautiful secretaire – until I recalled the reason for my being there. Consequently, I also pointed out all the deficiencies and relativized my interest in the object so as to be able to beat down the price, in case we would arrive at a purchase agreement.

The man was silent. For a moment, we looked each other over. He was of middle age, slim, but made a physically strong impression. The most striking features of his face were his pronounced nose, his full lips and his three-day beard.

Black curly hair protruded from under his gray brown felt hat. The clothes he wore were different from the common collar shirts and woolen pullovers of the local inhabitants. He was wearing a white long-sleeved undershirt with a dark green, sleeveless jacket over it. His hands were hidden in the pockets of his white jeans.
And the black rubber boots, stained with soil, indicated that the man sometimes moved around in marshy terrain.

I introduced myself and told him that I'm living and studying in Bern. With a certain feeling of pride, I added that restoring and selling furniture would be a part-time occupation of mine. He replied that his name was Nestor.

For a while we informally talked about furniture and its restoration. In the course of our conversation, it turned out that he was the owner of the house, and that he himself also was familiar with furniture restoration. He didn't seem to know much about Mari Egli and the piece of art in his stable; it had already been there when he purchased and took over the house, he added.

Finally I told Nestor that I would be interested in the secretaire. I deliberately did not mention anything about purchasing or paying, because I knew that people sometimes appreciate it when they can get rid of their rummage for free. Nestor, however, did not want to give the object away. He explained that Mari Egli's secretaire belongs to this place and nowhere else. I tried to talk it over with him, but he was stubborn and didn't want to change his mind. When I started to mention money and payment, he abruptly ended our conversation by wishing me a good evening and disappearing in his house.

On this day I returned to the village with empty hands, but I decided to stay another night. I was confident that I could persuade Nestor to sell the secretaire, after all, because my impression was that he was not really interested in that piece of art, and that he simply tended to stick to his possessions – even if that was old useless rummage.

So, on the following day I again drove up the left side of the Emme, to that piece of furniture that I wanted to have, by all means. Nestor, however, rebuffed me another time.

»I don't understand you,« I told him, »you could benefit from it.«

»You really don't seem to understand,« he replied. »This particular piece of furniture is not restored that easily. It requires a high degree of attention to handle it correctly. If you are missing that attention, this piece of furniture would rather cause more harm than benefit.«

»I'll take care not to damage it. I'm always alert and mindful,« I assured him. Nestor remained silent, and so I kept talking at him.

»You don't have to make a decision right away,« I finally said. »I can come back later, once you've made up your mind. I can wait, no problem.«

Nestor looked at me inquiringly. »You can? How long can you wait, what do you think?«

I shrugged; his question came as a surprise to me.

»Well, let's say till tonight?« My idea was that I would spend the intervening time down at the pub, getting a good meal and reading some papers.

»That's not much time.« Nestor shook his head, then he said it would be time for me to go.

To me, Nestor's attitude was somewhat provocative. I wanted to show him that I'd be able to wait for a longer period of time. So, a week later I returned to the Emmental and asked him once more to sell that secretaire. Nestor was, in my view, a smart wheeler dealer: he kept me in suspense so as to push up the price of the object. He could afford it because he had quickly realized how much I cared about that secretaire.

Consequently, Nestor was not surprised at all when we met again. I tried to convince him with logical arguments, explaining that he'd no longer need that piece of furniture, anyway, that it would just rot in this place, that I could restore the secretaire to something valuable and useful, and that I would pay generously for it.

And as I expected, he finally relented. We agreed on confirming the deal in writing. However, Nestor named two prerequisites that had to be fulfilled, no fail, before he would sell the secretaire. The first prerequisite was unusual and laborious: he insisted that the restoration be done here on his property. This meant that I would not be able to have the object at my disposal until the restoration would finally be completed. In addition, he demanded that no one else than I was supposed to work on it. I pointed out that it would be too expensive and time-consuming to me to drive from Bern into the Emmental every day, but Nestor offered me a room on the upper floor of his house where I could live for free as long as I would work on the restoration. To me, this was an inconvenience I readily accepted, knowing the secretaire would be mine once the restoration was finalized. Nestor's second prerequisite, however, was not the least bit surprising to me: cash in advance.

1

A Recalcitrant Secretaire

On the following Monday, I started with the restoration of Mari Egli's secretaire. I assumed that I could restore it back to an impeccable and sellable condition within ten days – but that soon turned out to be impossible.

To my chagrin, Nestor frequently intervened into my way of going about the restoration from the beginning, without me having asked him to do so. This was not only insulting, as he questioned my skills in this way, but also annoying because it mixed up my habitual work rhythm and delayed the outcome. When I tried to talk him out of his frequent interventions, he immediately reminded me of the terms and conditions of our purchase agreement: he, and only he, had the secretaire at his disposal until the restoration was completed. I had no choice than to yield to his terms. As an example, on the very first day already, he forbade me to use an electric sander. Nestor seemed to attach great importance »to me restoring the piece of furniture »under my own steam«; he said any and all energy I invested into the secretaire had to be my own.

The actual reason, however, why the restoration took longer than I expected was not Nestor's frequent intervening but a phenomenon of a totally different nature: working on this particular piece of furniture seemed to have an adverse affect on my physical condition so that I was forced, time and again, to take longer breaks.

On the first day, when I applied the lye solution to one side of the object to strip dirt and varnish off of it, a strange kind of tiredness overcame me. With each stroke of the brush, my arms became heavier, my movements slower. I was affected by some kind of drowsiness which I sometimes experienced after a rich meal or on a boring rainy Sunday afternoon. Too often, I had to leave the stable to stretch my legs or to sit down on the bench in front of the house. There I was searching for reasons which could explain my weak condition, and I blamed myself for the frequent slowdowns and interruptions which delayed the restoration. I was upset that I couldn't strip the varnish off of the secretaire in one go: when the lye solution dried for too long, scraping it off was more laborious and took longer.

Due to this persistently recurring drowsiness I needed all day to apply the white smeary liquid onto one side of the secretaire again and again, but I could scrape off only parts of it. And at night, when I wanted to retreat back to my room, I was annoyed by Nestor's question, certainly well-intended, whether I had made any progress. Back in my room, I ate some of the food I had brought along with me and went to bed early.

The next morning, Nestor was nowhere to be seen. Perhaps he had gone somewhere or he was still asleep. But actually it was quite alright with me that I was able to start my work without having to exchange trite banalities with him.

In the stable I proceeded to apply varnish remover on the remainder of the side I had started with. Initial feelings of success made the drowsiness of the previous day seem to be an exceptional experience. But then, all of a sudden, scraping off the varnish with a spatula and fine steel wool caused a strange dispersal of my attention. My thoughts started to flow and carried me away farther and farther, just as if I was close to falling asleep. The moment this entered my consciousness I tried to resist it, tooth and nail, and forced myself once more into concentrating on the job to be done. But in the further course of my work, this unpleasant state of dispersal extended all over my body in a drastic way: my pulse quickened and caused me to breathe faster. My hands started trembling. Frightened, I ran out of the stable where the trembling ceased as soon as it had started. My breath came back to normal, my body started to relax.

What had happened? This sudden uncontrollable state of my physical functions was alarming. Perhaps a dizzy spell or some sort of sudden qualm, I calmed myself down; after all, I rarely had a real breakfast in the morning. And as it was almost lunchtime anyway, I decided to get something to eat.

After lunch I resumed my work. But I had hardly picked up the spatula again when the next wave of this strange uncontrollable state came over me: my body heated up and started to quiver and tremble. All hyper, I staggered outside and plunged into the grass. My breath went so fast as if I had run around for hours like a madman. For a while, I kept lying in the grass so as to catch my breath.

I didn't realize that Nestor was present until he bent over me. He was wearing a hat, and the leather bag hanging over his shoulder was filled with something. He raised his eyebrows and looked at me questioningly.

I sat up straight, still trembling and nervous. I was embarrassed that he had found me lying in the grass the way I did. I told him that I didn't feel particularly well. And as I was afraid that he might be alarmed at my strange behavior, I explained to him – with a confidence and conviction that was unusual for me – that everything was alright; I merely had suffered a dizzy spell, stuff like that happens.

Nestor dropped his bag and crouched down beside me. He didn't put up with my excuses; rather, he wanted to know exactly what had happened.

»That was no dizzy spell,« he disagreed after I had reluctantly described the symptoms to him. »A dizzy spell manifests itself in a complete *loss* of strength. Then everything turns black before your eyes and you just collapse. But in your case it is rather that *too much* energy has flown through your body – more than it is able to stand.«

»How can it be that too much energy is flowing through my body?« I asked surprised.

He looked over to the stable thoughtfully. »Perhaps that secretaire is causing you some discomfort or qualms,« he replied and finally laughed.

I couldn't laugh about his joke but had to admit that he was right: these strange fear-instilling conditions did indeed show up only when I was busy restoring the secretaire. I got up, assured Nestor that it was nothing serious and went up to my room. There I laid down on the bed and searched for explanations for these strange fits and attacks; I thought I was able to recall similar conditions heralding a flu or other illnesses.

Time went by, but the symptoms didn't flare up anymore, and no fever broke out. I no longer suffered from any discomfort. In the evening I said goodbye to Nestor and drove home, just to be on the safe side.

In the week following these events, I was well and in good health. So I decided to drive out to Nestor on the weekend to resume the restoration. But the disillusion was sobering: I had hardly started to apply the lye solution onto the side of the secretaire when the exact same symptoms showed up again and kept me from scraping off the white mass. And again, it started with an impairment of my ability to concentrate, followed by the quickened pulse, the faster breathing, the heat within my body and the trembling – all this was so intense again that I didn't have a snowball's chance in hell of continuing my work. For a while I tried to defy the physical signs, but a sudden piercing pain in my abdomen almost took my breath away and drove me out of the stable, writhing.

I tried to grasp the phenomenon: perhaps it had to do with some form of electromagnetic radiation. Maybe there was some kind of electronic device somewhere in the stable which was the cause of my physical and mental complaints; some apparatus emanating some sort of radiation, perhaps strong electromagnetic waves, to which I reacted with allergic-like symptoms. I searched through the entire stable two, three times, but I couldn't find anything. To be sure for real, I wanted to take the secretaire outside, but I realized that merely trying to move this piece of furniture caused my body functions to go on strike again. And my suspicion that this particular electronic device could possibly be found in the secretaire itself could not be confirmed. Because, all the drawers jammed and could not be opened, as I already had found out. I abstained from taking violent measures in order to open them; too strong was my fear of damaging this rare piece of art which might have reduced or even wiped out its value. But this notion of an electronic device installed in a piece of furniture which generated intense waves or vibrations, strongly perceptible to me, had captured me – only to be confirmed every time when my body was coming up against its limits.

I spent the rest of the day trying to get to the bottom of these strange physical sensations. I resisted the notion, though, that the symptoms were caused by my restoration work on the secretaire. To disprove this, I tried all possible and conceivable things in sort of an insane game: did the sensations really show up every time I was working on the object? Did it play a role what part of the secretaire I was working on? How fast I was moving to go about the restoration? Or what tools I was using?

After a number of attempts I couldn't deny any longer that my body reacted adversely to each new activity of mine on the secretaire. Merely touching it didn't cause any sensation. But as soon as I exerted some slight pressure on the surface by moving the brush or the spatula, a queasy feeling took possession of me which quickly escalated to become uncontrollable. So was it possible at all that some device, hidden in the object, could cause these strange phenomena? Perhaps that device emanated its radiation in periodic intervals?

I couldn't find any peace of mind until I knew exactly how far I could go: so I moved the secretaire in a series of little steps, covered it with plastic wraps, attached the brush to a long stick to be able to apply the lye solution from a longer distance, tried to scrape off, time and again, the dried substance with different tools – none of it helped.

At the end of this evening, I had to admit that the restoration work on Mari Egli's secretaire was so exhausting that it was virtually impossible to continue the job. My only explanation for this curious phenomenon was that certain rays or vibrations caused this particular effect, even if that raised new questions for which I couldn't come up with an answer: was it possible at all that some kind of vibration or radiation could have such an immediate and drastic effect on a human being? If so, was it possible to house a device with this energy output in such a small space like that of my secretaire? And how in the world did a device with that power fit into a piece of furniture aged more than 100 years, the drawers of which just couldn't be opened?

The Perfect Restoration

On the next day, I tried my luck on the secretaire again, but the result was the same. The rest of the morning I sat in the stable, perplexed and helpless. I saw no other way out than to ask Nestor if I could take the secretaire along with me, home to my place. My idea was: once I had it at home with me, it would be child's play to find out whether, and if so, how the object caused effects in other people. All I'd have to do was ask a friend to give me a helping hand with the restoration work.

Of course I hadn't forgotten the written agreement between Nestor and me: the restoration had to take place on his premises exclusively. But I was confident that I would eventually be able to convince him, all the more because there was no cogent reason for his request – except perhaps that, as a former restorer, he wanted to take a look over my shoulder to play a part in the job by giving me hints and tips, but at the same time voicing his requests and assuming a certain air of importance. The upcoming lunchtime seemed a favorable occasion for me to discuss it with him.

Nestor had cooked some potatoes for us. He poured them onto a quartz glass plate, chopped them up coarsely, seasoned them and spread some diced cheese and herbs over them. I myself wanted to contribute some cold meat to our lunch, but Nestor informed me with a derogatory comment on the consumption of meat that he was one of those more stubborn vegetarians. So for a while we were engaged in a discussion over the consumption of meat, in the course of which he did not deviate a fraction of an inch from his position, namely that the consumption of meat was a big error in our society, and that human beings on a higher awareness level had canceled meat from their diet. And although this was not the first discussion I had on the subject – believing I had steeled myself against all possible arguments of vegetarians – he somehow managed to instill a bad conscience in me. So at the end of our lunch I decided to postpone the discussion about taking the secretaire home with me until the evening.

When I had finished lunch, Nestor unexpectedly asked me about the progress of my restoration work.

»So-so,« I said halfheartedly.

»What do you mean: so-so?«

»I need longer than I had expected.«

»Then Mari Egli's secretaire is causing you some trouble,« he concluded.

I hesitated before answering. The straightforward way with which he voiced his words prompted me to seriously consider the possibility that he knew exactly what my problem was – either he was familiar with the phenomenon or he was the one who caused the trouble all along.

»I'm just not used to these particular surroundings,« I lied.

Nestor looked at me penetratingly. »So you want to take the secretaire along with you,« he concluded quite correctly.

I told him that I just couldn't concentrate on the job in this place, adding as possible reasons the cooler temperature and the more humid climate conditions. »At home, I'd be able to work faster,« I tried to make him believe.

»So it's supposed to go fast, « he soberly stated.

»I don't want to spend the rest of my life with this particular restoration,« I justified myself. Nestor smiled and scraped off the last remnants of food from the plate.

»Can I take the secretaire home with me?« I finally asked.

»Forget it.« He looked at me as if I had illegally trespassed holy ground. With his adamant voice and admonishing look, he stripped me of any hope that I might be able to convince him.

»We have an agreement, don't you remember?« he added. »Once the restoration of the secretaire is completed, you can do with it whatever you like.«

»Why is it so important to you that the restoration takes place here?« I asked him after a while.

Nestor didn't answer, and at that moment I believed to know intuitively why he was refusing to leave the secretaire at my disposal: for sure he was a lonely man; perhaps he had withdrawn into this remote solitude because life and his experiences with people had been just too disappointing for him. Understandably though, he was longing for company. And that was the reason why he had chosen these particular terms and conditions for the sale of the secretaire, because I would be forced to visit him in regular intervals. He was smart and cunning.

Of course, I didn't tell him all this directly; I just implied that I would still come around and visit him, even when the secretaire was over in my place.

»So gsehsch uus – a likely story!« he answered, put his plate aside and leaned relaxed against the wall. But then he seemed to think it over.

»Do you think,« he asked, »that you can load the secretaire into your car at all?«

»If you help me lift it – why not?« I asked back, ignoring the thought that virtually every contact with the object caused my body to shiver and tremble. I had to keep a straight face now and not show any weakness – not right now, the very moment he started to give in.

»Well all right,« he relented. His sudden change of mind made me a little suspicious, but I believed he realized that his demands were no longer tenable. As a gesture of friendship, I offered him some chocolate, but he refused to accept it.

We went over to the stable were Nestor took a look at the secretaire. With his hand, he glided over the dried and partially scraped off lye solution.

»That looks like a battlefield,« he remarked.

»Not for much longer,« I replied with regained self-confidence.

I drove the car under the roof of the stable, as close to the door as possible. Together, we lifted the secretaire and started to move it towards the door slowly. The car was right nearby, just a short distance, and I was confident we would make it. But after taking the first few steps, all my confidence vanished: an ominous feeling of fullness spread throughout my abdomen. It was a feeling of pressure which quickly intensified so that I was not able to take a deeper breath.

I continued to keep a straight face, as best as I could. My eyes were fixed on the surface of the secretaire, and I tried not to feel anything but rather just to »function« so as to get the job done. My feet became heavy like lead, but still I went on: another step, and my body turned hot; one more step, and my arms and legs started to tremble; and yet another step, and my strength finally seemed to leave my body altogether.

»It's enough.«

As if speaking from a far distance, Nestor's voice penetrated the mist of my illusions and banished my delusory idea of being unsusceptible to these strange phenomena. For a moment, I didn't know whether his command was directed towards me or the secretaire. In any case, his words made me give up my fixed stare onto the object. It was like a release, but his words made me realize that I also had to admit my defeat. We carefully put down the secretaire – and I was close to fainting.

Trying to catch my breath, I sat down on the ground. Thoughts rushed through my head like crazy. It was upsetting to me that he had to intervene the way he did; I felt like a little child that needs to be shown its limits because it is yet unable to determine how far it can go before overstraining itself.

»Did you feel that, too?« I gasped.

Nestor wanted to know what particular physical inconveniences I was experiencing, then he answered that he had felt nothing of the sort. I asked him once more and tried to get him to speak up. I just couldn't imagine that he hadn't experienced the same strange symptoms I felt. Nestor, however, answered that he didn't have a problem at all with a small piece of wooden furniture like this one, and that he was far from having his legs turn to jelly over it.

»The way it looks, you lose to the secretaire,« he said and sat down on one of the bales of straw. »This particular object demands quite a bit of you – more than you are used to invest in an ordinary restoration job, and more than you are able to give in your current condition. That creates the conflict you experience. Your skills do not suffice for the restoration of this particular secretaire.«

»Nonsense, this has nothing whatsoever to do with my skills as a restorer,« I answered angrily, surprised by his naivety. With all my patience, I tried to get across to him that I was indeed capable of working with wood and restoring old pieces of furniture. If I failed on this one, it had nothing to do with me and my skills. In this context, I also voiced my suspicion that there must be some kind of electronic device inside the secretaire which impaired my physical functions.

»An electronic device in a piece of furniture from the 19th century?« Nestor shook his head in disbelief.

»Someone must have installed it somewhere inside.«

He looked at me skeptically. »And you think I have actually placed something like that inside this secretaire?«

I kept silent.

»Forget it. Instead of cooking up conspiracy theories, you had better make up your mind how to deal with that pressure the secretaire is generating within you.«

»Pressure? How can a piece of furniture generate pressure within me? That's impossible,« I replied, slightly desperate.

Nestor laughed, and his laughing made me angry. This was the beginning of a longer discussion between us. I blamed him for having known all about it, and in my raging anger I even accused him of having committed the crime of physical injury. I tried to get him to confess that he had somehow manipulated the secretaire – or at least, that it was a certain force independent from me which had an impact on me from outside my body, barring me from continuing my work. Nestor, however, kept asserting that my potential success in the restoration was a question of my own energy level with which I could withstand that particular pressure. It was obvious that we had our wires crossed. But I was suspicious that he was deliberately beating around the bush.

Right in the middle of our dispute, I realized that I was arguing with him. I did this as a matter of fact, as if I had known him for a long time already. I fell silent immediately – it was embarrassing to me.

»I just don't understand what's happening,« I said, after calming down again. »If you know anything about it, Nestor, then please tell me.«

Nestor looked at me serenely. »Basically we are being confronted with ourselves all the time,« he started philosophizing. »But because we don't realize that, we tend to make differences. It's for this reason alone that certain objects or people exert more influence on us than others, consciously or unconsciously. So if you look at a beautiful piece of art, it can cause certain feelings in you. Or when you have your favorite dish in front of you and you smell how good it will taste, then quite a few happy hormones will be released, and your mouth begins to water. In the same way, looking at an attractive human being can trigger feelings of joy and happiness in your body.«

»It's not about releasing feelings of happiness. This object makes me gasp for air, and I can't hold my hands still any longer,« I stated with a dry voice.

»That's what can also happen to you when you look at a beautiful being,« Nestor said and grinned. But then he admitted that Mari Egli's secretaire was indeed quite extraordinary – the way it obviously had an impact on me spoke for itself.

I was fed up listening to him. Obviously, Nestor wasn't willing to help me. And somehow he was able to hold his point of view – that I myself caused these extreme physical conditions – with more conviction than I was able to hold my viewpoint. Annoyed and upset, I left the stable and spent the time until the evening in my room where I tried to find reasonable answers to what had happened.

In the evening I once more talked to Nestor about the recent events. He sat on his bed next to the oven and looked out the large window, as if mesmerized. The evening had set in, and across the valley a beautiful romantic atmosphere had spread. The setting sun made everything glow: sky, mountains and hills.

I informed Nestor that I had no use for a piece of furniture which I neither could restore nor transport. I thus demanded back the 600 Swiss Francs I had paid him for the secretaire.

Nestor complained in a tone of voice which I couldn't really take serious: he lamented that, given these business terms and conditions, he would never get anywhere. I wasn't in the mood for jokes and repeated my request.

»You're giving up too soon,« he replied with a smooth voice. »There is, despite everything, a possible way to restore Mari Egli's secretaire.« For a moment, he wrapped himself in a mysterious silence and kept looking out the window. Then he started talking about an approach that would enable me to learn the trade in such a way that I knew my craft and became a complete master at it. In the course of this, I learned to focus all of my attention on the secretaire and thus were able to cope with the pressure of the object. Nestor emphasized several times that I had to perform this *perfect restoration* in order to be successful in my endeavors.

I shrugged. Of course I firmly believed that each and every restoration I had ever done on a piece of furniture up to that point had been complete and perfect.

»That's not the same,« Nestor replied. »The perfect restoration isn't just about stripping varnish, sanding surfaces and replacing broken parts. Rather, it demands the highest degree of attention of you in everything you do.«

»I'm always alert and watchful when I'm working on the secretaire.«

»Not alert and watchful enough,« he countered. Now he turned towards me and looked at me penetratingly. »If you were, then you would realize how this pressure that you can feel comes about. And then you would approach the secretaire in a different way.«

»How does the pressure come about?«

»You impose your expectations and ideas on the object. With that approach, you're trying to see this piece of furniture as something which it is not. This is what you always do, with all objects, and with people as well. Mari Egli's secretaire, however, is like a mirror: it reflects the energy of your ideas and concepts directly back to you.

The crucial question is: what exactly do you impose on the object; what kind of ›input‹ is it? As soon as you realize this and change your approach, what will reflect back to you will change as well. In this sense, the ›perfect restoration‹ means that you engage in a serious and thorough exchange between you and this object.«

I was dismayed. What Nestor was telling me was sheer nonsense, some kind of weekend esotericism, at best. According to his words, the »perfect restoration« would turn me into one of those »love and light« characters who were mostly concerned with sending out their »positive energies« into the world so as to prevent wars and other catastrophes.

»This is my offer to you,« Nestor went on, noting my irritated silence. »Everything else you'll have to find out for yourself.«

»And what exactly is this perfect restoration about?«

»It is a totally different way of approaching the piece of furniture when restoring it,« he answered. »This is all you have to know for now.«

This prospect caused a certain reluctance and antagonism within me. After all, I wanted to restore and sell a piece of furniture – and not spend an eternity with a new and, on top, esoteric method of restoration.

I dared to make an advance: »How about if *you* restored the secretaire? I'll provide you with all my tools and take care of the sale afterwards. We share the proceeds 50% for me, 50% for you, what do you think? That would be much easier for both of us.«

Nestor kept silent for a while, and I believed he was thinking my proposal over carefully. But then he reminded me that it was my secretaire, and I had to restore it all by myself.

»Instead of wasting thoughts about how much money you will be able to make with the secretaire, you should begin to work on the perfect restoration. If you focus your full attention on the object exclusively, you'll be able to restore it.«

I was suspicious. Once again, I had to think of the possibility that Nestor had installed some kind of electronic device in the secretaire. The notion crossed my mind that the next thing he would do was to sell me a course teaching an allegedly safe method of restoration which would bear fruit for sure – precisely the moment he turned off that device.

»How did you get to know about this perfect restoration?« I asked him skeptically.

»I've learned the trade.«

»Did you just learn the method, or did you develop it yourself?«

Nestor wasn't willing to talk about it. He said that this particular knowledge wasn't helpful in getting the perfect restoration done.

I asked him how much he would charge if he taught me the perfect restoration. I was in an awkward position because I had no idea at all how much such a course would usually cost. But all that Nestor replied was that there's always work to do around his house. I was uncertain. When I told him that I would drive home first of all and think it over, he just smiled.

»Come back soon,« he prompted me. »We have already started with the perfect restoration.«

Dissolving the Small World in the Picture

Actually I didn't have a choice. Neither was I able to restore this particular piece of furniture, nor could I transport it or do anything else with it as long as it wasn't my property. And, according to the terms and conditions of our contract, the secretaire was not my property until the restoration was completed. There was no doubt on my part that Nestor was behind all this, and that he himself had »engineered« the whole thing. He left me with only two choices: to forget the whole thing or to accept his approach, the perfect restoration. Despite all my reservations about Nestor and his behavior, I decided to at least give his method a try: after all, 600 Swiss Francs was quite a bit of money which I couldn't afford to waste in a careless manner.

On the next weekend, I obtained a first impression of what Nestor called the »perfect restoration«. And what he showed me already on the first day with a piece of wood was remarkable: he was extremely adept at using tools effectively. His motions differed from mine; they were stronger but at the same time more economical in terms of effort, and more targeted. Saw, file and sandpaper – Nestor held them all loosely in his hands, and yet he controlled them with a high degree of precision. In the afternoon of the same day, I tried out the new techniques, but I had a harder time than I expected, to saw, file and sand like Nestor.

At dinner time I expressed my respect for his craftsmanship and my confidence that Mari Egli's secretaire could be restored swiftly, applying these particular techniques.

»It's not just about technique,« Nestor replied to my surprise. »The work on the object is but a small part of the perfect restoration. Much more important is with how much attention and presence you can get the work done. Your motions will change as soon as you yourself change.«

»Change myself? So you really believe that this trembling and throbbing will cease once I'll change myself?«

»Yes.«

»And how should I go about changing myself, according to you?«

»You should stop to always ›make the most‹ of those things you're dealing with. And you should become a little bit more generous,« he answered. I laughed because Nestor's words seemed just like idle talk to me. He laughed as well.

»So you want me to turn into another *Santa Claus*?« I asked.

»No,« he replied, »it won't be enough to be *Santa Claus* in order to restore this piece of furniture.«

On the next day, Nestor wanted to take me along into the woods to look for burl wood which could be used to build a miniature chair from it. After breakfast, he took care of doing the dishes. In my oppressive idleness, I offered to help him dry them, but he dismissed it. At first I believed he just did so out of hospitality, but when I asked him about it he knitted his brows. There was no need to dry the dishes, he said, as they would dry by themselves – naturally.

When Nestor was done we left the house and followed the road further up the hill. Soon it ended in front of a creek ditch where we climbed up the hill and wandered through thick fir woods. Nestor, quite obviously a well-trained hiker, went ahead at a fast pace. And while speedily walking along, he talked to me effortlessly, directing my attention to this or that peculiarity along the way: a strange mushroom, beautiful rock formations, a deer – and I was gasping while acknowledging him.

I was surprised about the many things Nestor saw out in nature, all the little details that caught his eye. Next to him, I felt like someone who was walking through life with his eyes closed. On the other hand, my impression was that Nestor tended to exaggerate. In any case, it seemed incomprehensible to me why certain things could fill him with such enthusiasm. When I asked him about it, he replied that the perception of the picture depended on our *strength* or *energy*. Once we developed strength or energy within ourselves, he said, it would help us to better recognize and appreciate the beauty of nature around us.

We had been hiking for about an hour and found a few nice wave-shaped pieces of burl wood when we arrived at a hillside place clear of trees. We sat down in a sunny place on the edge of the woods. Nestor took off his hat, unpacked several files, a few sheets of sandpaper and a crosscut saw and asked me to carve a small seat out of the wood. He himself took a piece of wood as well, showed me once more the important points to watch for, and we began working.

To me, the whole thing was a more or less a »necessary evil«. I would have preferred to undertake the perfect restoration directly on the secretaire. So I sawed, filed and ground away on this piece of wood in a hurry until it eventually looked like a small chair. When I asked Nestor about his opinion, he rebuffed me: he said that I could work out the details much more, and that the chair was still be too asymmetric and much too crude.

Impatiently, I continued my work, filing off some wood here and there, and showed him the whole thing again. This time he became upset. He showed me every single flaw on my work and even implied that I had deliberately overlooked these.

»I know that you can take great pains in your work,« Nestor said as if he knew me for years already. »But this particular piece of burl wood doesn't seem to be worth the trouble to you.«

I wanted to justify myself and make him believe that, after all, I was not as adept at this as he was. And that this particular piece of wood was just a practice object anyway. But Nestor didn't accept my objections.

»See, this is exactly where your problem lies,« he started. »You have certain preconceived ideas of what is valuable and what isn't. But in this way, your judgment of the things in the picture is mistaken. You want to restore Mari Egli's secretaire because it is valuable; the burl wood here right in front of you, on the other hand, does not have any value to you. This particular attitude, or shall I say mindset – overestimating the value of certain objects and expressing contempt for others – is what affects you so drastically whenever you work on the secretaire.«

I couldn't believe my ears: Nestor took a small, trivial piece of wood as a cause to criticize my general behavior. Before I was able to reply something, he continued and said that all these preconceived ideas represented my own »small world«, and that I brought this small world into the picture. Consequently, all that I was able to get out of the picture in terms of experiences and perceptions were »valuable« things on the one hand, and »worthless« ones on the other.

»I'm having a hard time understanding your language, Nestor. What do you mean with the ›picture‹?«

»That's the picture,« he answered and pointed towards the environment around us. »The ›picture‹ is what we can perceive at any given moment. In this case, it's the hills, the woods and the mountains.«

»So you mean our world?«

»No, not the entire world. Just our field of vision, the things we can see right now. I call it *the picture*.«

I was joking that this particular comparison was a little flawed because pictures – I thought of paintings or photographs, of course – were pretty flat, two-dimensional, after all, and not in motion. Nestor replied that the comparison with a photograph was quite appropriate indeed.

He asserted that, at every single moment, our picture was quite flat as well and not in motion.

I asked him how he arrived at such a notion. He didn't answer directly but told me that I'd have to learn to see for myself what the picture actually is.

»You cannot see what your picture is, after all. Because what you see right now is a ›decorated‹ or ›adorned‹ picture. You are adorning your picture with your own beliefs, ideas and thoughts. So you're decorating it with your *small world* – and thus you alter it continuously.«

Nestor instructed me to take a look at the hills in the distance. He explained that what I was seeing was just a pure unadulterated picture – at first. But the next moment, and without me being aware of it, I imposed my thoughts, ideas and wishes on the picture.

»You're putting your small world into the picture,« he stated, »by judging it, interpreting it and thinking about how it should be. You're comparing it with ideal pictures of beautiful places and events in your memory of the past. That's what I mean when I say that you're putting the world, your own small world, into the picture. In that way, you're turning the picture into the world – but basically, all there is, is the picture.«

Nestor laughed when he saw the question mark written on my face. I told him that all he did with his words was just confuse me.

He took this as an invitation to express himself more precisely and comprehensibly. One's own small world, he explained patiently, consisted of all our beliefs and ideas, of all our knowledge of the world we had acquired. He talked about the knowledge of all the achievements of the human race, of planet Earth in its entirety, of the oceans, the continents, the countries with their political and cultural borders, and of the people with their different opinions, viewpoints and problems. Our knowledge of the world, according to him, was based upon recollections of what we have seen, heard and felt in the past. But most of our knowledge was not something that we had actually experienced in practice but rather learned in theory. Therefore, the small world was not even our own world but one which has been taught to us, and which we eventually adopted.

»The whole thing is a vicious circle,« he went on. »The picture which you alter with your small world is affecting you in turn again. It reconditions your ideas and beliefs of hill and dale, undulating landscapes and of beauty as such. And you in turn put this newly conditioned, readjusted small world back into the picture.«

I shrugged my shoulders and replied:

»That's normal, after all; everybody's doing it. Everyone has his or her own way of interpreting what he or she is seeing or perceiving in general.«

»Yes, right. The point is, though: we're not able to see what the picture basically is, how it is constructed or what its cause might be – all because we're imposing our small world with all its beliefs and concepts on the picture.«

Slowly I became impatient. I would have rather talked about restoration techniques than about the human incapability of recognizing the world as for what it really is.

»What does this have to do with Mari Egli's secretaire and the perfect restoration?« I asked him.

»If you want to perform the perfect restoration,« he said with some seriousness in his voice now, »then you'll have to learn to dissolve your small world in the picture.«

I scrutinized Nestor's face, but there was absolutely nothing I could read off of it which would have dispelled my uncertainty: the earnestness in his words, as well as his facial expression, convinced me that he really meant what he said; but *what* he said caused me to seriously doubt this earnestness.

»Dissolving the small world in the picture – doesn't sound too difficult, after all,« I wisecracked, still helpless. He grinned.

»Dissolving the small world in the picture means, first of all, that you don't put your attention on anything else but the picture itself. If you take a look at your picture right now, it certainly is filled with your small world. Nevertheless, concentrating on the picture is the only way to find out what it is. For example, you can begin by putting your full attention on your carving the burl wood while carving it – and on nothing else whatsoever.«

»But that's what I'm already doing.«

»No, you're not, not at all. In your head you are haunted by thoughts circling around Mari Egli's secretaire which you wanted to restore and sell a long time ago. In this way, you're constantly reconditioning your small world in the picture.«

I didn't know what to answer.

»You'll have to be aware of all this when you're working on Mari Egli's secretaire,« he went on. »For the work on this particular piece of furniture is a situation which does not allow for your habitual thinking and acting. The secretaire is reflecting your small world back onto yourself – in your case with such intensity that you're shivering, shuddering and trembling.«

For a while we remained silent. Nestor was indeed a strange person, just like that piece of furniture in his stable. For a second, the silly notion crossed my mind that both of them were »carved from the same wood«.

»How did you get to know all these things?« I finally asked.

He said he knew a lot about the picture because he had managed to dissolve his own small world in it. And he took the opportunity to remind me once more that I had to do the same thing if I wanted to perform the perfect restoration.

»The picture is real, for it is there right this instant,« he argued. »The small world, on the other hand, is elusive and ephemeral, just like warm air. It is constantly changing, and it goes far beyond that which we can perceive at the moment.«

»So to you, all of reality is restricted to what you can perceive this instant?« I summarized what he said, expressing my disbelief with my tone of voice.

»Exactly. Reality is always what I see right at this moment.«

I had to laugh involuntarily. My initial suspicion was confirmed: Nestor was an armchair philosopher. I reckoned he had read some classic epistemology works, and now he believed he was in the know about God, the world and everything in it. With pleasure I explained to him that he had contradicted himself: on the one hand, he asserted that we, as human beings, didn't have access to reality because our perception was dimmed by the »small world«; and on the other hand he now argued that reality was that which we can perceive at this moment – the unreal small world.

Nestor thought this over for a while and then replied that both was correct. »The more you succeed in being in the place you're looking at,« he pointed out, »the more you dissolve the small world in the picture – and the more you will find that reality only consists of that which you can perceive at each given instant. He went on: »Interestingly, the word ›perceive‹ itself already contains that message: per-ceive, to take and inspect something thoroughly, and thus to recognize the truth or essence of it. Actually you can only perceive and take the truth out of the picture because, ultimately, there's nothing ›false‹ in it that you might be able to see. The truth of the picture becomes more prominent, though, the more your small world disappears out of the picture. Performing the perfect restoration therefore means to have the piece of furniture become more truthful and authentic.«

»I think that secretaire is already true and authentic enough to me,« I objected.

»No. To you, Mari Egli's secretaire is a wooden object full of wishes and dreams,« he dissented. »It is a part of your small world. Your small world, however, places restrictions on your consciousness and your body – so that you can't cope with this extraordinary situation requiring so much strength and stamina.«

»But that's exactly what I don't understand yet: how can it be,« I asked, »that an ordinary piece of furniture can exert such an influence on me? I mean, isn't that dangerous? Where's the borderline? The pressure could become even stronger, after all, and kill me at some point.«

»Then you had better watch out,« he replied. »You see, in the final analysis it's not the secretaire doing this. That's what I've been trying to explain to you all along: it's all about you and yourself – all that's reflecting back on you is the small world you put into the picture.«

Seeing the Picture as a Whole

After breakfast on the next day, I wanted to take over washing the dishes before Nestor would, as he had done the day before. Nestor however answered that it wasn't necessary to do the dishes every day as there were enough cups, plates and everything for two or three days. I replied in a playful way that he might not object to me doing the dishes after all, would he?

»To me, it doesn't play any significant role,« he answered, »but to you it does. The perfect restoration is not only a mind game but a very practical thing. It embraces your daily life as well. And it's always about not dispersing and wasting your energy. In other words: the perfect restoration means acting properly in the right place at the right time. So, in all matters and concerns you should carefully ponder about the time, on the one hand, when you have to act, and on the other hand, when the time has not yet come to do so. In this way, each dish washing turns into a ›complete‹ dishwashing.«

He laughed about his remark, but I couldn't really share his humor. Even if what he said was certainly meant to be an encouragement, it still resulted in me feeling inhibited and self-conscious. Nestor's world was completely different from mine, not familiar to me. And even though I wasn't really interested in his way of living, he behaved in a way as if I had to deal with it in a serious manner – just to restore a secretaire.

The rest of the morning I spent alone, working on my wooden chair. I realized with how much endeavor and engagement I worked on the job, trying my best to arrive at a perfect result. I didn't want Nestor to find anything on the chair which he still could criticize. Around lunchtime I packed up my belongings. Then, before I drove back to Bern, I showed him the chair.

He looked it over carefully. »Looks much better than yesterday,« he stated. »You've done a good job – even if it wasn't for the purpose of the chair itself.«

His insinuation made me assume a defensive attitude at once. »Isn't it irrelevant, really, why someone tries hard at whatever he or she does? Bottom line is, the result is satisfactory, isn't it?« I argued.

»*By no means* is it irrelevant whether you act out of, for instance, joy or out of a sense of duty,« he answered. »You must know what exactly your motivations are, because they are part of your small world and therefore important when it comes to performing the perfect restoration. But as soon as you're able to dissolve your small world in the picture, then your motivation behind doing all the things you do is neither joy nor a sense of duty or even fear – you just do them for the sake of doing them. And it's not until then that true pleasure and joy begin to show up.«

I moaned and told him that his idea of dissolving the small world in the picture was an illusory one: because, the way I had understood Nestor it meant not to think about anything any longer – something I didn't consider desirable or possible.

»Basically it's not just about thoughts and ideas,« he answered. »Your deepest feelings, mostly unconscious, also belong to your small world. They express themselves in your fixed convictions and preconceived ideas about how the world is set up and how it should be. Views of that nature have consolidated themselves since your earliest childhood. Of course you can't shake this off just like that, as if it were dust on a jacket sleeve. And because these feelings and fixed convictions are part of your small world, you cannot dissolve this small world simply by engaging in certain thoughts and ideas.«

Nestor explained once more that the dissolution of the small world in the picture can only be achieved by concentrating on the picture – a form of focused concentration which leaves all feelings and thoughts behind. In everyday life this means that we pay full and unrestricted attention to the things we are doing at any given instant. Aside from that, however, there was a more direct way, according to him, to concentrate on the picture: by seeing.

Nestor began talking about seeing the picture, but what he told me didn't make any sense to me at first. Slowly it dawned on me that he aimed at something very specific when he talked about »seeing the picture«: it was more than merely looking at that which was located in our immediate field of vision. To Nestor, »seeing« was a way of focused inspection, close to scrutiny.

»You have to *see* the picture,« he said. »You have to see it *as a whole*, because it's not until then that your small world will be dissolved.«

»What do you mean by *seeing the picture as a whole*?«

»I mean seeing the picture as one single unit, as one entity, after all.«

I accused him of teasing me. To me, it was obvious that this was ultimately impossible. Because, I argued, who was able to see the picture as one single unit when it actually consisted of many objects and details?

Nestor replied this was a matter of perception, after all, and that the quality of perception was something a human being can work on in a very targeted and conscious manner.

»At this time, the picture consists of many different parts in your view,« he explained. »That's because you're always directing your attention to these parts, keeping them separate from each other. It is your small world that creates the differences in the picture. But as soon as you succeed in seeing the picture as a whole, there are no more differences. Then you have dissolved your small world in the picture.«

Nestor explained that perceiving the details in the picture was correct and necessary when it came to surviving in this world. But in order to perform the perfect restoration, it was just as important to be able to see the picture as a whole. He suggested I should try it right away. I was skeptical but at the same time curious about what would happen next. I agreed and we sat down on the bench in front of the house.

The day was sunny, with only a few clouds in the sky, and we had a clear view down the valley and across to the range of hills on other side, majestically towered by the Hohgant.

Nestor glanced over the landscape. He told me to focus my eyes on one of the Alpine huts or stables at the foothills of the Hohgant. »Just take your time,« he added jokingly, »after all, there is a wide range of choices. «

The small wooden huts and stables on the other side were spread evenly across the brighter green of the pastures which were divided into single segments by the dark green of the firs lined up along the ditches. My eyes focused on a hut which was located higher up the foothills. There was no road leading to it, so I assumed it was a stable.

Nestor instructed me to look at this particular stable and to observe what I could see. I focused my eyes on the stable. It was so far away and so small that I could hardly recognize any details. I could distinguish between roof and walls; otherwise, it was just a brown spot against a green background.

The immediate surroundings seemed quite peaceful, but the stable itself looked vacated. I was thinking about whether it was still used at all. Then I tried to estimate the age of the stable – something which was a little problematic, of course, over this long distance. I supposed it was very old, because I knew that there were wooden buildings in this region aged 200 years or even older. To me, it was fascinating that I had the chance to touch an object with my hands which had been touched by other people as well long before I had. Buildings like that, I knew, had quite a few stories to tell – if they could speak. Because they couldn't, we had to retrieve their stories with the help of scientific analyses.

Then I slowly became aware of the silence, or at least some sort of silence. Because the ever-constant rush of a creek in our vicinity, the whistling of birds and the weak drone of agricultural machines in the far distance – all this wasn't particularly noisy, but it filled the air quite well with sounds of all kinds.

Minute after minute passed by. Slowly I became nervous. It came to my mind that I actually wanted to restore a piece of furniture – instead, I sat in this place and stared at some confounded stable. And this was what Nestor called the »perfect restoration«. I felt like a stupid fool. I waited for another moment, then I thought I had spent enough time sitting there and »looking at the picture as a whole«. I looked over to Nestor.

He asked me what I had seen.

»Well, the stable of course. What else should I have seen, according to you?« I answered slightly annoyed.

Nestor smiled. »It's not so easy to see the picture as a whole. It doesn't just happen overnight,« he gently said. »But as long as you can't concentrate completely on the picture, and as long as you still bring in your thoughts and feelings into it instead, you will not be able to continue the restoration.«

I voiced my doubts that I actually had an easier time working on the secretaire by staring around here in the environment. Undeterred by this, Nestor repeated what he had already told me the day before:

»To see the picture as a whole, and thus to dissolve the small world, is an important approach to the perfect restoration. To you, this might be an unusual method to go about the restoration of a piece of furniture – but it is one that helps. You'll see.« He laughed and repeated his last words: »You'll see.«

Nestor encouraged me to try it once again, and this time, to look at the building of my choice with all my attention. While I kept looking at the stable this time, I suddenly believed to understand what he meant by his encouragement to see the picture »as a whole«: because I realized that – though I kept looking at one tiny spot in the picture – I could also perceive the environment not in my direct line of vision. For example, I could also notice the few tall firs around the stable. Or I could perceive the course of the ditches, or other houses. In this way, I gained the impression that I was able to see everything in the picture simultaneously.

40

I told Nestor of my perception. He considered my observation to be good but added that this did not have anything to do with concentration and seeing the picture as a whole – only with a state of dispersal.

»Trying to concentrate on something in the picture without directly looking at it – that doesn't work. All it does is impair our attention. We can easily grasp this, considering the fact that we cannot see the details of objects far outside our line of vision; at best, we can perceive their color, their rough shape and whether they are in motion or not.«

I called Nestor's attention to something which seemed contradictory to me: on the one hand, he asked me to see the picture as a whole. On the other hand, in order to achieve this, I was supposed to concentrate on one single spot in the picture. I couldn't wrap my wits around how I was supposed to bring these two together and juggle them properly.

»You can't see yet what the picture basically is,« he replied. »All you can do is to look at the single objects in the picture. It's like with a mirror: if you just take a superficial glance into a mirror, you don't see the mirror itself but the many things reflected in it. But our only chance to recognize the mirror as such is to look into it with all our attention. So if you want to see the picture as a whole, you must begin to focus more and more on one single spot in the picture. In this way, you come closer to the entirety of the picture, because this is the way you're dissolving your small world.«

Nestor made no secret of the fact that »dissolving the small world in the picture« was something very difficult because we are usually quite content with that small world of ours; we settled for the knowledge that we could retrieve from the single objects with superficial attention. He maintained that human beings did not progress with their concentration because they were afraid of losing their small world. Therefore they always concerned themselves with objects, feelings and ideas of one kind or another which distracted them from seeing the picture as a whole.

I opposed him and his, in my view, too generalizing statement that people only engaged in superficial concentration. As a counter-example, I mentioned leading scientists which could hardly be accused of doing their work with superficial concentration. Nestor countered this by saying that even these people, who perhaps were capable of pondering over something for a longer period of time and with heightened concentration, were just as unable to focus on one single spot in their picture for a longer period of time. This was so because they didn't practice this kind of deep concentration.

»What we are actually doing all day,« he explained, »is nothing else than repeating our small world – so as to maintain and perpetuate it.«

»I'm repeating my small world?«

»Of course. After all, you want to keep it. This is only possible, though, by repeating it. Do you think it is a natural state for human beings to have so many thoughts and ideas rushing through their heads, and to subdivide the picture in so many different objects and concepts? If you dropped the effort of constantly repeating your small world, then it would gradually fade out of the picture.«

Nestor kept on asking me to try to see my picture as a whole. I concentrated a few more times on a spot in my field of vision, but my perceptions didn't seem to conform to his expectations. Obviously I hadn't succeeded in dissolving my small world in the picture.

I got up and stretched my limbs. I was out of patience, and my butt was hurting from sitting on the hard surface for such a long time.

»Do you really think it's possible to see the picture as a whole and to dissolve the small world?« I asked Nestor.

»It is. I know it. But it takes some time.«

»Do you know it because you have experienced it for yourself?«

»Yes.«

»And what exactly did you experience?«

»There's no use in talking about it at this time. You'll have to find out for yourself.«

I tried to persuade Nestor to let me in on some more, but he blocked all further discussion.

»Then I'm supposed to believe you blindly?« I teased him.

»Blindly? Certainly not. I told you before: look at the picture and become aware of what you see.«

»I don't know if I'll succeed in seeing the picture as a whole,« I expressed my concern.

Nestor remained silent.

»What do you think, how long will it take until I'll be able to continue my work on the secretaire?« I finally asked.

»It all depends on how fast you're making progress in seeing the picture as a whole. Perhaps it'll take days until you can continue, perhaps weeks, perhaps months. I'd suggest you practice every day.«

I thought he was joking. Just the idea that I would stare in the far distance like a halfwit for months on end made me laugh.

»Perhaps even years?« I asked jokingly so as to carry it to extremes. Nestor looked at me thoughtfully and rubbed his chin. Then he started smiling.

»Perhaps. Perhaps it'll take a little bit longer in your case.«

The Attractive Force of Matter

During the time I spent in the Emmental, Nestor continued to teach me the perfect restoration. As he had already told me, this meant to him, first and foremost, the skillful handling of the picture. This included his instruction to me to sit down regularly and to look at the picture with all my concentration. The handicraft, on the other hand, the skilled handling of tools, was something that was put aside, touched on only casually along the way; only a few times in between, Nestor had me work on a piece of wood so as to refine my practice skills.

Still I yielded to the temptation, time and again, of working directly on the secretaire – clandestinely, while Nestor was gone. Each time I had a spark of hope that I would still be able, after all, to get the work on it done and thus to evade that strange »perfect restoration«. The source of this die-hard optimism didn't seem to run dry, but all my confidence and hope still couldn't cover up the harsh reality of my unpleasant physical sensations – namely that I just wasn't able to restore this secretaire in the usual way.

If it was correct what Nestor had said – that I myself was the determining factor whether, and to what degree, this piece of furniture affected me –, then my goodwill and optimism obviously didn't suffice to get the restoration of the secretaire done. So I came up with another idea: if the secretaire actually emitted some kind of electromagnetic waves, which I still suspected, then all I had to do was to shield the object with proper materials which would diminish and absorb these energies. First I tried it with aluminum foil which I had brought along on one of my visits in fall.

It came in handy for me that Nestor wasn't home on this cold cloudy day when I arrived. I went into the stable and unpacked the aluminum foil – with mixed feelings, though. I knew: Nestor wouldn't have agreed at all with my plan and approach. But what he had suggested I should do so as to complete the restoration hadn't shown any effect whatsoever.

I started to wrap the aluminum foil around the secretaire. This took quite a while, because the pressure this generated within me forced me to take frequent breaks. Finally though, the secretaire stood in front of me, completely wrapped into the silvery shining foil; to be on the safe side, I had wrapped two layers around the object, and in doing so I took great pains to make sure that everything was covered up – except one little spot which I had left uncovered so as to do a little »pilot« on it, applying some of the lye solution and removing it afterwards. But the moment I started to scrape the spot with a spatula, the pressure in my abdomen started to increase, just like before, and my body reacted with the same familiar symptoms I hated which drove me out of the stable, gasping for air.

I didn't give up. As soon as I had recovered somewhat, I wrapped a second double layer of aluminum foil around the secretaire and scaled down the spot I wanted to work on by half. But this attempt ended just like the previous one – with the ungentle capitulation of my body. The aluminum foil didn't seem to have any effect whatsoever – unless the difference in radiation still emitted was too minute for me to perceive. So in order to make very sure, I wrapped two more double layers of aluminum foil around Mari Egli's secretaire.

My apprehension that I was about to fail again caused additional hot flashes within me, on top of the symptoms I already suffered from. Gradually, I sagged into a fever-like condition, with nothing else on my mind than the strong wish to get it over with this asinine secretaire – a state of mind in which it was impossible for me to simply give up and drop the whole thing. My impatience and desperation escalated dramatically, and the enforced breaks I had to take contributed their part to it. I had become so deeply absorbed into the work that it escaped my attention that Nestor had entered the stable in between.

»What in the world are you doing there?« he asked me, giving me a nasty shock which abruptly ended my fixation on the object. He took his hat off, and I saw how he knitted his brows in disbelief, making a sympathetic face with a slight smile lifting the corners of his mouth – a facial expression which, given the hyper state I already was in, provoked me even more. It took all my strength to hold back, keep cool and not to yell my frustration straight into his face. I was trembling with anger. Nestor started laughing out loudly and asked me if I wanted to take the secretaire along to a party out somewhere. Without looking at him, I walked by him and left the stable.

After I had returned from a pleasant and refreshing walk in the cool air, I felt the need to talk to Nestor about the aluminum foil, and to tell him everything I had on my mind. I found him in the kitchen where he fired the oven.

When he had listened to my idea, he tipped against his forehead with his finger. »You never give up, do you? What comes next? Are you going to put the secretaire in a metal cage? Or sheathe it with a lead cover?« he teased me.

»It was a good idea,« I defended myself. »It could have worked.«

»Forget it,« he said sharply. »That doesn't work at all.« Then he put up a friendlier face, but his tone of voice still had an insistent sound: »You should really stop to treat the secretaire just like a valuable article.«

»But that's what it's all about,« I explained. »To me, this piece of furniture *is* a valuable article. I want to restore it so as to be able to sell it, after all.«

»Once you've restored it, its value will be higher than you can imagine,« he assured me. »But up to that point you should see it for what it is, in the final analysis: a piece of wood.«

Nestor's words evoked sudden doubts in me as to the actual value of the secretaire. Did he know something about it which I had missed or that I couldn't know? I asked him about it, but he shook his head.

»As I just said: you're not asking for the object as such but for its material value. But in order to be able to restore Mari Egli's secretaire, you'll have to stop thinking about the *dough* you might make with it. Otherwise, the perfect restoration will never succeed, not in a hundred years.«

Nestor repeated that I judged and treated the individual objects in the picture too much according to their material value. He pointed out that the pleasure I take in material objects increased in direct ratio to their material value, and that I treated »valuable« things accordingly. As an example he mentioned my car: always bright and shining, and certainly not some cheap model. Or the fancy clothes I was wearing – not affordable for everyone.

I protested and explained that I was by far not so materialistically oriented as he tried to portray me. Of course, I strived for a certain standard of living. But the car was a chance purchase, and the clothes I had bought at a clearance sale.

Nestor, however, reminded me of my heavy upset over a torn pair of trousers which went by the boards during a hiking trip on the other side of the Emme while trying to climb over a cattle fence. And during my last visit, when we were following animal tracks through thick brushwood, my gold chain ripped off my neck and fell down into a ditch where I couldn't find it anymore. According to him, I hadn't stomached the loss for days – not to mention my leather cowboy boots which I had ruined on one of our first trips in the swampy pastures.

»You're clinging too much to certain objects – those which you consider highly valuable in terms of money,« Nestor was convinced. »You say: this is more valuable than that; this is what I want, and this is what I don't want. This is the viewpoint you walk through life with, and this is what thwarts the perception of the picture as a whole. These are also the ideas and concepts with which you look at the secretaire. The secretaire, however, reflects your ideas back to you. And that's what you can feel, more than you can tolerate.«

I accused him of trying to take away my joy in life and explained to him that I wasn't willing to live the life of an ascetic. Nestor replied that it's not about taking away someone's joy in something. Much rather, the aim is to take the attention off of the individual objects to which it was so overly attached, and to redirect it to the picture as a whole.

»You won't be able to experience true joy until the moment you succeed in letting your attention flow into the whole picture in an undiscriminating way,« he asserted. »And at that point you will have ceased to assign a special material value to Mari Egli's secretaire.«

»I don't think I'll ever succeed in that.«

»Well, you just have to make an effort and try hard. You already have the willpower to do so, don't you? Someone else would have cut and run long ago so as to look for another piece of furniture. But you're still sticking around and cook up all possible methods to win over this confounded piece of furniture.«

»I've invested 600 Francs, Nestor,« I replied.

He wrinkled his nose. »As long as you focus your attention on just making a profit with the secretaire, it'll always repel you,« he prophesied. »But this willpower is exactly what will help you, once you're able to redirect it – into the picture as a whole. Do this with the exercise I instructed you to do. That'll help you gain a balanced view of all things, and to treat them accordingly.«

In late fall I didn't visit Nestor regularly any longer. At the university, the winter term had started, and I had to concentrate on my studies. But whenever I was at Nestor's place, we mostly talked about the picture which, according to him, ultimately represented a complete whole. He encouraged me again and again to sit down, focus on an object with my eyes and to look at it with all my concentration.

During this time I became a little more familiar with the immediate surroundings around Nestor's house. If the weather allowed it, I hiked through the woods all by myself to look for those places which Nestor deemed favorable for seeing the picture as a whole. They were brightly lit places out in nature: clearings in the woods, sunny pastures or a place somewhere alongside the young Emme where it was possible to sit down somewhat comfortably and relax so as to direct all of my attention into the picture. The object of my choice varied: a log cabin, the green tip of a fir, a piece of tree bark, a stone, a mushroom, a puddle of water. Nestor had emphasized several times that I could use virtually everything as my object of concentration, as long as it could be distinguished well from the surroundings.

During these numerous attempts to see the picture as a whole, I gradually became aware of my inability to keep my eyes directed continuously to one single spot; a few slight movements of my eyes caused me to constantly realign my look at the object. These fine eye movements occurred in a reflex-like manner, independent from my volition.

Nestor wasn't surprised by my observation. He confirmed that we newly aligned our attention on the picture with each motion of the eyes. As our attention is impaired by the small world, though, all we did was to constantly put our small world into the picture. He asked me to deliberately stop realigning my look. In doing so, I was supposed to closely observe what happened with the picture.

Actually, I was close to desperation trying this, because I had to deal with a reflex I was supposed to overcome. It wasn't just about preventing the eyes from moving but also about not blinking for a certain period of time. Because each blink, according to Nestor, also was a realignment of my look.

After numerous attempts I was finally able to notice that, avoiding all reflexes, my look tended to drift downward to the ground. I recognized this because after some time I wasn't looking at the spot on an object any longer which I had started out with, but on a spot slightly below; it seemed as if something pulled down my look.

When I told Nestor about this, he talked about the *attractive force of matter* which caused this, affecting our visual system. I asked him how it could be that my look was pulled down by this attractive force. Nestor responded to this with the unbelievable allegation that it wasn't my look which is being attracted by this force but the picture which I just couldn't keep a hold of yet.

»When you try to see the picture as a whole,« he explained, »then you basically try to hold on tight to it. But the moment you try to hold on to it, it'll vanish.« Nestor made a gesture as if he wanted to grab an object with his hand, only to reach into empty space. He laughed; the whole issue seemed to amuse him big time.

»Why do you talk about ›holding on‹ now?« I asked. »How could it be possible at all to hold on to the picture?«

»I've told you that our picture is flat and unmoving – that holds good for the moment. Over time, however, we have to deal with many pictures which are in constant motion. It is like a movie: that which we see is a stream of images, a sequence of individual pictures which are projected on some kind of screen, conveying the impression of a moving picture. And that which we call ›concentration‹ is basically the attempt *to hold on to* the picture we see at the moment.«

The notion of a stream of images and of holding on to the pictures had something provocative – not the least because of the implicitness in Nestor's tone of voice. I pointed out to him that he was trying to make speculations look like facts.

»I'm talking about things which I can see for myself,« he answered.

»You mean you can see that the world is a sequence of individual pictures?«

»Yes, I can,« Nestor calmly replied. »But what I'm trying to explain to you is something else, namely why your look drifts downward when you want to focus on a spot in the picture. And because you cannot see this directly yet, you'll have to use your imagination for the time being. Think of it this way: that which we can see as human beings consists of several individual pictures in constant motion,« he repeated. »We now have the problem that we're never able to really look at the things; they vanish as soon as we start to concentrate on them. That means, these objects disappear with the entire picture – the picture is pulled downward by the attractive force of matter.«

»I can only observe that my look, which was directed right at the spot in the beginning, drifted downward,« I objected.

»Perhaps you had the feeling that your look is pulled downward. But basically, what happened is that your eyes followed the old picture which was moving downward for a little distance – just because you were not able yet to hold it still and in suspension.«

I started to object to Nestor's allegations. »The picture doesn't just disappear like that. After all, I can keep looking at something all day – and by the end it's still there.«

»Your impression is that you look at the same picture all the time. But that impression is misleading: with each new motion of the eyes, that is, the realignment of your attention, a new and different picture comes into being. But when you sit down to see the picture as a whole, what you actually do is to practice holding on to the same picture for a longer period of time.«

Nestor continued to explain that we are usually lacking the will to concentrate enough so as to be able to hold on to and keep looking at the same picture – something which was no wonder or surprise because nowadays the opposite process, the constant realignment of our attention, was stressed on a large scale: this *faster-faster-faster, more-more-more* – no matter if it's the pictures on TV, the flood of news in our age of information or the broad range of consumer articles we can choose from – all that dulled the awareness of people to the point that they become addicted to even more pictures and stimuli and even faster sequences.

»This constant overstimulation drains the people of their energy and leaves them nervous, restless and ›shallow-brained‹,« Nestor said. »And if there is a sudden lack of stimuli, people can become aggressive very quickly. People living such a lifestyle will never be able to find out what the picture basically is.«

Following Nestor's instructions, I spent the rest of the day finding out what actually happened with the picture if I did not realign my attention. I realized once more that I had a real hard time sitting down calmly and to look at an object in my field of vision with all my concentration. And no matter how hard I tried – I just couldn't notice anything which would have confirmed Nestor's allegation: still it appeared as if my look was pulled downward while the picture itself did not move an inch.

At night I was slightly upset because I felt as if I had wasted my time dawdling around all day. Nestor was very empathetic. Without me having said anything, he admitted that my endeavor was quite a difficult one, but he kept encouraging me to stick to my regular practice exercises.

»I can't imagine that the picture can be pulled downward just like that,« I replied. »The picture always remains precisely in the place where it is.«

»The picture is moving,« he assured me. »This is something you realize the moment you stop realigning your attention for a longer period of time. Then you'll also see what actually happens with the picture.«

»What is it?« I asked.

»It is converted into an *afterimage* with complementary colors. When we look at these converted images we can recognize that the picture is movable and pulled downward by the attractive force. So the moment you realize that your look is gradually sinking lower, you are not looking at the actual material world anymore but at the afterimage. That's what I wanted to explain to you today.«

»But I didn't realize that I was looking at an afterimage,« I objected.

»When your look is flowing downward, you are following the converted afterimage,« he insisted. »You just weren't alert and attentive enough to realize this.«

I ignored the criticism in his words and asked him instead how it could be that the attractive force of matter could exert an influence on these afterimages.

»The attractive force influences everything,« he answered. »It takes effect in the picture and through the individual pictures. As we are also a part of the picture, we're also attracted by this force: our body, but also our concentration, our attention and ultimately all of our consciousness. And the weaker that will to concentrate is in a human being, the more he is subjected to the attractive force of matter – and the more materialistic in turn is his attitude and mindset. So you see, your preference for shiny cars and trendy trousers is the reason for your lack of concentration and the fact that your picture is pulled downward towards the ground.«

Nestor stated that we, as human beings, battled against this force all our life. Each form of motion, including thinking and just about any attempt to stay alert and conscious, basically represented an effort to overcome that attractive force of matter. In order to be more successful at that, people rather resorted to exterior sources of energy and auxiliary means: they are driving around in cars, flying through the air in planes and consume tons of stimulants. Only when we are forced to capitulate – like when we fall asleep or in the end, when we are about to die – we relinquished our body and consciousness to that attractive force, turning blissfully unconscious in the process.

»With our visual system,« Nestor went on, »we can witness our fight against this attractive force directly: we fight against it involuntarily by trying to hold on to the picture, which means: by concentrating. But soon we succumb to the attractive force and are thus not able to hold on to the picture, with the result that we immediately realign our look at the new picture – that's relaxation.«

»I don't understand why holding on to the picture is supposed to be concentration, and the realignment of the look is supposed to be relaxation,« I said.

»If we want to know what the picture basically is,« he explained, »then we have to be able to hold it in suspension and to look at it calmly. Holding something in suspension, though, is an effort whereby you have to gather your strength and align it to this particular goal – and that's *concentration*. *Relaxation* takes place the moment you end your concentration and realign your attention.

Looking at it this way, most people are lacking the ability to properly concentrate on something. We can't concentrate for long enough so as to hold the picture in suspension. So with each new moment we realign our attention onto the new picture again. This one, however, we cannot properly see, either, because it is already being pulled down by the attractive force. And because we cannot properly see the picture, we predefine it, for the most part, with our thoughts and actions. So we think that we see the world in our picture the way it really is; but the truth of the matter is, we can only perceive the surface of the picture – our small world.«

Nestor kept mysteriously silent for a moment and looked at me with bright eyes.

»As soon as we succeed in holding the picture in suspension for a longer period of time, we'll get to the point where our small world is dissolving, and where we can see the picture as a whole. And then we'll also be able to see what it really is that we're looking at each single day.«

Acquiring a Taste for It

The winter set in fast. During the time when everything in the Emmental was covered with a thick cold layer of snow, I visited Nestor only once. It wasn't so much my studies that kept me from the trip into the Emmental but the frosty cold.

In spring of the following year, Nestor reminded me of many things which I had neglected or lost sight of during wintertime. His encouragements made me eventually resume the exercises pertaining to the perfect restoration.

In addition, Nestor began talking about one of his neighbors, a farmer. It was the first time that he mentioned another person living on the left side of the Emme like him, and with whom he had contact. He described that man in very friendly terms, picturing him as a quiet, hardworking fellow and raving about his exquisite culinary skills. As a gesture of friendship, Nestor said, he visited him now and then, bringing along some food as well. He wanted me to accompany him on his next visit and help him take along some of the mushrooms and berries he had collected in fall and dried or preserved in jars. I agreed to come along because I was confident to find out more about Nestor and the perfect restoration with this visit – and perhaps even about Mari Egli or her secretaire.

The day Nestor chose for that visit was an unsettled day in spring; the two mirabelle trees in front of his house were already budding, and the snow at this altitude had mostly melt away. After breakfast we started our trip, packed with food for our host. For some time, a narrow path led us through thick woods. Then, when we arrived at a small pasture, we walked down the hillside along the edge of the woods, in the direction of the valley where the Emme was flowing.

After walking a while like this, I realized that the surroundings became increasingly barren and lifeless; whereas snowdrops and crocuses used to show their white and yellow blossoms here and there before, and hundreds of little black spiders used to crawl over last year's dead plants, the ground now was hard and stony. This barrenness, together with the silence all around up here, created some kind of spooky effect and gave me the feeling that there might hardly be any other place in the world where one was more lonesome than here.

Once however, when I briefly turned around, I recognized the contours of a human being next to a group of barren fir trees. According to the brief impression I had, it must have been a woman, dressed with a long skirt or an apron, who walked along deeply bent forward, as if she was searching for something. Immediately, I looked back to the trees where I believed to have seen that woman: there were dead firs, interwoven with one another, but no person.

Nestor, who was walking ahead in front, had turned around towards me and gave me a questioning look. I told him of that woman, bent forward and searching, which I believed to have seen – a perception which he at first dismissed as a daydream. But then, after we had kept on going for a while, he suddenly stopped.

»You saw the coal woman,« he grinned.

»The coal woman?«

»A long time ago, an old woman, a healer, had lived somewhere around here,« he began to tell. »Her healing powers were outstanding, but she was also known for her greed. One day, she met a small dwarf who was injured. The woman knew about the dwarfs' wealth, and she sniffed a chance of a big reward if she managed to heal that manikin. She did, and the dwarf, healthy again, led her to a huge oak tree in the deepest woods. At the foot of this oak tree, the entrance to the subterranean town of the dwarfs was located, invisible for human beings and animals. The dwarfs were overjoyed when they saw their fellow again, after having missed him for days, and they were only too willing to reward the woman's good deed. So they started to gather pieces of coal from the deep ground and placed them in that old woman's apron – as much as she was able to carry.

Of course, the healer woman hadn't expected to be rewarded with ordinary coal. What was she supposed to do with that black pile in her apron? Disappointed and upset, she started her way back home with that uncoveted burden. On her way home, she simply threw away a part of the coal, and a number of pieces just fell out of her apron. But when she arrived at home and poured out the remaining pieces of coal, they were all made from pure solid gold.«

Nestor looked at me, somewhat amused.

»What do you think the woman did once she made that discovery?« he asked me.

»Well, I believe she went back out to find the remaining pieces of coal she had dropped on her way back,« I answered spontaneously.

»That's exactly what she did,« he laughed, »but she couldn't find one single piece of it.«

Nestor found that the old woman had acted wrongly: she hadn't assigned any particular value to the coal and thus had handled it carelessly – because she only knew her small world which made her evaluate the situation accordingly. If she, on the other hand, had been able to see the picture as a whole, she wouldn't have distinguished, in terms of value, between gold and coal.«

»Would she have taken the coal then or not?« I wanted to know.

»That's beside the point. What's really important in any case is that, to her, the material value of things wouldn't have been the decisive factor any longer.«

»If seeing the picture as a whole deprives a person of his or her power of judgment,« I concluded, »then that woman might perhaps have been better off with her small world: after all, she had brought home a little bit of the gold which she then could make use of.«

»No, she couldn't,« Nestor countered me. »Her stinginess made her set off into the woods again so as to find the remaining pieces of coal. And she's still looking for it up till today – you've seen her for yourself, after all.«

We continued our trip, and soon we arrived in the place where Nestor's farmer friend lived. It was a large lynchet at the foot of a rocky, steeply rising hill ascending to our left. Towards the right, the lynchet rose up a little further at first, but then it bordered on a hillside sloping down steeply. Close to this precipice there were two buildings we were heading towards. I was surprised that none of them was an ordinary farmhouse, as I had expected. Instead, there were a small wooden hut and a larger house made of stone close to each other. The rocks and boulders spreading across the entire lynchet made it impossible to utilize the soil for large-surface planting of field crops or efficient pasture farming – it was inconceivable to me how a farmer could settle in a part of the country as barren as this one.

I asked Nestor where the farmer planted his grain or vegetable crop or where his cattle grazed. He answered that the man wasn't active as farmer any longer; all he did was to plant some vegetable in his garden.

»Then why do you call him a ›farmer‹?« I asked.

»I call him *the farmer* because he used to work as a farmer, and that was what enabled him to arrive on the left side.«

»I don't get it. Doesn't he have a real name?«

»All names are falling short as soon as a human being arrives on the left side. They are merely reminiscent of things of the past.«

I wanted to know from Nestor whether he referred to the left side of the Emme, and what was so special about it, that is, arriving here. He assured me that we would pick this up and talk about it some other time.

We passed by the smaller hut which probably was used as a shed, walking in between large rocks here and there, and arrived at the farmer's house. It was built from stone and mortar, had a slate roof, and its front faced the mountain. Parallel to the front of the house, and placed in regular intervals, plants with thick fleshy leaves were growing; their red-colored tips ended in a sharp spike. These leaf rosettes close above the ground were forming a line which included the well and the garden next to the house. Nestor explained that these plants are named »houseleek«.

»They protect against rock slides,« he said, as if it was self-evident, and called my attention to the fact that the stones breaking off the mountainside now and then and dropping down on the lynchet reached, in part, very close to the line of plants but didn't pass over it. I tried hard, but I couldn't find one single, ever so small, piece of rock anywhere beyond this line of plants. Indeed, it appeared as if the fleshy plants would fend off rock debris in an almost magical way, thereby protecting the house. I for my part, however, rather suspected the farmer of clearing away the debris around his house in regular intervals.

Finally we entered the house. There was just one single room in this small hut, and there were even less furnishings and fittings than in Nestor's hut: a big wooden cabinet, a mattress on the floor in a corner, covered with brown woolen blankets; in the middle of the room there was a square-shaped wooden table upon which Nestor placed his backpack; and in another corner, black frying pans and pots were hanging next to a small stove.

In between an oblong wooden table with various tools and an impressive beam balance scale made of brass on top of it, and the tiled stove which had a big old scythe attached to its front – eye-catching because of its slightly curved and adorned wooden handle – the only colorful piece of furniture in the room was a red leather chair in which the farmer was sitting. The man's body was calm and motionless so that I assumed he was asleep. But then I could recognize that he had his eyes slightly opened, watching Nestor and me with a blank and expressionless look.

Nestor seemed to ignore him. Calmly, he started to unpack the food from the backpack and placed it on the table. I did the same. Only when we were done, Nestor turned around to greet the man in the chair with a few words. Then he pointed towards me and explained that I was very hungry, and that I have come along to join them for a meal.

»We'll take the five-course menu,« Nestor demanded.

I could see how a slight smile showed up on the farmer's face. When the man looked at me, I gave him a friendly smile, nodded and took the opportunity to introduce myself. But he didn't respond to my gesture at all.

»Henusode!'« he called out instead and suddenly rose up from his chair. He stretched himself full length which resulted in several loud cracks, and once he stood up straight he appeared as tall as a giant. He was taller and brawnier than Nestor.

Without saying anything, the burly man began firing the stove, while Nestor and I went to get water from the well beside the house. Nestor told me once more that the farmer was an excellent cook, and that I had the chance to witness his outstanding culinary skills today by enjoying a five-course meal. To me, this was nothing more than idle talk; I didn't believe for a second that the farmer would actually serve us a five-course menu.

Inside the house, the stout man began to chop up various kinds of vegetables which he had spread out on the table. Nestor sat down in the leather chair after he had filled some of the water into a pot on the stove. I for my part, however, didn't want to sit around idle like Nestor and asked the farmer politely if I could be of any help to him.

»You can't help him,« Nestor answered in his place. »Only he himself can prepare the food in such an excellent way.«

So I sat down and watched the stout man doing his work. In the process, I realized that he chopped up the vegetables in a quite peculiar way: at first, he halved a potato, carrot or celery. Then he took the right half of each vegetable and chopped it up into many small parts. For the left half of each vegetable, however, he took the knife in his left hand and chopped it up into just a few large crude pieces. After he had poured the minced vegetable into the pot, he went through the same ritual with other vegetables. When all the vegetables in the pot started boiling, the farmer took a brief scrutinizing look at the dried mush-

---

[1] Swiss German for "well in that case".

rooms we had brought along. He took some of them and chopped them up the same way he had done with the vegetables.

I didn't only wonder about his strange approach but also about how deeply he was immersed into his work, as if chopping up vegetables in this way was the heaviest work one could imagine. All that time, he didn't say a single word, just like Nestor and I. To me, this »prayerful« atmosphere had something oppressive and absurd at the same time.

Once he was done with his work, the farmer sat down on his mattress and leaned his back against the wall. I could see how he was breathing deeply and slowly.

Nestor was the first to break the silence. He told the stout man that I had seen the coal woman today. I objected that I had merely believed to see a woman in the far distance. The farmer, though, appeared thoughtful and massaged his gums with his tongue.

»Back then, I used to see her often,« he remembered. He uttered his words in a calm and slow way, his voice sounded monotonous. »I've seen her often. But that was only because I was so similar to her. I also used to distinguish between coal and gold all the time. That was the way I lived and acted.«

After a long, almost unbearably long, pause he went on: »So my farm, which I still had around that time, became bigger and bigger. And the fields surrounding it became more and more. And the cows became fatter and fatter. And I even began to imitate them ...,« he laughed with a low voice and looked at me. »When you see the coal woman, it just means that you are similar to her.«

»But that's only a tale,« I tried to lift the conversation back up to a rational level. »How is it possible that you have seen this woman?«

»I did see her,« he insisted stubbornly. »She's the greed in person. She wants gold only and no coal. She leads a miserable life because she's only seeking the better part and not the whole. That's why she'll never be able to satisfy her hunger. And that's why you still see her around today, in the woods and pastures.«

»So you also see her from time to time?« I concluded, playing a long the naïve game.

»Of course not,« the stout man replied harshly. »I don't see her around anymore these days. I'm no longer like her. Today I don't care, I don't attach importance anymore to the question whether I'm dealing with coal or with gold.«

»And how did you manage to do that?« I asked skeptically.

»I made a deal and swapped my farm and my cows for this piece of land here.«

I laughed. Undoubtedly, he wanted to pull my leg and make fun of me. I was convinced that no human being with some reason left would trade an entire farm, including all the cattle, in for this worthless stony lynchet. The farmer looked at me penetratingly and kept on massaging his gums.

»It was a good deal, after all,« he finally explained. »Here I succeed more and more in satisfying my hunger completely.«

»I don't think the hunger can be completely satisfied at all. As long as we live, we also have needs and wants,« I argued.

»The hunger can't be satisfied with the individual things in the picture; the satisfaction is only temporary,« Nestor admitted. »But it can be satisfied with all there is, in the entire picture. The moment you succeed to see the picture as a whole, there'll be no more hunger to be satisfied.«

The farmer nodded silently, stood up and walked over to the stove where he tasted the soup. Obviously he was satisfied with the result because he placed the pot in the middle of the table. Then he went to the cabinet and took out some soup bowls. He didn't just place them on the table, however, but walked around it counter-clockwise and put down one of the bowls on each of the four sides of the table.

The fact that he placed four instead of three soup bowls on the table made me assume that, before long, another person might join us for the meal. But when I asked him about it, he shook his head and said »no«, to my surprise. I looked over to Nestor but he also kept silent. By now, the atmosphere had markedly cooled down again. We still remained silent, even when the stout man began to fill up all four bowls, in the same sequence and procedure as he had placed them on the table before. For each bowl, he filled the soup ladle all the way to its rim. Then he gave me a spoon and pointed towards the four bowls around the pot.

»Am I supposed to eat all this?« I asked, slightly confused.

»This meal will not just satisfy your hunger; it will also show you how you can satisfy your hunger completely,« the farmer replied mysteriously. Then he asked me to start with the bowl he had filled last. I was supposed to walk around the table clockwise and eat out of each bowl as much as I liked.

The fact that this meal was prepared and arranged with so much painstakingness made me laugh. I couldn't come up with any other explanation for the entire situation than the one that these two strange men wanted to tease and kid me for some reason or another. Nestor and the farmer, however, looked at me with no particular expression in their face whatsoever. And the earnestness I could see and feel in their behavior caused me to feel uncomfortable and to start justifying my nonchalance. I told them that I could see no sensible reason for the absurd »staging« of this particular meal.

»You'll acquire a taste for it,« was the farmer's laconic reply.

I looked at the soup in the first bowl. The gray-brown cloudy liquid didn't look appetizing at all. Only the pieces of carrots and potatoes swimming around in it created some kind of colorful variety. I took a spoonful of it – and almost spat out the liquid at once. The soup was extremely bitter!

Nestor and the stout man broke out in laughter. The latter reminded me with a sneer only to move on to the next bowl once I'd have enough of the bowl I'm currently tasting. But I wasn't willing to continue playing their game like a stupid fool. I accused them of amusing themselves at my expense. But both of them assured me with an innocent mien that this was not their intention. And Nestor emphasized once more that I had to taste of the soup in all four bowls at least once in order to »savvy« the farmer's *création.*

Reluctantly, I went on to the next bowl. This time, however – expecting the bitterness –, I only took a little sip. I was all the more surprised, though, when I realized that the soup in this bowl didn't taste bitter at all – instead, it tasted *sour.*

Even before I was able to judge the sour flavor more precisely, the question struck me how these entirely different tastes could be explained at all. Because I had observed for myself how the stout man had filled all four bowls out of the same pot in the center. I asked him about it, but he made the impression that he didn't really want to tell me about it; he said everything arose from the One in the Center, and it further subdivided in four directions, in this case four different flavors. I, on the other hand, suspected that the farmer had clandestinely added some flavorings or taste-producing substances into each of the bowls before filling them up with soup.

In contrast to the bitter soup, the sour one wasn't repelling; it even had an interesting taste. I emptied the bowl halfway, but then I felt that I had eaten enough sour-tasting food.

Moving around the table clockwise for another quarter circle, I stood in front of the third bowl. And as I had expected, the soup in this bowl had a different taste again; it was spicy and aromatic, just like I would have expected from a »regular« soup. It was well salted, too, but not oversalted. I liked the smooth and racy taste which was slightly burning on the tongue. With each new spoon, my appetite increased, and the unexpected treat caused my resentment to vanish quickly. I almost emptied the bowl, but then I realized that the hot spices were a little hard on my stomach.

The soup in the last bowl had a fruity-sweet taste. I didn't particularly like the sweetness and ate less than half of it. It struck me that there were only a few pieces of vegetable in this bowl, but they were larger than, for example, those many pieces in the first bowl. The farmer must have taken painstaking care of the »correct« distribution of the different pieces of vegetable.

Before I could ask them about it, the stout man encouraged me to taste the soup in the pot in the middle of the table. I was quite curious what particular flavor I would encounter this time, and followed his invitation. To my surprise, the soup in the pot had no taste whatsoever. I took a second and a third spoon because I thought my sense of taste might have been strained too much by the preceding treats. But it seemed as if the liquid in the pot was completely neutral in terms of taste.

When I wanted to tell the two men about it and ask them what the entire exercise had been good for, I felt a sudden strange sensation in the region of my jaw. I lost the feeling of sensation around my mouth, and soon I could only feel the back region of my jaw- and cheekbones. Otherwise, the lower third of my face felt almost numb. I couldn't even have told whether my mouth was open or closed. Startled, I looked at Nestor.

»That leaves you with an open mouth, eh?« he said.

I rubbed my cheeks and my chin. This seemed to help, because soon after, the feeling of sensation returned to the region around my mouth – and a certain state of relaxedness remained. Soon this feeling extended from my face to my entire body. I sat down in the easy chair.

Nestor and the farmer didn't take any further notice of me but started to talk to each other with muted voices. Finally, they sat down at the table where they shared the remaining soup in the pot. At times, they looked at me in a friendly manner and smiled, then they continued slurping up the soup, smacking their lips loudly.

A strange contentedness had taken possession of me, perhaps only a slight drowsiness. I tried hard to follow their conversation but couldn't. I only heard the words they spoke but not what they actually said.

At some point, my look fell on the table next to me. All around the majestic beam balance scale, there were quartz crystals in different sizes. I saw that the farmer made various pieces of jewelry from it. He cut and ground the crystals, then he combined them with gold and silver to manufacture amulets, brooches and finger rings. I was not a jewelry aficionado, but the finished pieces lying around made a very fine impression. I even went so far to believe that I could recognize a style of its own in the farmer's works: most of the pieces had an even number of roundly ground gemstones – four or eight – which were inlaid into some precious metal which surrounded another quartz globe in the center which was slightly larger than the others.

These forms somehow filled me with extraordinary fascination. The kind of jewelry the stout man created was nothing fancy, eccentric or modern; the underlying basic principle was simple, almost banal. And still I felt that these pieces of jewelry were »full« and »complete«; any add-ons would have resulted in a fatal decline of their originality.

In some strange way, incomprehensible to me, I felt so intensely connected with the farmer's artistry that nearly all my thinking and feeling was absorbed by it. I regretted that the everyday world could not be as simple and at the same time so complete as these pieces of jewelry, but I took comfort in the belief that this kind of simplicity actually existed, and that it constantly exerted an influence, no matter if it could be perceived or not. With this blessed certainty I fell into a deep sleep.

Nestor woke me up. He signified that we would return to his house. It was already late afternoon. I still felt a little drowsy. And I felt a slight pressure in my stomach. When I stood up, my eyes were again caught by the wonderful pieces of jewelry.

»Nice, eh?« the farmer said who had taken a seat on the tiled stove in the meantime. I confirmed this, and the stout man told me that, at the time he still distinguished coal from gold, he had hammered dozens of these quartz crystals out of the bedrock of the mountains and hoarded them for years. Today he manufactured jewelry from them.

Spontaneously I asked him if he was willing to sell me one of these amulets. He replied that he already had a customer for each of those pieces of jewelry. But instead, he would give me one of his crude unworked quartz crystals as a gift, namely the first whose weight I was able to guess straight away.

»Guess it?« I called out hopelessly. »How am I supposed to guess the weight of such a stone?«

»With the weights of the scale,« he answered and explained that I should take a quartz crystal in one hand and the corresponding number of weights in the other so as to compensate the crystal's weight. If I had the feeling of equal weights in both hands, I should place the objects into the scale pans to see the result.

I agreed and tried my luck. Again and again, I balanced one of the quartz crystals in my left hand with a number of weights in my right, and vice versa. Finally, when I thought their weight was in balance, I placed them in the brass pans of the scale. But I was far off in my estimation of their relative weights: the quartz crystal always turned out to be lighter than the weights. With each new crystal, I tried to place less and less weights into the scale pan – but each time the crystal was up and the weights were down.

The burly man seemed to visibly enjoy the game while my impatience in turn was growing. And when he encouraged me to continue after several failures, I explained with some bitterness that all of the weights were too heavy. To express my resentment, I placed the next quartz crystal into the scale pan and tried to balance it with only one weight, the lightest of them all. It was totally clear to me that this small weight would never suffice to lift the quartz crystal, but contrary to my expectations the scale balanced out evenly and stayed in that position.

Relieved and upset at the same time, I accused the farmer of having manipulated the scale somehow. He denied this and claimed instead that what I really had done was to balance gold with coal; in doing so, however, I had assigned too much weight to the gold. According to him, I behaved just like the coal woman, and this was also the reason why I had seen her today. Then he took the quartz crystal out of the scale pan and handed it over to me.

»That one's yours,« he said and lowered his voice: »This crystal is valuable – not because you can turn it into a lot of gold, but because its clarity will help you find *your own* clarity,« he explained with a seriousness that was hard to accept for me.

After we had said goodbye, Nestor and I walked back to his house on the narrow path without saying anything. Still slightly drowsy, I was pondering over the events that had taken place in the stout man's house. What was particularly unsettling to me was the fact that I had fallen asleep just like that; it was not alright with me at all.

I asked Nestor for how long I had actually been asleep. He noticed my concern and answered that it might have been the food of the farmer that could have caused me an upset stomach.

»This meal was supposed to show you that it is possible to gain more energy by consciously dealing with the sense of taste – just like we can gain more energy by consciously dealing with all our senses. What the meal has shown you, though, is that your sense of taste is not balanced, and therefore you have some trouble coping with stronger energies.«

It was not the first time that Nestor was talking about »energy«. But it wasn't until now that I started to comprehend that he was aiming at something very specific – something a human being was able to accumulate by behaving correctly.

»Consciously dealing with the sense of taste means that we bring about a balance in the different flavors,« he said and explained that people with an intact sense of taste were not able to eat bitter food in larger amounts. Things tasting bitter should be eaten with caution; a little bitterness could be beneficial or even act as a healing agent, but often the bitter taste indicated the toxicity of a plant.

»Sour food has a stimulating effect,« he went on. »A little amount is refreshing, but too much of it constricts everything within you, and finally you yourself also ›turn sour‹. Basically, some of the food which tastes sourish is already spoiled.

Salty and spicy flavors in turn make you become active, pushing and prompting you. Too much salt and spice, on the other hand, heat up the body and dry it up. This expresses itself in nervousness and can even lead to aggressiveness.«

Finally, Nestor praised the sweet taste. According to him, we could eat as many sweet things as we wanted to, provided the food was not unnaturally sweet, because then it just made us fat and lazy.

»Primitive peoples living in remoteness or seclusion,« he went on, »sometimes have to rely on their sense of taste to be able to tell whether a fruit or a tuber will be edible or not. We, however, are spoiling our sense of taste with all possible kinds of garbage. Entire industries live on man's spoiled sense of taste. The fact that something can be bought in the supermarket is enough for us to classify it as ›edible‹.

When your sense of taste is out of balance, it can lead, over time, to upsets and physical complaints. The more natural your nutrition is, on the other hand, the better you will be at determining the correct ratio of these four basic flavors. This is something you'll also be able to feel – just the way you could today.«

»So when my nutrition is balanced and correct, I'll constantly fall asleep?« I sneered.

Nestor considered this funny and laughed. He finally repeated that the correct use of the sense of taste resulted in more strength and energy flowing through the body. And he claimed that I was not yet able to consciously experience that much energy within my body – and that is why I had fallen asleep.

»Even if so,« I told him, »why are you telling me this?«

»If you really want to restore Mari Egli's secretaire,« he answered, »you'll need much energy, as much as you can possibly muster up. A part of this energy becomes accessible to you when you succeed in correctly using your senses. With regard to the sense of taste, this means that it plays an important role what your nutrition consists of.«

Nestor stopped and looked at me penetratingly. »You'll have to change your eating habits,« he said to me as if he had just announced my death sentence. »You can't afford any longer to stuff yourself with garbage.«

The Afterimage of the Secretaire

Nestor's demand to change my eating habits was something I had a hard time to digest. This was the first time that he told me directly and relentlessly that my habits in this regard were simply wrong. Perhaps my diet wasn't particularly that which was always recommended as »balanced« and »healthy« – but that was my own business. Nestor and the farmer, though, behaved like to evangelizing health apostles, perhaps because they believed to have picked up all »grains of truth«. I wasn't willing to accept this behavior, and so I decided to talk to Nestor about it on my next visit.

Meanwhile, I knew that he was a tough negotiation partner, so the first thing I did on this occasion was to express my admiration for him, as he obviously managed to live his ideals for real. Then I assured him of my general willingness to continue our cooperation. After this display of my goodwill, I now believed to be in the position to voice my request. Politely but firmly, I pointed out to him that our cooperation suffered if he tried to act as a »guardian« for me, for example when it came to diet and nutrition. Nestor laughed and claimed I was already be »spoon-fed« from all sides anyhow.

»That's not true,« I defended myself, slightly provoked. All at once, he had obliterated my formality.

»Of course,« he insisted. »In all your thoughts and actions, you orient yourself to ideals which you have adopted as your own, and which you have gotten used to. The sense of taste is no exception in this regard. It had been affected all along by the habits of people around you. In this way, you have your preferences and antipathies – independent from what is really nourishing.«

»And who decides what is nourishing and what isn't? You?«

»If your sense of taste is balanced and in a natural state, you'll know for yourself what is best for your body. But as long as it isn't, you'll have to choose your nutrition in such a way that your sense of taste will get there.«

Nestor repeated that it is important to balance the sense of taste and to recover its natural state by ingesting natural and unprocessed food, as far as possible. And I should balance it by taking the different flavors into consideration accordingly. But if, on the other hand, I primarily lived on nearly spoiled, too salty or too sweet food, I was far from balancing my sense of taste and recovering its natural state.

»The correct use of the sense of taste will release energy within you,« he said again. »You'll feel it when this energy flows through your body. And then you'll be more successful with the restoration of the secretaire.«

This and other conversations on the subject of eating habits finally made me adapt my diet to Nestor's menu plan – for the sake of peace and out of respect for him. This meant that, for the time I spent in the Emmental, I would live on vegetables, bread, cheese, nuts and honey – all natural and unprocessed, of course.

The change of my diet was something that was difficult for me at first. Not just because I deprived my sense of taste of the usual stimuli, but also because my giving in was a concession to Nestor. And whenever I wanted to cover up my injured pride with the voice within me that praised my peacefulness and adaptability, another voice imposed itself on me which accused me of a low fighting spirit and a lack of assertiveness. At any rate, the effort to arrive at a balanced nutrition was so strainful that I stuffed myself, as if I were out of my mind, with all possible and impossible things as soon as I had returned from the Emmental to Bern – a bad habit which I wasn't able to get rid of for a while.

The following summer was so extraordinarily hot and dry that, even in the Emmental, water became scarce in some places. I enjoyed driving up to those higher altitudes, leaving the city heat behind me. During this time I finally succeeded in completing the first step of the restoration: cleaning off the entire secretaire. I wasn't able, however, to answer the question whether or not the change of my diet had played a role in this.

On this bright sunny day in July I accompanied Nestor on a hiking tour alongside the Emme. We drove down the valley, crossed the river and followed it downstream. Nestor then told me to turn into a small side road which led us to a traditional farmhouse, remotely located on the banks of the Emme. From there we hiked upstream. The valley floor was relatively spacious in this region, the river bed wide and shallow. Only the right bank of the river, strewn with stones, was accessible; on the left side, however, thick woods reached all the way down the riverbank.

Nestor walked barefoot from the start. I for my part preferred to have my shoes on my feet and not in my hands. But a false step which cost me the dryness of both shoes and socks made me change my mind, and I also started to walk barefoot. My unprotected feet were not used to the hard rocks, though, and when the ground of the shallow bank turned increasingly rough and bumpy, and the size of the rocks varied more widely, it became increasingly difficult for me to walk without shoes.

It was not until now that I was able to correctly judge Nestor's performance: obviously he was very adept at walking on rocks. Clever and adroitly, he kept on walking with the same speed he was used to, while I stayed behind time and again. After each step I had to look out for the next rock which I considered safe enough to put a foot on. This permanent concentration on where to place my feet while walking was straining, and I was relieved when we finally took a break and sat down on a little sandbank in the shadow of some broad-leaved trees.

I made a joking remark on the stresses and strains of this hiking tour, but Nestor took the opportunity to point out to me what a poor physical condition I had.

»Then I guess it's not enough to just eat a healthy diet, is it? The way I understand you, I'll also have to improve my physical condition so as to be able to perform the perfect restoration?« I sneered.

»A good physical condition is also an expression of strength and energy,« Nestor replied undeterred. »If you'd walk over these rocks for just an hour each day – your stamina, and thus your strength, would increase quickly and markedly,« he claimed and explained that walking on rocks is actually similar to the perfect restoration: because, while walking on them I had to take every step with full awareness of the ground because each step was a different one. There were no repetitions because the relative distances between the individual rocks differed each time.

»When you walk on rocks you can't engage in absent-minded day-dreaming; much rather, it demands all of your attention in the picture,« he stated. »Each moment demands a quick decision of you; there's no room for doubts or speculations. If you hesitate, you'll always stay behind. Or even worse: you'll take a wrong step.

The perfect restoration also means that you put all of your attention on what you do at any given instant – because the picture itself changes with each new moment, there are no repetitions. If you approach Mari Egli's secretaire in this way, you'll soon be done with the restoration.«

Nestor made no mystery of the fact that only people with a high energy level were able to experience the picture as always new and without repetitions. People with a low energy level, on the other hand, arranged their everyday life in such way that it looked like an ever-repeating ritual without any differences. In this way, according to Nestor, they only had to pay a minimum of attention to the picture – so as to be able to withdraw back into their thoughts and daydreams as soon as possible. Those, he said, were the egoists.

I objected to his ridiculing people's everyday routines – an inevitable result of being caught up in the working world –, and that he excluded himself from it.

»We're all egoists,« I replied.

»You too?« he asked.

»Yes, me too. And you. All of us,« I said without hesitating.

Nestor looked at me amused. »You don't consider yourself as egoistic as you claim, do you?«

»Of course,« I answered slightly impatient. »Why should I be an exception?«

»Well, what exactly is it that makes you an egoist?«

This question came as a surprise to me, and it was embarrassing that I couldn't come up with a concrete answer. Actually I had never really thought about what made me an egoist. Evasively, I told him that this was only my business, and that he didn't have to deal with that. Nestor laughed; he had quickly recognized my awkward position.

»Your problem is that you don't really know yourself,« he pointed out to me. »You should earnestly try to become aware of your feelings and notions, and that means: converting them into energy. Then, and only then, will you really know yourself. Up till then, your admission to be egoistic is just an alibi exercise of your mind.«

I protested and claimed he deliberately alleged this. But it was useless: my protest was outweighed by Nestor's persuasiveness. And the fact that I had to admit he was right deprived me and my clamor of the last remnants of credibility. He had caught me out in an unprecedented way.

We continued hiking, Nestor at a faster pace, me at a slower. In regular intervals he waited for me, and in doing so he directed my attention to natural phenomena he seemed to greatly enjoy: he admired the rocks located in elevated places, between tufts of grass and small bushes, which had adopted a reddish hue, obviously due to their contact with algae and lichen. Then again he was astounded by the bizarre forms created by mud and interwoven roots and branches within it. The almost intact shells of hatched water flies, which often were sticking to the rocks on the bank, also had a certain appeal to him. And once he had discovered a massive tree trunk washed up to the bank which showed carvings of religious symbols of different cultures. Obviously he was familiar with this particular trunk; he told me of the place near the spring of the river where it used to stand before.

Nestor's observations put me in a tight spot. I also tried to look out for something peculiar around us, but I couldn't find anything worth mentioning. I attributed this to the fact that I had to concentrate so hard on my steps while walking. I envied Nestor for his ability to hike at such a fast pace, and to still find the time to admire the surrounding nature. My envy, my poor condition and my painful feet eventually led me to admit that I had run out of steam.

»The rocks literally have an edge on you,« Nestor claimed amused when I suggested to take a rest. »To beat you, they don't have to do anything else than just lying around.« But he himself didn't object to taking a rest, either, and to get something to eat.

Nestor began to prepare the vegetables we had taken along. He instructed me to find five stone slabs with which I was supposed to build a kind of oven. According to his explanation, everything was quite simple: the vegetables were placed on a flat stone; four other slabs had to be arranged around it in an upright position, and another one was finally supposed to be placed on top. Then he would spark a fire on each side of the oven and on the upper slab – *et voilà*.

I didn't want to be impolite, but I told Nestor that I had my doubts that this would work out. And this was too laborious and consuming too much time, I added. Nestor, however, insisted on the necessity of this stone slab oven, but the reason he gave me was incomprehensible to me: he said, time doesn't have to be our concern, now that the rocks have kept me, so prematurely, from hiking on. He considered that, at this point in time, we weren't able to advance all the way to the spring of the river, and we didn't have to, either. But in order to do this, it was inevitable to master the elements. The first thing I had to do was to consciously deal with the stones and to try to do something creative with them. So whether the vegetables turned out well done or not depended on whether I had the »right touch« for the stones.

I couldn't think much of what he said, but somehow I liked the way he wanted to encourage me to build this oven. He tried to awaken my consciousness for a mysterious world in which other ways of thinking prevailed – and which people with common sense might have called »irrational«. At this moment I felt like doing it, and I was willing to support his fantasies and to play long – somehow like an adult condescending to the level of an infant so as to immerse into a magical world with the kid.

The magic vanished, however, the longer I played along: the search for suitable stone slabs was laborious, and the ovens I constructed either collapsed quickly or they had gaps so large that any firing of the oven would have been useless. Only with a lot of effort and Nestor's help was I able to find five suitable slabs and to assemble them to a relatively compact oven.

When the vegetables were finally put in the oven and the fire around it started to light up brightly, Nestor expressed his admiration for the nature around us once more. This time his attention was caught by a rock face which was rising up steeply and forming the opposite riverbank. He called my attention to the strange rock formation: countless round stones of different colors and sizes were sticking in a kind of porous solidified mass. And the water leaking out in some spots obviously flushed out minerals as well and changed the *Nagelfluh*[2], as Nestor used to call the formation, to reddish and yellowish hues. He could find many additional details in this rock face which he enjoyed and called my attention to.

I became impatient. I found myself in the same situation that occurred each time when we were on our way together: in my view, Nestor tended towards exaggerated descriptions, no matter what he had discovered. He was virtually raving about nature.

»Well,« he sighed when he saw that my reaction to his discoveries was conservative at best, »perhaps I'm the only one seeing the beauty in such ordinary things like these stones. Perhaps all the beauty out here is just there for me.« He said this in a friendly thoughtful way while he was fishing for the vegetables in the oven with a small stick.

Perhaps it was the way he spoke; perhaps it was the fact that he virtually excluded me from the beauty surrounding us; perhaps it also was his »overshooting«, because it was not the first time on this day that he had said things like that – at any rate, I became exasperated. I tried to explain to him how arrogant it sounded when someone claimed that all the beauty was just there for him only, the sun only shone for him, and clouds only moved along the sky for the same purpose – in short: the entire picture was there just for him only. To rational people – and I

---

[2] Southern and Swiss German term for sedimentary conglomerates.

included myself in this category – utterances of that kind were just absurd chitchat.

»How do you come up with the idea that everything is just there for you only?« I quarreled with him, »you're not the only person around here. As it happens, I'm here as well.«

»You?« Nestor laughed. »You belong to the setting of my picture. You're wallpaper.«

I kept silent. My exasperation was so strong that I wouldn't have been able to reply something sensible anyway. But Nestor soon propitiated me by stating that, of course, every person had their own picture. We all saw our own picture and influenced it in doing so. And eventually it depended on our energy how the picture presented itself to us.

While we were eating I speculated that, in that case, he was something like a *solipsist*, someone who considers the world to be nothing more than a product of his own ideas, a person who does not grant the world an existence as such, independent from his own ideas and thoughts. By referring to the philosophy of solipsism I also wanted to point out to him that ideas and notions of that nature were nothing new to mankind.

Nestor didn't seem to have heard of these particular philosophic teachings. Instead, he showed a childish joy in the word »solipsist«. Countless times he repeated it, stumbled with pretended awkwardness over the seemingly tongue-twisting *psisht*[3] and teased me by calling himself a solipsist, time and again. But to me, his histrionic fuss was nothing else but a subterfuge he resorted to so he wouldn't have to show his true colors.

»Who are your role models, after all, if not the solipsists?« I asked him.

»I don't have any role models, I only have that one picture which is the whole, after all,« he replied, and with a majestic gesture he pointed towards the environment. His pretended elevatedness made me laugh.

»Ah, come on, somebody must have taught you – directly or indirectly. You don't really claim that you have newly invented your philosophy, do you?«

»That's no philosophy,« he replied insistently. »I don't care about philosophy. Philosophy means that you ponder over the picture and break it down into different fragments – in other words, you're bringing your small world into the picture. When it comes to the perfect restora-

---

[3] In Swiss German the third „s" of „solipsist" is pronounced „sh".

tion, though, you are dissolving the small world in the picture. And that has to do with *seeing*, not with *thinking* like philosophers do: you learn to *see* the picture as a whole.«

On this evening, after we had returned from our hiking tour, I sat down across from Mari Egli's secretaire in the stable. I wanted to practice seeing the picture as a whole by concentrating on the center of the object. I wasn't able to focus my attention, though, because my thoughts kept carrying me away to the events that took place during our hiking tour on this day. Fragments of memories were chasing each other, evoking this or that feeling within me at times.

At first, I concerned myself with the fact that Nestor took my clumsy behavior regarding the stones on the banks of the Emme as a measurement standard to judge my progress in the perfect restoration: on the way back he opened up to me that my trouble with the stones, namely walking on them and building an oven with them, was characteristic for my difficulties with the secretaire. He urged me to make more and direct contact with the ground, the stones and the soil so that I was able to gain additional energy from the ground. This made me stronger and more alert, and this in turn positively influenced the restoration of the secretaire.

My eyes were caught by the inlays on the object which showed rings and lines extending, on the one hand, over all three steps, and adorning, on the other hand, only a few single drawers.

I had to think of the way back which I had experienced quite in the sense of Nestor's »contact to the ground«. Nestor and I hadn't taken the same way back we had set out on; rather, we left the bank of the Emme by climbing up a steep rock face overgrown with grass and small trees. Our climbing fun ended abruptly, though, when I – halfway up the face – couldn't make any further headway and had to cling to some tufts of grass. My strength was waning, and I was close to sliding off. Nestor had to put my attention on a root right next to me which I could hold on to so as to pull myself up and to reach safe ground. This lack of attention had almost cost my physical integrity. By now I realized that Nestor had pointed out to me this lack during the entire hiking tour by showing me his high attention level in the picture.

There were two kinds of lines adorning the secretaire: the horizontal zigzag line extended over the two bottom drawers while the vertical line rose up, more or less straight, between the six drawers.

Indeed, Nestor was able to display an extraordinary high level of attention. He didn't merely perceive the objects in his field of vision, but he actively dealt with them and created an emotional affiliation in this way. And now that I began to get an inkling of how much he was capable to be »in the picture«, that is, in the know about the environment surrounding him, I myself started to deal more consciously with the picture. Compared to Nestor, my interest in the tangible, living environment was rather poor; he was able to look behind things I merely looked at on the surface. On the other hand, it were small, unimpressive, even trifling things he could get excited about: forms, patterns and colors on stones and plants – why, after all, should I have dealt with petty things like that? To me, there were things far more important, greater, loftier than a few rampant weeds and scattered rock debris.

The top and center drawers on the left side showed little dot-like images.

I pondered whether Nestor really had the ability to perceive the picture newly and free from repetitions at each given instant. At that moment I became aware that this was precisely what I was *not* doing: I sat in the stable and looked at the secretaire – but I hardly perceived it because I was almost exclusively preoccupied with things that didn't happen here and now. With awakened fervor, I concentrated on the object and deliberately tried to look behind it, not just at it: the inlays consisted of three different kinds of wood, each with a different hue. A reddish-brown formed the background on which the mysterious line- and ring-shaped figures made of bright yellowish and dark-brown wood seemed to float. The large-surfaced leaves of wood extended over all three steps. This was remarkable because the builder had to subject the thin wood to a longer and quite elaborate adjustment procedure. Why all this effort? And why were there only dots on the two upper left-hand drawers? It struck me that I had never asked Nestor about it.

»Look behind it, not just at it.« Hoping for some idea, some answer, some spontaneous inspiration which would reveal the sense of these inlays to me, I concentrated on the center of the secretaire.

Gradually, the flow of my thoughts was ebbing out, and the memories in my head faded.

I had been looking at the secretaire for some while when I suddenly could clearly perceive the lines and circles of the inlays. Their rims had changed color and lit up intensely now. This brightly luminous, green-bluish hue on the rims made the inlays, and therefore the entire secretaire, protrude from the picture.

I tried to keep my look focused on the center of the object with full concentration so as to perceive only that which took place in the picture. Each new alignment of the look, no matter how small, seemed to renew the brilliant glow of the inlays. It also looked as if the patterns of the inlays were in slight but constant motion, just as if they wanted to drift off towards the left or the right. Newly aligning my look ended this drifting until, after some time of concentration, it repeated itself.

At some point I closed my eyes which had started to feel tired from staring for such a long time – and I saw the greenish glimmering circular patterns as afterimage. When I opened my eyes again, I could perceive the afterimage on the walls of the stable, at the ceiling and on the ground, on my legs and hands – everywhere I looked at. I could see it so clearly that I just couldn't help but look at it. The longer I gazed at it, however, the more the image seemed to escape my look. Even if I held my eyes still, this glowing spot seemed to be in constant motion, particularly downwards.

Once the notion crossed my mind that this afterimage I could perceive was the actual »inner essence« of Mari Egli's secretaire. In fact, the behavior of the afterimage seemed to point to the behavior of the secretaire as such: just like the afterimage escaped my observation, so had the secretaire denied me access to it, time and again. This thought evoked a strange kind of exhilaration within me: Mari Egli's secretaire behaved elusive, I just couldn't get a hold of it. So this piece of furniture had a character of its own, and I had denied it this special property and fought against it instead. It became totally clear to me now that I would have to arrange myself with the secretaire so as to be able to restore it – otherwise it would always »escape« me. In fact, Mari Egli's secretaire demanded respect of me, and I began to appreciate it for that.

When I put my attention back on the afterimage again, I recognized that it was not in such a strong motion as before. I was able to keep it up at the same height for a longer time, and thus I could see it better before it started to flow down slowly. Without hesitating, I grabbed the brush and started to apply the lye solution on the surface. While the solution was drying up, I stared at the center of the object again until the afterimage of the secretaire began to show up. I played with it for a while, pushed it over the walls of the stable and the secretaire as such until I wasn't able to see it any longer.

Then I took the spatula and started to scrape off the dissolved varnish and dirt, and with a piece of steel wool I removed all remnants. I could feel how the pressure within me had built up and how my heart pounded while I did this – but aside from a slight tickle in my abdomen, my body stayed calm. Much rather, I was surprised about the effortlessness and certainty with which my hands were moving: it was as if they knew by themselves what motions they had to go through and how much effort they had to apply.

I repeated this procedure a few more times, then I fixed some scratches and unevennesses with coarse and fine sandpaper. Finally, I took an old rag and wiped off the wood dust that had remained from sanding down all surfaces – until the entire secretaire was completely cleaned off. By now I realized how easy and »matter-of-course« the work had been; I had even worked on the object at the same pace I used to work with on other objects. And after I had put down the tools late at night, my relationship to Mari Egli's secretaire had fundamentally changed: I liked the beautiful piece of furniture, I even had fun with it.

2

Afterimages

The next morning I went into the stable, first of all, to take a look at the secretaire: the lye solution was completely removed, scratch marks were smoothed out with sandpaper, and all remnants of wood dust were wiped off with a rag. The working utensils were still lying around.

I would have never even dreamed that I could feel such a childish happiness over the success of a trivial activity like stripping the varnish off a secretaire. As there was no obvious reason why I was successful last night without encountering the difficulties I had previously, I was soon concerned with the question whether, and if so, how Nestor's perfect restoration might have played a role in this success: was it the concentration exercises? Or had I even succeeded in seeing the picture as a whole? Did my small world dissolve in the picture, as Nestor had said? Did diet or nutrition have an influence? Or was it a combination of all these factors?

Nestor stuck his head through the stable door and ended my pondering. »How's our chief restorator?« he asked amused but didn't wait for my answer; instead, he took a look at the secretaire. »Oh,« he said and lifted his eyebrows in surprise. »You managed to clean off the secretaire completely.«

Proudly I told him what had happened and what I had done. When I mentioned the afterimage of the object he became thoughtful. For a moment it seemed as if he wanted to say something, but he kept silent. Instead, he was beaming, as if it was a success worth celebrating.

»You probably think that the exercises for the perfect restoration have played a role in my success, don't you?« I speculated.

»What else do you think it was?« he asked back.

»I'm not sure. Do you think I've managed to dissolve my small world in the picture?«

»Well, a small part of it.«

I didn't know whether I should be pleased or upset: if Nestor was right, then the perfect restoration did indeed have an effect. On the other hand, it had taken me a full year to celebrate this »triumph« – over something that usually would have taken me two days.

I didn't want to imagine what it would have meant to transfer these time dimensions to the upcoming work on the secretaire.

»Dissolving the small world completely in the picture is something that will take more time,« Nestor picked up my considerations. »Because you'll need a lot of energy to do so. And energy is not something which you can acquire overnight. But you've made progress and came closer to your goal – *judihui*[4].«

After breakfast I helped Nestor gather some wild berries. We left the house, climbed up the hill and got into a marshy area furrowed by creek ditches. We followed the narrow strip of trees alongside the ditches and found small strawberries and raspberries. Then we combed through large forest areas further up the hill separated from each other by pasture strips. The flora was wild and untouched, beautiful to behold but hard to penetrate.

Nestor called my attention to the mighty old sycamore maple trees which could be seen here and there. Not without some irony, he started to talk about the history of the Emmental which used to be dominated by deciduous virgin forests. But with the colonization of the valley floors, all these trees had been cleared until the Emmental had almost turned into a flatland due to the many landslides and floodings. Today, he regretted, the fir trees – so suitable for reforestation because of their quick growth – deprived the inhabitants of the Emmental of any sense for beauty with their evergreen dreariness.

While Nestor told me this, the first signs of a thunderstorm showed up. There were still blue spots in the sky, but a heavy, dark ring of clouds was already hovering over the Hohgant mountain. And the thick cover of clouds behind the Schrattenfluh mountain began to squeeze itself through the numerous peaks of the mountain, creating a spooky effect.

Nestor assumed that we wouldn't be able to make it back to his house in time. But he knew of an empty stable nearby where we could find shelter. We were still hastening through the woods towards that stable when the first drops of rain fell, announcing a heavy thunderstorm.

And we had just barely arrived at the hut when the clouds' heavy burden came down onto the Emmental with unrestrained volume.

The stable was relatively small, a two-story building which provided space for six to eight cows. Previous visitors had left their »marks« in the wooden wall next to the entrance, and some of these revealed the old age of the hut:

---

[4] Swiss German for *hooray!*

I. B. 1955
E. L. Sch. 1874
M. E. 1882
F. von Gunten 1937
O. M. St. 1865

In the front part of the stable there was an opening in the ceiling through which we climbed up to the second floor. Up there, Nestor opened a large gate which was used to bring in the hay onto this barn floor. We sat down at the wall across from this gate, and for a while we listened to the roar of the thunderstorm.

Nestor took off his hat and began asking me about the greenish afterimage of the secretaire which I had perceived last night. He asked me precisely about its form and color and wanted to know how it was correlated to my eye motions. The expectant attitude he assumed in doing so caused a certain distrust in me.

»Was this the kind of afterimage which comes about when I don't realign my look for a longer period of time?« I asked, picking up his theory on the afterimages.

»Exactly. Your success last night is directly linked to this afterimage.«

I was just about to answer that I couldn't understand this when I remembered that I myself had linked these two factors as well: I had interpreted the afterimage as some kind of mirror image of the secretaire, and I had extrapolated from its behavior to the secretaire's »readiness« for the restoration.

When, after some time, the afterimage tended to flow downward less strongly, and I could hold it in suspension for a longer period of time, I assumed, as a »matter of course«, that I would be able to work on the secretaire without encountering any trouble – which, curiously enough, was the case. I told Nestor about it but also added that the analogy between afterimage and secretaire was an arbitrary one, only existing in my imagination. So this could not at all explain my success on the previous day.

»That was more than just imagination,« Nestor answered back with a resolute tone of voice. »That was *direct seeing*. And because of that, you had acted correctly. Last night you have recognized something very fundamental: your ability to hold the afterimages in suspension is a direct indicator for the degree of success with which you can work on the secretaire.«

80

»But linking the afterimage to the piece of furniture in this way was illogical and improper,« I objected. »After all, there's no direct relationship between an object and its afterimage.«

»Today you're judging everything in perspective of your small world again,« he countered. »But yesterday your small world had kept quiet, and you didn't have to deal with the existence or non-existence of direct relationships. All you had done was just seeing and acting.«

Nestor explained that last night I had succeeded in holding the image in suspension for a longer period of time without constantly realigning my look. Due to the higher degree of attention with which I had seen the picture, I had been able to render it more energetic and thus less material. And this had resulted in the perception of the afterimage.

»I rendered the picture less material?« I asked.

»Human beings like us have this potential,« he confirmed. »When we're able to put our energy directly into what we are looking at, then our picture becomes more energetic. A more energetic picture means that the energy is less absorbed in material objects; thus, the picture is less material. Yesterday you were successful because you were able to establish a little distance to the material world and its values because you were not so concerned with it. You were more relaxed, but at the same time you were able to better concentrate your attention. You've acted very much in the sense of the perfect restoration. And because of that you were able to hold the image in suspension for a longer period of time, and to perceive the afterimage clearly on the inner screen.«

I thought that Nestor tended to overestimate these afterimages; as far as I knew, they came about quite naturally as a result of physical stimuli in the eye itself, for example when we briefly look at a source of light or when we fixate our eyes on objects for a longer time. Nestor, however, took the phenomenon out of the context of everyday experience and placed it in the realm of his own quite peculiar worldview. What was particularly irritating for me was the fact that I myself was part of this explanation: Nestor took my experience from the night before to confirm his viewpoint on the importance of these afterimages.

»It's not difficult to generate afterimages,« he admitted. »And it doesn't play any significant role how an afterimage comes about, whether by briefly looking at a source of light or fixating the eyes on an object for a longer time. At any rate, the challenge is to *hold* the afterimages *in suspension* on the inner screen, and to be able to *see* them for a longer period of time. And this you should practice.«

»Practice to hold the afterimages in suspension?«

»Yes. For you, seeing the afterimages is now a part of the perfect restoration,« he said, firmly convinced. »When you were filled with strength and energy, you had discovered the inner screen for yourself. Now start to develop this inner screen. Work with it. The fact that we have an inner screen at our disposal with which we can work consciously – that's something we have to experience, first of all. Because from the beginning of our life we haven't learned anything else than to put our attention on the outer screen, the material world perceivable with our senses. By concentrating on the afterimages now, you'll get to know your inner screen.«

»What are these screens?« I asked him.

Nestor thought this over for a while before he answered. In thoughts, he played with his hat.

»The more you succeed in dissolving your small world in the picture,« he finally said, »the more you will see that our picture is comprised of different projection surfaces. I can't tell you more about these surfaces than that we project our small world onto them. I call these surfaces ›screens‹, and there are two kinds of them: an outer and an inner screen. On the outer screen we project our material world; the inner screen is the projection surface for our feelings and thoughts.«

»But you said I was supposed to get to know my inner screen by concentrating on the afterimages?«

»Yes, the afterimages are part of the inner screen, because they are memories of the material world; they are converted conglomerates of feelings and thoughts made visible in this way.«

I didn't follow up on this further but asked him whether he really believes that concentrating on the images could help in the restoration of the secretaire.

»When afterimages come into existence while looking at the picture as a whole, then that is the first sign that you have started to dissolve your small world in the picture,« he replied, again firmly convinced. »If you concentrate directly on the afterimages, you start to detach your attention from the material world, and instead, you shift it to the inner world. And the length of time which you are able to hold the afterimages in suspension shows you how strong and well developed your attention, that is your energy, already is. That's why you should concentrate more on your inner screen and try to hold the afterimages in suspension.«

I kept silent and listened to the pattering of raindrops that was only occasionally drowned out by rolling thunder. Nestor still seemed quite thoughtful, his eyes wandered over the dull and cloudy landscape.

»Your perfect restoration becomes more and more confusing,« I finally remarked. »It removes itself farther and farther from my original intention – to just restore a piece of furniture.«

»You know for yourself that your original intention was by far not only the restoration of the secretaire,« he countered. »If that had been the case, the restoration wouldn't have caused you any problems. But your attention was not devoted to Mari Egli's secretaire but to your idea of how much *dough* you will be able to make with it. The concentration on memory pictures of the past will further counteract such an attitude.«

The thunderstorm became stronger. Nestor stretched his legs and placed his hands on the ground. His movements caused a reflex in me, and I did the same. At that instant I became aware that I imitated him. Immediately I pulled my right leg back to my body.

»Why didn't you tell me from the beginning that the perfect restoration centers around these afterimages?« I asked him.

Nestor smiled. »If I had told you that beforehand, you would have had an even harder time comprehending this than the point of concentrating on the outer screen; you would have dismissed it as some lonely man's flight of fancy. But now you yourself had a successful experience with these afterimages, and that will motivate you to keep practicing.«

»I'm not so sure about that,« I objected. »I still think that it's mumbo-jumbo.«

»Perhaps. But now that you have made this experience it's your own mumbo-jumbo.«

Later in the evening, the rain ceased and we returned to Nestor's house. I was very tired and went to bed immediately. In this night I had the first of a number of strangely real and vivid dreams which kept repeating in regular intervals, though they were a little bit different each time.

While being asleep, I suddenly became aware that I was dreaming. But I wasn't able to wake up. I felt the urge to move around, to stretch my body, but that turned out impossible: if, for instance, I wanted to lift the leg or the arm, I met some kind of resistance. A feeling of powerlessness, of despair started to overcome me, but soon this feeling turned into blind rage. In an attempt to free myself I started to flounder and struggle, kicking my legs in all directions. All my efforts were in vain, though: I stayed right where I was.

Exhausted, I laid on my belly, breathing hastily. It was cold and damp. In a moment of relative silence I looked around and recognized that I was in some kind of cavern. The walls were so close up that they almost touched me on all sides. Slowly and cautiously, I began to creep forward. For a while this worked out alright, but each single motion took that much energy that, before soon, I was lying flat on the rough ground, completely exhausted. I wanted to turn my head and look behind me, but there wasn't enough space to do so. And in front of me, I couldn't see the end of the tube because the close and narrow walls soon passed into a deep, all-embracing darkness. Another time I tried to pull myself together and to keep going, but again my strength was waning too soon.

The following morning I began to plan the next restoration steps on the secretaire. The task now was to fix the damaged spots on it. Of the three circular symbols on the top left-hand drawer, the inlay of the right circle was damaged. There was a hole with frayed margins stretching from the center of the circular figure over the ring all the way beyond the figure. Here the task was, for the purpose of simplicity, to cut out a generous triangle which contained the hole. The matter became a little bit more complex due to the fact that the new wooden leaf, which would replace the old damaged one, would have to be assembled from three different kinds of wood: one kind for the center of the figure, another one for the outer ring and the rest for the part outside of the circular figure. This job I wanted to tackle next.

Nestor entered the stable the moment I was busy marking and measuring the size of the spot that had to be cut out. I explained to him what I intended to do. For a while he sat on a bale of straw while I continued my work.

»You should not be blinded by your success and rush the job,« he suddenly said. »Two days ago, circumstances were favorable, and that's why you had strength − enough to get the secretaire cleaned and prepared. What you plan to do now demands even more attention of you. You should gather more strength, first of all, by concerning yourself with your inner screen.«

I was irritated that Nestor expressed doubts of my capabilities; somehow, this thwarted the momentum with which I started out.

»So instead of restoring the secretaire you want me to stare at its afterimage now?« I sneered.

»Leave the secretaire alone for a moment,« he replied calmly. »I know a place which is better suited for seeing afterimages: the chicken house.«

Nestor led me to a small room under the hayloft. There he opened a small low door, ducked down to step inside and disappeared in the darkness. I looked inside but couldn't see anything. Instead, a musty odor entered my nose.

»That's supposed to be a chicken house?« I asked skeptically.

»This is the chicken house,« it sounded from inside. Then a dim light fell into the interior. I saw that Nestor had removed a blanket which covered the only window.

The »chicken house« was a small room with a length of perhaps ten and a width of about six feet. It was completely empty – aside from piles of dust and cobwebs in the corners. But nothing seemed to indicate that this space was previously used as a chicken house. Floor, walls and ceiling of the room were painted black, and this blackness absorbed much of the little light that fell through the plate-sized circular window in the wall on the other side of the entrance door.

The strange window which Nestor cleared of cobwebs and dust attracted my attention: it seemed to consist of two parts, an outer circular ring and an inner disk. The light shining through the outer ring into the space seemed brighter than that which fell through the center part; it was almost unnaturally bright which led me to assume that there was an artificial source of light behind that part of the window. On closer inspection, though, I could see that the window actually consisted of two single glass panes separated by a fine wooden ring. The glass pane in the center had a slightly concave form and acted similar to a diverging lens which created the optical effect of a brightly illuminated outer ring.

The exercise Nestor explained to me then didn't sound too difficult: all I was supposed to do was keep my eyes focused on the window for a while, as if I would practice to see the picture as a whole. Then I was supposed to see the afterimage of the window on the black walls until it faded out – and then the whole thing would repeat itself from the beginning. Nestor encouraged me right away to try seeing the afterimage.

Unmotivated, I followed his instructions, positioned myself at the back wall and looked at the window. After a while I unfixed my look and turned towards the black wall. Now I could clearly see the colored afterimage moving through the dark room. After it had faded out, completely absorbed by the surrounding darkness, I focused my look on the window again, and then back on the afterimage. I repeated it two more times, then I lost my patience: I decided that I had seen enough. I told Nestor that I didn't have any difficulties at all with seeing the afterimage.

He seemed upset about my statement and accused me of not thoroughly looking at the afterimage, even claiming that I didn't *want* to see.

»It's not about merely looking at the afterimage,« he said insistently, »you have to hold it in suspension in order to see it properly. You're not alert enough.«

With these words, Nestor left the stable and came back soon after with two wood blocks of identical size and a narrow board. He put the two blocks on the ground and placed the board on top of them, parallel to the wall with the window. Then he asked me to step onto the board. When I stood up there, he corrected my posture. Finally, my feet stood parallel to each other, my knees were slightly bent, arms and legs were relaxed and hanging loosely. Once Nestor was satisfied with my posture, he stepped back and looked at me in an amused way.

»Like the cock on the roost,« he said and made us both laugh with his words. Actually the situation was so absurd that it would have been embarrassing to me if someone from my circle of friends had seen me at that moment.

»If your body is too relaxed, you'll grow tired quickly and your thoughts wander off,« he said to explain the necessity of the wooden board. »At the same time, though, it is important that you don't strain yourself too much. This particular posture here will prevent both of these extremes. In this way, you should succeed in focusing enough of your attention on the picture.«

Once more I looked at the window and tried to hold its afterimage in suspension so as to take a thorough look at it and to examine it. Just like two days ago, I realized that the afterimage tended to flow downward. If I wanted to keep it in my field of vision, I had to constantly realign my look. As the afterimage was flickering too much, though, and because of its alterations with each new realignment of my look, I didn't succeed in capturing its actual form — as far as I could establish, its form was similar to an accumulation of a number of these round windows.

After I had told Nestor about this, he explained that I couldn't see the afterimage in its pure form because I also realigned my look in those moments I was still looking at the window. In this way, I didn't just constantly renew and superimpose the picture but the afterimage as well. To avoid this effect, according to Nestor, I was supposed to just take a short look at the window each time.

Nestor's advice helped. With my next attempts I wanted to determine the exact color of the afterimage, but I realized that I couldn't: it seemed to be a mixture of yellow, green and blue. Which of the colors dominated in each case depended on the intensity of the afterimage: first I could see it in bright yellow hues; then, after a while and with diminishing luminosity, the color changed to green and then blue until the after-image of the round window was so weak that it was hardly perceivable any longer.

Nestor kept giving me advices on how I should align my look at the window, and what I was supposed to do with the afterimage. His prompts went always in the same direction: in order to keep the after-image in the field of vision for as long as possible, I was supposed to gently shift it back and forth with my eyes, or to hold the afterimage in place and tilt my head back and forth slightly. These movements, with the eyes or the head, I was supposed to execute until the image on the inner screen had lost its luminescence and was absorbed by the dark-ness.

Gradually, my ability to concentrate dwindled, and keeping the bal-ance on the narrow board became increasingly difficult. Instead, another circumstance captured my attention: I was surprised how suitable the black walls of the room were for this particular exercise. Not only that they acted as a contrast to the afterimage, thus making its luminosity appear more intense; the evenly spreading darkness, in addition, de-prived the eyes of the opportunity to stick to some material object so that the concentration on the afterimage was not impaired by anything – I began to understand that this room was specially prepared for the purpose of seeing afterimages.

After Nestor had me stop the exercise and step down from the board, I asked him whether it was him who had painted the walls and built in this window. He answered that he had found the room already in this condition when he moved in. Of course I was interested who, besides him, had such a strong interest in these afterimages – so strong that he had set up a room exclusively for that purpose. But Nestor's brief an-swer made me understand that I shouldn't ask him any further questions about the chicken house.

Finally I asked him if I could apply this exercise on Mari Egli's secre-taire. But Nestor advised me against doing so. He suggested that I should first of all learn to see the afterimages correctly.

»But why not on the secretaire?« I wanted to know. »Do you think I wouldn't be able to reproduce the afterimage of the secretaire?«

»Oh no, sure you'll be able to,« he answered. »But right now you're full of expectations. Now you think you can continue your work trouble-free. These expectations impair the ability to see the afterimage. And thus you lose your distance to the outer screen.«

»I'll surely notice that if it happens,« I said, shrugging.

»Indeed you will. You already know how the secretaire lets you know when you're trying to enforce the work on it,« he reminded me.

Then he repeated that I should make myself familiar with my inner screen, first of all. Usually, he explained, we tended to bring our intention, our will, into the material world because we have learned from our experiences that it is the only world in which we are able to act. But the moment we paid attention to the afterimages and learn to hold them in suspension, we would retrieve our willpower from the outer screen, and an inner world with new possibilities would gradually open up for us.

Nestor's prophesying words made me come up with the idea that he considered the afterimage a kind of means of transport enabling a human being to escape this material world.

»Do you think we can leave the material world behind us by holding the afterimages in suspension?« I asked him straightforward.

My question seemed to surprise Nestor. For a moment he kept silent.

»We're not leaving the world,« he finally said, »we're dissolving it in the picture by holding the picture in suspension with our look and putting in our energy. In this way, we're able to find out what the picture basically is. And the afterimages are already closer to reality than the material world.«

Circular Figures with Double Membrane

Nestor associated the phenomenon of the afterimages with my first partial success in the restoration of the secretaire and combined it adroitly with his system of the perfect restoration. The fact that he had mentioned, even announced, these afterimages already before led me to question whether it was a coincidence that I now had to deal with them – and also, whether there were any existing rules for the perfect restoration that Nestor adhered to, whether there were any boundaries in his world and where these were located; or was he just a clever speaker who adopted all possible and conceivable things to his system, simply plucking the respective explanations out of thin air?

If the perfect restoration was a system with clearly laid out rules and practical instructions, the credibility of the system would have received an enormous boost, at least in my view – simply by the single fact that it would then show a certain degree of rationality, be transparent and thus not be dependent upon an individual's arbitrary caprices.

Considering it soberly, I was working with a system I wasn't able to comprehend with my rational mind. Nestor hardly answered, if at all, my questions about nature, origin and scope of the »perfect restoration«, as if he seemed to evade a clear-cut statement. According to him, there were no generally binding rules. The objective of all we did was to gain clarity and certainty about the picture as a whole – for me with the result that I was able to restore Mari Egli's secretaire. And when I kept asking questions he took this as a cause to reproach me by telling me that I concerned myself with all possible things in the picture but not with the picture as a whole.

So when Nestor interpreted or explained certain facts or appearances in the sense of his perfect restoration, I only had two options: to either believe his explanations or to dismiss them, that is, to take his exercises to heart or to neglect them. And that was unsatisfactory because Nestor talked about a subject I virtually didn't know anything about so that I couldn't come up with anything to counter it. I started to rebel against this kind of relationship when I began to search for the rational, medical explanation of the afterimages which I wanted to confront Nestor with. My intention was to relativize his romantic, misty-eyed interpretation of this optical phenomenon, and to introduce him to a more realistic perspective with regard to origin and significance.

In late summer of the following year, the day was there when I took all the information I had gathered on afterimages and went up into the Emmental to visit Nestor. After my arrival it didn't take long until we addressed the subject of afterimages, because he announced that he had built a more stable *Hüenerstängeli*, as a roost is called in Swiss German, that I could use for seeing the afterimages in the chicken house.

I grabbed the chance and immediately countered his thesis, casting doubt on the effectiveness of seeing afterimages, and explained this with the results of my research.

»In the human eye, there are two kinds of photoreceptors: the longer rods and the shorter uvulas,« I read to him from my notes. »In the case of the uvulas, science distinguishes between three different kinds: those that respond to red, to blue and to green light. Our physiological visual system is based on the so-called additive color mixture; this means that the different colors we perceive are produced by different levels of stimuli that these three kinds of uvulas are subjected to: for example, we see blue when only the blue uvulas are stimulated, and we see yellow when the red and green uvulas are both stimulated to the same degree. If we see white, all uvulas are equally stimulated. All colors we can perceive are a mixture of the three basic colors red, green and blue.

If we look at a red object for a longer time, for example a red cup, then the red uvulas are stimulated. Over time, however, the red pigment in these uvulas are subject to exhaustion and depletion which means that their performance gradually deteriorates. Therefore, if we now look at a white surface, the performance of the red uvulas which we had strained more than the others is very low while the blue and green uvulas still perform a hundred percent. The result is that we see the afterimage of the cup in the color blend blue and green, turquoise, which thus is the complementary color to red. This turquoise-colored cup is called a ›negative afterimage‹.«

I looked over to Nestor. He shrugged his shoulders and made a defensive gesture.

»This is scientific knowledge, Nestor,« I confirmed my explanations. »This is scientifically proven knowledge.«

»It is no direct knowledge,« he replied. »That's why this knowledge will not help you in getting the perfect restoration done. Who cares, after all, how the afterimages come about? In order to know what they really are, you have to *see* them, not *read* or *think* about them.«

»Afterimages are the result of a deteriorating performance of photoreceptors in the eye. This is scientifically proven.«

I passed my notes over to him. He took the sheets and looked at them. But he didn't read them; he merely glanced at them superficially, and this made me angry.

Nestor shook his head. »And now?« he asked me. His voice sounded serious, and he gave me a stern look.

»You haven't read it,« I accused him.

»I don't have to. I know what afterimages are,« he claimed.

»But you're distorting the facts,« I called out enraged. At this moment I felt a stinging pain below my navel which in turn caused my heart to start pounding, as if I had run for miles without taking a break.

My voice was trembling when I tried to defend my viewpoint. »You're talking about the afterimages as if they would represent a real world, analogous to our world. But they are nothing else than physical stimuli and biochemical processes in the eye itself.«

»Right,« he acknowledged me with a certain tone of irony in his voice. »Your whole life consists of physical stimuli and biochemical processes – there's nothing else.« Nestor returned my papers to me.

»Don't be naïve,« he said gently. »Don't try to cling on to that scribble. The afterimages are actually a real inner world. A world you need to learn to see, first of all. What we're dealing with is not a scientific knowledge of physiological processes in the eye. What you have noted on your sheets there may be true for the scientific world – but it is of no value to us. What we are interested in is to become familiar with the afterimages and getting to know the inner screen. But in order to do so, you'll have to stop to reduce your experiences to material processes only. If you do that, you constantly put your small world into the picture, and this is what distracts you from perceiving the inner screen.«

It dawned on me that I wouldn't be able to match up to Nestor. I wanted to convince him of my viewpoint, but he neither gave in, nor did he show a basic willingness to accept compromises. This realization caused me to withdraw and »shut up«. I didn't say anything. I could feel Nestor's look resting upon me, but I couldn't look into his eyes.

»You're having a hard time digging that, don't you?« he concluded correctly. His voice was calm, but I had the impression that he sounded a little disheartened. »I admit, it's not that easy to grasp. If you feel that you doubt the effectiveness of seeing afterimages,« he advised me, »then just remind yourself of the success with the afterimage of the secretaire. This will convince you to keep on practicing.«

For a while we remained silent. To distract myself, I looked down the valley through Nestor's large window. Dusk had set in meanwhile and I observed how the village houses slowly faded in the dark, until all that could be distinguished was the ground, the sky and clouds. While the picture was gradually cloaked by the surrounding darkness, my heart rate slowly reduced again and I calmed down. A pleasant feeling was spreading throughout my body, together with a strange satisfaction and relaxation. It felt as if the dark emptiness of the picture had extended over to my body.

Nestor broke the silence and suggested a hiking trip to a place farther away for the next day. He wanted to collect egg-mushrooms and the last porcini of the season. I wanted to show him that I was neither vexed nor bearing a grudge and agreed to accompany him.

When we left Nestor's house on the next morning it was much too early, much too dark and much too cold. Secretly I scolded myself for having gotten involved into this hiking trip. But the moment we had arrived on top of the hill and were able to look down into the valley, I forgot all the inconveniences of this early morning. The scenery in front of my eyes was breathtaking: day had broken and the waning moon stood closely above the Hohgant; it was still shining brightly despite the increasing brightness. The sky had a deep dark blue color, and feathery cirrus clouds with a mild red hue covered the sky here and there like a fine stroke of a brush. The snow-covered peaks of the Hohgant were already glowing in the same red.

For about an hour we were hiking over wooded hills and through moist ditches when we finally arrived at a place on the edge of the woods with two large overthrown trees. They must have been lying there for quite a while, because they were rotten, and there was moss, bushes and even small fir trees growing on top of them. Here we took a rest.

Nestor took out two apples from his backpack and held them in my direction for me to choose one of them. The one in his left hand looked appetizing. Its skin was smooth, and the light was reflecting in it. It appeared fresh, ripe and juicy. The other apple, on the other hand, had already a few dark spots, and its skin had started to shrink.

I was in a conflict. Of course, my choice would have been the better looking apple. But I knew how to behave myself, and I left the choice up to Nestor. He just shrugged, took the nicer apple and gave me the other one.

»This one looks much better than the other one,« he explained his choice and laughed.

We ate our apples. Nestor seemed to be in a good mood; every time our eyes met he smiled at me. With visible pleasure he bit into his apple and smacked his lips loudly; from time to time he nodded, and with a childish *goody-goody* he signaled how delicious the apple of his choice was. I, on the other hand, was busy trying to convince myself all the time that I didn't really care which of the apples I was eating. I wasn't so much upset about the fact that he was allowed to eat the nicer one but rather that he had deliberately chosen the nicer apple for himself without any restraint – and that he even pointed this out in an overly manner.

When we had finished our small meal I asked Nestor why he had chosen the nicer apple when, according to his claims, he could see the picture as a whole which consequently meant that everything in it was of equal value. He replied it was nonsense to ponder over that – I should have made my choice when it was still my turn. I admitted that he was correct but still insisted on an answer.

»Which one would you have chosen?« he asked me.

»The other one,« I hastily lied so as to defend my ideal.

»Well, that's the one you had, after all.«

It annoyed me that Nestor had managed to fool me so easily, and he seemed to take visible pleasure in it. But then he told me that acting in life, on the one hand, and seeing the picture as a whole on the other, were two totally different things.

»You cannot do both at the same time. If you want to see the picture as a whole,« he explained, »then you practice the exercise of not making any differences between objects in the picture. Rather, you try to view everything in such a way that it is of equal value. And that doesn't have anything to do with thoughts, feelings or actions but with direct and immediate seeing. But when you need to act you'll have to make some distinctions.«

»But if that's so then any kind of action counteracts this seeing the picture as a whole.«

»Not if we act in such a way that we sit down as often as possible so as to be able to see the picture as a whole.«

»What does that mean in concrete terms?«

»I don't want to tell you how you should act in your everyday life, what you should do in each particular case. That's up to you. Let me just point out this: if you aim at seeing the picture as a whole, you'll always have to make appropriate decisions. You'll have to ponder over each single decision with respect to this goal, and as such, there are only good or bad decisions for you; each thought, each feeling, every single action and just about everything related to you in some way will be good or bad.«

I expressed my vigorous disagreement with what Nestor just had said, arguing that it oversimplified matters if one subdivided the world only in »good« and »bad«. Reducing the diversity of the world to merely »good« and »bad«, I explained, distorted reality, and therefore this was not only incorrect but also highly questionable.

Nestor replied that he would understand my objection – but the reason for my disagreement, according to him, was that I wasn't able to recognize the two absolute opposites as such in the picture. He didn't explain any further what these »absolute opposites« were supposed to be; he just pointed out that my reality had a diverse quality due to this particular inability: in my distinction and evaluation of objects, people and experiences, there was an infinite number of gradient steps between »good« and »bad«. That is why my world was so complex, and this is what kept me from seeing the picture as a whole.

»But actually I wanted to explain something else to you,« he went on. »Once you set this one correct goal for yourself – seeing the picture as a whole –, and once you're aware of this goal of yours whenever you engage in activities, then your activities do not contradict seeing the picture as a whole – even if it brings about differences.«

Once again I got annoyed over his »absolutizing« tone of voice which had crept in this time when he mentioned the »correct« goal.

»There are as many correct goals as there are people, Nestor,« I objected.

»Well of course,« he called out, laughing. »Come on, let's quit the blah blah.« He got up and stretched himself.

I was surprised. It seemed as if, from one moment to the other, he was about to drop everything he had proclaimed so vivaciously just before. I asked him if he didn't really mean what he had said.

»Of course I mean what I say,« he replied, picked up his backpack and placed it on his shoulders. »But at the same time I also know that, in the final analysis, it doesn't matter whether I'm right or you, or anyone at all. This is just two small worlds colliding with each other, and this keeps us from seeing the picture as a whole.«

»If that's your conviction, then why did we have a discussion on this subject all along?«

»This is exactly what I wanted to point out to you: we're not idle but we are active, making distinctions in the picture in the process. But when our actions are focused on attaining that particular goal – consciously realizing that the picture ultimately is a whole – then we are less fixated; we enjoy more freedom with regard to what we do – which in turn helps us to open up more and see the picture as a whole.«

»So all I'll have to do is to now and then think of the fact that the picture is a whole – and this will set me free? Sounds too good to be true.«

»I didn't say that it would be enough to think of it now and then; what I pointed out was that you should act with this particular awareness in mind. And this awareness comes gradually into existence the more you succeed in seeing the entire picture. So both is needed: acting in every-day life and seeing the picture as a whole.«

After a longer hiking trip on the edges of the woods where we had found a considerable number of porcinis, Nestor led me into a relatively large and flat recess, far aback in a broad ditch. The area was overgrown with tall plants similar to water lilies. Blueberry bushes grew over a wide area on some of the hills close to the edge of the woods, and egg-mush-rooms of a size surprising me time and again were hiding under their branches and small leaves, down in the moss.

Later, on the way back, we came up to a small but deep ditch which we had to cross somewhere. It wouldn't have been a problem to climb down into it and up the other side again. But Nestor had discovered a tree trunk further up the hill which laid square across the ditch, and with playful but confident movements he balanced over the trunk on the other side.

The admiration I felt for him and his physical dexterity at that mo-ment, but also my envy for his skills, put me in a tight spot. Hesitantly, I climbed up on the tree trunk. I was wavering: one voice within me ad-vised me against the risk, calling me to reason. The other voice de-manded more self-confidence and determination of me. But where was the borderline between unrealistic overestimation of my capabilities and healthy self-confidence?

The first steps were not particularly difficult – here, the trunk was still resting on the forest floor. Now I took some further steps. I tried to stay optimistic: yes, why not? Why shouldn't it work out? Wasn't it a question of believing in myself, after all? And this voice of reason, al-ways spoiling the game – wasn't it this particular voice which wanted to get me scared? A voice which relied on everyday experience, knowledge acquired and skills trained, and which thus only restricted me, nailed me down and clipped my wings, time and again?

Speaking of wings: in between, I was almost in need of some. For a moment I thought I would lose my balance – when I had almost reached the middle of the ditch. I balanced myself carefully and paused for a moment in my position until I calmed down.

Of course it was frivolous to do something like that, because it was foreseeable that it wouldn't work out. This tree trunk was so narrow that I couldn't even place my feet side by side. What was the point? Did I have to prove something to myself? Did I still have to live something up like a pubescent boy? A little extreme here, a little radical there? Of course I liked adventures and risks of some sort – but not without a reasonable level of safety.

The last steps over to the other side demanded an enormous degree of concentration of me: limpingly, I made it across the second half and onto the other side.

After this adventurous crossing, I felt as if I had deserved some complimentary words by Nestor. After all, I had made it across to the other side in one fell swoop without landing in the ditch. Nestor, however, directed my attention to the fact that I had almost fallen off the trunk; he criticized my lack of balance. I was not in the mood, though, to be exposed to my deficiencies and denied him a judgment of my balancing skills.

»You're out of balance,« Nestor insisted. »I can see that not only in the way you balanced over the tree trunk – your imbalance already shows up in the way you usually walk.«

»In the way I walk?«

»Just watch yourself: when you walk, your left arm is hanging down slack, but your right arm is moving back and forth like crazy. Is that what you call balance? That's not a relaxed body – that's a ›stressed-in‹ behavior pattern.«

Nestor's critique of my body embittered me. I protested. Nestor, however, didn't respond to it but rather showed me a series of physical exercises which were supposed to reveal my unbalanced state to me, and to bring me more into balance. They were symmetric exercises addressing both sides of the body, the left and the right, one after the other. He instructed me to go through the motions of these exercises. I tried my best to stretch my body equally wide in both directions, but I had to realize that one side of my body actually wasn't as flexible as the other one.

»In order to perform the perfect restoration, you have to be in balance – in everything that you do,« Nestor explained. »Equal balance starts with your body. When your body is balanced, you'll also be more balanced in your consciousness. And then you'll be able to better keep that balance in this contradictory world – a world which always consists of two sides or poles, in which there is always a pro and a contra. This means that you're completely aware of these two sides without losing sight of your ability to act, or forgetting about your goal.«

Nestor said that many people were not able to resolve this dilemma; they committed themselves, mentally and emotionally, to that side which they feel will correspond with them and their viewpoints. This side, according to Nestor, is the one they clung on to with all their energy while dismissing the other one. But that was similar to sitting in a boat out in the middle of a lake and rowing with the paddle on one side only. That is why they were moving around in circles. That is why they had such a hard time to give up their fixed and preconceived ideas. And that is why they always had to chew on the same problems and suffer the same troubles.

»When you take care of a physical, emotional and mental balance, that is, a balance on the outer and inner screen, then you'll be more flexible and concentrated while working on the perfect restoration – and not just there but in everyday life as well.«

I felt that Nestor definitely tended to overreach himself here. Not only that it almost sounded as if he had found the solution to all problems plaguing our society or even mankind; he also contradicted himself with what he said.

»You said a while ago that each activity can either be right or wrong – depending on the goal we are pursuing.« Nestor confirmed this. »But now you're talking about balance: you said that we have to bring about a balance between things we do on the outer screen and on the inner. So what is it that counts when we are engaging in activities: ›right and wrong‹ or ›the balance‹?«

»It's actually interconnected,« he replied. »The opposites ›right‹ and ›wrong‹ exist within time when you have to act with respect to a goal. The balance, on the other hand, is something we need to keep in the moment. The more you can live in the moment, the immediate here and now, the more balanced you will be; there is no ›right‹ and ›wrong‹ in the moment.

It's just the same as with the tree trunk earlier on: our goal was to return to my house; to do so, we have made the right decision to cross the ditch and to get over on the other side; and we have decided to do this directly by balancing over the tree trunk. But in the individual moments along this way we had to be balanced; otherwise we would have fallen into the ditch instead of attaining our goal.«

On the following day we cut the collected porcinos into thin slices and placed them on the oven to let them dry. In between, Nestor started to talk about the process of seeing afterimages.

»If you want to see the afterimages you'll encounter two barriers which reduce the length of time you'll be able to see them,« he prophesied. »The first challenge is that the luminosity of the afterimages diminishes until they are so faint that you're no longer able to see them. And the other problem is that you can't hold these afterimages in suspension – they're floating around in your field of vision and disappear downward. That is, they're subject to the attractive force.«

Nestor added that the first barrier was nothing we had to be overly concerned about. The length of time I'd be able to see these afterimages would extend – the more I'd be able to hold them in suspension.

Then he introduced me to an eye exercise so as to master the second challenge. He said I could learn to hold the afterimages in suspension by pulling them towards me with the eyes and letting go of them again. For that purpose, I should concentrate my look for a certain length of time until the image of the left eye and the one of the right would start to drift apart.

»You want me to cross my eyes?« I asked him.

»There's two ways how you can see double images, that is, two pictures side by side: when your eyes are tired and you stare into the far distance, that is one way of seeing double images. But there is no activity in this; it's merely a letting go of the eyes. This is useless, though, when we want to hold afterimages in suspension. The other way how you can see double images is by tensing your eyes and consciously pulling your point of view towards you so that both pictures drift apart – that's what I call *doubling*. It is an act of concentration, both physically and mentally. It requires strength and willpower – exactly those things we need to hold the afterimages in suspension.«

Nestor instructed me to try this doubling. He suggested I should concentrate on some object for that purpose. It would be an advantage, though, if there was something *standing out* from the picture, perhaps something that was shining or giving light in some way.

I looked for a suitable object, and eventually I stared at my tea glass which reflected the light. After a while I gave up – nothing whatsoever happened. There was no doubling of the picture. Nestor was writhing with laughter. According to his facial expression – that was supposed to mimic mine – all I did was stare at the glass saucer-eyed instead of directing my eyes inwards, to my inner screen.

He suggested that I should start with gazing at the tip of my nose, because that also was a form of doubling. I had a relative easy time at that, but when I wanted to lift my eyes and look into the farther distance with »double vision«, both images immediately attracted each other and rejoined to one single picture.

I told Nestor about my problem. He confirmed that doubling would require a lot of strength because it is all about concentration. Then he opened up to me that there was a trick how I could practice this doubling better.

After we had spread all the porcinos on the oven to dry, Nestor instructed me to draw two circular figures of equal form and size with a pencil. Such a figure was comprised of two concentric circles which offered two surfaces that could be painted in: a disk in the center and a circular ring around it. While drawing these figures, I was supposed to observe that the surface area of the center disk be of the same surface size as that of the circular ring.

When I was done, Nestor took a piece of coal out of the tiled oven and told me to blacken one of the two surfaces of each figure. On one figure, I was supposed to blacken the outer ring while the center disk remained white; on the other figure, I was to blacken the center disk while the circular ring remained white. Coal, according to Nestor, was particularly suitable for this purpose because the blackened surfaces didn't display an even black throughout; rather, there were brighter and darker areas within it. The same held good for the surfaces that remained white, because the white of the piece of paper neither showed an even white throughout. This would contribute to a stimulation of our eyes and thus our consciousness.

Eventually, Nestor instructed me to hang both figures up on a wall, side by side – the one with the dark center disk to the left, the other one to the right – and to practice doubling with them in this particular arrangement. The idea was that these figures would double from two to four as soon as I would increase the distance between them with my eyes. At some point, the images of the two doubled figures should merge and superimpose on one another so that, instead of four, I would only see three images. In this way, I would be able to rest my eyes on the superimposed circular figure in the middle. As a result, my look would be kind of fixed, and I wouldn't have to exert an additional effort to keep the picture doubled.

Nestor encouraged me to experiment with the relative distance between the figures. I was supposed to find out for myself how far away from each other I should hang up the figures, and at what distance I should sit down in front of them.

»The wider the distance between the figures, the more you'll have to concentrate to get the figures superimposed. But you'll grow tired faster and start to get lost in thoughts. If you, on the other hand, bring the figures closer together, you won't have to concentrate that strongly. But at any rate, you should always be able to perceive these circles sharply focused. Because only when you see them in sharp focus you'll be there, that is, you'll be able to direct your full attention onto them.«

»How did you arrive at this particular figure?« I wanted to know.

»It's the simplest way to express two opposites,« he replied and explained that the mergence of these two opposites to one superimposed center image would in turn bring about a balance in the person practicing this exercise. This balance would be helpful in holding the afterimages in suspension longer, and in seeing the picture as a whole. Nestor also mentioned that this exercise would help me get to know my own eyes and their opposite characteristics, and to find the balance between them.

»This exercise will help you to be more present and to live more in the here and now,« he explained. »Because, you always use one eye to look into the future, but the other one to look into the opposite direction, the past. Then you try to superimpose these two tenses so as to combine them to present time in the center. In general, the two circular figures stand for all opposites we are familiar with: sun and moon, for example, or the male and female principle; or day and night, or even feelings such as love and hate.«

Nestor really gathered momentum while explaining this to me and searched for some more dichotomies which he could assign to both double circle figures. The whole thing seemed to amuse him, and I surmised that it was so because he realized that my patience was running out.

»Don't take these assignments and classifications too serious,« he said in a conciliatory voice, as an answer to my expression of resentment. »That's just the same as ›putting the small world into the picture‹. All you are interested in is to learn this particular doubling so that you can hold the afterimages in suspension longer and see them properly.«

Wanting to Know

It took me quite a while until I was able to merge the circular figures to one single image by using the technique of doubling. In the beginning, this concentrated method of applying double vision seemed almost impossible. I wasn't able to randomly direct my eyes inwards and look at the figures at the same time – I was missing the special feeling for this approach.

At first I tried to concentrate on the tip of my nose and maintain the special position of my eyes while then directing my look to the circular figures in the background. But right that moment, both images merged back into one each time. Eventually I helped myself by looking at the tip of my index finger which I held closely in front of my face. This had the advantage that I could see the circular figures in the background, despite concentrating on the tip of my finger. And when I moved my index finger back and forth in front of my face, I could see how the two doubled circular figures in the background either approached each other or drifted apart. At the correct distance between finger and eyes, the figures merged and superimposed one another. And at that point it wasn't too difficult anymore to direct my look from the finger directly onto them.

The problem, however, was now that I could only see the circular figures as blurred, out-of-focus images. But Nestor had explicitly told me that the exercise was only beneficial if I was able to perceive the figures sharply focused. For quite a while I tried in vain to see the superimposed double circles sharply focused until I realized that the degree of focus and definition of the image depended on how strongly I was doubling, that is, how far I pushed both images apart. The more I was doubling, the more the picture went out of focus. Consequently, I reduced the distance between both figures so that I didn't overstrain myself while doubling, and as a result I was now able to perceive the merged images sharply focused.

It was around this time period of practicing and exercising when it dawned on me that the circular figures displayed the same principle as the window in the chicken house: a larger outer circle with a smaller one inscribed into it. I didn't immediately assign any significance to this, but then my attention was caught by the inlays which adorned Mari Egli's secretaire. These circles showed the same principle: a disk in the center was surrounded by a circular ring, and the wood chosen for both parts showed strong contrasts. The creator of this particular piece of furniture had attached great importance to the emphasis of this contrast between outer ring and inner disk.

Now it obviously suggested itself to assign some deeper significance to these two-colored circular figures – based on the fact that Nestor used a symbol which had been in use more than a hundred years ago. The question I wanted to answer was whether Nestor used this remnant from older times just for the purpose of inspiration, interpreting it in accordance with his own viewpoints, or whether he was a representative of some traditional line reaching back to Mari Egli and perhaps even further back into the past.

On a cold rainy weekend I drove up the Emmental for the last time before winter set in. The temperatures had dropped quickly, but at the altitude of Nestor's house the snow was still melting away.

I found him busy chopping wood when I arrived. He welcomed me with an exuberance of feelings from which I concluded that he was very delighted to see me again. Together, we chopped the remaining wood and stacked it at the outer wall of the house where it could dry, protected from rain and snow, under the mighty roof. While working away like this, we discussed some subjects in world politics and global economy, and it turned out that Nestor was interested in subjects like these. I was surprised how well informed he was when it came to major world events, and with what a keen sense he was able to grasp the conceivable intentions behind political decisions, concealed in the background. The ironic tone of voice he used while expressing his opinions on the subjects, however, showed me that he couldn't take much pleasure in the course of ongoing world events.

In the evening, the subject of nutritional habits came back up again after I had observed how Nestor had cut a banana in slices and mixed it with honey and a handful of grapes and nuts. In the months before my visit to Nestor I had engaged in a thorough study of different nutritional systems, including the thermic effects of food. With this knowledge I wanted to explain to Nestor what he was about to do: I pointed out to him that, during the cold season, it could be problematic to eat a fruit like the banana because of its strongly cooling effect on the entire body.

Nestor looked at me with his brows knitted and replied that he wasn't really afraid of his stomach freezing solid by eating what he intended to. When he put his glass plate into the small interior compartment of the tiled oven so as to warm up the food, I insisted that he would take a risk – a small but unnecessary one – in doing this: namely an imbalance of his physical energies. In order to avert such an imbalance, nuts and honey – neutral in terms of their thermic effects – wouldn't suffice to bring about a balance in this regard; it didn't play a role, either, whether the banana was eaten warm or even hot. I recommended to him to spread some powdered cinnamon over the food because cinnamon had a strongly warming effect.

»What's the matter with you?« Nestor called out in disbelief. »You weren't that picky and finicky before, were you?«

»I'm just trying to arrive at a more balanced state with proper nutrition and to raise my energy level,« I defended myself with Nestor's own words.

Nestor, however, didn't accept this as an argument and asked me once more how I arrived at notions of this kind. I explained to him that I was experimenting, inspired by him and the farmer, with different nutritional practices for some time already. But in doing so, it wasn't enough for me to merely orient myself to Nestor and his habits. In my opinion, he didn't pay enough heed to the amount of certain types of food he ingested. His solution was a very simple one: vegetarian, as natural as possible and in moderate amounts. That was all very well but, in my view, a better directed intake of food could yield much more in terms of health and energy.

I described to Nestor how I had lived, at first, on uncooked vegetarian food, later on food combining. Once a week I put in a fast day to cleanse and detoxify my body. In addition, I controlled the amount of calories I took up with a food chart that I always carried along with me – which was a little laborious but also very informative. Then I began to study the thermic effects of certain sorts of food, and I cooked my meals according to those criteria. And I avoided bread because I had heard that the human stomach was used, throughout the ages, to mammoth meat and wild berries but not to bread.

I didn't drink any liquid until I was done with the meal because I had read that this was beneficial to our digestion.

I mixed spices, seeds and kernels into the food so as to avail myself of the gratifying effects associated with them – and asked myself how I could have stayed healthy all these years without these. Then I heard that it would be optimal for the stomach to fill it only halfway with food, to one quarter with liquid and to leave the last quarter empty for optimum digestion. To be able to follow this rule, I established the intake capacity of my stomach and determined the precise volume of my meals by mashing the food into a kind of puree from then on.

I thought Nestor would approve my efforts because, according to him, a conscious intake of food was part of the program of the perfect restoration, after all. But he just burst out in laughter.

»It is very good that you now take the effort to carefully watch over your nutrition,« he said with a conciliatory voice. »But when you force yourself to practices of the kind you just mentioned, you won't really do yourself a favor – it will only lead to the other extreme again.« Nestor explained that this excessive back and forth – in this case, the radically disciplined nutrition regimen I followed on the one hand, and the exorbitant out-of-control stuffing with garbage on the other – was also part of learning the perfect restoration. According to him, this would still accompany me for a while until my sense of taste had learned again to appreciate untreated and natural food, and to stick to a moderate diet so that malnutrition would finally be a thing of the past.

Nestor's accuracy in estimating the situation baffled me: in fact, I had never managed to continuously adhere to any one of these eating habits and practices. In regular intervals, I experienced excessive behavior patterns, moments when I ransacked the fridge and ate whatever I could put my hands on – only to blame myself for these »blackouts« later on. Stubborn and narrow-minded, I kept trying to convince him of the value of a well-directed and disciplined nutrition regimen, but Nestor interrupted me.

»If you want to eat in this way, go ahead and do so,« he said, »but leave me alone with that. My sense of taste is balanced, and I'm eating whatever I consider best for me. I neither have to count calories nor pick certain kernels, and I don't have to do without my banana dessert just because someone out there claims that it would excessively chill my stomach.«

On the next day we talked about Nestor's doubling. I told Nestor how I had been successful, eventually, in bringing together the two circular figures. In the process, I also told him of several optical effects which struck me while practicing. For example, it seemed that the two images doubled became smaller the wider I placed them apart.

»Doubling is a form of concentration,« Nestor explained this perception. »And what you concentrate on becomes increasingly smaller but also more intense in turn.«

»I also realized that the two superimposed circular figures constantly alternate in terms of their dominance,« I added. »Either the left figure stands out or the right.«

»Yes, the eyes alternate in their dominance and take regular turns,« he confirmed. »In the beginning you can only perceive one or the other of the two pictures. Now, you shouldn't just look at the figures but rather try to see the picture as a whole. The more you succeed in that, the sooner you will see the mergence of these figures into one instead of two images superimposing one another.«

Nestor advised me to also increase the distance between the two figures, close to the point where the doubled and superimposed center picture would start to go out of focus. The intention behind this, according to him, was that, over time, I should be able to see that blurred center image more sharply focused.

Then I steered our conversation to the symbolism of the circular figures so as to find out if there actually was some kind of esoteric or philosophic tradition behind this, and if Nestor was involved in this »movement« somehow.

»Why do I have to look at these circular figures, of all figures that exist, Nestor?« I asked.

»You don't have to take these circles; you can practice doubling with any two objects. You can also practice it with just one object, but then there won't be any kind of superimposition of two identical forms in the center which have an ›anchoring‹ effect. That's why practicing with two objects of equal shape is more beneficial.«

»But you had me draw these particular circular figures for my practices – why those and not some other ones?«

»Because they are particularly suitable for doubling.«

»Why's that?«

»I told you before that, by nature of their form and color, they represent the most natural and simple opposites you can conjoin when practicing doubling.«

»Was Mari Egli familiar with these figures?«

Nestor looked at me in surprise, but then a knowing smile showed up on his face.

»You mean because she adorned nearly half of the secretaire with circular figures of that kind?«

»Yes, and the round window in the chicken house also has this form. There is some kind of connection, after all, isn't there?«

»Since when are you interested in things like that?« he asked. »I thought all you'd be interested in was the restoration of that secretaire?«

»Exactly. But you'll certainly understand that I'd really like to know about the origins of this symbol, this way of thinking and living and the exercises which I'm supposed to practice here. So: has Mari Egli seen the same significance in these circular figures as you?«

»How am I supposed to know? I've never met Mari Egli, after all.«

»But how come that you both use the same symbol? Haven't you adopted it from her?«

»I haven't adopted anything. I've seen these double circles already before I had moved into this house here.«

»Where was that?«

»On my inner screen.«

»I mean: where have you seen them out in the material world?«

»Not out in the material world, just on the inner screen.«

I kept silent. Obviously, Nestor wanted to fool me. Because, in order to see these figures as afterimages on the inner screen, one had to, first of all, gaze at them for a while in the material world.

»What is it that you really want to know?« he finally asked me.

I told him of my assumption that these circular figures might represent traditional symbols carrying a certain significance for a certain group of people – a symbol which must have the effect of lending this group of people a certain identity and creating a certain feeling of togetherness and interconnection.

Nestor thought this over for a while, as if he had to ponder over what and how much he should tell me about it.

»It is correct that these figures have a certain significance for certain people,« he eventually explained.

»For what people?«

»For those living on the left side and close to the spring.«

I was quite surprised and puzzled that Nestor referred to a geographically restricted place in which this symbol had a particular significance for the people living there. I tried to find out how strong this symbol was actually tied to the place mentioned by Nestor, and whether these figures could be spread elsewhere and be well-known to others not living in this particular geographic region. Nestor's answers indicated that living on the left side of the Emme was the key factor to understanding the significance of these circular figures. For people on the right side, as he called all others, it would be absolutely necessary for them to change over to the left side so as to really understand the principle behind these figures.

»What's so special about this left side here?« I asked him.

»The left side is the place where the ›order‹, the fixed regimens and rules of human beings, are reduced.«

»What regimens and rules?«

»The regimens and rules of the small world. The regimens and rules determining our thinking, feeling and acting – in short, our entire being and existence: what sort of thoughts are correct, which ones are not; how should I think and feel and act in what specific situation; how do I grasp those things happening around me; how do I approach them, and what kind of an effect do they have on me – all this is going off within us human beings according to specific patterns. These are the multifaceted regimens and rules I'm talking about.« Nestor put up a somewhat evil smile. »This is exactly what you're doing right now as well,« he added. »You're trying to integrate your experiences here into the regimens and rules of your small world.«

I was joking that I would have to expand and enlarge my small world considerably so as to find a place in it for all this. Nestor laughed and replied, I shouldn't expand my small world but rather dissolve it in the picture.

»So you're saying that people on the right side differ from those on the left with respect to these regimens and rules? Those on the right side have them, those on the left don't?«

»Not quite. There are also regimens and rules on the left side, and in principle they don't differ from those on the right. But they are the foundation on which the complex, detailed and rigid system of the right side is built up. The regimens and rules existing on the left side unite everything in a few basic aspects; these are the essence of the system on the right side. These two circular figures with double membrane are the symbol for one of these aspects: the duality. Being able to see these absolute opposites – that is an achievement of those people living on the left side.«

I objected that the natural opposites of life, such as »man« and »woman« or »day« and »night«, would be something that all people experience in their everyday life. To talk about the perception of these opposites as an achievement of the people on the left side seemed unrealistic to me. Nestor replied to this objection by saying that opposites such as »man« and »woman«, »day« and »night«, »good« and »bad«, would only be recognizable with the help of the right-sided system of regimens and rules of the small world. The circular figures, however, would not just symbolize these multifaceted opposites known from everyday life; rather, they would represent the original *duality*, that is, the opposites in their absolute and most abstract form.

»This abstract duality is the origin of all opposites,« he explained. »Without them, there would neither be day nor night, neither man nor woman – there would be nothing at all. And the people of the left side are able to see this duality on their inner screen.«

»As afterimage?«

»Afterimages are not the only thing you can see on your inner screen,« he replied mysteriously.

But when I asked him further about it he just dismissed it and replied that it wouldn't make any sense at this time to talk about it.

Hurt by his refusal, I fell silent. Finally it was Nestor who picked up the conversation again. He came up with a very general theoretical explanation for why the people on the left side were able to see this alleged »abstract duality« on their inner screen: according to him, normal people created, due to their living conditions, an infinite quantity of this duality for themselves by always evaluating this one duality differently, in terms of quality. In this way, they didn't just create their entire small world with »day« and »night«, »man« and »woman«, »good« and »bad«; they also moved farther and farther away from the one abstract duality. The people on the left side, in comparison, had reversed this process: they had stopped to evaluate the duality, and thus to multiply it. And this they did with such consequence that they could see the duality on their inner screen.

I didn't want to judge or criticize Nestor's statements. To me, these were ideas that had turned into ideals. And I just couldn't imagine how this was supposed to have an effect in concrete everyday life.

»What's the use of seeing this duality on the inner screen?« I asked him.

»Seeing the duality is not what we are striving for. We try to see the picture as a whole – but in order to do this, we have to deal with the subject of duality in a different way. So all we can do is to keep a balance of the duality, these absolute opposites, and thus to overcome and resolve them. This is the way to strive for wholeness.«

I told Nestor that I couldn't quite follow all of what he had said. He replied that this was so because I didn't live on the left side.

»So that means: all I have to do is to settle on the left side, and as soon as I have, I'll understand the meaning of the circular figures, and I'll be able to see the duality on my inner screen?« I teased him.

»It's not easy to arrive on the left side, let alone to live here.«

»But that's not true,« I objected. »I'm here now as well, and I live and work in your house. Why should it be so difficult to live on the left side?«

»With your body you are here, but with your feelings and thoughts you are still over on the right side. Only if you would live here permanently, you would gradually change. Could you really imagine living your life out here?«

I was just about to answer »yes« to Nestor's question when I realized that I really had quite a hard time to stay at Nestor's place. Several times I had observed on myself that I experienced feelings like joy, affection, satisfaction, but also misemotions such as resentment, reluctance and sadness much more intensely than at home in Bern. In addition, these feelings were much more inconsistent, even changing into their opposite at a time I expected it least. This inconsistency of my state of mind was scary because it made me distrust my feelings and even brought about self-doubts. I blamed the environment, the silence and the place here for my unsettled temper – not to forget Nestor: meanwhile I got along with him well, but still I always felt a certain relief, even a release, when I said goodbye to him and returned home. Only the prospect that I would someday be able to finish the restoration on the secretaire and to take it along with me, made me return to this place time and again.

»So life on the left side is more ambitious and sophisticated because the human system of order, with all its regimens and rules, is suspended?« I tried to understand the essence of Nestor's message.

»Not suspended, just reduced to a few fundamentals. Here, diversity is being united beneath duality. Those living on this side of the river can see this directly. And those who can see this are striving for wholeness. This is what I'm doing here.«

I called Nestor's attention to the fact that, as far as I could remember, this was the first time that he provided information about his activities in such a forthright and outspoken way. To him, however, this didn't seem to be anything special: he replied that he had tried to explain this to me all along; the point was just that I often was not open enough to listen, let alone internalize the things he said.

The following winter I spent in Bern again. But the notion that Nestor could be a follower of a hundred-year-old tradition of seekers in the Emmental didn't let go of me. The longer I thought about it, the more I was convinced that he was an advocate of a belief system; a belief system with concepts, rituals, symbols; with a description of the world, adjusted to the enhanced perception of the individual, and with the mystic goal to overcome the duality and to see the picture as a whole.

I tried to find out more about this mystic tradition whose members used the circular figures as common symbol and practice object. The name Mari Egli, the year 1888, the place and the two-colored double circles were the source points from which I started my research.

Soon I had found out that the Emmental was, and still is, home to a considerable number of religious groups and sects – among them also groups which had come into existence in the Emmental itself. The remoteness of this region and the adverse social and economical conditions the inhabitants had to live in had been a breeding ground for religious activities outside of the established churches for centuries. This held good in particular for the 19th century: economical distress and technological revolutions in industry and agriculture had led to an exodus of workforces, to unemployment and poverty. In uncertain times like those, people were much more receptive for religious activities outside of the established churches, and part of these were in particular movements with inward-mystical orientations. So it was definitely conceivable that the mystical teachings of salvation which Nestor represented had their origins in the Protestant Emmental of the 19th century – perhaps it even was Mari Egli who had started that movement.

My search for groups outside of the established Christian churches, for sects, mystics in the upper Emmental, however, was a failure; according to the information I could gather, there were no religious movements outside of Christianity in the recent history of the Emmental. It wasn't until the second half of the 20th century that other religious groups started to spread their teachings here. Nestor's teachings, however, didn't seem to fit into the picture of popular belief, either – a belief that was deeply rooted in this region, and which was fought by the established churches.

Contrary to Nestor's teachings, their practices aimed at worldly salvation: they tried to fend off, with the help of magic objects and symbolism, misfortune in the form of evil spirits, natural catastrophes, illness and death, and to guarantee prosperity and fertility of the soil; a mystical overcoming of the duality was not part of their goals. The name Mari Egli wasn't of any particular help, either: all I was able to gather in terms of information were some data about her life and some names of family members. But because I didn't know Mari's hometown, it wasn't even clear which of the Mari Egli's in question the owner of the secretaire was.

These flops didn't mean, however, that there were no religious movements aside from Christianity. Perhaps the group around Mari Egli had never been documented because it was small enough and able to keep a low profile. Perhaps the followers didn't reveal their identity, mindset and affiliation on purpose. And perhaps they had every reason for that if one considers that followers of a different faith and members of religious groups outside the established church were prosecuted in the Emmental as well, as the example of the religious movement of the Baptists has shown in the time period after the Reformation – and the members of that group were referring to the Bible, after all, understanding themselves as Christians. But all this remained speculative.

In the following spring I told Nestor about my research activities. It was a cold cloudy Tuesday in April when I informed him that I had been searching for information about Mari Egli and the tradition on the left side of the Emme. He seemed to be surprised about my endeavors. Smiling, he said he wouldn't have believed that I invested that much energy to get to the bottom of the significance around the circular figures.

I ignored his insinuation and told him about my failed search efforts. Then I hazarded the guess that this tradition must have been a mystical movement which hadn't been discovered or identified as such so far. I hoped that Nestor would come up with some more detailed information about Mari Egli and the seekers on the left side of the Emme.

»Why do you want to find an old tradition here?« he asked instead. »Do you need that as a confirmation for the exercises you're practicing here?« He gave me a broad smile and added with his usual irony: »Yeah, the older the exercises and the higher the number of people practicing them, the more effective they must be, he?«

»You said there was a tradition of Emmentalers which use the two-colored circular figure as symbol,« I defended my research activities.

»I never said anything about Emmentalers or some kind of tradition,« he contested my assertions vigorously. »I said that there are some people here striving for wholeness. The circular figures with the double membrane are just one of several aids or tools for that purpose. And they symbolize the absolute opposites. But I had you draw these figures so that you look at them and practice doubling, not that you ponder over them.«

»But obviously there had been people in the past who also strived for a unification of opposites – perhaps with exactly that symbol which, after all, is still being used today,« I insisted. »Perhaps Mari Egli was just such a person.«

»There have been people striving for wholeness, for the unification of opposites, at all times,« he replied evasively.

»But here, Nestor. Here on the left side of the Emme, as you always say. These circular figures refer to a certain tradition, don't they?«

»I do not think much of any tradition,« he dismissed my assumptions. »Tradition creates boundaries: it divides the whole into two parts separated from each other. Either you belong to it or you don't; either you are an advocate of it or you oppose it. So tradition is something that creates and maintains opposites; it doesn't contribute anything to their unification.«

Nestor kept talking about the disadvantages of a tradition, but I didn't listen to him any longer. To me it was obvious that he didn't want to go into the question of whether there had been, and perhaps still is, a traditional mystical religious community. I asked myself what his motive could be for remaining silent around this subject: was it such a secretive tradition that »outsiders« were not only denied access to the group but even knowledge of its existence? Or was the novice introduced to the movement without his explicit knowledge and only with a practical approach? And if so, wasn't I already a student in this sense?

At any rate, I was still convinced that there was some history connected with these exercises and that particular symbol which spoke in favor of a system with clear goals and auxiliary tools of its own. If this should be the case, and if Nestor, for whatever reason, would continue to keep silent about this tradition, then the only way for me to find out something substantial about this movement was to continue making myself familiar with the perfect restoration.

In the late afternoon Nestor left the house. I tried to immerse myself into a text which I had to study in preparation of a seminar. But my thoughts were still circling around that tradition of the left side which I assumed to exist. And the frustration resulting from not having received any confirmation for my research activities caused the situation to be nearly unbearable for me. I dropped into an erratic and unsatisfactory pondering: why did Nestor remain silent? What was really hidden behind that perfect restoration?

When I succeeded in shifting my attention more and more to the exterior world, the picture, I suddenly felt irritated in the environment I was in. All of a sudden, the silence in this place was unbearable to me. And Nestor's living room constricted me somehow. My seat was too soft, my foot rest was too hard. I was thirsty but didn't like to drink anything. I couldn't sit still but didn't want to move my body. Then I noticed again that many thoughts rushed through my head, but I wasn't able to focus on one clear thought.

Finally I went outside, after all. It was like a little release but didn't last very long. The discontent was following up on me like a shadow. I took a deep breath of fresh air and had to think of the everyday mixture of smells in the city: exhaust fumes, cigarette smoke and irritant perfume smells – smells which I detested under normal circumstances but which I had almost preferred at this moment.

I took a look around me. In front of me, there was the wide expanse of the valley. To my left, the Hohgant was towering. The only sound I could hear was the ever-bubbling rush of the creeks flowing around Nestor's house. It seemed as if there was nobody else in the entire world but me.

I stepped into the chicken house to see the afterimages. But I wasn't able to successfully concentrate myself here, either. Instead, I kept on pondering over the symbol of the double circles. In my feverish state I came up with the idea to take the measurements of these circles and to compare them so as to eliminate any coincidence. So I calculated the ratio between the center and the periphery surfaces, both of the glass window in the chicken house and of the figures on the secretaire. The result only confirmed that the size and surface of these double circles were the same: in each case, the surface sizes of the core portion and the outer circle were identical.

Frustrated, I sat down in front of the secretaire and stared at it. I really would have liked to know who had built this strange piece of furniture, and what he or she would have to say about the circular figures which – and now I realized it for the first time – were not randomly spread across the drawers; there were always two of them which formed a group. On the center drawer there were four of those groups of two, arranged in equal distances around a concentric circle in the center. On the left top drawer there was another group of two, again with the larger circle in the center. Only the sphere on top, plastically worked out of the wood, was an exception, in two respects: it was neither part of a group of two, nor was it surrounded by such a feature; in addition, it didn't just show a core in its inner part but several circular rings. Staring at the center of the secretaire, I tried to grasp the intention behind the arrangement of these circular figures.

After a while I became aware how much I had concentrated on the secretaire: suddenly, the contrasts between dark and bright emerged clearly, and parts of the picture started to flow into each other and to drift apart. Then I could recognize that an afterimage had come into existence: the secretaire's edges started to glow. I unfixed my look and moved the afterimage across the back wall of the stable with my eyes. The fact that I could see the afterimage signaled me that I would be able to continue my work on the object. The pleasant anticipation outweighed the circumstance that I couldn't manage to hold the afterimage in suspension on the spot – time and again, it drifted downward.

Filled with excitement, I took the steel ruler and the knife and started to cut out the triangle which I had drawn into the damaged wooden leaf on the upper left-hand drawer. But once again, the disillusionment was sobering: my pulse immediately started to quicken, and soon after the old well-known symptoms showed up again. I braced myself, but I barely managed to keep the blade of the knife running alongside the ruler. Then my body reacted with involuntary convulsions.

That was no reason to give up, however; after a short break I sat down in front of the secretaire again and tried to see the picture as a whole. But I couldn't really concentrate as I constantly had to think of the high degree of precision this particular work required. Because, if I couldn't hold my hands still this might have resulted in a damage of the inlay work.

It took some time until the afterimage showed up, and again I tried to hold it in suspension, but to no avail. After it had faded out, I placed the steel ruler on the secretaire and cut the second line; it didn't take much time or effort, because the grain of the wooden leaf was in line with the direction of my cut.

I repeated the process one last time, but while cutting the third line the pressure below my navel increased markedly: when I was about halfway through with the cut of this line, my body started trembling and shivering. In my overeagerness I ignored this shivering, but then something happened which shouldn't have: my hands took on a life of their own, and I was lacking the strength to keep the ruler pressed against the secretaire. The result was that I broke off a portion of the inlay work with my knife.

Exasperated, I dropped the tools and tottered away from the object. But the exasperation was superseded by an outright horror when I had to realize that the unpleasant sensations would not subside. I went outside to take a breath of fresh air, but this didn't bring any alleviation or relief, either – quite the contrary: the unbearable pressure below the navel region increased even further and took my breath away. My heart was pounding in my breast faster than ever, and when I had to gasp for air, a panic seized me which drove me back into the house. I could see the afterimage of the secretaire everywhere, now more clearly than ever before.

I laid down on the sofa. For a seemingly endless time I laid there waiting, trembling, breathing hastily and superficially, wishing the symptoms would finally cease. At some point I became aware that I wasn't trembling any longer but doing small involuntary movements: I played with my hands, circled my shoulders time and again, opened and closed my mouth, turned my head towards the left and right side – I just couldn't manage to hold my body still.

I got up and began to put all of my attention on these body movements. They didn't occur simultaneously but in a certain sequence or rhythm. And I realized that they had aligned to the frequency of my heart beat. I had the strange impression to »know« these movements just seconds before I went through them. But when I deliberately tried to go through a movement, or prevent it, the immediate result was some kind of disturbance or disharmony that expressed itself in new uncontrollable shiver attacks.

Then I could feel some kind of release within me. As if dammed up for a long time, strange, absurd but well coordinated and harmonic movements were flowing through my body. I started dancing. I was dancing with such a certainty and lightness at the same time – as if I had been moving this way all my life. This dancing evoked intense feelings within me: this deep calmness in the midst of dynamic movement; this deep relaxation in the midst of straining tension – I was in an extraordinary euphoric condition.

I didn't know how much time had passed by when I became aware that my movements were not as light and relaxed as before; I had to enforce them more and more. I noticed how exhausted I was and how much my body had heated up while going through these movements. Again I became aware of the excessive pounding of my heart, again I felt the blood pulsating in the temples and rushing through my body. Fear, timidity, apprehension and doubt now superseded any previous euphoria.

I went up to my room and laid down on my bed, hoping to fall asleep soon. But my eyes stayed open, just like the wooden eyes on the ceiling and the walls which seemed to look at me, between the dancing lines, with sadness, anger, affection and indifference.

Once I saw Nestor's eyes; they looked friendly and gave me the feeling that everything would be alright. The eyes kept looking at me for quite a while, even when I closed my own. These two bright purple-colored circles wouldn't fade, but they started to take on different shapes: they morphed into entire faces and humanoid bodies which were moving and dancing.

Thereafter, I became aware of the increasing darkness. It left its domains, crawled out of the cabinet and from under the bed and emerged from drawers so as to gradually spread throughout the room. This darkness scared me because it devoured all clear lines and boundaries between the objects, and it eliminated any distance. There was no more means of orientation, no more clearly arranged order. Ceiling, floor, door, cabinet, closet, fireplace, bed – due to the darkness, these objects could be everywhere and nowhere at the same time; they had become movable, blending into each other. They all dissolved in an all-embracing dark void. The picture seemed to be a whole.

This darkness was threatening – not just because it was boundless but because it constricted me to such a degree that I could virtually feel it around me. It even became rigid and stiff and deprived me of any freedom of mobility. In a desperate attempt to free myself, I wanted to lash about, but all that I could reach were cold moist walls everywhere around me.

Water was dripping on my body. I took a look around. It wasn't as dark anymore as at the beginning. I had the impression that the brightness depended on my physical activity: if I stayed calm and motionless, the picture seemed to be little bit brighter, and I could see farther into the darkness than when I was moving around.

I recognized my immediate environment: it was a narrow cave. As cautiously as possible, I started to crawl down the duct on all fours. For a longer time I followed this tube-like duct which had no curves. The walls were smooth and even, always the same distance apart, and virtually seemed to lead into infinity.

Suddenly, and totally unexpected by me, a wall showed up in front of me, out of the void, making any further advances impossible. Helpless, I cowered down. I couldn't turn back; at best, I could crawl backwards. In my desperation I hammered against this wall – and startled: from the spot where I had hammered against the wall, circular wave patterns spread in all directions as if I had hit a smooth water surface. When the waves ceased, I cautiously touched the wall with the palm of my hand which triggered a strange sensation: I could feel a tickle, at first in my fingertips, then in the entire hand. Fascinated by this feeling, I applied gentle pressure on the wall, whereon my fingers penetrated the surface of the wall. What seemed to be hard rock before, felt like a viscous mass. I applied even more pressure, but the resistance increased the more I pushed my hand and my arm through the mass. Still I tried to penetrate the wall with all of my body – hands and head first. But the increasing resistance exhausted my energies, and the wall »spat« me out again. I was stuck.

The Inner Pressure and the Flow of Energy

On the next morning I drove back to Bern without having talked to Nestor. I was mad at him, simply because that which wasn't supposed to be possible was possible here in his place. And I didn't want him to give me one of his usual comments because I had an inkling that he would explain my hallucinations of the previous day in the context of his perfect restoration, and in the most convincing and plausible way.

I avoided the Emmental during the next two months. I needed some time to »digest« my experiences and to determine how much the restoration of the secretaire was really worth to me – which included the question whether I would risk my physical and mental integrity in the process. Finally I decided to abandon the restoration. Perhaps, I told myself, I just wasn't the right kind of character for such an endeavor – perhaps *no* rational human being was fit for breakneck activities of that nature.

At any rate, it was clear to me that safety and well-being should have top priority during all activities. But obviously, precisely this wasn't the case when it came to the perfect restoration: this one turned out to be a hazardous game with my health. And if there was something I really didn't need, then it was a hazardous game with my health. As I still couldn't come up with a rational explanation for these extreme physical and mental conditions I encountered, I couldn't estimate either how intense the symptoms, obviously caused by the secretaire, could flare up at all; could it have been worse, with my body completely giving up on its functions, or, perhaps even worse, with my mind lost in the neverland between two worlds? No, this was something I really didn't need – even if it was connected with a loss of six hundred Swiss Francs.

On a very cloudy but dry weekend day in early summer I drove out to Nestor to inform him of my decision and pick up my tools. He was out in front of his house, tying up twigs and branches to bundles. When he saw me he smiled and interrupted his work. He stated that I hadn't been here in a long time, and that he almost had sold the secretaire on to someone else.

I didn't go into this but just briefly told him my decision that I would abandon the perfect restoration. First I tried to make him believe that I wasn't interested in Mari Egli's secretaire any longer because I had found another piece of furniture which I could restore faster and sell with more profit. Nestor, however, just laughed and said that I didn't need to hide behind fine excuses.

»When you were here the last time, you really had *dr Gack i de Hose ghaa⁵*, didn't you?« he hinted at the fear I had experienced during this intense extraordinary condition.

Nestor's crude and direct way of addressing what had happened provoked me. I forgot my excuse and explained to him that, in my view, his exercises and, for that matter, the perfect restoration, were reckless and dangerous if they had the potential of evoking extreme physical conditions the like I had experienced.

»Yeah alright,« he calmed me down. »Just tie those branches here together to *wedelis⁶*. That's for sure not dangerous. I'll go pick up another load of wood.« He put on his hat and pulled a hand cart along a small footpath up into the woods.

I was upset that he was so brief with me on this point. But when he later returned from the woods, my anger had evaporated. Tying those bundles of twigs had distracted me and calmed me down. Nestor came up to me and we continued the work together.

»I must have scared you with my condition the last time I was here,« I assumed and picked up our conversation again.

Nestor didn't answer directly. Instead, he talked about his return from the shopping trip into the village at nightfall. First he had looked for me in the stable. When he saw the damaged inlay work on the secretaire and tools spread around it, it dawned on him what had happened.

Nestor wanted to know what I had experienced. I told him in detail what I was still able to recall.

»You're talking about your experience as if you had undergone an illness,« he finally observed.

»I've been hallucinating, seeing things that don't exist. That's not normal, and it can't be healthy, either,« I tried to get across to him. »I'm sorry, but I'm not interested in further subjecting myself to influences of that extreme kind.«

»You had heightened perceptions of your senses,« Nestor analyzed. »Those were perceptions which had the same degree of reality at that moment, compared to what you see now. You shouldn't evaluate them with medical or psychological terms.«

---

⁵ Swiss German for *shitting your pants in fear*.
⁶ Swiss German for *bundles of twigs or branches*.

»I know what I have seen, Nestor,« I insisted. »Those were hallucinations. And that has nothing whatsoever to do with reality.«

»Hallucinations,« he mimicked me with an ironic tone of voice. »Well yes, if those were hallucinations, you should really watch out: hallucinations threaten your ability to perceive the world in orderly terms and correctly. And that is dangerous, because just imagine everybody would perceive the world in their own individual way – that would be sheer chaos. So when those hallucinations don't cease, they have to be treated with psychiatric methods. There's meds for that. And health insurance pays for it.

But if we really want to be resolute, we must not dream anymore, either,« he went on. »Because when we lay down at night and fall asleep, all that is playing on our inner screen are just hallucinations as well. But in this case it seems to be alright because it doesn't occur in our daily consciousness, and because we can stow it away in the drawer ›sleep and dreams‹. But if someone sees things in everyday life that others don't see, than he really has a problem.«

»What are you aiming at?« I asked him, provoked by his cynical comments. »That I had the vision of the century?«

He looked at me attentively. »Of course, it's not about playing up heightened perceptions of that kind, either,« he replied. »What you've seen still belonged to your small world, and it's not difficult to create perceptions of that kind. There's people around that even manage to sell their particular perceptions as prophetic visions. Sometimes that results in great religions, but in most cases these self-proclaimed prophets find only a few people they can relieve of their money – but they either stay prisoners of their own delusions or they deliberately lie to the people. The solution is not to classify these perceptions as illness, and neither to blow them up to divine visions; instead, consider them a chance.«

»A chance for what?«

»A chance to free yourself from the fallacy that there is only one correct way of seeing the picture,« he said with an assertive tone of voice. »A chance to recognize the value of the inner screen, and to seriously practice with it.«

I informed Nestor that I was light years away from believing that there was only one correct way of seeing the picture. And aside from that, I was perfectly satisfied with my world, so it didn't make any sense to me at all to escape into a different reality, no matter how that reality came about. Nestor countered my statement by saying that I perhaps was open enough to think of the picture differently, but not open

120

enough to *see* the picture differently. That's why the concentration on the inner screen made more sense than I myself believed.

I started to become angry. It was this disgusting way in which Nestor judged me in a condescending manner. And I detested him for the certainty he always expressed when rendering these judgments. I conjured him that he hardly knew anything about me, and that he therefore couldn't be certain when he was talking about my life.

»So that's the reason why you hardly tell anything about yourself,« he replied with a smirk. »You don't want to commit yourself but keep sitting on the fence. You don't want to be judged and screened. Why not? What are you afraid of?«

»I'm not afraid of anything.«

»But you keep silent about so many things concerning you and your person.«

I snapped at him and demanded he should stop. It was none of his business to judge me, I said, and he should quit telling such nonsense. When I was done, I felt totally exhausted. Nestor smiled and gently remarked it was amazing with how much fervor and commitment I defended my small world.

I realized that it was senseless to continue a discussion with him. There was no discussion anyway, at least the way I was used to lead them: where the individual participants tried to explain their viewpoint so as to arrive at a compromise in the end. Because Nestor didn't talk to me about his view of the world; no, he integrated me directly into his world. The only thing I could hold against him was silent defiance.

We kept silent for a while. I tied some more twigs to bundles and pulled the knots more tightly. Gradually, my anger ceased and was superseded by a strange sadness: I saw myself in that state of blackout again, that powerlessness during the recent attack when I felt that overwhelming power in me which gave me the feeling to be a nobody.

»I was scared like hell,« it came out of me so spontaneously that I was surprised myself.

Nestor shrugged. »You've hit the boundaries of your daily consciousness for the first time,« he said, as if it was self-evident. »You've gotten to a point where your small world – which was so safe and solid for you all that time – turned out to be a shaky house of cards close to collapsing. All of a sudden, you were confronted with different perceptions. And you didn't know how to deal with these; you couldn't distinguish any longer between what was real and what wasn't – and of course that had scared the hell out of you.«

I had to agree, he was right. It seemed as if he knew exactly what had happened to me and how I felt about it.

»But it's exactly this confrontation with the emotion of fear which unfixes our worldview and philosophy of life; it forces us to reinterpret the perception of the picture and continue to develop our consciousness,« he added. »This is what I mean when I advise you to see it as a chance.«

»This ›chance‹ had almost killed me,« I replied. »I felt as if my heart was about to jump out of my chest.«

»You were afraid of dying,« Nestor brought the issue to the point. With his words, he triggered my memory of that extreme physical condition. I felt the presence of that horror I had experienced, when my heart was pounding and I had to gasp for air; when the structures in the picture seemed to dissolve, when I wasn't able any longer to register what was happening in front of my eyes. That's when I, for the first time in my life, felt a deadly terror, an agony, accompanied by feelings of reluctance and remorse about the fact that it had come that far in the first place.

I qualified the description of my experiences and made a general remark to the degree that more or less all people would be afraid of dying.

»No,« Nestor replied with a determined tone of voice. »Most people are not afraid of dying. Now and then perhaps, they are concerned about the notion that they will die one day and not walk this earth any longer. But most people don't feel a real fear of death – what they are missing is the experience of being scared to death, the feeling of deadly terror in their own body.«

Nestor began talking about death: encounters with death were frightening because then we experienced, in the most impressive way, that it brings along with it an unthinkable change; that our death was like an inevitable black hole devouring anything important to us, anything we believed in.

His words caused me to become nervous. I told him that I couldn't see any sense in this conversation because there wasn't anything anyway about death which could be established as certain or predictable. And everybody knew that death will eventually catch up with us, after all.

»Exactly, everyone knows it,« he replied sharply. »And this is probably the excuse for us not to deal with death as such but to deny and repress it. Everyone knows it – so why deal with something that is known and that will occur sooner or later in any case and without our ›active support‹? So why sound out one's own death?«

I didn't allow myself to be thrown by his irony: »Yes, why? I don't know.«

»Because in this way we can overcome our fears,« he answered. »The most extreme way of dealing with death is the immediate experience of deadly terror in our own body. Those experiences in particular give us strength because we can learn from them. Therefore, consider your experience an enrichment.«

I informed Nestor that his hymns of praise concerning fear and death almost sounded as if I should deliberately seek the confrontation with death – in my ears a direct demand to do without any joy in life.

»It is unnecessary and reckless to seek death directly,« he replied calmly, »but when we practice the perfect restoration, then we cannot evade the confrontation with our fears, including the fear of death. And if we make experiences of that nature, it shouldn't be a reason for us to give up and run away – but rather, to walk through the world with more joy in life.«

Nestor repeated that my encounter with death was a good experience. He talked about my progress in the perfect restoration which had become possible as a result of my regular practices. Immediately, he reminded me not to lose sight of the exercises, and he announced that there was something else I should know.

At this point I felt forced to express the original intention of my visit once more: I had come to pick up my tools and say goodbye, once and for all. I pointed out that his perfect restoration had taken on alarming proportions, and I didn't see myself in a position to live in this way, as he obviously could.

Nestor discontinued his work. He seemed to ponder over the answer, taking his time. The longer he kept silent, the more nervous I became. The notion that I might disappoint him with my decision made me feel pretty miserable.

»The perfect restoration is no easy job,« he finally said. »It's the most difficult thing there is. But at the same time it's the only thing in the world that can offer a conscious life free from fear and full of realizations, thus really freeing us from all restrictions. In order to get there, it needs a lot of strength and willpower; we have to work hard at it and always do something to push in that direction. Nothing ever happens all by itself.

It also needs a lot of patience: setbacks are part of the agenda; advances are difficult to make and can hardly be estimated by other people. And even though every human being is capable of it, there are only a few who are given this chance. And out of these few, there are even fewer who take on the challenge on their own volition and with sincere aspirations. Perhaps you are one of these people, perhaps you're not. No one can take that decision out of your hands.« He got up and went into the house.

I remained seated. His words had caused something unexpected within me: it nettled me that Nestor simply left the choice up to me. I had been convinced that he would try, by all means, to talk me into staying and continuing the restoration – but the way he behaved it didn't seem to matter to him whether I stayed or left. At first, I was upset about Nestor's unbounded cheek, but soon after, I had to laugh: I suspected that this was just a clever move on his part to provoke me and make me stay, after all. The thought of having seen through his strategy cheered me up.

I tied the remaining twigs and branches to bundles, and when there were none of them left I felt happy. I decided to stay at Nestor's place overnight.

After dinner we both sat silently in Nestor's living room. All that time he sat motionless on his bed next to the oven and looked out the window. He seemed to closely observe something out there in the setting dusk.

»When you started dancing in that intensive state you had been in,« Nestor suddenly started speaking up, »you acted correctly, guided by your intuition. With the movements, you succeeded in letting the increased energy within you flow, and this resulted in the removal of blockades in your body. And this in turn helped you to dance better. In this way you managed to deal with your inner pressure.«

»What is this ›inner pressure‹ you're talking about?«

»The energy in your body generates an *inner pressure*,« he answered and looked at me, scrutinizing my face. »When Mari Egli's secretaire affects you the way it happened the last time, then this basically means that a very strong force is impacting on and in your body. You couldn't do anything with this energy, though, because you were blocked. That's why your inner pressure rapidly increased until you got it under control with your dancing movements.«

Nestor explained that it was inevitable to be able to deal with the inner pressure when it comes to the perfect restoration. Blockades in the body and stagnating energy forced me to become active and divert the inner pressure with unconscious movements and thoughts. If, on the other hand, I got the energy to flow freely, then I would be able to do my work calmly and focused, despite the increased intensity. This was precisely the condition I was in when I had managed to strip the varnish off the secretaire.

»And how am I supposed to get the energy to flow freely? By dancing?« I asked.

»By doing physical exercises that help you to increase your stamina and flexibility, be it dancing or whatever – any exercise accomplishing that will do. It doesn't matter what it is; the only point is that you go through the exercise with full awareness and all your energy. The more you train your body, the easier it will become for you to get the energy to flow freely. And this will result in you becoming stronger, which in turn helps you to work creatively with even more energy, and without your body doing the strange and uncomfortable things it used to. And without those visions and feelings of losing yourself, or – in an even more extreme situation – actually losing your consciousness altogether. I guess the best would be if you practice this dancing,« Nestor advised me.

»I doubt that I'll ever be able again to dance the way I did. The experience of this dance was too unique.«

»Let it be unique but not a one-time thing,« Nestor replied insistently. »Learn to dance and get that energy to flow.«

Admittedly, the prospect of dancing again the way I did before was quite alluring. But the effort I had to make – if I followed Nestor's advice – was something I heavily objected to. I informed him that I was no sporty character at all, and that I could never really get into sports and athletics.

Nestor answered that my physical appearance signaled precisely that. »Breathing and other physical exercises enhance the strength and beauty of a human being,« he asserted. »But you, you are of such a slight build, only skin and bones; you're pale, you're missing the natural glow in your face – where's the energy in your body? You're lacking a certain inner pressure. And that little bit of energy in you cannot flow freely. With such a weak and feeble body, how do you intend to bear up to the pressure of the secretaire?«

»So, according to you, I'd also have to dance for that piece of furniture?« I asked, slightly annoyed. The way he criticized my body was insulting to me.

»Not just dance. It is indeed necessary to get the energy to flow freely so as to deal with the inner pressure. But at the same time you have to systematically build up your inner pressure so that there will be more energy in the first place that you can make flow. And breathing exercises will help you with that. Watch your breath closely as often as possible, and try to take deeper breaths. Because usually you're breathing too shallow and too often. Breathe deeply and consciously.«

Nestor then started to talk about breathing exercises that, according to him, should be as simple as possible: »Take a deep breath, hold it, exhale slowly again, and if you want to, take a small break between two breaths before you start all over again – that's all it takes.«

»And for how long should I hold my breath?«

»As long as you feel comfortable about it, until you think it's enough. It's not necessary to take a stopwatch and measure the time. You don't have to watch for rhythm or a certain number of breaths. The crucial point is the breathing itself, that you pay conscious attention to your breath; inhale consciously, exhale consciously. Breathing consciously means nothing else than tensing up more and relaxing more. And this is what it's all about: we human beings are always moving between these two opposites. Having a high level of energy means to be able to tense up more and relax more.«

Nestor claimed that this increase in tension and relaxation would even become visible in the picture. He demonstrated to me the way he was breathing deeply.

»Feel the breath, how it flows through your nose,« he instructed me. »Feel how your belly and then your chest expand, how the pressure increases within you. If you take a deep breath and tense up, you become big and the picture becomes small because you take all the energy out of it.«

»The picture becomes small?«

»Exactly. When you're big, the picture is small. So you inhale and hold the breath, and at that moment the picture is not only small, it also stands still. But inside of you, everything is moving. There's all that tension, and everything is revitalized and cleansed: the heart starts to beat faster, and the blood shoots through your body. Keep that tension, that pressure for a while until you feel it's enough.

When you exhale eventually, it's like a big relaxation. You yourself become small and return the life energy back into the picture, making it big again. Breathing is a communication with the picture: you take energy out of the picture, you convert it, and you return it back into the picture.«

»You can't really make the picture small and big, do you?«

126

»Well of course, what you think?« he called out. »Everyone on the left side is capable of that.« Nestor inhaled deeply, looked tensely into the distance and pretended that he would spot something out there which he could hardly recognize. Then he exhaled, threw his head into the neck and opened his eyes widely so as to demonstrate the sudden overwhelming size of that which he had looked at. His comical gesture made us both laugh.

Nestor then repeated that I should dance and breathe correctly so as to build up my own inner pressure, and to get the energy to flow freely. This would remove the energy blockades in my body and would allow me to use my energy creatively.

»Are these blockades actual material obstacles in my body, or do you refer to my mental inhibition?« I asked.

»You cannot separate the one from the other,« he replied. »They are impurities in the body, the result of a wrong lifestyle and bad habits inhibiting your flow of energy. And that has an effect, both on the outer and inner screen: on the inner screen it means that you are inhibited, and that you have to ponder over things and live through sudden surges of emotion depriving you of your calmness; on the outside, it happens that your body cannot bear up to the pressure and starts to move or tremble nervously. Also, you'll get sick more often when your energy is stagnating. But when your inner pressure is strong enough and the energy can flow freely, you'll be much more able to bear up to the pressure around you, including the pressure of the secretaire.«

The next morning I went into the stable; I wanted to check up on the extent of damage I had caused on the inlay work. Obviously, Nestor had the same idea: he was already in the stable, cowering in front of the secretaire and painstakingly scrutinizing it.

I paused in the doorframe. Nestor turned around to me and pointed to the damaged inlay work on the top left-hand drawer – the spot I wanted to restore when my body started to play tricks on me.

»Looks like you wanted to cut away this piece here?« He clicked his tongue and shook his head. All of a sudden, I didn't feel the urge anymore to inspect the drawer more closely. Undoubtedly it looked like a complete botchery.

»What gave you the idea to start the actual restoration on the upper left of the secretaire?« he asked me thoughtfully.

I shrugged. »I always start on the upper left.«

»He always starts on the upper left,« Nestor sneered, pretending to talk to an imaginary listener. »Just like that, by habit. After all, he also starts to read and write on the upper left.«

Then he got up. »When you approach this piece of furniture, you'll have to leave any and all habits behind. Your small world has no place in the perfect restoration.«

»Where would you have started with the work?« I asked him, annoyed by his rebuke.

»Take a look at the afterimage of the secretaire,« he said as if it was self-evident. »It'll show you where to continue with the restoration.«

His answer surprised me. This was the first time that he assigned a comprehensible practical function to the afterimage – though I couldn't imagine how the afterimage could have been of concrete help in this case. Nestor suggested that I should find out right away. His suspicious confidence sparked my curiosity, and I sat down in front of the secretaire.

I had no difficulties to produce the afterimage of Mari Egli's secretaire; I fixed my eyes on the middle of the object, and soon after, the edges of the contrasty figures started to change color, and the afterimage effect took place.

The afterimage lit up in the same green-bluish hues as before. It was pulled down by the attractive force, and I tried to hold it in suspension without newly realigning my look. Then I had a spontaneous inspiration: I bent the upper part of my body forward and looked down to the ground – and when I looked at the afterimage from above, it stopped flowing in any direction.

Excited, I told Nestor that the afterimage doesn't flow downward anymore when I looked at it in that way. He replied that this would be totally understandable.

»Yes, it doesn't flow downward anymore because you are looking in the direction of the attractive force,« he explained. »But you won't overcome the attractive force by looking in its direction; you'll overcome it by holding the afterimage in suspension while you look at it in your usual way – with your face held up, your eyes looking straightforward, either sitting or standing.«

Nestor instructed me to look at the afterimage again. After a few more attempts I was able to identify a brief but somehow special condition of the colored spot that differed from the usual impressions: there were moments when the afterimage clearly stood out from the background. Its glow lost any irregularity, any flickering, and instead became so even and strong that I had the impression it had turned into a steady, intensely glowing mass with actual substance. But this perception lasted only for short while, because as soon as I tried to hold the afterimage in suspension at the same height, the flickering turned on again.

Nestor commented on this perception that the flickering came about through a steady realignment of my attention: »You're looking at the afterimage which is being pulled downward on the inner screen. But because you want to hold it up in suspension, you constantly realign your attention – and a new picture comes into existence. And then another one, and another one. These superimpositions cause the flicker effect. It's similar to looking at the picture on the outer screen. There you were also forced to constantly realign your attention if you wanted to look at a single spot and hold in suspension. When it comes to the afterimages, you can perceive this repeated realignment of your attention optically as a flicker effect.

If you, on the other hand, do not constantly realign your attention, the afterimage doesn't flicker because for a while you're looking at the same picture. However, as your concentration isn't focused enough yet, the attractive force makes you follow the afterimage downward with your eyes. That creates the effect of a steadily glowing afterimage in those moments when you follow its movements.« Nestor advised me to direct my attention to the steadily glowing afterimage as best as I could and as long as possible.

I turned back towards the secretaire. After a while I managed pretty well to perceive the afterimage as an intensely glowing mass. It needed a certain sensitiveness in the eyes: with a precise and strong but brief look upwards, I lifted the afterimage into my upper field of vision. Then, in an attempt to hold it in suspension, I followed it downwards. But during these few seconds everything appeared more intensive. Not only that the shimmering colors of the afterimages were stronger; the darkness surrounding it was deeper as well. During these moments my thoughts seemed to come to a standstill, and I almost forgot the intention behind my activities.

When I looked at the afterimage in this way it suddenly struck me that its intensity of glow was not even throughout. Some more attempts confirmed this impression: on the left side, the afterimage of the secretaire was brighter, particularly in the upper half. In the direction of the lower right-hand half, however, it lost some of its luminosity – not much but clearly perceivable. When I looked at the secretaire's legs on my inner screen, I could only perceive them as a weak shimmering.

I told Nestor what I saw. He seemed to be satisfied with my observation and said I should continue the restoration of the secretaire in the spot where the glow of the afterimage was the weakest – on the legs and on the lower right-hand side.

»You think the secretaire won't exert any pressure on me when I continue there?« I asked.

»It won't be as strong as on the upper left.«

Somehow this didn't satisfy me. The thought that such an extreme condition, the like I experienced two months ago, could possibly recur had something alarming to me. I told Nestor that I really didn't want to subject myself to that devastating influence. As long as the secretaire exerted pressure on me, I would not continue to work on it, on no account.

Nestor knitted his brows and made a derogatory gesture. Obviously he was upset by my statement. »You won't be able to restore the secretaire if you keep withdrawing all the time. I already told you what you have to do so as to overcome the pressure: you'll have to build up your own inner pressure and get the energy to flow. Now it's your turn.«

The authoritative tone of voice in his words outraged me. I blamed him that his perfect restoration was totally arbitrary, and that he wanted to fool me with some weird exercises. First it was all about seeing the picture as a whole; then I was supposed to practice concentration and holding the picture in suspension; this was followed by seeing afterimages and staring at the circular figures with double membrane – and now the success of the perfect restoration obviously depended on my inner pressure and the free flow of energy. What would be next?

Nestor allowed me to explain my views without interrupting me, but his look was so penetrating that I felt I had to argue against this look and nothing else. When I ran out of words I could feel my heart pound, and I was trembling slightly. It was almost as if I had foolishly puttered on the secretaire in a spot where I wasn't supposed to; it was as if arguing with Nestor also had the effect of rapidly increasing my inner pressure.

»From the very beginning you haven't done anything else than to increase your inner pressure,« Nestor explained. His voice was calm and he appeared relaxed. »All those exercises and advices I have given you aim at increasing this pressure within you. You can increase the inner pressure by sitting down calmly and concentrating on the point on the outer screen, or by looking at the afterimages. And most of all, by breathing correctly.«

Harnessing one's own energy in an economic way, however, was the key to the perfect restoration, Nestor added.

For that purpose we should be aware of the fact that we, as human beings, were in a constant exchange with the picture, by taking up and giving off energy.

»We take up energy from the picture in the form of nutrition, the air that we breathe and the sunlight,« he explained. »First I had pointed out to you that it depends on the quality of this energy. We should take care to take up, as much as possible, fresh natural energy, be it with the nutrition or with deep breaths of air – just with everything we pick up. The question is now what to do with this energy.« Nestor looked at me. »What do you think – what can we do with it?«

»All possible things. Everybody is using his or her energy in their own way,« I was convinced.

»We only have two choices,« he claimed. »Either we use our energy to keep on running our small world. This includes all activities with which we subdivide, discriminate and judge the picture. One example is the chase after material commodities; another is the constant repetition of our viewpoints with respect to this world, how it is, how it should be – including all ideas and beliefs regarding our self-image, our personality which we nourish and cherish. In this way we pin down our life energy to material objects, feelings and beliefs, and disassemble the picture into many parts. In other words: we are creating our small world.

The other choice, however, is the perfect restoration: by living a proper and adequate lifestyle we reclaim our pinned down and bound energy, increase the inner pressure, get the energy to flow freely again and remove energy blockades. As a result, we'll dissolve our small world in the picture. And when that happens, then we'll be able to give our energy into the picture as a whole in an undiscriminating way.«

I asked Nestor what it meant exactly when he talked about reclaiming our »pinned down and bound energy«. He explained that we had to know ourselves better and become aware of our feelings and beliefs. As we should, first of all, free our energy from its entanglement with material objects, we would have to clear up our feelings and beliefs with respect to these objects.

»People with a high degree of ownership expectations have the longest and most rocky road to the perfect restoration,« Nestor explained. »What they'll have to do, first and foremost, is spend less energy in the acquirement of material objects. They'll have to learn to take only that which they need for their livelihood and subsistence, and not more than that. No greed, no gluttony.

Then they'll have to learn to give. They still can't put their energy directly into the picture as a whole, though, because that energy is still pinned down to material objects. Consequently, people clinging on to their possessions have to free this energy from their ownership expectations. This expresses itself in the phenomenon that they no longer watch over their possessions with a jealous mind; instead, they make their possessions become available to others more easily and free of charge, or they even give away excess possessions for free. With the energy freed up in this way, their inner pressure gradually increases, and they have to get this energy to flow freely in their body with corresponding exercises. In this way they will be, at some point, able to put their energy directly into the picture, and in the process they will free themselves eventually. As a side remark: this approach would solve a lot of the problems existing on this planet.«

»That's a good idea, Nestor. I think something like that is called a ›Utopia‹,« I teased him.

»Stop that yakety yak about the ›Utopia‹,« he replied with a sharp tone of voice. »That's just excuses, nothing else. There are no utopias for the individual striving to live and act according to the perfect restoration. A person putting his or her energy into the picture in an undiscriminating way will also change the picture.«

I asked Nestor how it was possible to give off one's own energy in such a non-discriminating way. I reminded him of his own words according to which any kind of activity meant making discriminations in the picture.

»When you put your energy directly into the picture as a whole, that's not the same as acting in life. It is not a form of concentration, either. It's not something that you do but something that just happens. And you can feel that.«

»What kind of a feeling is it?«

»It's energy that flows out of the body,« he replied. »You'll be able to perceive it as a certain *prickle*. This feeling will tell you about the magnitude of your inner pressure: the stronger your inner pressure is, the more often and intensely you'll happen to feel that prickle. And the more intense it gets, the more energy you put into the picture as a whole.«

»And what is it supposed to be good for, after all, to give away one's own energy in this way?« I asked.

»What is it supposed to be good for?« Nestor looked at me as if he couldn't understand why I asked that. »Because you animate and vitalize the picture in this way: it'll become more intense in all respects, more colorful and luminous, sensible and conscious. And this prickly feeling of energy flowing out of your body – *that's just mind-blowing*.«

Developing the Emotional Body

Nestor was right. Indeed, the afterimage of Mari Egli's secretaire turned out to be a reliable guideline for the sequence in which the damaged parts of the object had to be restored. In the following fall I thus succeeded in repairing the legs of the secretaire that had shown a dim glow in the afterimage.

I was stunned about the amount of effort that the artist had put into the elaboration of these legs: skillfully artistic, incredibly detailed carvings with motives of nature, both animate and inanimate, spread relief-like and plastically over the entire length of all four legs. It wasn't so much that there were adornments on the legs; each leg in itself was an adornment.

As such, the right back leg showed fine carvings of motives like rock crystals, slate and miniaturized mountain ranges. Ivy entwined around the right front leg, and a large number of blossoms, mushrooms and lichen, both known and unknown to me, barged in between the leafs of the vine. On the left front leg there were animals, animal eyes, animal faces and body parts of the most different species: snails, worms, fish, sheep, cats, foxes and at the upper end an eagle whose spread wings projected from the leg. Human figures, faces, mouths, eyes and noses formed the left back leg. Men and women – provided they were shown with their full body – were displayed, in part naked and performing sexual intercourse – something which wasn't necessarily part of the cultural repertoire of the Emmental at the end of the 19th century.

The two legs to the left were mostly intact, but on the right-hand legs several parts had to be replaced: on the back leg, the tip of a protruding rock crystal was broken off. And on the leg with the plants and blossoms, a large piece of wood was missing which deprived the ivy of some of its leaves. This restoration work would also take longer than under usual circumstances, because: although the pressure impacting on me during the restoration of the legs was actually less than during the work on other parts, I still took painstaking care to stay moderate in my efforts. And that meant to me: rather too little then too much work on it. When my pulse started to quicken, when I had to breathe faster, and when sweat began to cover my palms, then I dropped everything and immediately withdrew from the secretaire.

Nestor considered this delay a neglect on my part. He criticized that I now had lapsed into the opposite extreme, touching the secretaire only with velvet gloves to avoid any exaggeration by any means. According to him, I could allow myself to work on the secretaire for a longer period of time without having to be deterred by the slightest physical reaction. But despite his affirmations I kept exercising caution and finished these restoration works – slowly but surely – in the fall of that year.

Following the realization that I had to work my way on the secretaire from the lower right to the upper left in order to perform the perfect restoration in the correct sequence, I next directed my attention to the only handle of the object which hung on the bottom right drawer. As so many other things on this piece of art, this handle was quite strange as well: it was a delicate brass handle with two arcs of different length. Whereas the lower end was not fixed to the drawer, the upper part opened out into a sphere which was embedded into a corresponding metal mold screwed on tightly to the secretaire. It could be turned from below to the upper left, but not to the right.

The handle showed corrosions in some spots and had to be replaced. In an antique shop in Bern I bought a new handle which I considered suitable for the secretaire. It was an artistically adorned, gold-plated drawer handle from about the same time period. But I couldn't fix the new handle on the drawer. The moment I tried, I experienced such a rapid increase of my inner pressure that it was impossible for me to keep my hands still and continue the work. In the sense of the perfect restoration, I assumed that my inner pressure still wasn't strong enough; obviously my energy couldn't flow freely enough so as to be able to work on this part of the drawer. To my surprise, however, Nestor didn't attribute my difficulties to physical-energetic or psychosomatic circumstances this time. According to him, the villain was the handle.

»You probably think you could attach any old piece of metal on Mari Egli's secretaire?« he called out, visibly amused, after I had shown him the new handle.

»Does it make a difference, after all? It's just about a handle.«

»It's not just about a handle,« he disagreed. »Everything on the secretaire has its space and purpose and belongs to a whole. You cannot replace this handle with any old other handle without causing a drastic change on the entire piece of art.«

»So, according to you, the reason why I'm not able to attach the handle to the secretaire is that it doesn't tolerate drastic changes on itself,« I concluded dryly.

»No,« he countered me, »you cannot attach the handle because you're not acting in the sense of the perfect restoration. Because the perfect restoration always aims at overcoming barriers and boundaries, at connecting things separated and combining the parts to a whole. With this handle, however, the inherent unity of the secretaire would get lost.«

Then he said that he didn't blame me for what I had intended to do. Because, in order to establish whether a handle was the correct one, I had to be very familiar with the principle underlying Mari Egli's secretaire; but once I was, I wouldn't have any problems with the restoration.

The fact that Nestor talked about a principle underlying the secretaire in such a natural way confirmed my idea that he stood in an old tradition of wisdom. Of course I wanted to find out more about this principle and its effect on the choice of the handle, and I was also interested in the question how come that Nestor had knowledge of all this.

»We cannot talk about this principle just like that,« he replied to my questions. »Because it can't be described with words only. But don't worry, all that will come at the proper time. Now it is essential to find the right handle.«

Around lunchtime we left the house. Nestor wanted to introduce me to a woman who lived in this area. The thought of this supposedly eccentric lady made him laugh time and again – obviously he was looking forward to meeting her. He called her *the danseuse*, because for many years dancing was her way to strive for wholeness.
Nestor said that there might be a good chance to find the right handle in the woman's place; in her attic one could find just about everything that people could collect.

For while we followed the path leading up the hill into the woods. Due to the recent thunderstorm, the ground was still soft and moist, and the little creek ditches were filled with moldy branches, twigs, roots and rock debris washed down by the deluge of water.

When we arrived up on top of the hill we sat down, took a rest for a while and enjoyed the impressive view: the valleys bordering to the right and left were covered by thick fog. Both covers of fog slowly flowed together at the peak of the *egg*[7] and pushed further down in the direction of the plains. Out of this ocean of fog, the hill across from us emerged in a spooky way – narrow like a dark green dorsal fin of a marine mammal, only occasionally speckled with yellow and red spots.

---

[7] Swiss German term for an elevation between valleys or ditches.

Nestor made a remark on my physical condition. He stated that, in comparison to our previous hiking trips, it had markedly improved; he assumed that this was the result of my breathing- and physical exercises. With a clean conscience, I could confirm that I regularly practiced them. In the beginning I had a hard time to interrupt my habitual work rhythm to practice the exercises, but meanwhile I had fun with them. Moving my body had something refreshing and brought about a higher level of concentration during my work.

We kept silent for a while. A moist wind swept across our hill in the direction of the valley. There it stroke over the cover of fog, causing single billows to emerge from it and to rise up slowly into the sky. Occasionally the sun broke through the upper layer of clouds and sent its mild autumnal warmth onto the billows rising up from the ocean of fog which then started to dissolve, creating wondrous forms and shapes.

Suddenly Nestor started to talk about dreaming. He said that, over time, the physical exercises would also influence my dreams.

»You'll experience your dreams more consciously, they'll become clearer and more real,« he prophesied. »That's part of the package, because after all, you're practicing the exercises so as to feel better in your body; this feeling reaches all the way down into your dreams. In addition, you regularly direct your attention onto your inner screen. This is also something promoting lucid dreaming. Because the inner screen is not only the place of the afterimages but also the projection screen for your dreams while you are asleep. For this reason you will deal more and more consciously with your *emotional body*.«

I wanted to know from Nestor what that emotional body was. He answered that this particular body was more subtle and flexible than the physical body. And it wasn't just active in our dreams but also in our daily consciousness: the emotional body was the place where we generated and experienced feelings.

»But the emotional body can only unfold its full activity when our consciousness has withdrawn from the material body, that means, when we're already asleep,« he went on. »However, this we can only experience when we can maintain our consciousness in the emotional body. If our consciousness withdraws even further and we fall into a deep sleep, we strip off this emotional body as well and dwell in the *mental body*.«

»Is there a difference whether we are dreaming in the emotional body or in the mental body?«

»Usually people don't dream in the mental body because they haven't developed it enough, and they are unable to maintain their consciousness during a phase of deep sleep,« he replied. »Only people on the left side can dwell in this body consciously, and this allows them to experience that kind of consciousness which can exist without these three bodies. We'll talk about the mental body later. For you it's important, first and foremost, to raise your awareness of your emotional body.«

Nestor explained that the ability to consciously deal with the emotional body was an indicator for an individual's progress in the perfect restoration. Small children had the easiest time to act from within their emotional body because their consciousness was not yet completely absorbed by the outer screen. But when a person started to build up and maintain its small world according to the ideals prevalent in our society, then he would gradually lose the ability and strength to counteract the attractive force by orienting himself towards the inner screen – and thus he would also lose the ability to consciously dwell in his emotional body.

»The result is that most people are, for example, not any longer able to fly in their dreams, like kids often still do. If adults dream at all, they rather experience situations in which they are not getting any place, where every single step ahead is strainful and exhausting; they get wasted, bog down and petrify in their nightmares – and wake up dripping with sweat.

But when we get our life energy to flow again by practicing physical exercises that not only increase our awareness of our physical body but also of our emotional body; and when we direct our attention onto the inner screen time and again, then we can again become aware of the abilities of the emotional body.«

»Then we'll be able to fly in our dreams?« I asked.

»Flying is one of the most advanced abilities of the emotional body. It can also move faster and jump higher than the physical body. It is lighter, more flexible and shapeable than that one. The emotional body also has the ability to renew itself constantly. And it can breathe underwater and even walk through walls.«

To Nestor, particularly the ability mentioned last was testimony for how far the emotional body had already been developed. He explained that those people who, in their dreams, were able to walk through matter, walls, doors and rocks, had overcome the notion of solidity and consistency of the sensual material world. Nestor made no secret of the fact that this was one of the most difficult things a human being could do with his emotional body.

His words sparked my interest. I told him of that dream in which I had been stuck in that cave, trying in vain to penetrate a viscous wall.

»Your small world has still acted too strongly on you,« he interpreted my dream. »You fell prey to the illusion that your body was actually not able to penetrate walls or the like – just like you know from your everyday experience. Still it was a good dream because you realized that the solidity of the wall was not absolute, after all. If you had been conscious and aware enough in your emotional body, you could have given your small world a *gingg, a kick in the butt* by walking through this wall.

But you're still lacking energy to do so. So you do experience more and more lucid dreams in which the abilities of your emotional body now reveal themselves in part, but in many other dreams you're still not able to counteract the attractive force, and you're not aware enough. There you're still moving on the borderline between emotional and physical body. This can go so far that your physical body reacts when you dream: then you're talking in your sleep, you're moving and struggling; it can also mean that your body heats up, that you wake up from a nightmare dripping with sweat, or,« – he gave me a smiling wink – »that your dream can also become a little wet in between.«

I wanted to know from Nestor how I could awaken my emotional body in my dreams. He answered that I shouldn't proceed from the point of dreaming because we could hardly, if at all, deliberately influence our dreams. Likewise, while dreaming it is difficult to act with an emotional body that has been made conscious without waking up in the process.

»If we want to explore our *emotional world*,« he said, »then we have to proceed, above all, starting from the physical world, from our daily consciousness. Because that's where we have the strongest influence, that's where we can practice and create an effect on the inner and outer screen. Basically, it's not about the dreams themselves but about having access to the emotional world and the emotional body in your daily consciousness. The dreams can show you how much this is already the case: the more lucid your dreams are, the more awake is your emotional body in everyday life.«

Nestor got up and pointed in the direction in which we continued our hiking trip. The path led us down from the hill into a small valley overgrown by flowers. All kinds of tall grasses and plants with large leaves reminiscent of water lilies adorned our way and animated the small valley. At its end we arrived at an extraordinary wide and flat moor range.

For a moment I paused and let my eyes wander over the grasses and mosses with their dominating red and orange colors. A strange fascination emanated from this area but I just couldn't put my finger on what exactly it was: my feelings remained just as vague as the soft and moist ground which yielded to each footstep with a gargling sound. Everything that was still solid and hard around here seemed to be somewhat frozen in timelessness, like the low and bare birch trees here and there, patiently persevering in this lonesomeness.

Then I recognized a woman between the trees who was walking over the moor, bent over as if searching for something. She didn't seem to notice what was happening around her; she was completely absorbed into her search.

Now and then she paused and picked up something from the ground that she put into a basket. For a moment I thought I had seen the coal woman again, but then my attention was drawn to her movements: they were simple walking, bending and pick up movements, but the way the woman moved was so graceful that I couldn't take my eyes off her. I was certain that this was a young woman, a girl.

Nestor had kept walking on and headed directly for her. I followed him without taking my eyes off the woman. With each step in her direction, I became more and more nervous. To cover it up, I started to quiz Nestor about her. He confirmed that this was the woman we wanted to visit but didn't reveal any further information about her.

»We'll see if she can smell you,« he added with a smile.

As we came closer, the woman's braided long silvery shining hair revealed that she must have been of advanced age. Now her graceful way of moving her slim body across the pasture was even much more surprising.

Nestor stood almost in front of her when she looked up and recognized him – and I startled: her facial expression appeared hard, her eyes looked grim and penetrating. It seemed as if she was far from happy to see us. Without a single word of welcome she turned towards me.

»He's standing on the white moss,« she said with a threatening tone of voice and looked at me as if I had committed a crime.

»Who?« I asked slightly confused.

»He!« she called out.

Nestor started to laugh and turned around towards me. »She means you,« he explained.

I looked down to the ground and recognized that the spot where I stood was covered with a white plant of low growth between the otherwise green, red and orange colored grasses and mosses. I laughed along with Nestor because I thought the woman was just joking. But she in turn started to move suddenly and headed for me with such a fast pace and determinism that I jumped aside in a reflex. She was cowering in front of the spot where I had stood, carefully scrutinizing it. Obviously she couldn't find what she was looking for there, so she got up, walked on without saying a single word and left us standing right where we were.

»What's the matter with that woman?« I asked Nestor with a low voice.

»I told you that she's eccentric,« he replied. »Come on, we'll help her search.«

He walked across the pasture and looked around. Twice he picked up something and called me over to take a look at it. He showed me what the danseuse was looking for: small white twigs of moss, interwoven and carrying some kind of tiny buds; these were exuding a pleasantly smelling, refreshingly sweet, almost fruity scent.

This scent triggered an indefinable feeling within me. I was certain that I knew that scent from somewhere, but I was missing concrete memories as to where and when I had encountered it before. I wanted to get to the bottom of this feeling, but Nestor started to look for and collect these fragrant twigs and asked me to do the same.

After we had collected a considerable amount of these buds we headed for the house of the old danseuse. Nestor and the woman went ahead. They were chatting in a humorous way, constantly giggling and laughing. It seemed as if they were bosom buddies of one mind.

The danseuse's home was a big farmhouse in a small valley, between a forest with an orange colored fern field in front and a pasture sloping slightly upwards from which steam was slowly rising. A small creek separated the forest from the pasture, and a footpath led along that creek to the house. I could see that the woman was generating her own electrical power: the cables led to a small hut with a water wheel directly at the creek; obviously a generator was located there, driven with water power.

We entered the house, the front of which was covered with striking amounts of moss and lichen. Nestor asked me to fire the tiled oven while he and the old woman retreated in the living room where, as I could observe, they sorted out the moss buds. They cleaned them and placed them either on a piece of paper to dry, or they put them into a glass jar filled with some sort of liquid.

The stresses and strains of our hiking tour and the search for the moss buds had been so exhausting to me that I had a real hard time after our meal to keep my eyes open. On my request, the old woman led me into a room in the shed near the farmhouse. I laid down on the squeaking bed and fell asleep at once.

When I entered the kitchen the next morning, Nestor was nowhere to be seen, but the danseuse sat at the wooden table and had breakfast.

»Hey, hey, here's the boy!« she called out in my direction when she saw me; obviously she was in a good mood. I introduced myself to her and explained to her politely that she wouldn't have to call me »boy« but could call me by my name. Then I asked her for her name. She said she didn't have a name. I replied that the farmer didn't have a real name, either, and I asked her if the reasons for that were the same.

»People on the right side have names,« she clarified. »That's why they live on the right side, after all – because they have names. On the left side, though, there are no more names. The names are all used up.«

I meekly called her attention to the fact that Nestor lived on the left side and still had a name. The old woman asserted that Nestor didn't really have a name either, no matter how I called him.

»Is the boy hungry?« she suddenly changed the subject. »There are sweet *Pflüümli*[8].« She pointed to the food on the table, asked me to help myself and turned back towards her breakfast.

On the table there was the partially cut loaf of bread from last night next to a bottle with herb syrup, a bowl of milk and a small pot with honey, some walnuts and a good dozen freshly picked mirabelles. Everything was strewn all over the table. I was looking in vain for empty bowls, plates, silver – there was only one knife for cutting the bread. I cut off a small piece and filled a glass with herb syrup.

While I was eating my bread I watched the old woman – clandestinely and with a mixture of disgust and fascination – eating her breakfast: she cut off a small piece of bread which she pronged with the kitchen knife; first she dipped it into the honey, then into the milk, and finally she put it in her mouth, chewed on it with a loud smacking sound and gulped the food down with a sip of syrup. My assumption was that she softened up the hard bread in the milk so as to relieve her teeth. But then I realized that was far from it: now and then she cracked the shell of a walnut with her back teeth which sent cold shivers up and down my

---

[8] Swiss German term for small mirabelles.

spine. Then she removed the broken shell and skillfully freed the kernel from the wooden shell pieces. As far as I could observe, she made it every time to free the kernel in one entire piece.

»Do you know who Mari Egli was?« I asked. I took the opportunity to find out something about the tradition I surmised would exist. The old woman lived on the left side of the Emme, and from this one could conclude that she was a follower of that mystical teaching, just like Nestor and the farmer.

»Why is he asking me for Mari Egli?«

I explained to the danseuse that I intended to restore Mari Egli's secretaire, and that I was interested in finding out some more about her as the previous owner. When the old woman heard that, she started laughing loudly; she had to choke so hard on a piece of bread that she almost suffocated and had to cough heavily several times.

I didn't get irritated by her behavior. When she had recovered I asked her again for Mari Egli.

»She was out of her mind,« she replied, smacking loudly. Strange enough, I couldn't sound out any contempt or disdain in her words. It rather sounded more as if she admired Mari Egli for her madness.

»What do you mean?« I kept asking.

»He should just take a look at that desk. Does he believe that this piece of furniture has been built by a normal person? Someone who builds a piece of furniture like that must be out of his mind.«

»What do you mean? In what way was she out of her mind?«

The old woman laughed sneeringly. »She was simply out of her mind. Can the boy understand that? While building her desk she made a jump in her consciousness.

And from that moment on she was out of her mind.«

»So you believe that Mari Egli has built this secretaire?« I concluded.

»Who else should have built it, huh?«

I shrugged.

»Someone from her family. Or maybe someone unknown.«

»Nonsense. There's even her name written on it.«

Cautiously, and with an attempt to avoid the impression that I wanted to teach her, I tried to explain to her that someone else could have written the name »Mari Egli« on the secretaire. The old woman mimicked the seriousness and impressiveness in my gestures with which I obviously tried to convince her.

»The boy should know that the name ›Mari Egli‹ is meaningless,« she explained. »In order to build that piece of furniture, she had left her name behind on the lower right half and moved to the upper left side, to the shining spheres.«

The danseuse surprised me with her detailed knowledge of the secretaire. She knew exactly where to find what on it. What didn't surprise me was that she called the circular figures of the inlay work »shining spheres«: like Nestor, she tended towards mystically exaggerating her perceptions. This tendency was certainly a question of her character and a result of the remote solitude she lived in. The fact that she hadn't had a higher education also seemed to play a significant role here. To me it was clear anyway that the old danseuse had dealt with the symbolism on Mari Egli's secretaire and was quite familiar with what exactly was happening here on the left side.

She looked at me expectantly while she was chewing on her bread. Encouraged by her silence, I started to talk about the exercises which Nestor had introduced me to so as to improve my perception of afterimages on the inner screen.

»Nestor told me that the length of time in which I was able to hold my afterimages in suspension on the inner screen was an indicator for the amount of energy I could muster up for the restoration of Mari Egli's desk«. Even though I didn't really want to, I used her term »desk« for the secretaire because I hoped to find out more if I did.

»Nestor sure knows why he says that,« she replied lackadaisically.

»So you know about the inner screen?«

»Like the boy knows his dickie.«

I ignored her gruffness and asked her how she had found out about the inner screen.

»If I look at it, it's there,« she explained succinctly.

»I mean: who has told you that there is something like the inner screen and instructed you to look at it?«

Right that moment the front door opened and Nestor stepped in. The danseuse turned around towards him. »So you really let that boy dabble and mess around with Egli's desk?« she called out to him in disbelief.

»Sure,« Nestor replied, took off his hat and put it on a shelf next to three wicker baskets. »He has paid for the secretaire.«

Both broke out in laughter, and the woman slapped her hand on the table. Then her eyes were screening me.

»The way it looks, he's still paying: no wonder the boy is so skinny! The desk is wearing him out like the cat does with the mouse, huh?«

»Well, he's not really the born wrestler,« Nestor consented.

»He has to watch out that he won't go even skinnier, that he *nid vom Stängeli gheit*«[9] she replied with pretended concern.

»Yeah, he's already had trouble with that in the chicken house,« he joked and described how I strained myself to keep the balance on the board while looking at the afterimage of the circular glass window. The old woman burst out in hard laughter again.

Both now took ample time to cook up derogatory comments on my physical stature. One comment gave the other, and they tried to outdo one another with absurd pictures and ideas.

I couldn't really join their exhilaration and laughter. Just because I was a little smaller and lighter than most young adults, that still didn't give them the right to tease me in this rude way.

Nestor poured some syrup into a glass and sat down. He informed the old woman that I did physical exercises now to be able to stand up to the pressure of the secretaire.

»Some exercises will certainly do him good,« the danseuse confirmed. »But if he wants to restore Egli's old desk – that'll take some more.«

My patience had run out and I corrected the old woman halfheartedly: Mari Egli's piece of furniture, I explained, was a secretaire, perhaps a commode – but certainly not a desk.

The moment I finished saying this she interrupted her laughter and gazed sharply at me with a fierce and hostile look. Nestor fell silent, too. From one moment to the other, the atmosphere had markedly cooled down – so much that I even started to become afraid.

Without saying a word, the danseuse got up. She stretched herself and made some bizarre movements which caused loud cracking noises from all her bones. Then she started to move through the room. She did this very slowly and gracefully: she moved her naked feet gently but vigorously, and with her arms and hands she made elegant wave-shaped movements which were beautiful to behold. The old woman displayed a fascinating level of body control; she was indeed a true danseuse.

She slowly approached me with light dancing movements. Her face remained expressionless, and her fixed stare was directed at me, as if she didn't look at me but all the way through me. The seriousness of the situation and the immense amount of concentration with which she went through the movements had something terribly absurd. I sat on my chair, helpless as if paralyzed. Neither did I know what this was sup-

---

[9] Swiss German for becoming so slender that one feels weak and powerless (lit. "to fall off the perch").

posed to mean nor did I have an idea how I should react to the situation. Searching for help, I looked over to Nestor, but obviously the whole thing even seemed to amuse him. He lifted his eyebrows, and with a nod of his head he signaled me to look at the woman again.

The danseuse stood close to me now and slowly moved her head in my direction. She moved the side wings of her nose as if she had gotten scent of something. I myself didn't smell anything.

»What's the point of that?« I asked, offended. »Do I stink or something?« Again I looked over to Nestor to sound out what he thought of all this, but his face showed no expression at all.

Once more the old woman sniffed in my direction. Then she started to speak as if fully convinced:

»The slime is definitely dominant among the boy's juices. He wants to render the impression that he is open, urbane and adventuresome. But actually he is still, boring and likes to retreat and seclude himself.« She looked at me, perhaps to check my reaction.

A feeling of resentment rose up in me. The old woman was about to do something which I always had hated: she was about to judge me and rub my nose in my character.

The danseuse kept sniffing on me. »He could remain in his little snail shell for ages. Now and then he puts out his feelers from the hole – but he only comes creeping out when he's certain that everything is fine and calm outside. Or even better: if the people outside hail him and cheer for him.« She took several deep breaths through her nose and snorted.

»Uhuh,« the old woman suddenly called out – so loud that I cringed. »We have a boy here whom women are supposed to trust.« Nestor smirked. »For that he takes great pains to appear tender, sensitive and empathetic. He pretends to be a little shy, but that's exactly what creates a mysterious effect which is supposed to make him attractive and desirable. Because who knows what else could hide behind the shy calm boy? Perhaps a full load of explosive romanticism, huh?« She laughed at me in a stupid way.

I tried to stay as calm as possible. Of course I hadn't deserved such a treatment. But obviously the woman couldn't be approached with rational arguments, so I deemed it appropriate to let her have her way and just submit to the whole play – the wiser head gives in, after all.

But then it suddenly struck me that the old woman's chitchat about my strategy to just close my eyes until everything was over proved to be true right now. Hot flashes ran through my body. I felt the blood pound in my temples and started to sweat. I wanted to get up and vent my anger. But right that moment the old woman stomped on the floor vigorously and clapped her hands like mad, scotching my plan.

For a moment it was absolutely silent. My anger was gone; instead I felt miserable and also a little guilty.

»The boy has to be motivated,« she finally suggested. It sounded as if she herself was surprised by what she had said. She relaxed her body, turned away from me and sat back down on her chair. Nestor and the old woman looked at each other.

»To say the truth,« she explained coldly, »the boy is lacking quite some strength.« She shrugged and added with a casual tone of voice: »He's a weenie wimp.«

With a gaping mouth I looked over to Nestor. I was outraged and hoped he would come for my assistance, but all he did was to nod his head, signaling he concurred with her.

»You should put the boy into the cooking pot,« the danseuse advised Nestor.

»Even though there's hardly anything on him?« he asked.

»Until he's well done,« she insisted, and again both burst out in long laughter. I got up and left the house. I had to get away from these people, away from that madness.

Outside it was comfortably cool, but drearily cloudy. I went upstream to the hut with the water wheel and further on until I arrived at a small willow tree on the right side of the creek which attracted my attention.

Its low trunk, covered with moss and lichen, branched out into two big arched boughs. The right bough was strung out but not so high. The other one was higher and less elongated, arching over the creek towards the other side. From the upper side of both boughs, bumps were rising up in regular distances that looked like humps. Out of each of these humps, long thin orange-brown colored twigs were growing, bending upward. I guessed that the old woman was cutting off these extremely flexible twigs in regular intervals to weave baskets from it, the way I had seen them in her place.

Pondering over this, I realized that the danseuse had crept into my thoughts again. I sat down under a tree on one of the few stones that was relatively dry. The peaceful gurgle of the water had a relaxing effect on me and prompted me to bring order into my thoughts.

Unfortunately I had to admit to myself that I did recognize myself surprisingly well in the picture which the old woman had drawn of me. Perhaps my inner world had indeed been a place of refuge for me all the time to avoid conflicts as much as possible. But the relentless way in which she revealed this deprived me of any feeling of security so that I felt naked and helpless. And for that I abhorred her.

The creek flowed by me in an unconcerned way. I envied the water: you could curse at it and call it names, or you could praise and applaud it – it was simply impervious to any kind of emotional outbreaks. It always stayed cool and kept on flowing as if nothing whatsoever had happened.

Nestor came strolling in my direction. He sat down across from me on the left side of the creek, watched it attentively for a while and kept silent. I thought that he had come to apologize for their outrageous behavior and make it up with me.

»You're just like the water,« he pointed out instead and sparked my curiosity with that. »Water flows in those places where it meets the least resistance. Without additional pressure it'll stay in its predetermined channels. It can't free itself from that, it cannot break new ground. This is exactly the situation you're in. And the danseuse has recognized that.« His eyes were resting on me.

»That old lady is definitely nuts,« I mumbled.

Nestor didn't go into this but explained that she had directed my attention to a big problem – to something which would play a crucial role in building up the inner pressure, and even in the perfect restoration.

»You're too careless with your sexual energy,« Nestor brought the issue to the point.

»What do you mean?« I asked, more surprised than unknowing.

»You know exactly what I mean,« he said with a serious voice. »So far we haven't talked about it, but the correct handling of sexual energy is the central point of importance for any person who is striving to build up the inner pressure and get the energy to flow freely.«

Nestor began talking about sexual abstention which – if practiced consistently and with the appropriate knowledge – would considerably accelerate, perhaps even enable in the first place, the buildup of that pressure. He compared sexual energy with the flowing creek from which I had to retrieve the energy the way the danseuse did it with her water wheel.

He explained that a large portion of energy at the disposal of a person was tied up in the urge to procreate: the human body invested tons of energy into the production of spermatozoa and ovules. If we wouldn't waste this sexual energy but retained it for ourselves, this would help us most in raising our consciousness. He said the inattention with which I handled this energy was the reason why I made only very slow progress in the perfect restoration, and why the secretaire still had such a rapidly exhausting effect on me. Then he advised me to abstain from any and all conscious sexual activity as much as possible.

I evaded his look. I just couldn't believe that he wanted to give me advice for my sexual life. I simply refused to accept that he or the old lady were in a position to make judgments about my sexual energy and activities in that direction.

»The danseuse has smelt you. And she knows more than you can imagine,« Nestor replied implacably as if he had read my mind.

Cautiously I voiced my concern that abstaining from sexual activities would make me square and boring. With a smile, Nestor replied that I was square and boring already because I was lacking a lot of energy which I could regain through abstention. Frantically, I tried to explain to him that pent-up sexual energy would result in a person feeling nervous and aggressive, and it could even adversely affect his physical well-being.

»What are you afraid of? Do you think your ›best friend‹ might explode when you practice abstention?« he laughed out loudly. »Don't panic, you don't just pile up sexual energy; that would be senseless indeed. Rather, you're doing something with it: you're retrieving the energy that is physically tied up for the purpose of sexual procreation – and you do it through physical and mental activities, like the perfect restoration. In this way you're converting sexual energy into consciousness.«

Later in the afternoon, when we were having a meal, Nestor told the danseuse that I was looking for a handle for Mari Egli's secretaire. His remark came as a surprise to me because I completely forgotten the reason for our visit over the stirring events.

I confirmed Nestor's words and wanted to describe the issue with the handle to the old woman. But all she had to say was that the »junk« was up in the attic.

»If he finds something suitable,« she added, »he can take it along with him.«

I had finished my meal but remained seated. My intention was to look for a handle together with Nestor who was still eating. Meanwhile, the old lady explained to me how I could get up into the attic, and when I still remained seated she insisted that *dr cheibe Grümpu*, as the Swiss call *old junk and lumber*, wouldn't come down from the attic all by itself as if showing up at a beauty contest. In this way, she signaled me in an unmistakable way that I was supposed to go and look for a handle right away, by myself.

I left the kitchen and walked over to the shed where I climbed up the ladder to the attic. Up there, it looked worse than I had imagined. Junk was piled up on junk, and there was hardly any way through all the old disused objects, partially intact but hardly usable any longer. The amount of stuff up here collecting dust and going to seed was so much that, to me, it was impossible that the danseuse had collected all that herself; this looked as if at least three generations had worked on it.

I started to fight my way through brown paper bags and plastic buckets filled with rusty scrap metal, chains, nails, large screw nuts, steel brushes, cogwheels and the like; in other buckets I found tools, used dishes, old silver, wire whisks and scoops. There was a pile with bicycle parts: fenders, lamps, spokes and wheels, bicycle pumps, single pedals and a bag with old metal license plates.

In a wooden cart I found an antediluvian record player with a small jewel case on top that sparked my interest. I opened it, and inside I found a yellowed black-and-white photo of a walkable rock connecting two sides of a deep and narrow canyon. I wondered why this particular photo was lying around, kind of lost, in this case.

While I was ransacking the attic, I constantly had to think of the ridiculous instructions which Nestor and that old woman wanted to give me with regard to my sexual energy. Indeed, meanwhile I understood quite well that I had to build up an inner pressure within me so as to be able to withstand external pressure. But who could give me a guarantee that withholding sexual energy, of all things, could accelerate the build-up of inner pressure? And what did that old lady know anyway about male potency? After all, she was a woman.

Absorbed in thoughts around the subject, I continued to dig into wooden boxes with empty glass bottles, busted light bulbs, gas canisters and paint pots; I found parts of small broken clay figures, an ancient vacuum cleaner, a rusty toolbox filled with mirror shards, rasps, files and steel wool.

I was pondering over the question whether the old danseuse really had such a sophisticated olfactory sense that she was able to see through, or better »smell through«, other people. I rather liked to believe, though, that Nestor – who knew me better than her – had certainly talked to the old woman more than once during my absence.

Two horse harnesses were hanging on the wall, and immediately below it there was an uncovered horse sled in cheesy bright pink and blue

150

– how on earth did that get here? – and loaded with old heavy skis and ski poles. Old perforated jute bags, yellowed linen sheets and woolen blankets were hanging on the other wall.

Nestor was right: the old lady was eccentric to the core. Her impulsive mannerisms, her petite but strong body, her fascinating movements, her disgusting sniffing, her admirable but nauseating self-assuredness – all that made her a mysterious human being I would have liked to find out more about: how she had arrived on the left side of the Emme; what her viewpoint on Mari Egli's tradition was; what she knew about the perfect restoration – and of course what she needed these white moss buds for.

The thought of the moss revived my memory of the refreshing sweet scent which seemed so familiar to me but which I couldn't identify for some reason. I paused for a moment and tried to imagine this scent. Vague, intangible feelings crept up on me, accompanied by a prickle in my abdomen. But the clear images I was longing for didn't show up.

But then I had the impression that I would actually smell that fruity scent – at first only very mildly but then increasingly stronger. It must have been a hallucination: my imagination had become too vivid and led me to believe in having that sensual perception. Or was it exactly vice versa – that my thoughts were circling around that scent because I could actually smell it?

I dismissed these ideas and turned back towards the buckets and boxes to find a handle for the secretaire. But the scent kept sticking around, penetrating my consciousness even stronger – so strong that I eventually believed the old woman might have stowed away a sack with these moss buds somewhere up here. I followed the scent through all the junk and lumber, took a step forward, checked whether the scent became stronger or weaker, took a step back sometimes and on into another direction. After a longer period of this hot-and-cold game I was again standing in front of the hatch through which I had entered the attic. The scent of the white moss seemed to come from below.

To satisfy my curiosity, I stepped down into the shed. Then I walked back and forth for a while before I finally discovered a trap door in the floor. When I opened the door I was immediately surrounded by a cloud of this sweet scent. I climbed down and, soon after, found myself in a laboratory: there were porcelain mortars, several glass bottles with cork stoppers and chemicals in them, glass flasks of different colors, an old distillation device with wound glass tubes and transparent plastic pipes, a gas cooker, filters, small tumblers with scale units printed on it, test tubes, a thermometer – that old lady had quite some equipment.

On a low table I finally discovered the glass jar into which Nestor and the danseuse had put the moss buds on the day before. Although the bowl-shaped flask was closed with a glass stopper, enough of this obviously very volatile and intense scent could escape from it so that one could smell it all over the shed. Around this flask there were four other slightly smaller bowl-shaped flasks made of brown glass. And all five of them had strange labels in Latin attached to them: *terra fugax*, *aqua sicca*, *ignis umidus*, *aer rigidus* and *odor aureus* on the flask in the center.

When I left the laboratory I was still thinking about what these moss buds were used for. But the moment I had closed the trap door I realized that the scent was now even more intense than down in the lab. So there must have been another source for it. Again I walked up and down in the shed, sniffed into my room next door as well, but then my nose led me outside. I started to walk upstream alongside the creek, past the mill and the willow tree, up the open pasture.

In the meantime fog had descended, and soon it was so dense that I couldn't look twenty feet ahead. For me to move around in an area unknown to me and with visibility conditions as poor as they were, was not just irrational but outright idiotic. But my obsession with finding the source of this sweet-fruity scent swept aside all reason and suffocated any uncertainty. Soon I couldn't think of anything else and focused completely on the sense of smell.

I went on and on, over marshy meadows, through moist ditches, along the edge of the woods, still following the infatuating scent of these white moss buds. The fog became even more dense. Soon there was no more forest but only single fir trees covered with moss and lichen that seemed to appear suddenly out of nowhere; there were no more hills and ditches, only my steps up to or down from something, with both taking unexpected turns.

And just as sudden and unexpected, a strange disconcerting feeling entered my consciousness: it seemed as if I wasn't out somewhere but much rather inside, in a house, in a room. For a moment I paused to get to the bottom of the source of this impression. But all that came to my consciousness was the absurdity of this thought, and I walked on, focusing on that sweet scent again which seemed to become more intense.

Pictures were arising in my consciousness, vague pictures, somehow inextricably related to the scent. They were inklings of situations which were familiar to me but which I hadn't remembered in a long time. And while these pictures were arising in me, assuming increasingly lively forms, the spooky hunch imposed itself on me that, in reality, I was somewhere inside a room, snug and warm. But this abstruse idea did not disappear in the fog again like everything else; on the contrary, it increased in strength.

With all my might I began to fight that notion, that feeling. Time and again, I remembered myself that I was walking through a forest. To assume anything else would have been absurd. After all, I could see the forest soil, the mushrooms, the sparse foliage, the dead twigs covered with lichen; I saw the trees which appeared out of the fog as quickly as they disappeared into it again; I saw my arms, hands and legs and could feel how they moved. And there was something else that I could recognize clearly: a spot on my inner screen, lighting up with an intense deep blue color.

I couldn't tell how long this afterimage had already accompanied me. For a moment I put my attention on it: it was a constantly glowing spot, having more width than length, round towards the left and elongated towards the right. It was hardly moving but standing out more and more from the environment which was gradually cloaked in darkness.

I walked on at a fast pace. Dusk had already set in, and I wanted to be back before nightfall. But then I began to doubt whether I was moving at all. I felt a definite pressure on my right body half, on the temple and the cheek, on the torso and the legs. This feeling that I was lying on the side somewhere didn't let go of me anymore.

I could feel the fear creeping up my neck. In an attempt to distract myself, I began to talk to myself – and got scared even more: the sound that came out of me was not my voice; it rather sounded like an infant yelling. Time and again I tried to hear my own voice, but instead I only heard this yelling.

Now terror had its grips on me. I yelled from the top of my lungs. I tried to perceive and move my body so as not to lose control completely. But in the meantime it had become so dark around me that I could hardly see the hand before my eyes.

The only thing which clearly stood out from the dark was this wide yellow-white spot lighting up in front of my eyes in some distance. This calmed me down immediately because I knew: if I was able to see it, she would come around right away and dispel my fears. Still the silence had me in its grips, and I yelled into the darkness.

And then the door finally opened. The yellow-white light outside fell into my room and lit it up sparsely. A woman stepped in and immediately searched for my eyes. She wasn't very tall, had shoulder-length curly hair and was wearing a long orange-blue dress which I knew was pleasant to the touch.

She talked to me, her voice sounded tired. She came up to my little bed and picked me up. And as I laid in her arms, I felt that protection and security again I was longing for so much. She caressed me and gently stroked my head. Then she came so close to me that her forehead and nose touched mine. I liked her. And I liked that refreshing sweet smell that she was exuding.

For a while she held me in her arms, lulling me back to sleep. Finally she kissed my forehead and laid me back into my bed. She pulled the blanket over me and looked at me with loving eyes. Again she said something; her voice was low but full of warmth. Then she left the room and gently closed the door.

Dancing out of Mind

A yellow spot was glowing in some distance in front of my eyes. I recognized that it was a single sunbeam shining into the room through a crack of the closed window shutters, sparsely lighting up the room. Little strings of dust were floating in the beam, seemingly weightless.

I kicked back the blanket and saw that I had been sleeping in my clothes. It was almost lunchtime. Gentle rain fell outside, but at the same time the sun was able to assert itself against the clouds and lit up the autumnal colorfulness of the meadow around the house. I left my room and looked for Nestor and the old danseuse in the kitchen.

»Uhuh, the boy is honoring us again,« the old woman called out as a welcome. Nestor smiled at me.

I sat down beside them and was just about to tell them of my dream last night; it had felt so real that I was interested in finding out how active my emotional body had been during that dream.

»Go help yourself with breakfast, first of all,« the old lady prompted me before I could say anything. Actually I was very hungry. Just as the old lady did the day before, I dipped a piece of bread into the honey and then into the milk, stuffed myself with mirabelles and gulped down everything with that delicious aromatic syrup. The walnuts were the only thing I avoided. I was surprised how great this relatively simple breakfast tasted.

We were all in very good spirits. For a while we talked about trivialities. Finally Nestor casually inquired about whether I had found a suitable handle by now. This question triggered a strange nervousness within me. Yesterday's events moved back into my consciousness. Now I became aware of a puzzling inconsistency that I hadn't really noticed up to this point: I had indeed interpreted the hiking trip through the woods and the encounter with that sweet smelling woman as a dream. But I just couldn't remember the precise point in time when I abandoned the search for a handle and went to my room to go to sleep.

I told them that I hadn't found a suitable handle yet; I had discontinued my search because I had become too tired.

Both looked at each other and started chuckling.

»If he was so tired, why did he then go for such a long walk late at night?« the old woman asked me with a mischievous smile. She described the direction in which I allegedly had gone – it was the same direction that I had recalled in my dream.

Something within me started to heavily object to the idea that I actually had been out there in the woods. I knew myself as a rational and realistic person that was able to estimate what he could dare to tackle and what he couldn't. Walking around in a forest close before nightfall and with thick fog descending, without a flashlight and a poor sense of orientation – that did not belong to the things I dared doing.

I tried to shift the conversation to my favor by vigorously denying that I had been out and around last night. With a level of conviction I myself was surprised about, I tried to get across to both of them that I had retreated back to my room and fallen asleep. Then I told them about my dream, at least as far as I could remember it.

They both listened to me, now and then looking at each other in amusement again.

»How cute,« the old woman finally called out. »The boy has dreamed of his sweet smelling mommy.«

»Yes, that's cute indeed,« Nestor agreed and added with a smirk: »He really must like that scent if he takes on such a long hiking trip to get after it.«

»No wonder,« she chuckled, »wherever that smell prevails there is tender loving care. I guess he'll run after this scent for the rest of his life.«

»And whatever smells that way, he'll try to snap up as if out of his mind,« he added.

»For sure. I wouldn't be surprised if old Egli's desk would also smell like that stuff; otherwise mommy's boy wouldn't be so out of control.«

Suddenly it dawned on me that Mari Egli's secretaire indeed exuded the same sweet scent, even if only very mildly. The scent had struck me immediately when I had examined the secretaire for the first time, but back then I just couldn't identify it. And by now I could hardly perceive it anymore. It was possible that the varnish could have exuded similar scents, or that there was some object in one of the drawers smelling that way. But I heavily disagreed with their claim that my fascination for Mari Egli's piece of art was caused by this particular scent which I supposedly associated with feelings of happiness and security ever since my earliest childhood.

»I chose this particular piece of furniture because I like it. Because it is a piece of art, and because I thought I could sell it and make some good money with it,« I justified myself.

»Because it smells *smoochy*,« the danseuse answered back with a somewhat singing voice. Both laughed again.

My high spirits were gone. Stubbornly I tried to convince Nestor and the old woman of my viewpoint. A scent, I argued, could perhaps evoke certain feelings in me, but it could definitely not prompt me to engage in activities which would cost me a dear sum of money.

»He underestimates the scents,« the danseuse objected. »After all, he has followed such a scent through nearly half of the Emmental.«

»But that was just a dream« I called out in despair. »The scent I had smelled came from your basement but for sure not from the woods. How could I have smelled this scent over such a long distance?«

»That was no dream,« Nestor replied. »You had picked up that scent and followed it. When you had walked through the woods, your emotional body was more awake, and you had acted through it primarily. Your consciousness had shifted over into the emotional world without you having fallen asleep beforehand. So it was not a dream. But when your consciousness penetrated even more deeply into the emotional world, you started to have certain visions: you experienced yourself as a little intimidated child yelling for his mom.«

Nestor explained that I had to interpret this vision from two viewpoints: on the one hand, it had been a necessary experience because it had dissolved something within me so that I could become aware of that something. Now I knew, according to Nestor, about this particular scent, its significance and effect on me. And this would be useful for me when it came to the perfect restoration. On the other hand, a vision always meant that I had somewhat lost the relationship to the outer screen. This, however, must not happen during states of higher intensity, because it could result in fainting and a complete loss of consciousness – which precisely had happened, after all.

»Losing control and having visions is nothing special,« the old lady pointed out. »The only important thing was his hiking trip through the woods: hasn't the boy given and taken more of everything out there? Hasn't he perceived the world more clearly and more luminous?«

She looked at me impatiently. I looked over to Nestor, searching for help.

»The danseuse is talking about your state of heightened intensity,« he explained. »During that shift of your consciousness into the emotional world there was more energy flowing between you and the picture. If you managed to remain attentive enough, it actually should have resulted in the perception of a clearer, more sharply focused and brighter picture before the vision came up.«

I told them that I had not experienced something of that nature. Nestor asked me to try to remember as best as I could to really be certain. He repeated what the danseuse had said just before: in the final analysis, the only point of significance was the perception of a more intensive picture, and not the vision; the latter was only »small world«. I tried to remember if I had perceived a picture as described by Nestor, but no matter how hard I tried I just couldn't confirm their claims.

»Any old cow would've been more sensitive than this boy,« the old lady mumbled, turning away in disgust. »No wonder he hasn't made his way back.« With these words, the danseuse hinted at something that I hadn't thought about for a second, up to that point.

»If I actually had been out there in the woods and lost my consciousness,« I argued, »how did I ever get back? I know nothing whatsoever about that.«

»Oh«, Nestor said and pointed to the danseuse, smiling. »She has carried you back home.«

The old woman grinned and made a gesture as if she caressed a small child in her arms, rocking it gently. The notion of having lied in her arms was simply absurd. But all my objections were in vain. They both amused themselves with my dream of having lied in the arms of my mother while it had been the old danseuse that had carried me back to her house.

»That's nonsense,« I replied with a hoarse voice, and both burst out in laughter again.

»She couldn't possibly have carried me the entire distance,« I called out into the laughter, appealing to their sense of reason.

»She's a very strong woman,« Nestor grinned, »and you are a fly-weight.«

»But she didn't even know where I was. How could she possibly have found me?«

»Just follow your nose, boy,« the old woman snorted with laughter, »just follow your nose.« Then she waggled the side wings of her nose.

At this instant I felt a tickle in my lower abdomen, under the navel. I realized that I was in an uncomfortable situation in that I couldn't completely rely on my memory. At the same time I was convinced more than ever that the two were just out to tease and fool me. But for some strange reason, I didn't get annoyed by it any longer. I felt light and exhilarated, and it was as if a heavy burden was taken off my shoulders – the burden of having to defend myself by all means.

»How could it happen at all,« I asked them placeably, »that I had gotten into a more intensive state of being, acting with my emotional body? After all, I hadn't even worked on the secretaire.«

»It was the scent of the moss,« Nestor knew. »It has triggered quite something in you. This, by the way, is also the reason why the danseuse makes perfume out of it. And she's very successful at that: her *création* is so seductive that quite a few more people could get into dreaming over it.«

Another time I had searched for a suitable handle in the old lady's attic, but I couldn't find anything really fitting. Nestor deemed it best to manufacture a handle from scratch, using the old one as a kind of template.

Thus, in the following winter and spring it happened that I visited the farmer several times who was proficient at forging metal, who owned the necessary equipment and who was willing to help me out with my problem. With the help of that burly man I was able to forge new handles from the same sort of metal and with the same form, but no matter how hard I tried to replicate the original, I just wasn't able to attach any of these handles to the secretaire.

Eventually I even built a casting mold made of gypsum, following the farmer's instructions, using the old handle as model. I poured liquid brass into the mold and cast a handle in this way that was almost identical with the old one – it was impossible to come any closer to the original. But even this endeavor was in vain: the newly cast handle just couldn't be attached to the secretaire as my body went on strike again.

Nestor then changed the tactical approach: he advised me to put the handle issue aside for now, because obviously I still couldn't stand up to the energy affecting me when trying to work on that part of the secretaire. Nevertheless he instructed me to keep building up my inner pressure, and to get the energy to flow freely. In this way I would become capable of bringing about the same intensified state of consciousness more often that I had acted in when I had done the hiking trip through the woods and stripping the varnish off the secretaire. Nestor believed that I had the best chances to successfully work on the object in that particular condition – because I would then be able to act with the attributes and abilities of the emotional body, and all that in my daily consciousness.

Next to breathing and other physical exercises, Nestor encouraged me to dance. Dancing in particular, according to him, was the right way to shift my consciousness over into the emotional world, that is, the inner screen, and to be able to restore the secretaire. Several times he reminded me of that situation last spring when I had danced in a condition with a strongly heightened energy level. I could see that Nestor was serious about the dancing activities when he actively did something to really get me to dance.

This happened in the following summer. When I visited Nestor on a hot and sunny weekend he opened up to me, somewhat amused, that he was invited to a festival. This came as a surprise to me. In those nearly three years I had visited him he had never mentioned anything about a festival, a party or other festivities of that sort that he had attended. To me, Nestor embodied the ideal type of a human being that had turned his back on the world and, therefore, on social events as well.

He said he had promised to attend, and he wanted me to accompany him.

»What kind of a festival is it?« I asked him.

Nestor went back into the house and returned with a strikingly colorful flyer that he held out in my direction. It was a flyer announcing a Goa trance party! Surprised, I asked him how he had come across this flyer. My astonishment made him laugh. He replied that he knew a woman who occasionally helped to organize events like that. And it was her who had created this particular flyer. And she had invited him.

»We should go there together,« he said and explained that the party would take place close by, on an alp on the other side of the Emme.

»So you really want to go there?« I asked him cautiously.

»Yes.«

»But do you like that music at all?«

He smiled. »Who said that it's only about me? First and foremost, it's about you. It's about you moving your body, about dancing – and this music is just right for that purpose.«

»But I'm already doing my physical exercises.«

»Yes, you are. But you're still not moving with enough intensity. Now here's your chance to really dance for a longer period of time.«

»Is it really necessary for the perfect restoration, after all, that I dance?« I asked.

Nestor laughed and answered that it was typical for me to do everything so as to attain a goal I had set out to achieve – but whatever wasn't really essential and necessary so as to attain that goal didn't interest me *the least bit.*

Then he explained to me with pretended seriousness that dancing was absolutely essential because it is a mixture of breathing and physical exercises helping me to develop my emotional body. And this in turn was crucial for the restoration of the secretaire. Having said that, he looked at me with a mischievous smile.

»Is that enough reason for you?«

In the evening we arrived at the venue. The festival took place on an alp located in a wide, relatively even recess. On one side, the mountain range rose further up, on the other there was only a small hill before the pasture sloped steeply downward. We could hear the rhythmic dull thuds of the speakers already from far away; only occasionally, and then for a very short moment, there was a period of silence – and right afterwards the pounding beat went on and prompted the guests to keep on dancing.

On the way to the dance floor we passed by numerous camping tents with young people in front of them dancing, laughing, smoking. In other places the men and women, mostly dressed in colorful clothing, were busy erecting their tents. The general atmosphere was exuberant and expectant. Only the cows grazing in the immediate vicinity were watching the strange hustle and bustle with moderate interest.

We set up our camp a distance away from the scenery where the music could only be heard faintly. Nestor explained that he was too old to listen to that »boom boom« all night.

The main venue with stage, dance floor and decorative elements appeared like a futuristic UFO landing place. The towers of speaker boxes and the large framework structure with lighting floods and spots on top were covered with colorfully painted sheets. These sheets, partially also hung up on strings in the triangle-shaped form of a sail, always had the same typical bright colors:

yellow, orange, pink, blue, green and violet, mostly painted on a black background. The motives ranged from simple patterns such as spirals, circles, triangles and three-dimensional undefinable forms, all the way to religious symbols of ancient advanced civilizations or futuristic subjects such as extraterrestrials and Mars landscapes. The decoration also included numerous strings in the common fluorescent colors which were spanned in cross angular patterns resulting in star shape images or geometric figures such as circles, curves, three-dimensional triangles and pyramids.

Again Nestor encouraged me to go dancing while he went his own ways, and for quite a while I stood on the side of the dance floor, observing the wild crowd of people and listening to the Goa music.

The music didn't sound very sophisticated at first: there were fast regular beats dictating the rhythm, accompanied by all-penetrating bass sounds. Both made the crowd rant and rave. These beats continued for quite some time with varying intensity and slight rhythmic and melodic alterations.

I knew from previous situations that I could never bring myself to move my body out on a dance floor. When I visited a discotheque with fellow colleagues, all I did was have a drink and watch others.

In my eyes, dancing was some kind of contest, not to say cockfight, with everybody trying to outdo each other or steal each other the show. Of course I didn't need something childish like that.

The beat of the music was interrupted only occasionally and for short moments. Sometimes a melodic interlude replaced it that led from one rhythm over to another; at other times there were formless diffuse sounds, and the people on the dance floor didn't really know how to move their body along to it.

In comparison to previous discotheque visits, the situation now was a totally different one: the activity I was about to engage in had nothing to do with enjoyment or a contest; it was simply about making advances in the perfect restoration. Therefore I had a tangible reason for dancing. And my fellow workmates were not here, either.

Listening to the music, I realized that actual melodies were quite rare. The synthesized sounds, the partially conventional instruments and the chant with oriental harmonies were often distorted beyond all recognition; they acted as one-time inserts, frequently repeating themes or intercuts.

Hesitantly I stepped out on the dance floor, moved my body a little but couldn't stand it for a longer period of time. I was too nervous and uncomfortable. A little later I tried another time but left it at that and went searching for Nestor in our agreed upon location. He had placed himself on a hill; up there, he comfortably leaned against a rock and could overlook the entire dance floor.

»Dancing is fun,« Nestor commented the wild action around the speakers. I sat down next to him. »It raises the intensity in the body. The heart rate increases and breathing is more intensified. The people have more energy and become a little more open and exuberant.«

»Why aren't you dancing?« I asked him.

He confided to me that he had danced more than enough when he was young. As a result of dancing, his body had opened up so that his excess energy was flowing directly into the entire picture. That's why he didn't need so much physical exercise anymore. I had to laugh inside. His words sounded wise, but my impression was that they were just supposed to cover up the fact that he, due to his advanced age, couldn't move his body the way he used to any longer.

Silently we looked down on the dancing crowd. Then Nestor made a surprising remark about my dancing that he obviously had observed from up here.

»You're already moving your arms quite well,« he judged, »but your legs seem heavy as lead. You could move them a little more.«

»How did you manage to recognize me in the crowd?« I was wondering. »From up here one can hardly distinguish the people over the distance.«

»I can see very well, because everything in the picture is clear and big to me,« he replied and added with a secretive tone of voice that this was the result of his lifestyle on the left side. Then he repeated his critique of my dancing attempts.

»Well, seems that's just my way to dance,« I defended the way I moved.

»It's not just about dancing,« he dissented. »Your body movements are an expression of your consciousness. And you can change yourself by going through conscious movements. That's what I'm aiming at.«

»So then you know my consciousness now,« I sneered.

Nestor looked at me. »Yes. You are a down-to-earth human being, sluggish and inhibited. You like to stay where you are, both physically and mentally. You want to hold on to that what you know. And it's hard to enthuse you for something new – except if it will pay off for sure. All this becomes visible in the way you dance.«

At the first moment his words made immediate sense to me. It was as if bright light had suddenly lit up a dark cloudy spot inside me, and I could easily recognize myself in what he said. But when I pondered on it some more, my old familiar critical aloofness came back up. And even though I didn't outright reject what he said, his comments were not more than one possible interpretation out of many to me.

Nestor explained that the living conditions, particularly the education in a person's early years, could lead to a certain uptightness and inhibition that also showed up in body movements.

»Such people have a very hard time to ›let their hair down‹, so to speak, and really move their body. Their hands and feet are literally tied up. Their body is not open enough, the energy cannot flow freely. But this is exactly where dancing comes in, and it can be of considerable help. Discovering and moving the limbs, gradually feeling into the body, that is, becoming aware of the body – that is a big release.

The better you can feel into your body, the sooner you realize that you don't just consist of arms and legs but also of fingers, feet, pelvis, torso and head – those parts of the body want to be moved as well. When you move all your body parts you are channeling the energy through the entire body. And then you'll also discover that you are not consisting of individual limbs but rather that you are a unified whole in motion.« Dancing for real, he added, was a contest with oneself. The person dancing became acquainted with himself by moving and becoming aware of his movements.

The fact that Nestor criticized my dancing annoyed me and rendered me incapable of replying anything suitable. My opinion was that there was no »better« and »worse« when it came to dancing but rather only individual movements.

Still I tried to follow Nestor's advice whenever I went out on the dance floor again later that night – not just because I believed he could watch me. In the meantime I had understood his viewpoint that there was an advancement in all realms of human existence that also included dancing. And that I had to consciously involve my entire body in the process. In Nestor's way of thinking, »better« or »worse« simply meant »more conscious« or »less conscious«.

I also looked around to see how other people were moving: some emphasized the footwork while others mostly executed some kind of movements with their arms. But there were also some who were dancing with their entire body. A young woman struck me in particular; she executed wave-shaped movements with fingers, arms and torso, similar to the way the old danseuse moved her body. She went through all motions in a relaxed and easy way, obviously without any effort at all. There were only a few people who were dancing in this way; others did include their body in their dancing movements but it somehow looked ridiculous and grotesque. Their movements were too fast, too jerky, too nervous.

My own attempts to dance with my entire body didn't turn out so successful, either. Whereas I did move all my limbs consciously, I still had a hard time to harmoniously coordinate all my movements. The result was more like an enforced sequence of different movements instead of a body dancing in harmonious balance.

Throughout the next day I avoided the heat and did not dance. Instead I visited the large tents surrounding the dance floor. Just about everything that somewhat fitted the occasion was available: next to exotic drinks, sweets and candy, the visitors could buy clothing, shawls and pictures in the typical bright Goa colors. Then there were tents with smoking accessories and paraphernalia: tobacco and tobacco boxes, incense sticks and nicely adorned wood boxes as well as holders for the incense sticks. The entire place was filled with a scent mixture of sweet incense and spicy foods offered at several stands.

Later I met Nestor in a tent where Indian spice tea was served. He was talking to a woman. I sat down next to them on one of the large soft pillows lying on the ground around several low tables. As soon as I was seated, the woman got up and went behind the counter. I observed how she poured tea from a big pot into three thermos mugs. As soon as she had done that, several young people suddenly showed up that obviously had already waited for the tea.

I liked that woman right away. She had red hair with strong curls and lots of freckles in her fine face. Her green cat eyes looked penetratingly, almost hypnotizing.

When she was done with her customers, the woman came back up to us and resumed the conversation with Nestor. I realized that he was consorting with her in the same easy and informal way he did with the old danseuse: they laughed, joked and made expressive gestures. I admired and, at the same time, envied Nestor's disarming and winsome way, his spontaneousness and his humor.

Listening to what they said, I found that they made fun of the people on the dance floor. It turned out that the woman could be just as bitchy as Nestor sometimes was. She compared the people on the dance floor with a herd of cows always staring in the same direction – in whatever direction the leader of the herd turned its head.

The red-haired woman hinted at the fact that most of the people on the dance floor were facing the front, the stage with the DJs, because that's where the show and the action was, after all. I hadn't realized that when I was on the dance floor myself – perhaps because I just did what everybody else did. In response to her nasty remarks I tried to defend the people on the dance floor and thus myself. I told them that, to me, it didn't matter which direction the people faced when they were dancing, and that everybody should dance the way he or she feels was appropriate.

»But most people don't dance in a way they feel is appropriate,« the woman answered back assertively. »They thoughtlessly turn in the direction in which they are being pounded on the most. If, on the other hand, the people had enough self-confidence they would free themselves from all external stimuli.« She got up because she was needed at the counter.

»Guess that's hard to realize,« I gently objected; I was certain that this woman had no clue of the trials and tribulations associated with acquiring energy through the perfect restoration.

»For example, you can start by consciously integrating all four points of the compass, not just one,« she replied with a smile. Her quick-wittedness and her penetrating cat eyes made me look away in a reflex-like manner; I pretended to be interested in a group of young people smoking a water pipe at the table next to us. When I turned around to face the woman again, she was already back behind the counter.

During my dancing attempts on the following night I took care that I consciously turned my body in all directions. What the young woman had said to me was challenging, because I interpreted it as a personal critique: I had to assure myself that I did not belong to the »cows« that only were being »pounded on«.

In the beginning I had a hard time to turn towards the others on the dance floor because I felt that everybody's eyes were resting on me now. But when I could see that this was not the case I was able to bring myself to take these turns, and I enjoyed moving around so freely and in all directions. It actually felt like a little release.

But now there was something else causing me more trouble now: my stamina. To me, a strong stamina was undoubtedly a question of long-time training. I talked to Nestor about this, but he thought that I had trained my body for more than half a year by now so that my stamina should be sufficient. The reason why I danced only for short periods of time was that I didn't breathe correctly – according to him too fast and too shallow. He therefore recommended that I take slow and deep breaths.

»That's impossible,« I objected. »When I'm moving, my pulse rate increases, and therefore I'm also forced to breathe faster.«

»That's because your breath is still tied to the heartbeat,« he answered. »But the breathing exercises I taught you will help you to become more and more successful at separating the breath from the heartbeat. In this way you'll be able to breathe more deeply and calmly despite an increased heart rate. And this in turn means that you'll have much more stamina in everything you do.«

Nestor went on to say that accomplished dancers had even gained the ability to be in a more intense state not only with calm and even respiration but also with a calm and even heart rate. This was the highest form of increasing intensity that didn't have to be brought about by physical exercises any longer.

Encouraged by Nestor, I tried to watch my breath while dancing but I had considerable difficulties doing so. It wasn't only hard to concentrate on my body and the breath at the same time; even when I watched my breath and tried to consciously control it, I managed to do so only for a few breaths. Breathlessness cropped up too fast, and too strong was the urge to end the symptoms by breathing faster.

In the morning I laid down on my bed to rest a little. I realized that I was unusually relaxed and contented without feeling tired or sleepy. I really had fun dancing, and now I enjoyed it to simply lie there and look into the starlit sky.

Suddenly several individual muscles of my body began to twitch involuntarily. Those were muscles of the upper arms, the thighs, the fingers and the throat which were contracting and releasing in irregular intervals for fractions of a second.

These twitches were something I hadn't known and experienced before to this extent. I was concerned and tried to find an explanation for it: perhaps I had overstrained those muscles, or maybe I had simply not drunk enough liquid.

I turned towards Nestor and couldn't manage to hide my fear. When he listened to what I was concerned about, he calmed me down. To him, the twitches seemed to be a positive signal.

»Finally something's happening in your body,« he said.

»But isn't that harmful?« I wanted to know.

»Nonsense. Your body is going through a change, that's all.«

»What does that mean?«

»That means that you have begun to build up the inner pressure, and that inner blockades are slowly being removed. Don't worry about that, it'll pass by soon.«

In the third and last night, Nestor and I talked about the rhythmics that accompanied the music along with the basic beat. Nestor found that this music offered many interesting and sophisticated rhythmic possibilities for body movements – if I became aware of them and knew how to utilize them.

»You're tied to the basic beat too much,« he stated. »Just like most of the people here. They don't have any other option at all then to just join in with these basic beats and hop along with it. But this is something you should consciously overcome. Because being tied to the basic beat too much is an expression of immobility and bondage. There's no challenge in adopting and keeping something that is already under way. In contrast, it requires a lot of energy to break out of this basic rhythm and to play with it, that is, to change back and forth between fast and slow movements and following both rhythms and melodies.«

Nestor called my attention to a young man who was dancing in that way. In fact, this man did not let himself carry away by the basic beats, as it was the case with many other people on the dance floor. Quite the contrary: the rhythm of the music was owned by the dancer. He played with it and didn't mechanically jump from one leg onto the other with every single beat but now and then freed himself from them. Then he went through his own steps and movements, but without losing the basic beat.

I was particularly impressed by these sudden extreme changes from very fast dancing to very slow powerful movements which in turn were immediately followed by fast ones again. Nestor said that sudden changes of that nature were fascinating because they were an expression of strength. Because, the faster the transition from one extreme to the other, the more strength had to be mustered up to do so. In general, young people were more adept at these sort of changes – not just when it came to dancing but in their thinking and acting as well – because they had much unbound energy at their disposal.

»Somebody who can dance like that is very flexible,« he explained. »Not only physically but in his entire being. To be flexible also means to be conscious and free. So try to dance in this way.«

At a later point I stepped out on the dance floor again, and this time my intention was to integrate powerful changes of that nature into my

168

dancing movements. While I was moving my body I became aware of the fact that, under Nestor's influence, I had not only lost my reservations with regard to dancing but I also had some serious fun on top. He had also succeeded in sparking my ambition so that I tried to remedy the deficiencies in my movements and follow his advice and recommendations. I wasn't dancing any longer for the purpose of restoring the secretaire but because I enjoyed to discover new possibilities of movements.

Nestor had already succeeded in motivating me, time and again, for exciting and interesting things that I couldn't make any sense of at first. I began to wonder how he managed to do this, but then I suddenly realized that I was breathing more deeply and slowly although I was moving vigorously and with a fast heartbeat. My thoughts petered out and I was dancing for quite a while without interruption.

A strange sensation, not uncomfortable, took a hold of me. It felt as if something had started to flow in my body which had been blocked before. From one second to the other, I wasn't only completely aware of all my limbs but I could actually and directly feel the wholeness of my body.

This state lasted only for a short time, but in this short period I had these clear insights again that I knew from the first time I had been dancing in this way involuntarily: I understood that I was not a person that exerted control over my limbs by moving them; rather, I *was* the body movements, I was the dance itself. Completely being the body and the movement meant that I already knew everything. I knew how to keep an impeccable balance, and I knew movements that I never before had even learned and executed. Now all my movements were fluent, harmonic, coordinated – simply perfect.

A thousand light spots suddenly flashed up and were shining in my field of vision: white, blue, green, red ones – time and again, they faded out and flashed up again, accompanied by enormous bangs and the tolling of bells. I was surrounded by yelling and cheering people out of their senses. I felt an indescribable joy and danced with faster and stronger movements. I was all motion, direct motion beyond any doubt.

Soon I found myself standing on the edge of the dance floor. Gradually I realized that the people were cheering at the fireworks which had been lit in the midst of the night, and the loud bangs had obviously startled the cows on the pasture. Now I could feel how heavily I was breathing and how quick my pulse was. The thought of drifting into visions again scared me and made me stumble off the dance floor. I sat down in the grass a little bit away from the scene where I constantly checked my condition and the picture surrounding me. I moved my body, my head, my hands, my shoulders so as not to lose myself.

Pulse and breath soon returned to their normal rhythm; I calmed down, but there was a tickle, not uncomfortable, that remained in my limbs. For a while I kept lying in the grass. My thoughts were clear now and I felt more awake than before. I was watching a woman for some time that practiced fire-breathing. Whenever she blew her fiery breath into the night sky, the whole area was lit up brightly for a short moment. A wave of affection seized me, and when I admired the beauty in her activities and being in general, I felt a strong prickle in my legs. It had a relaxing effect on the entire body. I felt relieved and comfortable.

It was already dawning when I got up to look for Nestor. I found him in our agreed-upon place. Immediately I told him what had happened to me.

»You were out of your mind,« Nestor answered.

»What?«

»As I said: you were out of your mind. Out of your mind.« I thought I heard the old danseuse speaking through him. I looked at him questioningly.

»You mean I was out of my mind in the same way Mari Egli supposedly was when she had built that secretaire?«

»No, of course you were not *that much* out of your mind,« he laughed. »But your inner pressure has still increased enormously, the flow of energy was stronger, and some of the blockades were removed. Your consciousness has shifted from your intellectual into the emotional world, so you were literally »out of your mind«: your movements became more emotional and therefore lighter and more flowing. Your emotional body was more awake. This was ›dancing out of mind‹.«

Nestor then started to talk about the tickle and prickle feelings I had experienced. He said that a *tickle* in the body was always an indicator of a stronger flow of energy. But my body would not open up until I felt a *prickle feeling*, with the body hair standing on end in the corresponding body part, and then the excess energy would flow into the picture as a whole.

»The body opens up? What do you mean by that?«

»The body opens up when there's enough inner pressure, and when the energy is not stagnating due to blockades. If you feel a prickle, your body has opened up a little.«

»I still don't understand this opening up. Do you mean the pores of my skin will open up?«

»It is unimportant what exactly it is that opens up in your body. What's important is the prickle feeling. It means that energy is flowing out of your body directly into the picture as a whole.«

The thought that energy had »leaked« from my body, according to my understanding of Nestor's words, was displeasing to me. This was obviously contradictory to the original intention of the perfect restoration, I justified my skepticism.

»If the perfect restoration focuses on building up the inner pressure,« I argued, »wouldn't it be better to retain the energy in the body instead of giving it away?«

»I told you before: everyone of us is forced to give away our energy again. The only question is in which way this takes place, and what we are doing with this energy. This prickle is the right way to release the energy. And you can feel it because your inner pressure was strong enough. Don't worry, you've learned a lot tonight.«

I asked him what exactly it was that I had learned, and how this was related to the perfect restoration. Nestor explained that I had experienced the possibility of putting energy directly into the picture as a whole without having to act at that moment. The more I was able to release my energy in this way, the more my small world would dissolve, and the more alive and intense my picture would become. In this way I would also succeed in coping with my increased inner pressure.

»You think I would be able now to restore the secretaire?« I finally asked him.

Nestor smiled. »Now you're wide awake, eh?« He looked me over attentively and I answered his look. Indeed, I felt unusually awake and strong.

»Well, would you like to work on it?«

I shrugged and scrutinized my feelings. At this moment I didn't really feel the urge to work on the secretaire. I asked the question more out of a habit, like I mostly did when Nestor observed advances I had made in the perfect restoration.

Nestor pointed to the people; there was an obvious atmosphere of departure. They climbed up the hill and looked for good places to welcome the rising sun with a dance – a ritual that I had observed already on the day before, and which obviously repeated itself on these occasions.

»Come on, let's go,« Nestor suddenly said.

»Are we taking a look at the sunrise?« I wanted to know.

»No, we're taking a look at the picture,« he replied.

We climbed up the hill and sat down facing the snow-covered Alps. The sky was clear and cloudless. It was refreshingly cool but I wasn't freezing. The first rays of the sun made the dew shimmer, the grass shine and the people cheering and raving.

Nestor instructed me to use the still weak sunlight to create afterimages and shift them back and forth on the inner screen. I briefly looked to the left at the rising sun, then turned away and concentrated on the afterimages. I directed my eyes upwards with vigor to hold the afterimages in suspension as far up as possible.

At this moment I saw something in the picture rushing by from the bottom to the top. It went by so fast that I couldn't recognize more than just a dark spot. I repeated the same eye movement, and again I could see this thing rush through the picture. It was dark but transparent, like a haze. And it obviously was related to my eye movements.

I blinked my eyes a few times and rubbed them, because I believed it was something on the eyeball. Then I repeated the exercise. But the dark hazy spot appeared in my field of vision again this time: when I shifted the afterimage of the sun back and forth, a dark spot was swinging along with it but dwindled down continuously until it had disappeared out of my field of vision at the bottom.

I told Nestor of this cloudy spot. He was unusually interested and asked me quite a few questions, for example if that thing was rather bright or dark; what form it had; whether I could see just one or more of these spots. I described to him, as best as I could, what I had perceived.

»Is this spot in constant motion?« he kept asking.

»I'm not sure but I believe so.«

»Beliefs won't do for us here,« he replied sharply. »If you don't know it, just take a look at the spot.«

»Why? Is this important in some way?« I asked, irritated over his rebuke.

»It could change your life,« he answered.

Somehow his words had something threatening. At this moment I would have preferred to clarify the situation and ask him what exactly he meant. But Nestor urged me to keep on looking at the spot.

Again I looked into the rising sun and tried to concentrate on the afterimage. When I shifted it back and forth across the sky, the dark spot soon swung along with it again. Immediately I tried to look at it, but that didn't work out as it flowed out of my field of vision right that moment. I tried some more times but became desperate after a few attempts. It seemed as if I myself wiped away that spot with my eyes as soon as I wanted to take a look at it.

»I can't really see that spot, Nestor. It escapes me time and again.«

»Try to hold it in suspension just like the afterimages,« he advised me.

»Push it upwards vigorously. If you see it, shift it back and forth so that it'll remain in your field of vision for as long as possible. Watch how it flows.«

Gradually I was able to keep the spot in my field of vision for a longer time. In doing so, I realized that it was an overlay of rings and dots in different sizes – partially blurred, partially more in focus. I could only recognize them because of their more conspicuous contours, because they were colorless and completely transparent.

I told Nestor my observations. He seemed satisfied, smiled and found that this was actually a small realization of consciousness. He asked me to direct my attention to these spots from now on.

»But what is it?« I asked him.

He remained silent and seemed to take some joy in it before he finally answered.

»What you've seen,« he explained it with a mysterious tone of voice, »is a small detail of the picture's basic structure.«

»Basic structure?«

»Basic structure,« he replied laughing and mimicked my puzzled face. »The scaffold, after all, that holds the entire scenery here in suspension.«

3

Mouches Volantes

The significance Nestor attached to these opacities floating in the field of vision was incomprehensible to me at first. But his advice that I should now concentrate on them was not any more unusual than seeing the picture as a whole or looking at afterimages – actually the issue with the opacities did fit quite well into the collection of concentration objects he had in store for practicing the perfect restoration. Therefore, I regarded looking at them simply as a further step on this way.

During the following fall and winter weeks I thus tried, now and then, to look at these opacities – but only with moderate success. They were not always visible, and if so, they were quite dark, hardly perceivable and disappearing quickly out of my field of vision. Eventually I put this exercise aside, and because I had to concentrate more on other issues during that time, I had quickly forgotten about the opacities. But not for very long.

Without me having a hand in the matter, they now started to show up in my field of vision – first only sporadically so that I was able to ignore them, but then more and more frequently. What struck me in particular was that I was able to see them in places and under conditions that differed far from those that Nestor had described as favorable for concentrating on the outer and inner screen. They showed up although I hadn't even sat down calmly and concentrated, and without me having practiced seeing the picture as a whole or looking at afterimages prior to it. According to this, the phenomenon didn't seem to be linked to conditions of that kind but rather seemed to have a life of its own: it showed up when I expected it the least, and when I tried to look at it, it disappeared just as fast as it had showed up. At least I was able to establish again that these opacities mostly consisted of transparent rings and strands of different sizes.

Sometimes I experienced them as an amusing distraction, an entertaining pastime, for example when I was looking out the window during a longer train ride. But often they were annoying, for example when they flitted over the pages of a book, distracting me from my reading. And at times I also considered the distraction caused by these opacities dangerous, in particular during activities demanding my full concentration for the safety and well-being of others and myself – for example when driving a car.

Amusing, annoying or dangerous – one notion that crossed my mind more and more frequently and that didn't seem to let go of me was utterly alarming: could it be that the increased appearance of these eye opacities was the result of an injury recently incurred, a dysfunction or an illness in my eyes? Was it perhaps an abnormal phenomenon that could possibly lead to a loss of my eyesight? And the longer I pondered over it, the more I tended to make a connection between these opacities and the excessive strains and stresses for my eyes possibly resulting from Nestor's perception exercises.

I thus decided to tackle him about it – not just because he made me practice these exaggerated eye exercises but also because he obviously knew more about the phenomenon.

I visited Nestor on a cold afternoon in mid-January. When I got out of the car I saw a cat with red coat and white stripes on the back sitting on the windowsill. It looked me over attentively with its green eyes, and as if it had known about my intention, it jumped off the sill and placed itself in front of the entrance door, waiting. I opened the door and the cat quickly slipped through into the kitchen where Nestor was busy cooking a meal.

He welcomed the cat joyfully. The animal seemed to enjoy it when Nestor ruffled its fur in the neck, and it didn't refuse a bowl of milk with a few pieces of bread, either. Then he turned towards me.

»They all show up only when there's something to eat around,« he lamented and finally laughed. Then he threw a few additional potatoes for me into the pot.

I put my backpack on the table and started to unpack what I had brought along for him. Then we sat down in the comfortably warm living room and had a casual chat about the cat. Obviously it was a wild one, but from time to time it stopped by Nestor's place for a visit, and now it seemed to overwinter in his place. We watched the animal sitting down and cleaning itself when Nestor suddenly spoke up and observed that I must have an important reason for visiting him in the midst of the deepest winter, on such a dark snowy day.

I told Nestor about my perceptions and didn't make a secret of my concerns, either. He calmed me down with his usual compelling persuasiveness and confirmed that he knew quite a bit about the phenomenon, adding that he saw it every day, for years already.

»And what are you doing against it?« I asked.

»Do against it?«

»Yes. Aren't you disturbed by these things floating in your field of vision?«

Nestor scratched his head; obviously he couldn't follow me. »How could they disturb me? After all, I want to see them.«

»So then these opacities are part of the perfect restoration,« I assumed.

»They are the *key* to the perfect restoration,« he corrected me. »You should practice looking at them consciously and deliberately, just like you do with the afterimages.« Nestor went into the kitchen and put a pot with water for some tea on the stove.

»I'm not sure. To me, it feels as if I add to them by looking at them.«

»Yes, more of these dots and strands become visible the more often you concentrate on them,« Nestor confirmed. Obviously this notion didn't have anything alarming to him, quite the contrary: interpreting his tone of voice, I concluded that he considered it desirable and worthwhile to make them visible and proliferate.

»But I don't want them to proliferate,« I defended myself. »I just want to get rid of them: they're reducing my eyesight, they're distracting me from perceiving the world around me – perhaps they eventually even make me lose my eyesight.«

Nestor knitted his eyebrows and negated my concerns in a way that it seemed I had said something silly. He replied that the dots and strands did not deprive anyone of his eyesight at all.

»They are the basic structure of the picture,« he knew. »That which remains when your small world has completely dissolved in the picture.«

»You call these eye opacities the basic structure of the picture?« I called out, stunned about his naivety.

»They're not opacities in the eyes,« he countered. »They're dots and strands lighting up. But at this time you're still too far away from perceiving the light inside of them. At some point you'll be able, though, to see it.«

During our meal we continued our conversation about the dots and strands. It turned out that Nestor actually assumed the outrageous viewpoint that these things structured our picture so that we could perceive it as something sensible. I tried to find out how he had arrived at that notion, but he didn't want to say anything else about it. Nestor claimed that it was impossible to grasp this for someone who had just begun to see.

»You should consider these dots and strands an advancement in the perfect restoration, and you should concentrate on them,« he went on. »Because for you it's not a matter of course that you see them. You've striven for it.«

»What do you mean: I've striven for it?«

»You've become familiar with a lifestyle out here that is necessary for performing the perfect restoration: you've learned to put a part of your energy into the picture as a whole; and you've learned to concentrate on your inner screen. The result is that you'll now see these dots and strands, also located on your inner screen, more frequently.«

»But I never had the intention to see these dots and strands,« I called out in despair.

»They belong to the perfect restoration like the salt into the soup,« he replied. »You should be glad that you can see them.«

»Actually all I wanted to do was to restore a piece of furniture,« I complained wistfully.

»You will restore that piece of furniture, completely and to perfection. Your work is not done yet.« Nestor remained silent for a while and turned towards the cat that had jumped up on his lap. Obviously the two of them had gotten used to one another very much: time and again, the cat enjoyed Nestor's ruffling, and he cautiously took it up into his arms or teased it with the corner of a blanket or a pencil.

»It is good that you can finally see the dots and strands,« he eventually said. »It has taken you a long time, but the main thing is that you can now use them as concentration object.«

After we had finished our meal, we took a short walk through the snow. I asked Nestor once more if he wasn't irritated or disturbed by these dots and strands. After all, they distracted a person from perceiving the outer screen.

»If I want to concentrate on the outer screen, then I look onto the outer screen,« he answered. »If I want to see the dots and strands, I'll see them on the inner screen. You cannot concentrate on the inner and the outer screen at the same time. You'll learn to deal with it. Then you won't perceive it as irritating or bothersome.«

Nestor then started to explain the nature of these dots and strands. According to him, the most important point was that we could learn to exert an influence on them.

»In the beginning, these dots and strands flow about in your field of vision ›kind of automatically‹, and it seems almost impossible to take a real look at them. If we want to direct our attention to them, we therefore have to develop a fine feeling in the eyes so that we can push them back and forth in our field of vision without losing them right away again. Just as in the case of seeing the picture and the afterimages, in the final analysis it's all about *holding them in suspension* and realizing what they basically are.«

Nestor went on to explain that the specific light conditions play a significant role in this. It was more difficult, he pointed out, to see the dots when the sky was gray and dull. And at night I could only see them in the light of a candle or an electric light bulb. In contrast, they were visible very well outdoors in a snow-covered landscape because the snow reflected light so that everything became bright and clear. Finally he advised me to practice looking at them by daylight; an even blue sky was particularly suitable to take a closer look at them.

To me it was clear now that Nestor had made his experiences with this phenomenon, and that he wouldn't easily be argued out of his viewpoint he assumed with respect to it. I myself felt uncertain now. A few seconds ago I was convinced that this phenomenon was some illness or complaint of the eye. Nestor, however, asserted that it was the fruit of my endeavors.

At first I settled for the idea to consider these dots – whatever they were or caused – as practice object. Perhaps, I explained to myself, I was so skeptical because here I had something new and foreign to me, and because Nestor assigned such an outstanding importance to these opacities that I couldn't understand. I recalled the difficulties I had in the beginning, to accept the afterimages as part of the perfect restoration and practice with them. But this time I wanted to be more cautious: if these dots and strands were supposed to be a means to an end like the afterimages, then, I told myself, I would be able to work with it – independent from the mystic significances Nestor attached to them.

But as soon as I was back in my habitual living environment where everything had – and had to have – its rational explanation, my intentions and insights vanished quickly. I had to find out what it really was that was moving about in front of my eyes and that I was supposed to stare at – in order to eliminate any potential risk.

So I went to an ophthalmologist to do a check-up on my eyes. The man calmed me down and informed me that these opacities consisted of detached particles in the vitreous. He called them *mouches volantes*, an annoying and widely spread but harmless phenomenon. According to him, it was impossible to treat it, and I would have to learn to live with it. He advised me that it would be best to simply neglect it.

I, for my part, however, had to find out more about it and began collecting information on these opacities. »Mouches volantes«, I found out, is the general term for this phenomenon in both French and German ophthalmology. The common German term is »Glaskörpertrübungen«[10] or »fliegende Mücken«[11] and »Mückensehen«[12]. In the Anglo-Saxon part of the world, these dots and strands are known as *floaters*. In addition, there is a multitude of terms paraphrasing the phenomenon: dark spots, streaks, thin hairs, small black lint, fluff balls, dust particles, little worms, rings, flitter, as well as cobwebs, threads, circles and oblong strings – not to mention dots and strands and their belittled form.

Mouches volantes are classified as an »entoptic phenomenon«. This term refers to the perception of objects that the viewer believes to see outside of himself but in actuality are located within his eye. Mouches volantes are distinguished from other such phenomena, for example Purkinje's vessel shadow figures, that is the perception of small blood vessels in the wall of the eye when light is shining into them from sideways. Another phenomenon to be distinguished from floaters are the so-called »flying corpuscles« or »luminous spots« – small bright spheres moving in wound tracks – that can be traced back to leukocytes or white blood cells flowing in the capillaries (or capillary tubes) of the retina. Behind the term *mouches volantes*, however, a multitude of different viewpoints and explanations is hidden with respect to the nature of these floating particles as well as the cause factors and precise location in the eye.

At first at little excursion into history: *mouches volantes* are not a modern phenomenon at all. Different medicinal works, in part very old, of the Greek, Roman, Arabic and European culture mention the phenomenon and try to explain it according to the standard of knowledge in respective times. The German ophthalmologist Hubertus Plange was the last one to compile a historical account of the phenomenon of vitreous opacities.

In pre-Christian centuries, the Hippocratics, followers of the Greek medic Hippocrates, held that the cause for our perception of these dots and strands was to be found in the eye itself. Their explanation was that

---

[10] German term for *vitreous opacities*.

[11] German for *flying mosquitoes*.

[12] German term for *seeing mosquitoes*.

the particles, due to their mobility, were located in some kind of liquid or moisture, most probably in the area of the eye's pupil. Galenus of Pergamon, another prominent Roman doctor of the ancient world, traced the phenomenon back to a compression of the aqueous fluid located right behind the cornea. In general, it was assumed that the opacities were located in front of the eye's lens because the latter was considered the main element in the activity of seeing with the eyes. Even Galenus had already used the term »flying« or »floating mosquitoes«.

The Galenian theory of eyesight was prevalent throughout the medieval renaissance and even beyond, but it found its way into the European occident mostly via the Arabic medicine. Avicenna, or Ibn Sina, as his Arabic name was, continued to elaborate and refine the Galenian concept. He distinguished between different kinds of *mouches volantes*, according to their size, position and shape, and also named corresponding causes for them.

The idea of the lens being the central organ for the function of eyesight had been abandoned in the 16th century when discoveries in the fields of anatomy and optics presented new facts on the subject. The Swiss Felix Platter, a medical professor and Doctor of the City of Basel, explained for the first time that the actual place of eyesight was not the lens but the retina, the light-sensitive inner layer in the back of the eyeball. Nevertheless, he also assumed the location of *mouches volantes* to be in the aqueous fluid in front of the lens and the pupil.

In the 17th century, the French Jesuit and professor of physics, Claudius F. M. Dechales, found out that particles in the front portion of the eye, that is, on or in the cornea, the pupil, the lens and the anterior vitreous, could not project shadows onto the retina. To him, the location of the floaters was closely in front of the retina. His explanations for the opacities had implications: to Dechales, *mouches volantes* could have been caused by objects in front of the retina or by a damaged retina. With this, he was the first to speculate on a relation between eye floaters and damages of the retina. The visible black spots caused by bleedings of the retina, however, are today being called »scotoma« and do not, in theory, classify as »mouches volantes«.

A few years later, the French mathematician Philippe de la Hire distinguished between two kinds of spots: those that can be located in the retina and which stay in place when the eyes are being moved – today called scotoma – and those that constantly change their location, the *muscae volitantes*. To him, eye floaters could not be located in the vitreous, however, as he considered it not liquid enough to explain their high mobility. Instead he believed that *mouches volantes* would swim in the aqueous fluid.

In the mid-18th century, the German professor Albert L. F. Meister described eye floaters as tubules containing globules. He speculated that the phenomenon might be caused by lymphatic vessels with stuck blood globules within them. It is interesting that he, even after twenty-four years, could not observe any change in the appearance.

In the 19th century, the Czech physiologist Jan Evangelista Purkinje eventually explained the phenomenon of *mouches volantes* as shadows of particles projected onto the retina when the eyes are exposed to light. The particles floated freely in the vitreous, more or less close to the retina – to him the reason why the dots and strands could be perceived either more sharply or out-of-focus. With this description, Purkinje can take the credit of having correctly summarized the nature and character of eye floaters. Today, ophthalmologists mostly agree that *mouches volantes* are opacities of the vitreous.

When it comes to the cause of this phenomenon, though, there are many different explanations, according to respective viewpoints. This entoptic phenomenon is often treated as age-related opacity of the vitreous: the vitreous, originally a clear and jelly-like mass filling the eyeball, is steadily growing less solid over time. This results in liquefaction in some places and densification in others. Eye floaters are agglutinated structures coming into existence as a result of this process: they are projecting shadows onto the retina when the eye is exposed to light. In this context it is also mentioned that short-sighted people develop *mouches volantes* sooner because their vitreous is subject to liquefaction sooner.

The explanation that the vitreous is shrinking a little over time, separating itself from the back eye wall, points in the same direction. Some of the fine fibers containing collagen forming the matrix for the jelly-like mass come off and show up as eye floaters or »flying mosquitoes« in our field of vision.

Next to liquefaction or shrinking of the vitreous, there are other explanations for the causes of these floaters: misplaced impurities lodged in the vitreous, namely agglutinated proteins and cholesterol crystals; fungus-like infiltrates; white agglutinated blood cells as a result of inflammations; furthermore red blood cells and dead cells in both the vitreous and the space between vitreous and retina – just to name a few. They are all projected onto the retina when the eye is exposed to light, and they swim along in the viscous mass of the vitreous when the eyes are moved.

One specific modern medical treatise concerns itself with these particular cells. The author, the Japanese professor Shin-ichi Matsumoto, had researched the phenomenon of *mouches volantes* on himself for more than two decades. To him, they were strings of epithel cells without inherent active vitality, therefore persisting and not tending towards split-up or degeneration. He speculates on the cause and treatment of this eye complaint, describes and distinguishes between cubic and spherical cells strung together – some conspicuously pigmented, others hardly perceivable. The only thing he is able to establish with certainty in the final analysis, as a result of his own experiences, is the immutability of *mouches volantes* over a longer period of time – just like Albert L. F. Meister had observed two hundred years ago. For this reason, another explanation, besides the commonly mentioned causes such as mechanical dysfunctions, chronic inflammations and old-age deterioration of the eye wall, is conceivable to Matsumoto: he speculates that these strings of cells could be congenital; originally they could have been transparent cell remnants of embryogenetic nature that, over time, had accumulated a higher amount of pigments so that they finally became visible.

In general, eye floaters are regarded as harmless. They are considered a blemish showing up with advanced age and belonging to our life, just like wrinkles in the face or age spots on hands and arms. Basically and essentially, the opacities cannot be treated, and in many scientific articles it is recommended to just neglect them. Often people are being put off with the prospect that these molesters would disappear by themselves in the course of time – either due to the progressing liquefaction of the vitreous, causing the particles to slowly sink down so that they are perceived less often, or due to their becoming more blurred and vague, the more the vitreous separates itself from the retina. On the other hand, there are reports of people concerned stating that, in their personal case, eye floaters had increased in number and intensity with advanced age. Should it be the case, though, that the flying mosquitoes become stronger, larger and more dense within a short period of time, and that they appear together with other phenomena such as large-surface dark spots or glaring light flashes, then it is advised to consult an ophthalmologist. Because in that case a detachment of the retina is suspected that could cause a loss of eye sight.

Sometimes medical papers mention vitrectomy as a means for getting rid of *mouches volantes*. This is a surgical intervention during which the vitreous, in part or in its entirety, is extracted by suction and re-placed by water, gas or silicone oil. However, this particular surgery is usually only conducted in the case of very serious retina and vitreous damages, because this intervention can have grave consequences, in most cases an eye cataract and additional detachments of the retina from the eye wall – in some cases it results in a loss of eyesight over a shorter or longer period of time. Most physicians regard the phenomenon of *mouches volantes* as too harmless to justify a removal of the vitreous. Other physicians hold that a vitrectomy is not a safe method for the removal of eye floaters as there would always be some individual vitre-ous fibers remaining in the eye that in turn could project shadows onto the retina. In most recent times, however, this particular surgery tech-nique has been enhanced so that, today, the use of vitrectomy for the removal of *mouches volantes* is discussed controversially among ophthal-mologists: advocates point to patients' improved eyesight and thus en-hanced quality of life attainable by removing the disturbing opacities, with the respective surgery posing no major risk. Opponents are con-cerned that vitrectomies could, in the near future, be conducted as some kind of inexpensive ambulant lifestyle surgery on request of the patient.

The latter doesn't seem so much the case with the only alternative to vitrectomies: the vaporization of opacities in the vitreous with the so-called neodymium YAG laser. The method had been tested for the first time in 1978 in Switzerland, but obviously it couldn't really win recogni-tion. Today they are just three or four ophthalmologists worldwide that have specialized in this particular surgical operation. The prerequisites for a successful treatment that have to be fulfilled by patients with eye floaters are so strict that only very few of them come into consideration: certain kinds of opacities cannot be treated in the first place, for exam-ple when they are caused by damages of the retina. In addition, the number of floating particles must not be too large, and they have to be located in a sufficient distance from the lens and the retina. Laser treat-ment is also known to have its side effects, for example bleedings. Also there were cases with patients having perceived new eye floaters in their field of vision as a result of treatment.

At this point I felt that I had gathered enough information around the phenomenon of *mouches volantes*. What Nestor used to explain, in a misty-eyed romantic way, as the »basic structure of the picture« and as necessary for the perfect restoration, was nothing else than a physiologi-cal eye phenomenon, whether of embryogenetic nature, caused by a dysfunction in the eye or simply as a result of advanced age. Nestor's claim that he had learned to see these dots and strands was therefore absurd, if not even cynical. It was about the same as if a person of advanced age announced that he had trained for years to acquire wrinkles on the skin – to say nothing of senile dementia.

Near the end of January I visited Nestor as I wanted him to know about my research results. I didn't intend to »convert« him, though – this was something I considered impossible anyway. But I felt that he should at least know about the scientific explanations for the phenomenon.

»What I see is generally being referred to as ›mouches volantes‹,« I lectured. »The phenomenon is caused by a degeneration of the vitreous in the eye.«

»Mouches volantes. Degeneration,« he repeated as if he had to strain himself to memorize the terms. I could see him suppressing a laugh.

»›Fliegende Mücken‹ they're called in German,« I added.

»And in English?« he wanted to know.

»*Eye floaters.*«

»And in Italian?«

I paged through my papers. »*Mosche volanti.*«

As a courtesy on my part, I also informed him of the corresponding terms in Latin, *muscae volitantes*, and in Spanish and Portuguese: *moscas volantes* or *flocos.*

»*Flocos,*« he called out with a childlike voice.

I continued my lecture, but time and again, Nestor made fun of the terms *mouches volantes, flocos* and others so that I finally put down my notes in exasperation.

»It doesn't seem to interest you what I have to say,« I observed. Instead of answering, he quacked several times. I didn't understand what he went for.

»I know what you're doing,« he said, suddenly turning serious just when I started to regret my visit in the first place. »You desperately want to find an explanation you can understand. You're trying to integrate your dots and strands into the order of your small world – instead of dissolving your small world.«

»I'm trying to tell you,« I countered, »that your explanation of this entoptic phenomenon has nothing whatsoever to do with reality.«

»What reality?« he laughed and looked around as if searching for a reality. Then he added that it was indeed a question of what explanation would have nothing whatsoever to do with what reality.

In response to his evasive statement, I tried to show him that his viewpoint on *mouches volantes* did not match the empirical findings of science. As an example I mentioned an obvious contradiction:

»You said that it was the perfect restoration that had brought about my ability to see *mouches volantes*.« Nestor shrugged his shoulders defensively and signaled his agreement with a slight nod of his head. Now it was my turn and with pleasure I asked him: »But how can this be the case when many people get to know this phenomenon at some point in their life? We're talking about something here that can develop independent from our lifestyle, just like every human being will sooner or later have a wrinkled skin and gray hair – independent from our worldview, independent from building up an inner pressure or practicing certain exercises, or even doing nothing of the sort.«

»Nothing in and about the human being develops independent from his lifestyle. Neither gray hair nor wrinkles, dots or strands,« he answered back. »If many people can perceive these dots and strands, it means nothing other than that these people have already built up a certain inner pressure within themselves. Perhaps they haven't done so deliberately and in a targeted manner. But people who lead a moderately natural life without wasting their energy in idiotic ways will experience that the inner pressure will increase a little in the course of their life. In addition, some people have a higher inner pressure and unbound energy at their disposal from their very birth. That's the reason why some people are able to see the dots and strands already in their juvenile years – if they care to look out for it.

But that wasn't the case with you. When you came here for the first time, you were missing any and all inner pressure. Perhaps you wouldn't have seen the dots until you were sixty or seventy years of age – if at all. But as a result of practicing the exercises you've managed to live through this development in just a few years.«

»If I had known that your perfect restoration would bring me these particles in the eye, I would've never gotten involved in it,« I sneered.

»Don't look at them as particles in the eye,« he replied. »That's the explanation of people with a materialistic worldview. Of course they can't come up with anything else than ›particles in the eye‹. Instead, consider your dots and strands as an expression of consciousness.«

»Consciousness? Last time you said *mouches volantes* are the basic structure of the picture.«

»That's what they are indeed: these dots and strands are sections of a kind of framework, or better: a structure. And this structure is the picture without the small world, the naked picture, so to speak – that's why I call it *basic structure*; that which we call *small world* comes and goes at the outer brim of this structure.

But ultimately it is the consciousness forming this basic structure. So if you're familiar with it, you don't only know the buildup of the picture and thus the origin of all things in your small world; you will also understand this consciousness, that is you yourself, better.«

»What made you associate *mouches volantes* with consciousness in the first place?«

»Because these floaters always light up, and I can always see them best, when I'm more conscious. Consciousness means the ability to be *conscious*, to be *aware* – and this ability doesn't differ from the ability to *see* the dots and strands and make them light up.«

I started to argue with Nestor. I insisted that the phenomenon was nothing but some kind of particles in the vitreous having nothing to do with consciousness. As an additional argument I mentioned the fact that laser specialists and surgeons had successfully freed many people from *mouches volantes*. I confronted him with testimonials confirming this.

Nestor didn't say anything. I thought I had finally made him see reason with more rational arguments than his. But I couldn't really enjoy my small triumph because in my eagerness I had withheld certain information that could have been used to partially argue against *mouches volantes* as particles in the eye. In comparison to Nestor, I wanted to argue in a differentiated way, so with a little bit less enthusiasm I added the rest of my findings:

»Actually these medical procedures work very poorly; the prerequisites for a successful treatment of *mouches volantes* are so strict that only those patients come into consideration that suffer from serious damages or injuries of the eye. Patients, on the other hand, that only show harmless opacities of the vitreous are mostly rejected by professional and competent physicians. This holds good in particular for laser treatment, because what is commonly associated with »mouches volantes« cannot be objectively identified and thus not seen and photographed at all by ophthalmologists. With the laser, however, only those particles in the eye can be vaporized that specialists can identify and locate. In the case of vitrectomies, however, the situation is different: here the physicians are not concerned with establishing the existence of *mouches volantes* because, after all, the entire vitreous, or a part of it in the optical axis, is removed in the process.«

I told Nestor that our medical technology was not yet mature enough to identify all existing kinds of *mouches volantes* and treat them effectively and risk-free. This, however, was still no evidence that the flying mosquitoes were something other than particles in the eye.

Then I called Nestor's attention to a second problem closely connected to the problem of identification and treatment: the meaning of the term »mouches volantes« as regards content. From what I could establish after having read some of the technical literature on the subject, the term was not sufficiently well defined – even in the heads of those concerned – to distinguish between harmless eye floaters and phenomena indicating serious damages of the retina.

If the terms *mouches volantes* or *floaters* are mentioned, then a multitude of other illnesses and damages of the retina is resonating along with it – despite the fact that these are described totally different in their appearance than the single dots and strands: as motionless obscurations of the field of vision over wider areas, also called »scotoma« or sometimes described as »soot« or »soot rain«. In addition, there is the perception of bright light flashes, known as »photoma«, and finally the perceptions of yellowish or reddish spots – deposits in the vitreous caused by eye illnesses.

This might be the reason why these dots and strands, in the majority harmless and transparent, are regarded by some people as worrisome or even dangerous when they are called *mouches volantes* or *floaters*, with the result that they want to get rid of them at any cost. Here one could have argued that a person freed from his *mouches volantes* or *floaters* with successful laser treatment or vitrectomy had actually suffered from particles of some kind in his eye – but not those dots and strands that Nestor described as the »basic structure of the picture«.

When I was done we both kept silent for a while. I was certain that I had abetted Nestor, because with these arguments it would have been possible to simply explain away the material existence of these dots and strands – just a matter of how the term *mouches volantes* was defined. And I was certain that Nestor would now exploit this circumstance in a self-indulgent way.

But Nestor didn't respond to my remarks at all. »Don't think too much about that,« he only replied. »But take a close look at them. And don't worry: these flying mosquitoes will surely not bite you.«

»Do I have a choice? The way it looks, I have to spend the rest of my life with these *mouches volantes*,« I replied embittered.

Nestor disagreed. »If you think that way, and if you're satisfied with these explanations, you haven't searched long and far enough.«

Nestor's indifferent attitude towards my endeavors made me continue my search for information about *mouches volantes*. What was motivating me was Nestor's astonishing and provocative mystification of the phenomenon, as well as his arrogant claim that I hadn't searched long and far enough. I was intent on making him change his opinion in both cases.

On the Internet I found numerous articles and other publications on the subject of eye floaters. Many websites of medical professionals and private persons as well as forums established for discussing that very subject deliver information about and clarification of the subject, and users exchange their thoughts and opinions about the entoptic phenomenon.

One interesting realization is that *mouches volantes* are also listed as symptoms accompanying mental illnesses, most of all depressions. One report states that, even when a person is familiar with the flying mosquitoes for some time already, they are only perceived as disturbing or worrisome when the person is in a depressed mood. In cases like these, the fear originates in the idea that these opacities of the vitreous could increase in number and potentially lead to a loss of eyesight. As such, *mouches volantes* are partially also related to stress, everyday problems and personal crises that are often regarded as their cause.

Personal histories of some of those affected confirm this: they mention emotional and mental stress, partially accompanied by physical symptoms such as dizziness, drowsiness, tickle feelings and numbness in individual limbs. Some reports speculate on a connection between eye floaters and the tinnitus symptom of ringing in the ears when they mention that both phenomena had shown up for the first time more or less simultaneously in many patients. According to the statements of those affected, the sensation and perception of eye floaters is preceded by situations of that nature. I couldn't find any confirmation from medical professionals, however, whether these circumstances are the actual cause for the development of opacities in the vitreous.

Most persons affected with eye floaters and reporting on the phenomenon regard them as a problem. The worries and concerns people express about an increasingly clouded field of vision were totally comprehensible to me. The trepidation of these people is only alleviated in part, though, by exchanging experiences and words of consolation, because it is generally known that nothing can be done against these annoying objects in the eye – aside from a chancy and hazardous surgical operation. In some cases, the fact that nothing can be done results in quite some rage and anger that also expresses itself indirectly: a group of affected people in the USA, for example, is considering a lawsuit against their physicians because they don't know of any effective treatment for this particular form of eye complaint. Others are demanding the introduction of a new medical term giving consideration to this illness: *vitreous opacity syndrome*.

Some of the people affected, however, have found a creative way between self-help and artistic expression in order to deal with *mouches volantes*: they have done drawings and paintings of their dots and strands and exhibit them in *floaters galleries* on the Internet. Often these drawings reflect the persons' everyday perception of these dots and strands, but there are also some real works of art around, with colorful motives and adornments. Others in turn have developed *floaters* simulators – computer programs that can be used to optically illustrate the look of these dots and strands, as well as their behavior when the eyes are moved.

But despite all sobering medical facts: some people affected try to help themselves by speculating on the causes of *mouches volantes* and treating themselves. Accordingly, the number of good advices and recipes circulating among them and being tested is quite large. For example, one person reported that it was possible to reduce the number of *mouches volantes*, or even make them disappear altogether, by practicing relaxation exercises or by giving body and mind enough rest. When it comes to nutrition, some refer to certain vitamins or recommend uncooked vegetarian food with the objective of positively influencing metabolism processes. At any rate, people affected are told to avoid refined sugar, emulsifiers, milk, margarine and drugs of any sort. The advice to lower one's cholesterol level points in the same direction. And one woman reports that her flying mosquitoes have disappeared after she had stopped drinking coffee.

Alternative and pseudo-medical promises of healing are also widespread: in homeopathy, eye drops are offered against the annoying mosquitoes in the eye. In traditional Chinese medicine the cause of eye floaters is believed to originate in dysfunctions of kidneys, liver and colon; they thus recommend natural herb mixtures such as lady's thistle and dandelion preparations as well as acupuncture. And one company offers sunglasses that absorb ultraviolet rays one hundred percent which is supposed to counteract the proliferation of *mouches volantes*.

When I went out to Nestor with all these good advices, the snow in the Bern region had almost completely melted away. In the upper Emmental, in contrast, everything was still covered with glaring white snow on this sunny day.

Nestor was open for my further research work and carefully listened to the results I had obtained. He seemed to be irritated, though, about the efforts that people went through to get rid of their flying mosquitoes.

»Breathing exercises against *mouches volantes*; eye drops against *mouches volantes*; raw vegetables against *mouches volantes*; sunglasses against *mouches volantes*,« he grinned and threw up his hands in horror. Then he became serious. »Forget about that nonsense you dragged along with you there. The world doesn't have to be healed of *mouches volantes* but of ignorant and blind people.«

»Where's the difference, Nestor?« I objected. »Where's the difference between those offering homeopathic preparations, acupuncture and sunglasses against *mouches volantes*, and that what you tell about them? These people out there approach the phenomenon at least with serious consideration and with a more or less scientific background, whereas all you have to offer with regard to these eye floaters are things beyond good and evil, way past it.«

»The others are trying to make you believe that you are suffering from an eye illness,« he answered back. »I, on the other hand, tell you that these dots and strands are the first emergences of your consciousness that is forming a shining structure – that's the difference. Now it's up to you whether you prefer to become desperate over an eye complaint, or to pull yourself together, develop your consciousness and recognize the structure of your picture.«

»That sounds too simple – as if we had a choice. But for many people affected it's not that simple. They suffer from it,« I called to his attention and made him familiar with reports of people affected as well as the psychological findings that an increased preoccupation with *mouches volantes* as the result of a depression could lead to a problem, particularly when the result is increased fear of opacities in the vitreous when these in turn seem to increase in number. Following this line of thought in reverse, I surmised that a person affected, who finds himself rather in a manic mood, would mystify these dots and strands as something desirable and sensational – perhaps so as to repress his realization of the devastating consequences for the eyes.

I looked over to Nestor to observe his reaction. He remained silent. I interpreted his silence as a tacit consent and began to inform him of the different possibilities someone had at his disposal in order to get rid of *mouches volantes*. I cited a report of a person affected whose eyes had been massively clouded by *mouches volantes* for nearly three decades. Contrary to other persons affected, though, he had learned to live with it – and arranged his everyday life accordingly. Here's what he had to say:

»First and foremost, one has to break the habit of looking at *mouches volantes*,« I cited my notes. »In the beginning everybody will feel the impulse to look at them time and again. Here it is helpful to provide some kind of distraction. Over time, however, they won't be consciously perceived any longer because the brain learns to ignore them. On bright days, in sunlight, snow or fog, it is advisable to wear sunglasses with polarizing lenses. In addition, the interior walls of one's flat shouldn't be painted bright white; rather, wallpaper with patterns, structures or objects as motives are particularly suitable. In general, one should furnish the flat with decorative objects such as flowers, vases, bookshelves and pictures. People who often work on a computer or watch TV over a longer time are advised to reduce the brightness of the screen.«

When I had ended, Nestor shook his head in disbelief. »What you're telling there is incredibly naïve. To provide distraction, look the other way, turn off the screen and banish the light from the picture – so that's supposed to be the solution? What'll be next? Antidepressants on prescription? Forget it, you'll need the light because only in that way you'll be able to recognize what eye floaters actually are. And instead of advising people not to look at them, they should, on the contrary, learn to really see them to be able to judge for themselves what they are.«

»For those affected by them, *mouches volantes* are a curse,« I tried to explain to him. »They precisely *don't* want to have to constantly look at them.«

»Mouches volantes are only a curse when you don't know where the actual problem lies – because the fear of floaters is deeply rooted in them: basically, people suffering from them are afraid of a change in their personality. You mentioned it yourself: quite obviously, many people noted mental and physical complaints during the time when the dots and strands showed up. From that perspective, there's something to be said for a possible connection between eye floaters and states of depression. Feeling depressive means nothing else than feeling strongly that something is very awry in one's own life. And this is always a chance as well, because it could be an impetus for developing one's consciousness.

Those who see the dots and strands should accept them as an expression of personal change and not curse them as a cause of their misfortune. It's not enough to simply project one's own fears onto the dots and strands and to believe that the world would turn alright again once they're gone. If a person is afraid of the dots and strands, he should simply look at them until his fears are dispelled; those who want to know what they are should concentrate on them for as long as is needed to know what they really are.«

I didn't go into Nestor's explanations. Frustrated, I put my notes aside and told him that this was all the information I could gather on the subject.

»You said I should look for these *mouches volantes*, but I couldn't find any references anywhere that they could be more than a degenerative, age-related phenomenon that can turn into a serious troublemaker when personal problems arise.«

»You didn't listen to me,« he replied patiently. »I'm trying to tell you that you have to go beyond that paperwork here and begin with yourself: have you taken some time at all to really look at them? To see what forms and shapes your strands are adopting? And how they move?«

»I've looked at them several times,« I was able to counter.

»You've looked at them to confirm the findings of your research,« he claimed, and he did have a point there. »But you should look at them and learn to hold them in suspension to find out what they really are. After all that time you've spent here, during which you had practiced to see the picture as a whole and inspect its afterimages, I believed that you would arrive there by yourself. But you're still thick as a brick. You're running into the next library like a stupid boy and get into a tangle with explanations of some sort that won't help you at all.«

»But it did help me,« I insisted. »Now I know that these opacities are *mouches volantes*, that they're harmless. That was an important realization for me.«

»Mouches volantes – this term stands for an eye complaint, for a dysfunction in the eye, for an age-related phenomenon, at best. I told you already that ideas and concepts like these would be the result when you approach this issue with a materialistic worldview and try to inspect it just from the outside,« Nestor pointed out.

I blamed him that he just didn't want to admit that *mouches volantes* were nothing else than particles in the vitreous. To my surprise, Nestor replied that he didn't deny the possibility that they were particles in the eye – if seen from a materialistic perspective. And if he encouraged me now to learn to see my dots and strands as initial parts of a structure of consciousness, it didn't mean, either, that materialistic and scientific explanations were wrong – it's just that they were not sufficiently embracing the issue.

»If you want to examine your dots and strands in a scientific context, then the outcome won't be much more then the observation that something is wrong with your eyes. Only that Japanese fellow you mentioned the last time has gone a little bit further; after all, he had invested more than twenty years in observing his own dots and strands. But he was obliged to his scientific suppositions, and consequently he eventually could only observe that his dots and strands had hardly changed during this long period.« Suddenly Nestor started to laugh loudly. »Imagine, they paid the guy just so that he would stare into the blue for a while.«

»Then everything has been said,« I replied. »Science has solved the puzzle – they just don't have an effective treatment for it so far.«

»Wrong. The problem is that the methods of science can only cover a tiny aspect of the eye floater issue. As long as people only ponder over it and try to establish the existence of some kind of particles in the eye with some kind of machine or apparatus, they only describe the effects of the phenomenon. But they won't advance further to the point of cause if they don't learn to see the dots and strands for themselves.«

»I can see my *mouches volantes*, and I still don't know how you arrived at ideas of that kind.«

»Well, you yourself said that they are in constant motion. They flow away, out of the field of vision, when you try to take a look at them, right? So therefore you're not able to take a real look at them in the first place. Because, how do you want to calmly take a look at something if it tends to flow away all the time?«

»Are you able to calmly take a look at them?«

»Yes, I can. I've learned to see them and hold them in suspension so as to take a close look at them. I'm able to do this because I have trained my inner sense.«

»Your inner sense?«

»Yes. In order to recognize what this structure really is, it needs more than just the physical eyes; it needs the *inner sense*,« he explained. »The inner sense is like an inner eye. A person having trained his inner sense to perfection is a *seer*. He has trained his inner sense by concentrating, time and again, on the basic structure; because the moment he completely focuses on it, he withdraws energy from his outer senses and directs it to the inner sense.«

»This is the first time that you tell me about this inner sense,« I observed.

»Maybe. But you've already taken some time to train your inner sense,« he answered, »ever since you began to take a look at the inner screen.«

The Emmental Cooking Pot

My obsession with trying to identify Nestor and his »peers« as adherents and keepers of an old mystical tradition flared up again.

By now, more than a year had passed since I had been searching for testimonials of a non-Christian group or even movement in the Emmental, the members of which, as Nestor had expressed, were striving for a unification of opposites. But the search had been a failure, and I wasn't able to draw a secret with respect to such a tradition from Nestor and his neighbors that would have answered my questions. Finally I had given up that search, and instead I followed Nestor's advice and concentrated on the perfect restoration of the secretaire.

But now the situation was different. The following conversations I had with Nestor about *mouches volantes* always ended in dialogues about Nestor and his neighbors, who they were and what they did here on the left side of the Emme. According to him, they were exploring the origin and structure of the picture beyond duality; in order to do this, they were searching for answers in their own consciousness. As a result of their endeavors, they had revealed a so-called »basic structure« they could perceive with their »inner sense«. Piquant: this basic structure, he claimed, was not something aloof, detached or inaccessible; rather, the first emergences of this structure could be perceived by many, if not most people – ophthalmology identifies them as particles in the eye and throws them into the general pot »mouches volantes«.

The revelation and perception of the basic structure was a process that Nestor called »seeing«. And he called the people on the left side of the Emme, including himself, »seers«. It soon turned out that this term – that I had, at first, interpreted as a spontaneous inspiration and associated with fields of activity such as »prophecy«, »magic« and »occultism« – belonged to the general vocabulary Nestor used. Whenever he talked about »seers« he didn't only refer to the activity and the knowledge of the people on the left side in connection with it, but he also used the word so as to distinguish between them and other people that were not able to recognize the dots and strands as something that has come about through the basic structure of the picture that in turn was a product of consciousness.

As I had failed with my attempt to »enlighten« Nestor with respect to the eye floater phenomenon, I changed my tactical approach. Now the people on the left side of the Emme should be my object of study again. I wanted to find out about their knowledge and their viewpoints on *mouches volantes*.

In spring I started to visit Nestor on a regular basis again. On a warm day in April I told him of my efforts to hold the dots and strands in suspension, and of the specific properties I had noticed while doing so. I told him that I was now able to see them anytime, and also that I was able to exert a certain influence on them with my eye movements. For example, I was able to shift them back and forth in my field of vision. I noticed as well that only very few of the strands were simply empty; rather, they looked like small tubes filled with dots.

»You said that I should hold the eye floaters in suspension,« I finally reminded him. »But I'm not successful at that. I can't manage to hold even one single strand or dot in suspension, because it looks as if everything is interconnected: if I lose one dot, I'm losing it all. Is it really possible to hold these dots and strands in suspension?«

»It is. The dots and strands are your mirror image,« he answered. »They're moving because you're moving. Relax and calm down, then they will do the same.«

»But I *am* relaxed and calm when I look at them.«

»Not relaxed and calm enough. Even if your body isn't moving, you yourself are active – in your thoughts and emotions.«

»But that can't be the explanation for the phenomenon that the dots all flow downward,« I doubted his assertion.

Nestor shrugged his shoulders indifferently. »What do you expect? When flying flies fly after flying flies, then flying flies do fly after flying flies, after all,« he teased me, but he said it with such seriousness that I had to laugh.

»Here you're confronted with the same strong force barring you from correctly perceiving afterimages and the picture as a whole,« he explained. »It's the attractive force that pulls down your dots and strands. These strands are like little branches that you throw up in the air: they are attracted by the larger mass of the ground. In this way, you also throw your dots and strands – that are attracted by the larger mass of the basic structure – upwards, time and again, by moving your eyes accordingly.«

»There's a larger mass of the basic structure?«

»Yes, it's located below the section of the structure that you can see.«

»How do you know that there is a much larger mass of this kind below my dots and strands?«

»I know it from my seeing,« he replied. He pondered for a while, then he told me that I should imagine this entire basic structure to have the form of a water drop, for example. We were never able, according to Nestor, to see the entire form but only a section in the upper part, in the tip of the water drop.

»Why in the tip?« I asked.

»All living beings are traveling on a path in the basic structure, but not all living beings perceive it as such. That needs certain prerequisites with regard to consciousness. Man is capable of developing his inner sense and thus consciously perceiving this structure. And when he's able to see his dots and strands, then he has already traveled a certain distance in the basic structure and is situated in the upper region of this water drop.«

I asked Nestor about the inner sense with which we supposedly perceived *mouches volantes*. I wanted to know if that was some sort of sixth sense latently inherent in any person. Nestor negated this and explained that the inner sense was actually the tactile sense, only farther advanced. This sense manifested itself both on the outer and the inner screen. While it fulfilled its function on the outer screen as tactile feeling of matter, we could experience it on the inner screen as feeling of emotions and thoughts. The highest advancement of the tactile sense, however, was feeling the entire picture with the eyes, that is, seeing the basic structure. Concentrating on the basic structure meant to withdraw the five physical senses from the outer screen and to bundle their energy. Consequently, the inner sense was not only the farther advanced tactile sense but the summary of all five physical senses as well.

Then Nestor mentioned the attractive force once more, saying that it could only be overcome with a strongly developed inner sense.

»In the beginning, these dots and strands flow downward quite rapidly; your inner sense is weak. But the more you develop your inner sense, that is, the more you increase your inner pressure, and the more you exert yourself in the everyday world so as not to cling to the physical senses and trying to satisfy their hunger for stimuli, the better you'll be able to hold these dots and strands in suspension. Each time you sit down and direct your attention to these dots, you are detaching yourself from the outer screen and develop your inner sense instead. In this way you practice to gradually overcome the attractive force until one day you'll be able to hold the dots and strands in suspension, and only then will you be able to really see them. In the process, you'll also recognize that the basic structure is the first effect caused by consciousness; before anything else can come into existence, consciousness is split up into light and matter through this structure.«

I described to Nestor how the »first effect caused by consciousness« looked in my case: when my dots and strands were large and out of focus, they rather reminded me of dark spots clouding my clear vision. Then there were smaller, more sharply focused and transparent dots and strands, sometimes isolated and loose, sometimes in groups.

»I can imagine very well that the dots and strands give the appearance of a structure when they grow in number,« I said. »And I can even imagine that you can see them glowing brightly. But I just can't follow your idea that these little things are »the first effect caused by consciousness« – isn't that simply your own interpretation of these eye floaters?«

»As I said: your inner sense is weak and you're not a seer. That's why it is difficult for you to follow this,« he admitted. »And at this point it doesn't need to be relevant for you. First and foremost, it is important to understand that seeing these dots and strands goes much deeper than generally assumed. The fact that the dots and strands are part of the structure, with our small world emerging and decaying on its edges – that is the direct knowledge of a seer that right now seems incomprehensible to you.«

»So that means that you tap a knowledge that is only accessible to seers?«

»Yes. *Direct knowledge* is that knowledge coming about by seeing the basic structure when the seer is in a higher, more intensive state of being. You cannot acquire that direct knowledge independent from seeing, as it is the case with ›normal‹ knowledge.«

»But if you now tell me about things that resulted from your direct knowledge, I still adopt it as such, don't I?«

»If you want to. Only in that case it's no longer *direct* knowledge, and as such it has only limited value. As soon as a seer wants to pass this knowledge on to someone else, it loses its direct character and appears confusing and irritating. That's why you don't know right now what you are supposed to do with this knowledge that the dots and strands structure the picture and thus create the small world.«

»I really have a hard time to believe this, Nestor.«

»No one says that you're supposed to simply believe this,« he answered. »Keep advancing, then your inner sense will further develop and reveal the basic structure.«

To counter Nestor's claims, I was looking for objections I could raise. Finally I pondered this: if he was right with his concept of the dots, then the question posed itself why nothing whatsoever was known about it anywhere in the world. After all, we are living in a period of time in which so many people have so many possibilities of exchanging information; a period of time in which technology allows people to chase old wisdom and new ideas galore and in palatable bits around the globe at breakneck speed – in times like this, how was it possible that knowledge that, according to Nestor, was so elementary and universal, was unknown to the world?

I asked Nestor about it, and he replied that the problem did not lie in the number of people, not in the knowledge accumulated and not in the possibilities of communication – but simply in the fact that the overwhelming majority of people were not seers, and that they didn't make an effort in that direction, even if they had the chance to do so. This didn't mean, however, that there were no hints or clues pertaining to the basic structure in the wealth of knowledge mankind was keeping. As this structure was building up the picture in the broadest sense, modern science, in its striving for discovering the origin and laws of all phenomena, constantly revealed the principle of the structure in the process.

»In natural science in particular, in physics, chemistry and biology, the material basics of our live or the universe have been discovered and described. And these are, in principle, identical with the buildup of the basic structure of consciousness that reveals itself to a seer in his seeing.«

I started to listen attentively. Nestor was just about to lead himself up the garden path: he tried to use the discoveries of science to confirm the validity of his system. I asked him to explain this allegedly conforming principle in more detail, but revealingly he didn't want to talk about it any further. He implied that the hints and clues were never directly accessible but always had to be read off of scientific formulas, tables, graphics and descriptions. If I wanted to understand the relationships to the basic structure I had to be, according to him, a seer with direct knowledge at his disposal.

»The principle of the basic structure, however, cannot only be observed in the buildup of nature but also in the thinking of people themselves,« Nestor went on. »A seer is able to recognize hints and clues in many legends and myths. At the inception of religions, there were often seers whose direct knowledge of the world was packaged into stories that consequently adulterated that knowledge.«

»But why should they have done something like that? Specially if what you claim here is supposed to be universal truth: why isn't it written down in these myths and sacred scriptures in exactly the way a seer is able to see this?«

Nestor made an idle motion with his head. »Exactly because most human beings are not seers yet, after all,« he replied. »Seeing is indeed a concrete thing, but what you can see and relay to others is very abstract: dots and strands – who is able to make use of banal things like that? Of course, the people rather want colors, more complex forms, shapes and of course names. The people are seeking their happiness and salvation in something akin to them. They want stories, fantasies, concepts and suggestions they can follow. That's why the principle of the basic structure had always been packaged and relayed in stories and pictures – and adulterated until it was not explicitly clear any longer what actually was at the bottom of all this.« He gave me a wink and was beaming all over his face.

For a longer period of time we remained silent. Nestor sat directly across from me but I felt as if I was light years away from him. Of course I knew that his attempts at explaining the world were undifferentiated and speculative, all the more because he didn't even make any concrete statements at all. But somehow I envied him for his unrestrained ease and unscrupulousness with which he managed to adjust and straighten out his view of the world.

»Even if everything was just the way you claim,« I finally said, »what's the use in seeing the basic structure of the picture?«

Nestor smiled. He looked out the window over to the Hohgant that suddenly started to glow in bright red as dusk had set in. For a long time he sat there motionless, his eyes showing a fixed stare as well. He didn't respond to my question.

On the next morning, cool but sunny, I was busy preparing my breakfast when Nestor entered the kitchen. He was jocular and made a remark about the cereal I was just about to pour into a bowl. With a look at the grain flakes, he recalled the Spanish and Portuguese term for *mouches volantes*: *flocos*. Again he showed a childlike joy in the word and said that if I continued to eat as many *flocos* as I did, I would soon see nothing else but *flocos*. Then he had fun calling me »Floco«, time and again.

After breakfast I was routinely heading for the chicken house to practice perceiving afterimages, but Nestor mentioned almost casually that that wasn't necessary any longer for me. He explained that looking at afterimages and concentrating on the outer screen were actually preparatory steps for looking at the dots and strands.

»Now that Floco is able to see the *flocos*, Floco should concentrate directly on the *flocos*,« he was joking. »Because they are the most important part of the perfect restoration. The afterimages do relate to the inner screen, but they are not yet the basic structure of the picture. The dots and strands, on the other hand, structure the picture – the thinking as well as the emotional world with the afterimages and the material world.«

Then he abruptly changed the subject and asked me how I was getting along with transforming my sexual energy. This came as a surprise to me, and I had some initial difficulties to talk about it. Not just that the subject as such was uncomfortable for me to talk about, but it also cost me quite some effort to admit that I had actually tried to abstain from sexual activities for a while, as Nestor had advised. But I had quickly realized that this was nothing for me. Because despite great efforts I had taken, I couldn't manage to hold back the sexual energy completely.

Nestor patiently let me take my time to search for words and form sentences for an answer. Then he admitted that it wasn't simple to live in sexual abstention. He reminded me, though, that he had already told me that it was not about completely holding back sexual energy.

»You can't just turn off your sexuality as if you are dealing with some machine. If you try to suppress it, your body will revolt with just that much more force, because your body has its natural habits. And sexuality is part of that as well.«

»So why fight against it if we can't overcome and control it anyway?«

»We're not fighting against it. We are working with it. What we're trying to do is to transform as much sexual energy as possible, by engaging in creative work.«

»I don't know if I can do that. So far I couldn't.«

»You shouldn't give up now already,« he said. »In all those years you've gotten used to find comfort and relaxation in the energy outbreak accompanying the orgasm. And your body has gotten used to these little ephemeral pleasures. Now it'll take a certain time for your body to readjust and learn how to release the energy in a more creative way.«

»Is that really necessary, after all?« I asked meekly.

»People that want to develop their consciousness should definitely live an abstentious life for a while. It shouldn't be enforced, though, and if it doesn't work out then and now, it's not worth mentioning. What's important is that we keep trying again and again, that we don't let ourselves go beyond all measures, and that we don't stimulate ourselves artificially. What's also important is that we should always do something for our own creativity with the energy saved. Then our consciousness will rapidly advance to higher states.«

Nestor then began to describe the transformation of sexual energy with the metaphors water and fire. Water and fire, he explained, existed in every body, aside from the other basic elements. Usually water flowed down into the ground, but fire blazed up into the air – that's why water was located below fire in our body. If a person didn't take efforts to transform his sexual energy, it would just seep away like water; at the same time, his fire of life located above would gradually burn out.

»A person, on the other hand, that starts to transform his sexual energy is reversing the positions of these two elements: by leading an appropriate lifestyle, he pulls the water up above the fire. That means he's now using his fire of life to vaporize the water and transform his sexual energy. In this way, the inner pressure in his body increases, and in combination with body and breathing exercises he succeeds more and more in opening up his body and putting the transformed energy directly into the picture as a whole.«

I shrugged my shoulders indifferently. Meanwhile I was used to Nestor's use of metaphors now and then with which he tried to illustrate his ideas. But I felt that his water and fire metaphor in context with sexual energy was a little bit far-fetched. I couldn't do anything with it, either, as I couldn't relate what he said to me to any experience of my own.

Nestor noticed my attitude and insisted explicitly that the ultimate success in performing the perfect restoration depended on the location of fire and water in the body. He claimed that every person had arranged fire and water for themselves in one or the other way, and their consciousness would develop accordingly.

»You probably think that I have taken fire and water out of thin air and stamped it out of the ground?« he asked and laughed about his own pun so that I didn't want to say anything in response. Then he announced mysteriously that he knew a place where fire and water outside of my body could show me how fire and water within my body would take their effect. He wanted me to come along to that place with him.

Shortly after lunch we left the house and went into the direction where the Schrattenfluh mountain ridge gave way to the sun in the morning. After a longer and uneventful hiking trip we arrived at a relatively plain spot on the edge of a forest.

»There we are,«, Nestor announced. I took a look around: we stood up on a mountain terrace that sloped downward into a ditch. Trees didn't grow in this place anymore, only low bushes and moss sprawled here and there. Leaves and small twigs were lying around everywhere.

»And what are we going to do here now?«

»Be patient,« he said and walked up to a spot in the middle of the terrace. There he pushed aside the bushes and cleaned a circular spot between them with a fir branch. I was surprised when a large circular wooden plate appeared under the soil, leaves and twigs; obviously it covered the entrance to a sort of cave.

»What's that?« I asked.

Nestor didn't answer but asked me to help him lift the plate. Together we moved it towards the side and uncovered a hole of about five feet in diameter and eight feet in depth. The round stone walls inside were moist and rendered the impression at first that this was a small well, the walls of which narrowed down like a funnel. At the bottom I could recognize a smooth surface reflecting the light. But when I tossed a little stone into the hole, there was no splash of water but an unexpected glassy sound. Obviously the bottom consisted of a glass pane.

»This is the Emmental Cooking Pot,« he announced solemnly.

»The Emmental Cooking Pot,« I repeated as if hypnotized. Now I remembered that the old danseuse had maundered something about a cooking pot she wanted to stick me into. The notion that her words would obviously fulfill themselves now had something alarming to me.

Nestor announced that we had to clear the channel feeding the water from a small creek in the vicinity into the cooking pot of leaves, twigs and soil. Together we exposed a small stone channel that had been chiseled into the ground with great care. For a hiker or walker it was hardly visible because it was hidden under all that soil, debris and remnants of plants. The inlet of the channel was equipped with iron rods at small distances from each other that were supposed to hold off leaves and twigs carried along by the water. Right behind it, a steel floodgate controlled the volume of water flowing into the channel. Before arriving at the cooking pot, the channel branched out into four small furrows that led the water into the pot through four openings furnished with iron railings.

»Did you build all that?« I asked Nestor after we had removed all soil, leaves and stones from the channel.

»The Emmental Cooking Pot was designed and built by seers,« he answered. »And – no, I don't know who exactly it was that had built this construct and when,« he added quick-witted.

»But of course this knowledge doesn't matter in our case,« I replied in Nestor's sense, and both of us had to laugh heartily.

»The important point is that the cooking pot will help you understand how your handling of sexual energy will affect you over time,« Nestor pointed out.

»And water is being fed into the hole for that purpose?«

»The water doesn't just flow into the cooking pot like that but rather into different channels built into its interior wall.« He explained that stone furrows were built into the interior wall, channeling the water downward in a spiral. Usually the water was collected in a copper kettle located in a small space under the glass pane. A fire was sparked under the kettle that boiled and vaporized the water.

»But today we'll reverse the positions of fire and water,« he added. »We'll take the kettle out of the space below the glass pane, and we'll hang it up into the opening of the Emmental Cooking Pot and spark a fire inside of it. The water will then seep away into the ground. In this way, you'll make a first-hand experience what it means to live with fire above and water below you, that is, to allow your sexual energy to drain away unused instead of availing yourself of it to develop your consciousness.«

»What exactly will I experience?« I asked doubtingly.

»I can't tell you, it depends on you.«

»And all we have to do is to let water run into it and start a fire above?«

»I'll start the fire in the kettle,« he said. »And I'll let the water flow into the Emmental Cooking Pot. You yourself will be cooked well inside.« He grinned.

I had already apprehended that I was supposed to climb down into this hole. But I didn't like this idea at all: the thought of musty odor and the dampness as well as the amount of dirt, smut and perhaps even insects and other animals that might be found down there made me turn towards Nestor to discuss the workability and necessity of this undertaking.

»This cannot work at all,« I argued. »A little fire, a little water – and that's supposed to be enough to find out what effects my handling of sexual energy will produce? What's that supposed to be?«

»It'll work,« Nestor countered with much determination in his tone of voice. »The Emmental Cooking Pot is not just any old hole. It has been built by seers precisely according to the elementary principles of the basic structure. And that's what gives the cooking pot its effectiveness. Just like Mari Egli's secretaire has also been built by one or more seers perhaps.«

This argument alarmed me even more. If the secretaire could already exert such an immense pressure on me, how powerful was this particular device here? Just a few minutes ago I considered this whole thing ridiculous and unpleasant, but now I felt a real anxiety within me. I felt how the modest personality within me stepped forward, an identity that could restrict itself and didn't need or have to experience anything at all costs: after all, one could let it be because one was satisfied and everything was just fine.

In order to gain some time, I wanted to know from Nestor what these principles were that the seers had perceived in their seeing and that were the basis for the cooking pot. But just like the day before, Nestor replied it was too early to talk about it.

»Is there no other way to find out what effect my handling of sexual energy has upon me?« I then asked.

»Yes, there is,« Nestor laughed, »experiencing those ephemeral little pleasures for twenty or thirty years – if you're smart, perhaps ten years are enough.«

»I don't think that I have to experience that here and now,« I finally pointed out. »What for? After all, I'll find out for myself how sexual energy will affect me.«

With ostentation, Nestor sat down on an overturned tree trunk, as if he wanted to signalize that he had all the time of the world to discuss the issue with me fully and matter-of-factly. I felt as if I had upset him.

Nestor tried to bring home to me that I overestimated myself. According to him, now I was young and almost free from any complaints. I was doing well – not least because of the energy that had already accumulated with the exercises around the perfect restoration. This made me believe that sexual energy was something inexhaustible.

»Of course it's not easy for you to understand the purpose of transforming your sexual energy if you've never experienced on and in your own body how destructive it can be to lose too much of this energy. If we now bring about such an experience on purpose, it'll motivate you to further work on ›vaporizing‹ your sexual energy.«

Nestor's voice sounded calm but determined so that I didn't have any other choice in the end than to give the cooking pot a chance.

Nestor jumped up, full of zest for action, and said that we, first of all, had to get the kettle out of the space under the glass pane. We got into this space through a small tunnel that had its entrance a little distance away on the hillslope. It was just wide enough for one person to creep through it in a cowering position to the space under the glass pane. Soon after, we were in a small room of about seven by seven feet in which we could stand in an upright position. Floor and walls consisted of brickwork, the ceiling was supported with massive wooden beams anchored in the walls. It was fairly bright in the space because daylight could shine through the glass pane above.

On the ground, directly under the glass pane, a wide blunt cone was installed with a kettle on top of it; both were made of copper and fit so precisely into each other that they had direct contact on a wide surface. Nestor explained that the fireplace was located inside of that cone, and he showed me a little door in it from where it could be fired. In this way, the smoke was prevented from filling the space above; instead, it was channeled off through exhaust pipes.

Then he pointed upwards. I recognized four stone furrows, one on each wall. They protruded far enough into the space so that occasional water drops were loudly plopping into the overfilled kettle. Excessive water flowed over the brim of the kettle and disappeared through a grid that was built around the cone in a circular form. I was stunned about the perfection this space exhibited.

We took the kettle off of its blunt copper cone and emptied it. Nestor covered the fireplace with a circular piece of metal fitting exactly into the hole of the cone. Finally we dragged the kettle through the tunnel outside and up onto the terrace. Up there, Nestor instructed me to climb down into the cooking pot and to use the stone furrows as ladder steps.

I had a real hard time to follow his instructions, but the fear of humiliation that would have resulted from me backing down was bigger than following Nestor's instructions. So I carefully stepped down into the hole, and soon after I stood on the wet and slippery glass pane all by myself.

I was still busy freeing myself from cobwebs and the like – carefully so as not to touch the moist walls around me – when Nestor started to hang the copper kettle into the opening of the cooking pot so that the four bolts on its brim fitted exactly into corresponding notches in the surrounding walls. It became dark, but not totally: the bright ring shimmering around the kettle lit up the space inside the cooking pot sparsely.

Some minutes passed by. It was damp and the smell of soil entered my nose. Now I believed to know how it feels for a snail to be packed in its small shell. To distract myself, I inspected the stone furrows that I had used as ladder steps. They were small open conduits, chiseled into the wall, and I saw there were four of them, about two fingers wide. The water would flow down spirally in these four furrows, taking three turns overall and finally disappearing somewhere in the wall.

Then I could hear how Nestor prepared the fire in the copper kettle. He broke wood into smaller pieces and put it into the kettle. I could hear the first crackle of burning wood, and some smoke entered my nose. When the fire was finally burning powerfully, some time elapsed again during which nothing happened. Finally the water began to gurgle down the furrows.

I waited. Some more minutes, long minutes to me, went by. I would have liked to sit down; the gentle monotonous gurgle in the furrows had a slumberous effect on me. I began to play with the water and tried to dam it up with my fingers. Then it became quiet. Only now on then I could hear Nestor handling the fire to prevent it from going out.

Some more time went by slowly. Again, I became aware of the absurdity of the situation: I was standing in a damp, bad smelling hole somewhere out in the Emmental Forest to find out how an incorrect handling of sexual energy could affect me. Now I was upset that I had agreed to participate in this madness in the first place. How was it possible that I could so easily be lured into stepping down into this idiotic hole? Once again I regretted that I had such a hard time to assert myself in Nestor's presence. Somehow I felt at his mercy, like an animal in a trap.

These thoughts increased my resentment. I wanted to show Nestor that he was wrong, that his Emmental Cooking Pot didn't work. After all, what was it supposed to teach me? Negative consequences of a wasteful sexual life? If that was the case, I thought, then I felt quite well, considering the circumstances. How was I supposed to feel down here anyway? I felt like I always did. Everything was all right. I enjoyed the triumph over the cooking pot that didn't have any effect on me.

I called out up to Nestor that I had understood the purpose of the exercise, and that he could stop the whole thing, but I didn't receive an answer from him. Once more I called Nestor, this time a little bit louder. I knew that he ignored me. To me it was obvious that he did this to provoke me – to prove to me that his cooking pot was more than just a stinking hole. But of course I wouldn't be lured to fall into his crude trap.

Nestor was a pitiful fellow anyway in my eyes. He had to surround himself with all that hocus-pocus to attract people's attention because he didn't have anything else. In society he was a nobody, a dropout, a failure. He had nothing except his shabby little hut. He had never told me, either, what he is actually doing for a living. Perhaps he was too lazy for a real job, and instead he indulged himself in a life at society's cost. Quite possible that he was one of those seemingly disabled persons.

At this moment the gurgle in the stone furrows stopped. I called out to Nestor that he should take away the kettle, but nothing happened – the kettle stayed in place. I noticed how uncomfortable I felt and how hot my body was. I felt a constant itch on my upper arm. I scratched it but it just kept on itching. I couldn't find the exact spot of the itch which made me boil with rage. Nervously I scratched my entire upper arm, but I was certain that I hadn't found the spot with the itch – and indeed it started to itch again, this time even stronger, like a mosquito bite. The heat of the kettle was almost unbearable. I yelled up to Nestor that he should take away that confounded kettle now.

Just when I felt that I couldn't stand it any longer, I heard how Nestor extinguished the fire in the kettle. And finally he took the kettle aside. I blinked upward into the excruciatingly bright daylight where Nestor stood.

»You're well done now?« he asked me and put up a broad smile.

I didn't feel like joking. As fast as I could, I tried to climb out of that hole, but it wasn't that easy at all. When I stepped out of the upper opening I had to catch my breath. I felt worn out and exhausted, completely powerless. Standing in the hole all that time had taken away all my energy.

»Now what happened to you? Look at yourself!« Nestor called out and pointed to my arms and hands. Frightened, I noticed that my skin was completely dried out and not as tight and firm as it used to be.

»You've become older,« he said.

As it turned out, our way back was quite a challenge. As so often before, Nestor frequently called my attention to different peculiarities that struck him while we were passing by. This could be animals, plants, mushrooms, moss, stones, forms and colors. He pointed out everything that was somewhat unusual, funny, nice to look at and not trivial.

At this time, however, I didn't feel like talking or marveling at something, not to mention receiving instructions or teachings of any kind; a feeling of indifference towards the picture was all I could sense. Still Nestor kept demanding my attention as usual which, after a while, caused more and more resentment within me. I thought I had deserved a break after having brought myself to step down in that cooking pot as he had instructed.

Once Nestor called out something to me but I didn't want to react. He repeated what he had said, but I ignored him once again and tried to concentrate on my steps, but I wasn't really successful at it. Instead I was searching for justifications for my repellent attitude for which I blamed Nestor: why did he have to disturb me right now? He knew very well that I didn't feel like talking and listening right now. Quite obviously he was lacking a certain sensibility. And his urge of constantly trying to capture my attention with something was simply disgusting and inexcusable.

I remained silent. This was my strong point now: I was able to contain myself for quite some time. But I knew that, at some point, my good will would vanish, and even I wouldn't be able to hold back and keep myself under control. Nestor, and Nestor only, had it in his hands.

And as if he wanted to take his chances, a little later he pointed towards two deer playfully running around a tree and chasing each other which seemed to fascinate him. From one moment to the other, I blew up in a shameful way. I accused him of things that I later could neither understand nor justify; in fact, I didn't even want to remember them. But my anger didn't affect Nestor in any way. He laughed about my emotional outbreak and said that, obviously, I was still »boiling«.

I realized that I couldn't cause any kind of effect in Nestor, and my mood turned into self-pity. I regretted that I had done something I didn't want to. I regretted that I was completely at the mercy of the situation, not being able to cope with it. I regretted that I felt so miserable, and I regretted my regrets. I wasn't able anymore to feel joy in anything, nor was I willing to. I felt as if I had never left this hole, the Emmental Cooking Pot. The rest of the way back we walked in silence.

My bad mood lasted for the remainder of the day, and my indifference caused that I wasn't able to concentrate on anything else. I felt like padded in cotton wool, far away from everything, blind and deaf for the life around me. I retreated to my room, but an insatiable urge for consumption, to stuff myself with something, almost made me go up the wall: chocolate, TV, idiotic computer games, screwball lifestyle magazines – just about everything would have been good enough for me to be »gone« at least a little.

During my attempts to distract myself I even sat down once to take a look at the dots and strands. But soon after I gave it up again. They were hardly perceivable, too cloudy, vague and too dark. And on top of all, I was hardly able to hold them in suspension. They were pulled down by the attractive force so strongly that they immediately disappeared out of my field of vision.

All the time I stayed at Nestor's place I tried to evade him as much as possible. I didn't want to admit to him my urges and cravings, and I also didn't want him too feel repelled, either, so I tried to be as polite as possible and not ignore him when he was around but at least answer his questions briefly. But even that was hard for me to keep up for longer time because what I really wanted was to retreat and have my peace of mind.

A second confrontation between us arose out of a bagatelle. Once when our eyes met during dinner, I saw how Nestor wiggled his ears – something he did now and then. I always interpreted this gesture as a perfidious way to attract attention without saying anything directly. But at that moment his ear wiggling didn't only provoke me – I was outright pissed.

I blew up in his face why he had to wiggle his ears instead of telling me directly what he wanted from me. He looked at me surprised, then he grinned.

»You're taking things too serious and personal,« he replied with a friendly but determined voice. »If I wiggle my ears, it has nothing whatsoever to do with you. I wiggle my ears because in that way I'm pulling energy up into my head. You should do the same, by the way.«

No angry comment, no rebuke, no snub. The fact that I had wronged him once again made me feel miserable. I felt like wanting to leave, to leave Nestor and never return. Because I felt that I wasn't worth being together with a person like him – a person who was able to exert that much self-control and show that much understanding. I had a real hard time suppressing tears.

Nestor, however, didn't seem to notice or care about my state of mind. He began to explain to me why it was important to pull energy up into one's head.

»If you pull energy, that is, your sexual energy, via the spine up into your head, you're doing nothing different than to pull the water up above the fire. In this way, you're vaporizing your sexual energy and increasing your inner pressure. That's how you handle your inner Emmental Cooking Pot.«

Then he showed me how I was supposed to »vaporize« my sexual energy. It was a breathing exercise combined with tensing up certain muscles: while inhaling slowly and deeply, I was supposed to tense up the muscles of buttocks, back and head successively. The idea was that I should gradually develop an awareness in the back part of my body, from the pelvis along the spine up to the skullcap. This should enable me to »feel« the sexual energy flowing through the spine up into my head. Finally I was supposed to slowly exhale as soon as I could feel the energy under my skullcap; in this way, I would put the energy into the picture.

Nestor encouraged me to try it right away. Halfheartedly I inhaled a few times, but I had difficulties tensing up the muscles: I was lacking a sense of perception in my back and head muscles. Nestor advised me to continue my physical exercises at any rate.

»When the awareness in your body increases,« he explained, »then you'll learn to perceive and feel new muscles sooner or later – that also applies to the back muscles and those you use to wiggle your ears.«

My failure was pressing me so much that I admitted to Nestor in a kind of self-pitiful way how bad and powerless I felt, and how difficult and senseless all these exercises seemed to me. And how much I was fed up with retreating like a snail into its shell as soon as things turned out to be little more difficult.

This comparison made him laugh. »Well,« he said empathetically, »it's not so ...«

»Bad?« I interrupted him.

»... slimy as in the case of a snail,« he ended his sentence.

His humor made me cheer up. All of a sudden, things didn't look as dull and hopeless as they used to a little while ago. It was a state of mind, some mood that would pass by again. Now I almost felt a little stupid, having told him all these things.

At that moment a shiver went over my body, and for a brief moment it turned into an almost imperceptible trembling. Nestor certainly hadn't escaped that, as attentive and sensitive as he was when observing the picture.

»Your body has opened up a little so as to put energy into the picture as a whole,« he interpreted the trembling in my body. »But in your current condition this is hardly possible. Your energy level is pretty low right now; the Emmental Cooking Pot has drained most of it. The pressure in the picture is stronger than the counterpressure within you. If your body now opens up a little, you're lacking energy in order to balance out the relative strength between you and the picture. The tremble means that your body is mustering up additional energy.

What's more, the energy at your disposal cannot flow. It is stagnating in your body. That's why you're also forced to experience it in the form of negative feelings – as fear, aggression and self-pity. If you had enough energy and were able to make it flow, you neither had to be emotional nor feel a tremble in your body – then you would have felt a tickle or prickle, a feeling of relaxation and satisfaction.«

Nestor said that the picture, at this time, must look rather dull and colorless to me so that I was probably missing the verve to do anything at all. He was completely familiar with my poor condition and described to me my unbearable feelings: being stuck in a swamp of resentment and self-pity and being perfectly aware of that situation but unable to do anything about it.

»You're lacking the energy you should put into the picture as a whole to find joy and pleasure in your environment,« he said. »A human being gradually slips into such a condition when he wastes his energy in those little pleasures and amusements. But one can free oneself from such a condition if one builds up the inner pressure and gets the energy to flow. We draw the energy and the willpower it needs for that from a correct and appropriate lifestyle, for the most part from pulling up and ›vaporizing‹ our sexual energy. Then you'll be able to put your energy into the picture as a whole. The picture in turn will become more beautiful and colorful to you, and you'll be able to perceive the dots and strands more and more clearly. Finally the moment will come when you recognize that these dots and strands are actually the shining structure of your own consciousness that forms the world around here.«

The Layers of Consciousness

On the same evening I returned to Bern, but my hopes to leave behind, just like the Emmental, my state of powerlessness and irritation didn't come true. It took another two days and nights before I started to perceive my surroundings as I used to.

At first, I tended to lump together my recent experiences with previous ones, when the emotional body was more awake and at a higher energy level. On closer inspection, however, I could observe that these were two fundamentally different states of being: when my daily consciousness, as Nestor called it, shifted into the emotional world, I didn't feel tired or slack at all like in the past few days. I perceived the world much more intensely than in my usual state – so intense that I sometimes could hardly bear it. I wasn't irritable or resentful and did not experience any negative feelings, except the anxiety for my body that sometimes showed up when my heart rate was close to breaking all speed records. In states like that I had the feeling to lose the ground under my feet.

The experiences of the past few days, however, made me feel as if glued to the ground, powerless, lethargic. I was lacking any sense of handling situations that demanded more than just habitual actions and reactions. Consequently, I withdrew into my »shell« as much as possible, keeping life around me at bay. But the demands of daily life prevented me from constantly keeping up my role play, reduced to mere mechanics. Some small frictions or criticism were enough to make me feel inferior or react with unusual and unreasonable aggressiveness. When I considered those recent events, I didn't seem to make any headway, either: my thoughts were always circling around the same thing – who or what could I blame for the pitiful and undeserved condition I was in?

With these different extraordinary states of consciousness, Nestor made me experience firsthand that the way we, as human beings, usually recognize our picture, that is, our small world, is but a small portion on a wide scale of perception. Perhaps, I pondered now, it was indeed possible for man to advance in one or the other direction and develop his consciousness. In this context, the perfect restoration appeared in a new light: as a method to develop one's own consciousness in the direction of higher states of intensity, with the inner pressure being higher and the person being more open and creative. After I had experienced that it was much more difficult to perceive the dots and strands in a state of powerlessness, frustration and self-pity, I seriously considered the possibility that the appearance of *mouches volantes* was actually related to this specific development.

Until fall of that year, I didn't take any further trips into the Emmental for several reasons, but I continued the exercises of the perfect restoration, in particular seeing the dots and strands. In the process, I could ascertain that I had to do with the same dots and strands each time I practiced the exercise. Most strands did indeed change their form, and the dots their position, with each eye movement – but those were, by comparison, small movements and shifts. In relation to each other, the dots and strands had more or less their firm position in this structure. This went so far that some of the strands at the periphery of my field of vision that I had to fling to the upper left with vigorous eye movements in order to be able to see them, were immediately pulled back down to the lower right – instead of following the laws of physics, that is, describing a left-hand curve and eventually disappearing out of the field of vision on the left. In the same way, there were strands that I flung up from the left side to the upper right, only to have them disappear at once in the lower left-hand region of my field of vision again. It seemed as if these strands were attached to a sort of rubber band that had an additional effect on top of the attractive force, pulling the strands back to their original position.

This observation suggested that *mouches volantes* were not free-floating particles in the vitreous; rather, they had to be movable objects that were attached to something, possibly to the retina in the back. Many strands were limited to my field of vision, though, so that their connection to the retina that I assumed remained invisible. A second conceivable explanation for the relatively firm arrangement of the dots and strands was that they were embedded into the jelly-like mass of the vitreous; its viscosity would change their constellation only marginally and not permanently. This explanation, however, didn't conform to the fact that *mouches volantes* did not glide sluggishly across the field of vision but rather very fast and easily.

In any case, what I could establish was that the structure was movable on the one hand, visible with each eye movement when the dots and strands flowed down by themselves. But on the other hand, the structure had a somewhat firm arrangement as well, because no matter how vigorous my eye movements were – I wasn't able to change the arrangement of the dots and strands completely and permanently. Thus I became acquainted with my eye floaters in two ways: by their forms and by their constellations.

I also realized for the first time that the dots and strands I could see were partially floating in the left eye and partially in the right. This was clearly perceivable to me whenever I closed one or the other eye – even though it sometimes happened, particularly in very bright light conditions, that I could see dots and strands through the closed eyelid. To me, no further explanation was needed for this phenomenon: obviously, *mouches volantes* had formed both in the right and left eye.

In the following fall Nestor and I discussed this left/right separation. And it quickly turned out that he attached special significance to this fact that was fundamental in order to understand the perfect restoration: Nestor mentioned two »halves of consciousness« that we could perceive in our seeing.

»You have dots and strands in the *left* as well as in the *right half of consciousness*,« he explained on this occasion. »In the beginning you can only find out which of these dots and strands belong to which half by closing one or the other eye in turn. But if you get to know your dots and strands better over time, you'll be able to see directly whether they are part of the left or the right half of consciousness.«

I couldn't refrain from asking whether it was simply a matter of different dots and strands in the left and in the right eye. Nestor replied that this addressed the same basic question again, that is, whether I traced back the origin of life to matter or to consciousness.

»Those who want to see the material aspect of the world will certainly find matter to look at,« he pointed out. »Those who are consistently seeking consciousness, on the other hand, will certainly find consciousness to behold. You'll have to make a decision and live by it.«

Nestor often argued in this way. Meanwhile, I agreed with him that we basically had it in our own hands to adopt one or the other of these worldviews and live accordingly. He seemed to neglect the fact, however, that we had been influenced strongly by our social surroundings; therefore, changing our view of the world wasn't as easy as simply changing clothes.

»To you, the world is predominantly material because you've learned, just like everyone else, to perceive the world in that way, and because you still constantly learn that even today. You're anchored so deeply in this view that it is hard for you to strip yourself from it,« he admitted in response to my objections. »But you're also underestimating human willpower. If a human being arrives at a point where he does no longer want anything else than to completely understand what he's looking at – then he'll become able to change his worldview from one second to the other.

This is also what the seers have done. They have adopted a view of the world enabling them to unmask their character resulting from social influences as ›small world‹. If circumstances are favorable, changing that view can take place quite rapidly and spontaneously, but the subsequent work that needs to be done, dissolving one's own small world, is a process that takes years or even decades. In the end, this process results in the ability to see the picture as it is – and in order to describe this, the word *consciousness* fits best in this day and age. That's why I say that the dots and strands a person sees are his own consciousness, and that this structure of consciousness consists of two halves – a left and a right half of consciousness.«

Nestor addressed the subject of these halves of consciousness again. He instructed me to specifically practice perceiving them in my basic structure. I was supposed to become aware of both halves by acquainting myself with my dots and strands so well that I could tell what half they belonged to. Then I was supposed to put my attention on the left and on the right half of consciousness alternately.

»These two sides are of utmost importance,« Nestor went on. »We always recognize and experience these two sides that complement each other to a large degree on the outer screen as well: the human body, for example, consists of these two sides; as such, we have two eyes, two ears, two brain hemispheres – it seems nature takes much pleasure in symmetry anyway. Have you ever asked yourself why that is the case?«

»The seer knows the answer for sure,« I was convinced.

»The seer *sees* the answer,« Nestor corrected me. »Symmetries are predominant in our life because there are these two sides in the basic structure. The structure is the ›base frame‹, so to speak, of the picture, and so there are these two sides in every manifestation within the picture.

On the outer screen, however, we can observe that there are no absolute symmetries,« he went on. »We can recognize that most easily by looking at our own body: it is almost symmetric, but not quite. One half is always dominating; it's stronger, more sensitive, movable or whatever. The fact that there are asymmetries in turn originates from the halves of consciousness: one or the other half is dominating there as well. The seers now hold that a person belongs to the side dominating within him, that is, either the left or the right half of consciousness.«

I asked Nestor what it means to belong to the left or right half of consciousness. His answer was that right-sided people were not seers but ordinary people with the joys and woes of their small world. They didn't have the chance to overcome duality and see the picture as a whole.

»People anchored in the left side of their consciousness, by comparison, have lived through the right side to a point where they have overcome it. They have become seers, and all their actions aim at revealing the structure of consciousness and moving beyond duality. Therefore, the development of consciousness is a path leading from the right towards and into the left side of consciousness. You can find out what side you belong to by inspecting your own seeing.«

»How am I supposed to do that?«

»Take a look at your dots and strands. Those on the left side differ from those on the right. One side is dominating – analogous to our own consciousness.«

»What do you mean with ›dominating‹?«

Nestor put up a broad smile. »Look for yourself.«

The next two days I mostly spent with finding out which one of my halves was »dominating«. As best as I could, I compared the dots and strands in my left eye with those in my right. Of course I couldn't do this totally unbiased: on the one hand and according to Nestor's words, I had to belong to the right side of consciousness as I was a non-seer; on the other hand, I caught myself several times looking for something dominating in the dots of my left eye that was supposed to belong to the more desirable half. But I couldn't find any attributes that could have applied specifically to one or the other side: in both the right and left eye I had dots and strands, larger and smaller ones, that I perceived more or less sharply focused. My conclusion was that each dot and strand was somewhat individual, and that it didn't make any sense to talk about differences or similarities with respect to *mouches volantes* on either side.

On the last evening before I returned to Bern I informed Nestor of my observations. To him it was clear that I hadn't paid enough attention while looking at my dots and strands; otherwise I would have been able to tell the difference. Undoubtedly I was fixated in the right half of consciousness, just like all those people who were not seers. But then he admitted that the difference between the right and left half of consciousness, as regards seeing, would become the more visible the farther I advanced on the path within my basic structure.

The phrase »within my basic structure« made me sit up and listen to him attentively. Now and then, Nestor talked about a »path in the basic structure« – something I had always interpreted figuratively, simply as a synonym for the progress in the development of consciousness. But the variation with the word »within« sounded as if this path had to be understood as an actual advancement in the structure itself. I asked Nestor about this point, and he confirmed this. With further progress, the person practicing the exercises could observe for himself that he covered a certain distance within this structure.

»But that sounds absurd. If that were the case, the dots and strands would have to come closer and become larger when I move through the basic structure,« I concluded surprised.

»Now what a smart ass you are!« Nestor unexpectedly called out, and we both had to laugh. But eventually he confirmed my conclusion by letting me know that it wasn't enough to just understand this with the rational mind; rather, I had to be able to see it in my structure.

»So the dots and strands can really come closer and become larger?«

»That's what a seer can see.«

»But with some people the floaters also go down and degenerate,« I objected.

»Then these people do nothing for their consciousness as they obviously take the reverse path in the basic structure,« he replied dismissively. »If you only run after matter and pleasure and tie down your energy in this idiotic way, you'll move away farther and farther from the dots and strands until you can't see them any longer. If you, on the other hand, live an appropriate lifestyle and transform the energy still tied up within you, then you'll move forward on the path in the basic structure. So within the structure there is indeed a forward and backward, but there is only one single goal which is wherever we look to. Consequently, on the path in the basic structure we cannot turn around; we can only come closer to the goal or drift farther away from it. If we come closer to the goal, the dots will increase in size – so much that what we'll see are not dots and strands any longer but large spheres and tubes.«

»And how is that supposed to work out?« I asked skeptically. »After all, I can't just walk up to them.«

»Yes, you can,« Nestor answered. »Not with your body, but in your consciousness.« Nestor noticed my questioning look and added that this was not something easily understood; he still wanted to explain to me what I will experience through my own seeing.

»If you look at your dots and strands you'll recognize that some appear larger than the others. But in truth this means that the former are closer to you and the latter farther away. So the dots and strands are located in a space, that is, in different *layers* in this space.«

»Layers? What kind of layers?«

Nestor pondered over the answer for some time. Then he replied that he couldn't say more than that we projected our picture, both the inner and outer screen, onto an infinite number of layers for countless numbers of times. But in order to perceive them at all, a human being had to have a very high level of consciousness, that is, to put a large amount of transformed energy into the picture as a whole. Because only in this way the true nature of the picture would reveal itself to him.

He went on to explain that seers penetrated these layers in their consciousness. Ultimately it was this penetration of layers causing a significant effect in the act of seeing: the effect of dots and strands coming closer by leaps and bounds.

Nestor looked at me and waited. I remained silent. Once again he had steered me into unknown waters where I could neither reasonably endorse him nor dissent from him. He pointed towards my teacup and said:

»For you, this cup is always at the same distance from you. You could sit here for a lifetime and stare at this cup – it would always appear to be at the same distance from you. That's the case because your consciousness is very *stable* within a certain layer. This stability is something enforced on everyone of us – through education, impartment of values, viewpoints and ways of thinking. Thanks to this stability, we are perceiving all objects in the picture always at the same distance. And that's why we always see the same section of the structure as well, with the dots and strands more or less always in the same positions and with the same size.«

I was glad that I finally had found a point where I could enter into our conversation, and I pointed out to Nestor that the objects in the picture did not always have the same distance, that one could overcome the spatial distance in the material world – in contrast to the dots and strands.

»If I walked up to this cup here or if I pulled it towards me,« I argued, »then I reduce the distance to it, after all.« I took the cup and held it closely in front of my head to demonstrate to Nestor how I had reduced the distance between me and the cup.

He laughed. »Well yes, all right, you're reducing the distance in the sensual material world. But in order to do so, you had to invest physical energy, that is, you had to move your body. This is the only possibility for people who are not seers to come closer to an object. But you're not really closer, and I mean closer in your consciousness, to the cup. Because you're always projecting it onto the same layer in which you are stable. And because you can only light up this one layer of consciousness with your energy, you see the cup and even the entire small world only once – although they basically exist countless of times, that is, on each of these innumerable layers.«

Nestor paused for a moment, perhaps to give me some time to understand what he had said. I felt slightly annoyed because I wasn't really able to follow him.

»Now imagine,« he started another attempt, »the space between you and the cup consists of an infinite number of layers. If you pull the cup towards you, this doesn't mean that you're penetrating these layers; you're merely squeezing them together, you're compressing them. Even if you press the cup against your forehead – there is still the same number of layers in between them. That's why I say that you cannot come closer to the cup in your consciousness if you invest physical energy.«

Nestor took a sip of tea. »Man's nature is such that he naturally wants to unite with what he sees. Infants take everything into their mouth and want to unite with that. Adult persons are looking for partners they can unite with. Many people are eating too much: they're living the urge to unite with something via the food they ingest. People join together to groups, clubs, political parties – that's also an expression of the human desire for unity.

As a seer, however, I know that an amalgamation, that is, becoming one with the object of desire, the coveted person or group, is not possible. Because no matter how close we can come to that which we desire, we'll never be able to cover the distance completely and lastingly – not as long as we haven't penetrated the layers in the basic structure.«

After another longer pause Nestor went on: »Walking the path within the basic structure means to suspend our stability keeping us within a certain layer, and to penetrate the layers of consciousness,« he added. »We're penetrating the layers and approach our spheres and strands. As these are the cause of the small world, though, we are also coming closer to the material objects in our picture.«

»Where did you pick up all that knowledge, Nestor?« I asked, impressed by his attainments.

»I know that because I can see it.«

»You can see that the objects around you come closer?«

»Yes. The contents of the picture come closer and become more intense when I put my energy into the picture as a whole. One day everything around me will be so close that the inner and outer screen become one, and then I'll be able to enter into the picture, into the picture as a whole. That's the destination of the path in the basic structure.«

I didn't say anything. On the one hand, I just couldn't accept what Nestor said. The mystic unification he associated with *mouches volantes* here was perhaps the consequence of the uncommonly high regard he expressed for these dots and strands, but to me it was too far away from reality, at least the reality I was familiar with. On the other hand, I didn't want to object against Nestor because he had convinced me that he firmly believed in the possibility of entering into the picture via *mouches volantes*, and that this was his highest goal he was striving for with all his heart.

»You don't believe what I'm telling you, do you?« he correctly pointed out the reason for my silence. I confirmed this and added that I, after all, could neither see these things, nor had I ever heard or read about them.

He repeated that he had learned to put the largest portion of his transformed energy into the structure and thus into the picture as a whole. In this way he had succeeded to suspend his stability in one layer, and to be able to move freely through all layers.

»You, on the other hand, have learned to use the largest portion of your energy for keeping up your small world,« he went on. »In the process, you're stabilizing and preserving yourself within one single layer of consciousness. But that's idiotic. For you, there is only the possibility to retrain yourself and to put your energy into the basic structure. And this is something you're also doing when you sit down and take a focused look at these dots and strands.«

I didn't like his tone of voice. His claim that I didn't have another choice than to retrain myself and learn this had something repelling to me and caused me to build up resistance. His possessive character and the arrogance he displayed were simply disgusting. I told him that I was not his student, and that I could think of other things happening in my life than to enter into the picture by all means and at all costs.

»My young friend,« he replied calmly but with a certain emphasis, »what you are calling ›your life‹ is nothing more or less than a tremendous effort to keep the contents in your picture at a distance. If you were to refrain from exerting that effort only for a moment, you'd be able to take a clear look at what this world really is – if you were able to cope with the mind-boggling consequences arising from that.«

Before I left for Bern on the next morning, Nestor mentioned the layers of consciousness once more. He repeated that I still was too stable in my specific layer of consciousness, and this prevented the release of my *fixation* within the right side and the move over to the left side of consciousness. This didn't mean, however, that I was completely immobile and a change from one layer to another impossible; gradually advancing on the path in the basic structure would already lead me to moving forward from layer to layer – it was just that this happened so slowly and in so small leaps that I couldn't become aware of it at all.

»Seers, by comparison, are not fixated in the right half of consciousness any longer. There are so movable that they can, by taking big leaps, consciously move into higher, more intense layers of consciousness in order to perceive the picture in its foundation. But you have to find out for yourself that moves or changes of that nature are possible. Only in this way can you get a vague idea of the scope of seeing the basic structure.«

Nestor's talk about suspending stability and changing between layers of consciousness had something very disturbing to me – the more so as I still had a very vivid recollection of the experience with the Emmental Cooking Pot.

»But haven't I already experienced a change between layers of consciousness when I worked on Mari Egli's secretaire? Or when I was dancing? Or in the Emmental Cooking Pot?«

»Not completely. Indeed, you had managed to partially suspend the stability in one specific layer of consciousness. But with your light of consciousness you were not able to light up a new layer completely – otherwise you would have perceived the contents in the picture as larger and more intensive. But because you were neither able to be fully conscious in the old layer nor in a new one, you were missing the clarity and unambiguousness of the picture. That's why you were susceptible to strong emotions and perceptions with no direct relationship to the outer screen.

Still these situations would have been favorable for a complete change. Because changes of that sort always take place under circumstances in which people are in a more intensive state of being, in which they therefore have an increased flow of energy at their disposal. There's also people who don't consciously walk the path in the basic structure, and yet they sometimes experience a jump from one of their layers of consciousness to another – triggered by sudden, unexpected but drastic and far-reaching events.«

»Then it should follow that these people must see their dots and strands larger and more closely?« I concluded.

»Precisely not,« he answered. »Normal people cannot put any additional energy into the picture as a whole and use it for seeing. In their case, these changes remain just as incomplete, and they express themselves just as strongly in the form of emotional outbreaks, anxiety conditions, depressive states, hysteria or even euphoria, partially accompanied by so-called hallucinations and visions. And when too much energy is flowing, they pass out. That is so because they haven't practiced to handle the inner pressure, to get their energy to flow and thus to open up the body.

In the case of a seer, on the other hand, these changes between layers of consciousness are complete, deliberate and thus controlled,« Nestor went on. »He's able to put the released energy directly into the basic structure instead of having to let it out through emotions and actions. In this way, the seer's perception comes about that the dots and strands become larger by sudden leaps.«

I asked him how a seer was able to bring about a change from one layer of consciousness to another. The change as such, according to Nestor, was not brought about willfully. But the seers always chose their activities in such a way that a change was possible time and again. Two things were needed for this: a favorable situation with increased energy flow, and the ability of the body to cope with that increased flow, that is, to be open enough.

»The time around full moon, for example, is favorable for this purpose,« he explained. »The more the moon is waxing, the higher he's pulling the water, to wit, the sexual energy in the body of a person. Therefore, in those two weeks from new moon to full moon, the inner pressure within you is steadily increasing until it reaches its climax on the day of full moon.«

For a while, Nestor kept talking about the peculiarities of full moon, but I only listened to him in part. In my opinion, he overestimated the alleged strength of the moon. These professed effects on man and beast were pure hogwash, at least from my own experiences.

»In three days we'll have another full moon,« he suddenly said after we had remained silent for some time. »You should be here then. Perhaps you can then experience what it means to change directly and with full awareness from one layer of consciousness to another more intense one.«

»What are you up to?« I asked him, slightly faint-hearted.

»I can't tell you right now what will happen in detail. It's just that all circumstances must come together in a favorable way. Then it can happen that you'll be able to light up a new layer of consciousness with the energy released by these circumstances.«

»Well, I've been out in full moon nights before without having experienced something like a change between layers of consciousness,« I objected. »Why should the circumstances be favorable particularly during the next full moon?«

»Because a seer is ›staging‹ the event,« was his mysterious reply.

On the next full moon – it was a Wednesday – I drove up the Emmental with mixed feelings. My pride forbid me to back down and cop out; I had to show Nestor that I was able to stand up to that challenge – whatever it might be. On the other hand, the thought of what could be in store for me caused such an anxiety within me that I occasionally felt a nervous trembling all over my body. At any rate, I wanted to take painstaking care of watching closely for anything extraordinary so that I would be well prepared.

When I arrived at Nestor's place and entered the house, I first of all wanted to ask him some questions about the upcoming event. Nestor, however, already called out from the living room that I shouldn't leave the door open by no means. Startled by the urgency in his voice, I closed the door behind me right away. Nestor was busy, as I could see, catching flies in his living room with his bare hands and throwing them out the window.

I watched him for a while; he was very adept at this, and I was amazed about his fast and precise movements. Once he had caught a fly with one hand, he caught a second with the other one – sometimes even two or three in one fell swoop when they had placed themselves closely together. He caught the flies in all possible and impossible places: at the ceiling, on the walls, even on objects.

I commented on his skillfulness, and he explained that it needed both patience and swiftness at the right moment to be successful. He took this as an opportunity to encourage me to also learn to catch flies and thereby develop these qualities.

»Patience and swiftness at the right moment,« he went on, »that's also what a person needs in order to walk the path of the basic structure. It is nothing other than to practice deeper relaxation and higher concentration. The more adept you are at catching flies, the more you will succeed to hold the dots and strands in suspension,« he claimed.

Then Nestor instructed me to catch the remaining flies so as to practice patience and swiftness right away. He sat down in front of the house, leaving me with those flies and my doubts whether there actually were serious parallels between catching flies and holding eye floaters in suspension.

After several attempts I gave up. I was lacking a certain sense of touch in my hands; even if I was fast enough to catch a fly, I just squashed it. Nestor later commented on this and pointed out that I was thinking too much where I should simply be acting; according to him, this was also the reason for my inability to keep the dots and strands in suspension.

The remainder of the afternoon I spent with watching Nestor as closely as possible. I had to find out what he was doing; perhaps he was preparing something for the »favorable circumstances«. But nothing whatsoever that he did seemed extraordinary or different from what he usually did – and that wasn't very much: he cultivated some herbs or mushrooms, did household chores, chopped wood and fired the oven. Then he took care of the cat which was prowling around the house. And in between he sat down in front of the house time and again, staring into the sky.

Once he went into the forest – nothing unusual, either, but immediately alarming to me in the face of his announcements of what was to come around full moon. When he had returned I tried to find out what he had done out there, whether he had prepared the anticipated major event.

My thoughts seemed to make Nestor wonder. To my surprise he replied that, as far as he was concerned, everything was already set up and ready to go – he was just waiting for me all that time.

»What do you mean?« I asked.

»Well, today is full moon,« he pointed out. »This can help you in changing between layers of consciousness. I myself will stage the circumstances. That'll help you as well. What else do you need? Everything else is up to you and your body being open.«

»But what exactly is it that you have ›staged‹?«

»You don't need to worry about that right now,« he answered and smiled mischievously.

»And what am I supposed to do?«

»I can't really tell you what you're supposed to do – only that you should do it.«

The situation seemed to amuse Nestor. I myself was in despair. I had no clue what he expected of me and urged him to give me some kind of a hint. Nestor only laughed and puzzled about whether it was the full moon or his staging that already caused a certain effect here. But when I insisted on an answer he advised me to catch the remaining flies in his living room.

It was late afternoon when the steady »meow« of the cat yanked me out of my aimless musing and pondering. It sat in the kitchen and demanded food in an unabashed way. I got up and wanted to cook some potatoes and carrots for Nestor, me and the cat, but then I saw that Nestor's reserves were running low – it wasn't enough anymore for a full meal for all of us. I informed Nestor of our lack of supplies, and he suggested to go down to the village store and buy some food for the next days.

Usually Nestor only went to shop for food when there was nothing edible whatsoever around in his kitchen anymore. But here as well I believed to expose his »staging of circumstances«.

»Will the shopping tour cause me to change between layers of consciousness?« I asked him anxiously.

»Well, at least it'll cause you not to go to bed hungry,« he replied sharply. It seemed as if he was fed up with my nervousness. But then he admitted that, given the right circumstances and prerequisites, a change between layers of consciousness could happen virtually anywhere.

When we went down into the village we had the chance to witness the last part of a festive and ceremonial driving down of cattle from the mountain pastures into the valley. Oversized cowbells and girdles of flowers were adorning oversized cows. They were driven forward by farmers, dressed in traditional costumes, with sticks and *hoihoi* screams. Suddenly one of the cows broke out of the line and walked over to the pasture next to the street. Soon other cows followed it, and before long, nearly a dozen of the unhurried animals took joy in the lush pasture grass.

»*Heiland Tonnerwätter!*[13]« With curses, beatings and supported by his barking dog, a young farmer tried to drive the cows back onto the street, but it took him quite some time and effort.

»A little stress will certainly yield good meat,« Nestor ironically commented the scene while we were walking by; it was a perfect example that he immediately capitalized on to strengthen his position as vegetarian. »Here you can see for yourself that man is ultimately eating up his own aggressiveness.«

»There are also farmers treating their livestock with care and appropriate to the species,« I argued.

»Of course,« he replied without having lost his bitchiness. »And in the end a bolt is shot through the animal's brain – with care and appropriate to the species.« Nestor then repeated that it was about time for man to stop his consumption of meat wherever possible. With that we could do a lot for our consciousness and our physical well-being.

In the shop we bought everything needed for the next few days. On one of the shelves I discovered small plastic cans with the label:

Vliegenvanger
Gifvrij en geurloos[14]

I showed Nestor the Dutch flycatchers and offered him to buy some of these cans with which we could solve the problem with the flies in Nestor's living room.

»*Vliegenvanger*,« he read and lifted his eyebrows in surprise. Then he laughed and said that it was typical for me to solve problems preferably the comfortable way. He said that I had to catch the *Vliegen* I encountered on the path in the basic structure under my own steam. But when we had paid and stepped out of the shop, he sighed and said that he didn't even want to think of all those *Vliegen* that meanwhile might have accumulated in his living room.

Nestor's displeasure evoked a kind of malicious joy within me: after all, hadn't I offered him my help? And hadn't he turned it down a little prematurely? But the moment I noticed that malicious joy within me I

---

[13] Swiss German term for *gosh darn it!*
[14] Dutch for *fly catcher – non-toxic and odorless.*

228

immediately tried to release myself from it by declaring my solidarity with Nestor. Following an intuition, I suggested to him to postpone that *Vliegenvangen* and go have a drink, first of all. Nestor agreed.

When we arrived at the inn we sat down at a heavy dark wooden table in the back; its bleak appearance couldn't even be counterbalanced by the colorful arrangement of dried Christmas spices on top of it. While we were waiting for our drinks I took a look around the interior of the inn; in all those years it was only my second visit in this place.

The large room yielded a dark and gloomy impression even though there were small windows in three of the surrounding walls. Oil lamps made of white porcelain glass were hanging from the wooden ceilings, but instead of wicks inside them, there were energy saving lamps in their place. Last year's Christmas decoration was still hanging from the ceiling beams but adorned the large room only sparsely. An older man and a young woman sat at the table next to us and were talking, as far as I could follow their conversation, about the conflict of ethnic and enforced political borders. At another table four older portly gentlemen were sitting – perhaps the same ones that I had met here once before. As usual, beer in tall glasses was served, and the smoke of the gentlemen's cigars spread throughout the entire room. They tossed their cards onto the table with just as much vigor as their arguments and opinions in favor of or against political decisions at local or federal level.

»Now it has happened again,« Nestor suddenly mumbled, after having remained silent all the time.

His words made me wide awake at once. I looked into the direction Nestor looked, but I couldn't spot anything peculiar.

»What has happened?« I asked after a while.

»The surroundings have become louder.«

»Louder? What do you mean?«

»Louder, more noisy. The noise level has suddenly risen.«

I told him that I hadn't recognized anything of the sort. He replied that he always experienced the same phenomenon: when he enters a room, the noise level within it is moderate at first. But then, when he sat down to relax, a shift of energy takes place. The energy he usually needed to move his body now flowed into the picture as a whole. And the moment that happened, the noise level around him increased manifold, the people were more cheerful, laughed more, sometimes almost screaming and yelling.

I tried to tolerate Nestor's assertion as a purely subjective, probably also volitional, sensation. But he insisted that the loudness had increased clearly perceivable, comparable with turning up the volume of a stereo.

»Uh come on, if that were true you would have told me that already a long time ago,« I anxiously tried to get him to give in.

»I haven't told you that until now because now the circumstances are fitting,« he explained. »For a seer this is reality. The fact that what I say is actually the case is again associated with the layers of consciousness: most people cannot perceive that their surroundings become louder when they sit down and relax. That is so because they are situated too stably in a certain layer. So if they want to relax after an activity, they cannot put their energy directly into the picture and change layers of consciousness in the process; rather, they are forced to fidget and wiggle around, to constantly move their feet or hands. And even if they were able to sit still at some point, their feelings and thoughts would intensify.«

We interrupted our conversation when the drinks were served.

»When I say that ordinary people are situated too stably in their layer of consciousness so that they are not able to put their energy into the picture as a whole,« Nestor went on, »this does not apply to a seer. Due to his increased flow of energy, a seer is able to suspend the stability in his layer of consciousness and to penetrate several other layers.«

»And a seer simply does that by entering a room and sitting down?«

»Not by sitting down but by regulating his flow of energy with his expanded abilities of *concentration* and *relaxation*. In other words: depending on his activities, he changes his flow of energy and thus the picture surrounding him.

To ordinary people, the picture always looks the same, no matter if they concentrate or relax. If a seer concentrates, he draws very much energy from the picture; he makes its contents small and keeps them at a distance. This is what he can see directly. When it comes to relaxation, the opposite takes place: the flow of energy into the picture is increased, and in the course of that it becomes more intense – louder, for example.«

Nestor fell silent. His words somewhat made sense to me, but at the same time I defended myself against his explanations. It was precisely this knowledge, reaching beyond scientific findings, that fascinated me, but time and again I felt as if I had to oppose it. And the notion of this dilemma crossed my mind now with might and main: what Nestor was talking about was surprising and amazing, and I felt the urge to find out if he was right. The catch was only that I had to believe in Nestor and his teachings; I had to have almost implicit trust in advance in what he said so that I could practice, act and live accordingly without restrictions. The legitimacy of that trust, however, was something I constantly challenged, particularly when I was afraid that it could not only bridge outstanding experiences and missing insights but a lack of reason as well. To me, the perfect restoration had turned into a tightrope walk.

I tried to distract myself. The people at the table next to us had paid and left the inn. The four elderly gentlemen still tossed their cards onto the table. The radio presented evening traffic jam information. But the noise level remained unchanged. Obviously, circumstances had mixed up the persons: instead of me experiencing a change in between layers of consciousness, Nestor made that experience.

Somewhat bored, I was walking to the restrooms. In the hallway four strange ink drawings in wooden frames were hanging on the wall. It struck me that the pictures were not positioned side by side but one upon the other, with each upper drawing shifted slightly to the left, compared to the respective lower one. As the only decoration on the long and empty wall, the drawings yielded a somewhat »lost« impression.

All of them were drawn in the same style but covered different topics with no obvious interrelationship. At first glance they seemed to be realistic motives of some sort, but they were somehow disturbed in their harmony by a foreign, at times even eerie element.

The uppermost drawing showed a woman and a man on a mountain peak, facing each other. It wasn't clearly visible whether they were dancing or fighting. The woman had a fine face and bright hair flowing down the entire length of her back. It seemed strange, though, that she was dressed in the outfit of hunters, equipped with boots, horn, hat and shotgun. The bearded man had a hood on top of his head and was wearing a long dark robe with a shoulder scarf – the typical clothing of nuns. The full moon in the drawing – so large that it almost inscribed the two dancing or fighting figures – seemed to cover the woman, even if only transparent; the man, by comparison, clearly stood in front of the luminous disk.

The picture below showed a section of a rock face. At first, I couldn't recognize anything peculiar, but when I took a step back, I noticed that the artist had drawn the crevices and shades of this rock face in such a way that four human faces appeared in it. They were connected with each other in the shape of a cross by vortices that proceeded from the eyes.

In the third drawing, two motives stood out clearly: a kind of double arched bridge without supporting pillar leading over a narrow canyon, and a human being shown in profile jumping from the bridge over to the left side, with both feet in the air. The person jumping expressed confidence and didn't seem to be disturbed by the fact that the bridge ultimately couldn't be passed – that is, the connecting part between the left end of the bridge and the embankment was missing. Another strange aspect was that the two arches of the bridge imparted the impression of two ocean bays as if seen from an aerial perspective.

The bottommost drawing was both the most lively and surreal one. It showed a dairy farmer in an awkward situation: he stood in a ground hole up to his chest and tried to free himself out of it. Four little mythical creatures were bothering him below the earth's surface: the bottommost creature was a demon with glasses and a stick who was heartily biting the farmer in his buttocks. The second creature, a mischievously grinning goblin with large sharp teeth, ripped parts of the abdomen out of the farmer's body. In the farmer's stomach, a young dwarf lady smiled friendly and joyfully ate away the half-digested food. And on top a child, equipped with fork and knife, cut away a part of his heart.

I was still all absorbed into the drawings to discover more hidden details when suddenly someone opened the door to the restroom. As if yanked out of a dream by the unexpected sound, I turned away from the pictures and wanted to do my business now. I noticed a young woman leaving the ladies' restroom at the end of the hallway – the same woman that had served Indian spice tea at the techno trance party and had talked to Nestor and me. I hadn't expected at all to meet her here again, and I immediately stopped in my tracks. The red-haired, cat-eyed woman came strolling up to me.

»Do you like them?« she asked me.

»Do I like what?« I asked, slightly irritated by her straightforwardness.

She was casually leaning against the wall, and with a slight nod of her head she was pointing towards the four drawings. With an apologizing tone of voice I explained that I couldn't judge the artistic quality of those pictures as I had never studied the fine arts. She smiled, and with her smile all of her beauty and sympathy was blooming. I didn't want to yield the impression that I stared at her and evaded her look.

»Still you've taken a look at them,« she pointed out. I was a little abashed and searching for words, but I could only nod confirmatively. What struck me was the soft sound of her voice: she was talking understandably and with confidence but not loudly. I tried to guess her age – she must have been around thirty years.

She looked me over – for a moment that seemed like eternity to me. »Weren't you out at the Goa Open Air Festival with Nestor last year?« she remembered.

I confirmed this but couldn't really take joy in her inquiry: yes, she had remembered me – but obviously only as Nestor's companionship. I recalled situations in the past when I assumed different, often contradictory, roles towards different people. Embarrassment was guaranteed, however, when the people that I wanted to keep away from each other came together unexpectedly. In the same way, the role I would have liked to play towards this attractive woman stood in stark conflict with the one I assumed, both intentional and unintentional, towards Nestor: on the one hand, someone who liked to pose as an experienced, independent and self-confident person; on the other hand, the apprentice that had to cautiously inch his way forward through unknown territory under the guidance of an experienced tutor because he himself was lacking experience and a sense of balance and sound judgment.

»Nestor has told me about you,« she went on. »You're visiting him regularly to restore that piece of furniture.«

»I don't know if I'll ever get done with that restoration in this lifetime,« I wisecracked. She didn't laugh but rather concurred with me that this certainly was a difficult task.

»You're so right,« I bragged. »This particular piece of furniture has been built by a very special person, and I really would like to know who it was and what he or she has done in their life.«

She claimed that a close look at an object could already shed some light and give information about the builder and that which obviously was important to him or her in their life. I objected that that kind of »information« was merely an interpretation of things. In order to really find out something about the builder, one had to proceed methodically. I described to her how I had followed up the name on the secretaire, reviewing the history of the 19th century Emmental in the course of it so as to obtain the desired answers.

Then I started to talk about Nestor and the perfect restoration. I became quite talkative and started to rave about the difficult exercises that Nestor and me practiced for the purpose of the perfect restoration. I also told her about the *mouches volantes* that were particles of our material world's basic structure. With a strict disciplined lifestyle we could develop them within ourselves, enlarge them and thus – incredible but true – recognize them as a first effect of our consciousness. With an adventurous tone of voice I implied that Nestor, I and our neighbors on the left side of the Emme were some kind of secret society, a very old mystical community striving to overcome duality and attain perfection.

»For Nestor and me«, I finally added with some slight exaggeration, »the restoration of this particular piece of furniture is the key to understanding who the builder was and how that person had striven for perfection.«

I felt exhausted. For some strange reason, my explanations had demanded an unusually high degree of concentration of me. It was as if I had to press against an overwhelming force while talking to the woman so as to be able to even address and convince her. She was still leaning against the wall; all the time she had remained silent and listened to me.

»Yeah, the restoration of Mari Egli's secretaire will certainly continue to give you an exciting and eventful time,« she answered succinctly.

Her mentioning of Mari Egli's name made me listen up at once: how did that red-haired lady know that this was the name inscribed on the secretaire? I hadn't mentioned it all the time up to now.

»Do you know from Nestor that this secretaire originally belonged to a woman called Mari Egli?«

»No,« she replied in a childlike tone of voice. »I've seen that piece of furniture myself, many times. I'm visiting Nestor now and then, you must know.«

»You're visiting him now and then?« I asked, slightly confused.

»Of course, we're neighbors. My house is just a little bit further up the hill.« She gave me a smirky smile.

The blood was rushing into my head and my heart rate picked up. All that time I had believed that she and Nestor had met at the party by coincidence, and that their acquaintance had been cursory – in other words, that the young woman didn't know anything about *mouches volantes*, seers and the perfect restoration. But Nestor had mentioned several times that the only people who could permanently live on the left side of the Emme were seers. According to that, this woman was a seer and therefore completely in the know about everything! I didn't dare remember how I had bragged about all the activities and exercises just before. As cold as ice, this redhead had lured me into a trap.

I tried to stay calm and draw the attention off of that embarrassing situation with some informal remarks. But my willpower succumbed to my body: too fast was my heart rate, too irregular my breath and thus too shaky my voice. The shame and disgrace finally caused me to drop into a blocked silence. I was searching for a clear expression in the face of the young woman, for a sign of her exhibiting her triumph and putting me back in my place. But I was searching in vain – there was no expression at all in her eyes and face. To me, this was the final proof that the redhead was a seer, a woman who could put her energy into the picture as a whole and who therefore was able to be present in the picture with her full attention, without having to make a judgment or a change. Right at this moment I felt the same insurmountable ditch between us that I had sensed between Nestor and me several times.

Then the young woman started to talk about the drawings on the wall. I was glad that she changed the subject, tried to calm down and listen to her. But soon after I could feel how my attention was waning. A kind of mental sluggishness paralyzed me so that eventually I wasn't able any longer to follow the woman's thoughts. All I could do was nod affirmatively, but I didn't really know what she was actually talking about.

This realization made my heart rate pick up again. When all my desperate attempts to find the thread of our conversation again and to concentrate on it failed, I had only one choice left – escape. I took the next pause as opportunity to hastily say goodbye and turn away from her. I didn't even give her the chance to say anything in conclusion. With lowered gaze and a fast pace I walked up to the men's restroom.

»Hey,« she called out after me when I pushed the door open. I paused in the door frame and looked over to her, mesmerized. I expected her to say something about this situation that was so uncomfortable for me.

»It's a pity that the pictures are hanging here and not in some place where more people could see them. I've talked to the owner of the inn about it, but he doesn't really seem to care.«

The woman looked at me and seemed to wait for a reaction. I didn't know what to reply.

»Those are mine,« she finally declared with a micschievous smile and pointed towards the four framed ink drawings. All I was able to say was that I really liked her drawings. Then I disappeared in the restroom.

My body was trembling. I was so hot that I felt a strong urge to go outside and cool off. To avoid a second encounter with the cat-eyed seer woman, I climbed through the window and soon after stood on the backside of the inn, hidden behind tall bushes. Meanwhile it had become dark and the air had cooled off distinctly – a blessing to me. With some gentle movements I managed to calm down my body again.

After my senses and habitual thinking had returned I sat down with my back against the house wall and tried to recapitulate what had happened. Of course, I had experienced embarrassing moments often before, but in this case the reaction of my body was clearly exaggerated – almost as if I had enforced the work on Mari Egli's secretaire. This led me to the conviction that favorable circumstances had still arisen at last, and that I had changed between the layers of consciousness.

Through the leaves of the bushes I could see the full moon, that dark yellow circular disk that had risen just before, now hovering closely above the Schrattenfluh mountain range.

Listening to the Rushing Sound

It wasn't until the next day that I was ready to tell Nestor of my experience. He outright denied having known anything about the young seer lady and her presence in the inn last night. If she had been in the inn, he pointed out, he didn't have anything to do with it. He even regretted not having met her.

With these words he rejected my allegation that he had visited the young woman during a walk through the forest in the afternoon, and that he had instructed her to »run into« me in the village. As incredible as that sounded – it was the only »staged scenario« I could imagine with respect to my changing layers of consciousness.

Nestor laughed about my assumption. »If I had known that you would release your stability in one layer of consciousness so effortlessly because of this woman, I would have certainly staged a scenario like that.«

But then he explained that a seer's *staging* didn't have anything to do with letting some people perform a play. Rather, it meant that the seer put his energy into the picture as a whole and stepped up the intensity in the picture. If circumstances were favorable, this energy caused certain effects in other people, making them act and create favorable circumstances for a change between layers of consciousness. What kind of actions and reactions these were was not something the seer could influence. Therefore, staging something was only possible under the appropriate circumstances, but then again it also created the appropriate circumstances.

»Yesterday, the existing circumstances and my staging have resulted in you inviting me to the inn and meeting that woman; these new circumstances, as well as the young woman's staging, have eventually lead you to brag and boast in front of her.« Nestor put up a broad smile and added that I had actually danced attendance on a female seer.

I defend myself against Nestor's downplaying of this encounter as an everyday experience driven by instinct. The encounter with the woman had been quite some hard work for me, I tried to explain to him. He laughed so hard that tears began to fill his eyes. Eventually I myself had to laugh as well.

»But it is that way,« I insisted when we had calmed down. »After all, I had changed in between my layers of consciousness in the process.«

Nestor made a negating gesture. »You had reduced the stability in your layer, but you hadn't changed to another one – not to mention releasing the fixation in the right side of consciousness. Otherwise you wouldn't have had to cop out through the restroom window.« The mere thought of that made him laugh again.

»But you would've had the chance to do so,« he then went on. »Circumstances and staging were nearly perfect – only your body had gone on strike. But this time it was not because you were too open and didn't have enough energy at your disposal; rather, you had quite a bit of energy but it just couldn't flow. Your body hadn't been open enough and you were blocked, unable to do or say anything reasonable. This woman surely had made you hot, but unfortunately you were not able to put the heat as energy into the picture as a whole.«

I felt quite uncomfortable about the whole subject. In an effort to change to something else, I pointed out that I was surprised about the relatively young age of the woman. Because Nestor and the other seers that I had met on the left side were at least ten, twenty or even thirty years older than her.

»There's no age limit to seeing,« Nestor answered. But then he admitted that this particular woman was an exception. She had learned from early on what it meant to fully exploit one's own chances and opportunities in life, he added. She had walked the path in the basic structure with all her heart from the very beginning, so she had developed a strong willpower and had always been consistent in her acts. And now she was a seer.

»Are there many seers here on the left side?« I asked after a longer pause. Obviously this question came as a surprise to Nestor, or it was somewhat inconvenient to him. At any rate, his answer was rather evasive.

»Well, there are some. Sometimes one of them goes for a journey, at other times new people come to settle here.«

»Sometimes seers come to this place? Just like that?«

»The seer's inner sense leads him, time and again, to places corresponding to his seeing. The headwaters of the Emme is such a place: it mirrors pretty much what a seer is seeing.«

I looked around but Nestor laughed and said that this was of course not apparent at a glance, least of all to a non-seer.

»I'd like to meet all the seers here,« I told him.

»So that you're prepared the next time you run into one?«

»So that I can learn from them,« I tried to make him believe. Nestor put up a smile and knitted his eyebrows at the same time. This was the mien with which he used to express skepticism – with good reason. Indeed it was my idea that I could avoid an embarrassing blunder like yesterday once I knew all the seers around here. Because if I knew of a person that he or she was a seer, I would behave differently towards them, compared to ordinary people – that is, more passive, reserved and cautious.

Nestor assured me that I would meet all the seers around here in due time, albeit not at once. And as if he would confide a secret to me, he added with a low voice that seers were very busy people and their time was very precious. In addition, seers were quite hard to contact at times – it could happen that one couldn't get a hold of them for weeks or even months – not even on their *cell phone*.

The somewhat sincere and serious way in which Nestor elevated seers to the rank of VIPs made me laugh. In any case, I understood that I had to wait.

It took almost a year until I finally had an encounter with another seer. Until that summer I had traveled to the Emmental only a few times because my other commitments kept me busy all winter and spring. I was visiting Nestor only in irregular intervals.

During this time, however, he didn't only urge me untiringly to keep looking at the dots and strands and train my inner sense; he also encouraged me to pick up the work on the secretaire again. Indeed I had neglected the restoration for quite some time already – the restoration that I so boastfully had called »the key to understanding the mystical teachings of the artist«. Dealing with *mouches volantes* and the teachings of the seers had made too many demands on me.

All I did for the secretaire during that time were preliminary work steps such as procuring flexible wooden leaves that I needed for the repair of the inlay work. Nestor helped me find the corresponding sorts of wood: for the dark part of the circular figures we chose walnut, for the bright part maple. For the background we took pearwood.

The inlay work was damaged in several places. According to the afterimage of the secretaire, however, only the repair of the hole on the bottom right-hand drawer, still missing its handle, came into question for me. I didn't have much hope for success, though: not only because the work on this particular hole would be very intricate and involved as it was, just like the hole on the top left-hand drawer, in a place where all three sorts of wood came together; but also because I had already failed miserably on the handle some time ago.

On one evening in summer I was in a rather bad mood because for days I just hadn't been able to insert the wooden leaf pattern in its appropriate place. Taking precise measurements already turned out to be hard work: somewhere in this demolished spot there was the right tip of the zig-zag line that ran horizontally across the entire piece of furniture. Therefore, prior to taking measurements I had to prepare a precise drawing of the spot – at which I could hardly keep my hands calm. After several attempts it turned out that I just couldn't manage to glue the individual parts of the pattern into the hole. In my clumsy attempts I damaged the wood of the leaves to be inserted or, even worse, the wood of the trimmed edge of the hole on the drawer – with the result that I had to start all over again with taking measures and cutting the wood.

On that evening I lost my patience so violently that I just dropped everything, swearing loudly about the secretaire. Even when Nestor was around I remained edgy and fretful – banging doors, carelessly handling pots and glasses with loud noise, and swearing about Mari Egli's eternal construction site over and over. Nestor reacted to my aggravation with a nasalized quack sound that he uttered in a child-like way. He did that from time to time, obviously each time I was irritated, impatient, enraged or offended. Although I considered this sound disgustingly childish, it always made me reflect on my thoughts and feelings – this time as well.

»You've become more emotional since you have started to develop your emotional body,« Nestor observed when I finally had calmed down. »That's good, it shows that you have more strength and energy at your disposal. But you know that your emotional energy won't help you in the perfect restoration as long as you throw it against individual things in the picture – no matter if it's joy or anger.«

»I know, I know. I'm supposed to transform my feelings into energy by getting to know myself better and becoming aware of my motives,« I repeated his recommendations for dealing with feelings.

»Nicely memorized,« he smiled mischievously. »But just memorizing that doesn't mean that you've actually transformed your feelings.«

»I'm also applying it,« I defended myself. »I'm observing myself for quite some time already, and I get to know myself more and more.«

Nestor giggled ostentatiously. »But if it's only Floco looking at Floco, then Floco looks just like Floco looks. That may be enough for a life in a small world, but when it comes to the perfect restoration we need a specialist helping you.«

»What kind of a specialist?« I asked surprised.

»A real thinker,« he replied. »He is one of the seers here on the left side.«

»And what is he supposed to help me with?«

»He'll help you listen to your ›mind's ear‹, or let's say, your inner ear – so that you recognize what feelings actually are.«

I didn't like that. I believed to know my feelings and myself well enough. And if there was something within me that had to be brought up to the surface of consciousness, then I wanted to do this myself. After all, my feelings were nobody else's business.

»But isn't it possible to also recognize one's own feelings without a specialist?«

»Not in your case,« he answered, »otherwise you wouldn't be here.«

On the next day we went for a hiking trip to the place where the »thinker« was living. Nestor didn't reveal more about him than that he had his sheep graze on the pastures surrounding his house at this time of the year. To get to this house which was located higher up the mountains, compared to Nestor's, we first followed a small path through a dry and rocky area reminiscent of a stone quarry and somehow familiar to me: somewhere around here we had visited the farmer. Overall, the path sloped upwards, but after we had passed the peaks of two rugged hills it descended again.

Soon after, we were wandering through a fir forest for a longer period of time, alongside an ascending mound ridge. The shadow cast by the trees was a blessing on this hot summer day. We left the forest behind us, walked up a pasture and arrived in a more humid region. I noticed it immediately when I looked at a place where I could recognize those flowers with leaves similar to those of water lilies: wherever these particular plants grew, the ground was gargling. The path led us through a wide recess, past a pond full of water striders and tadpoles. Then we were hiking downwards alongside a creek. The rocky bed of this creek, lined with blueberry bushes and tall wild roses, had a fascinating orange-brown hue that, according to Nestor, was caused by iron deposits in the rocks.

A little later we left the creek behind us. The way led us up to higher altitudes again where we came into a high valley. Here, on a peaceful pasture strewn with yellow flowers, the twittering of birds and the distant humming of dozens of insects were the only sounds bearing witness of life and activity. We went on towards two buildings that I could recognize now at the far end of the pasture. One of them was so small that no one could live in there. When we came closer I saw that it was a bee house; there was a constant come and go of busy insects crawling in and out of the house through narrow gaps in the front.

Finally we arrived at the other building, a nice wooden frame house blackened by the sun, a little distance away from the bee house in a relatively free area, surrounded by sparse forest spots. From the other side, a wide drivable gateway led to the house, at the end of which I could see a yellow cabriolet, to my surprise. Nestor's only comment was that the thinker loved the color yellow.

The thinker was not at home. While Nestor was busy firing the stove and cooking some vegetables, I seized the opportunity to take a closer look at the house.

The thinker's home had the ground plan of a stepped pyramid, divided into three parts. Of these three parts, the small square-shaped room right at the front interested me most: it was the thinker's library in which old books were piling up everywhere. As far as I could see, the thinker had stocked up with literature from all over the world. I didn't know most of the books, and many were written in languages I didn't understand. What struck me was that a target stood in a corner and a large wooden longbow leaning against it; somehow they didn't fit into this library ambience.

The library was followed by the center section of the house: the lounge and a kitchen with a small storage room. The backmost part of the house, the empty stable, was the largest one. The low doors and ceilings indicated that there was only enough space for small livestock. The floor above the stable was divided into two parts: in one of them, straw and hay were stored, the other one was a room tenderly furnished with a straw bed.

Nestor and I had already begun our meal when suddenly the bleating of sheep could be heard, turning louder and louder. I could hear how the animals were led into the stable where they gradually calmed down. Shortly after, a wiry man entered the house. He was older than Nestor, with a strong suntan and wearing hiking shoes stained with soil, dungarees and an open shirt.

The moment he saw us, his eyes started to light up. He laughed and gave us a hearty welcome. Nestor returned the greetings and introduced the man to me as *the thinker*. Amused, the man so addressed tipped his forehead with a finger. Then he went to wash his hands and face. Finally he sat down with us at the table, filled his plate and started eating. Nestor and the thinker were constantly chatting about all possible things, in between talking big about people I didn't know and the thinker's sheep. The wiry man impressed me with his simpleness and joyful but modest disposition.

Finally the thinker turned towards me and wanted to know why I came to visit him. I answered that my visit was based on Nestor's initiative because I wanted to find out about my feelings.

»And you think I can help you with that?« the thinker asked.

»Well, after all those experiences I've made here on the left side, I don't want to rule that out.«

Nestor and the thinker laughed.

»You're very modest and polite,« the wiry man said. »But obviously you have your doubts. Why?«

I told him that I couldn't imagine how he wanted to teach me insights into my feelings. Besides, I added jokingly, a »feeler« seemed more appropriate to me for this particular job than a »thinker«. I, as a college student, was a thinker myself, after all.

»You're not a real thinker,« the wiry man answered back assertively. »You're only able to think correctly when you're familiar with your feelings, and when you have dissolved them into energy. Then, and only then, you will hit the mark – no matter in which direction you'll aim.«

I objected to this idea that someone had to get rid of his feelings in order to be able to think correctly. In a talkative way I pointed out to the thinker that, according to my experiences, feelings rather tended to fire and inspire the process of thinking instead of obstructing it. The same held good even for the scientific field, although it was of course dominated by certain rules and principles pertaining to the handling of feelings: feelings had no place in scientific works claiming general validity because works of that sort no longer met the criterion of general replicability.

»That's all very general,« Nestor commented with a smirk.

»That's why you can replicate it,« the thinker tossed in and laughed.

»The thinkers in science are therefore driven by their feelings, but they can deal with them because they are able to hold their feelings in check,« I concluded, ignoring their remarks.

»But it's not about holding feelings in check. Rather, it's all about getting to know one's feelings and dissolving them into energy,« the thinker objected. »Scientists pretending to be above and beyond their feelings are not just bad thinkers but also hypocrites.«

I thought that his harsh criticism was out of place – the more so as he obviously didn't know the modus operandi of scientific institutions.

»The thinker knows what he's talking about,« Nestor pointed out. »He had engaged in scientific studies for many years. He had even been a doctor.«

»Well, today I'm herding sheep but I'm still a doctor,« the thinker corrected Nestor and explained with a mysterious tone of voice that he was a language critic. Both of them burst out in hysteric laughter. I couldn't believe them.

»It's true,« Nestor assured me, »we do have a real honest-to-good-ness doctor in front of us here.«

»And why are you herding sheep today?« I asked the thinker.

»Because he's not just a good language critic but also a very determined one,« Nestor replied in his place and mentioned that the thinker, as a young college student, had been obsessed with trying to get to the bottom of reality. At first he had believed that he was dealing with a given reality existing independently from human beings and describable with a set of laws or principles. Over time, however, he had arrived at the insight that reality, as we know it, was a constructed reality.

Nestor laid his spoon in front of him on the table and explained what the thinker referred to with a »constructed reality«: »If we take a look at this thing here, then we all agree that it is called ›spoon‹; we also agree on its form and color as well as what we can use it for. It's not a matter of course, though, that we see a metallic spoon in this thing that we use for eating – that's something we have learned, it's our small world.

If I took this spoon now and used it to stir around in your food, you'd become angry, not sad or anxious. But this reaction isn't a natural matter of course, either. Rather, in the course of your life you've learned that stirring around in other people's food is something that you don't do. And you have learned to react to something like that with resentment so as to defend your view of the world – and of course your food as well. In this way, we create our day-to-day reality.«

He paused for a moment. I shrugged my shoulders. Basically, what Nestor had explained was nothing new in itself: the problem with the construction of reality had been known in the cultural-scientific disciplines for quite some time. The thinker laughed and fidgeted with his spoon in a childish way. Then he kept listening to Nestor attentively who went on:

»So after the thinker had accepted that our day-to-day reality was nothing existing independently from human beings, but rather that human beings constructed that reality, he began searching for the principle underlying this particular construction. That's why he had started to study language as such. Because he held that we constructed our reality by labeling the things in our picture time and again, thereby assigning certain ideas and notions to them.«

»Well, that had made you a linguist but not yet a language critic,« I turned towards the thinker.

»No,« Nestor replied again. »The problem was that language couldn't be that principle, either, as it wasn't something absolute but rather constructed by man. So he kept on searching for a principle.«

»And had he found it?« I asked Nestor.

»Not right away,« the thinker now answered. »I had compared languages and studied their historical development as well as their phonetic laws. I wasn't able to find the actual basic principle underlying language – because, after all, I had to use language in order to explore it.« The thinker made some awkwardly exaggerated movements with his spoon and added that getting to the bottom of language by using language was just like wanting to spoon out the spoon with the spoon. Nestor laughed.

»And what did you do then?« I asked.

»He had to find a way to get behind the veil of language,« Nestor went on. »The difficulty he encountered was that he had created quite a multifarious and complex reality as a result of all his scientific studies. And that one he couldn't dissolve just like that – even though he could conceive with his rational mind that it was just a construct. Because as a result of all that learning, repeating, applying what he had learned and expanding his vocabulary over the years, he had put his physical and emotional energy into this conceived reality – so that this reality finally had become actual reality.«

I looked over to the wiry man. He smiled at me and wiggled his ears.

»So what the thinker had to do was to dissolve the bound energy out of his numerous words and concepts.«

»I can't see how you can dissolve energy out of words,« I pointed out.

»Well for sure,« the thinker flared up. »I extracted it from the words by repeating each single term – first by articulating it, then by repeating it in my mind countless times. And I did this until all ideas, concepts and feelings connected with these terms were released as energy – until all that remained were the shells of these words, that is, the words without their significant meanings.«

»How were you able to judge whether all ideas, concepts and feelings associated with a word had been dissolved in this way?«

»I could hear it.«

I looked at him surprised and asked what exactly it was that he had heard. He replied that it was a certain rushing sound that became more clear and conspicuous the more the words' significant meanings faded out. Over time, all he did was listening to that rushing sound only, in the stream of which ideas and feelings had gradually become insignificant, but he in turn had felt an intense state of contentedness. In this way, he had managed to become silent, still and listening – after all those years of thinking, speaking and debating.

»It was the rushing sound of the structure of consciousness that he had heard,« Nestor explained.

»The structure can be *heard* as well?« I asked puzzled.

»Of course,« the thinker claimed. »By listening I am successful at deconstructing reality and raising the directness and immediacy of the picture with the energy so released. And the more successful I am at that, the more that emerges which is underlying all thinking, language and our constructed reality: a bright luminous web consisting of spheres and strands.«

I had a certain suspicion and asked him whether this rushing sound wasn't rather something like a buzzing or ringing in one's ears.

»If you want to call it that way,« the thinker answered and shrugged his shoulders. »Just like the water in the creek produces a rushing sound, we can hear the energy in the structure flow. The more you can become still, the more you will be able to perceive that rushing sound of the basic structure.«

»But that buzzing in our ears has physiological causes that have already been scientifically proven,« I informed him. Of course I thought of that ear disease called *tinnitus* that had shown up in some people who had also seen eye floaters. If these two phenomena were associated in some way, it certainly would have made sense when the thinker claimed to perceive this sound more strongly.

»The old question again,« Nestor tossed in as a cutting remark. »Is it a dysfunction of the ears, or is it the ability to perceive the picture more consciously? Is the world consciousness, after all, or is it matter?«

»Matter!« The thinker yelled ironically and stamped his foot on the ground vigorously. »After all, I can feel the solidity of all things.«

»The solidity of all things is a question of consciousness, that is, the energy that you can put into the picture as a whole,« Nestor answered. »The more you shift your consciousness into the emotional world, the more this solidity dissolves. Floco, for example, has already started to walk through walls in his dreams – even if those walls suddenly appear so real and solid that he simply gets stuck in the middle of it.« Both Nestor and the thinker considered this so funny that they had to laugh loudly.

Then the wiry man announced that he would make me an offer. With pretended seriousness he cleared his throat and solemnly declared that it didn't matter whether I wanted to penetrate the walls in my dreams, layers of consciousness or the nature of my feelings – the key to all that was raising the level of my state of intensity. There were many means and aids suitable for that purpose, but his suggestion was that I should concentrate on my own inner rushing sound.

»I'll try,« I assured him.

»I'm sure of that. But would the gentleman mind my humble offer to help him in this undertaking?« The thinker made a gallant but slightly exaggerated movement and announced that he possessed a very rare instrument that could help me particularly well to listen to my own rushing sound. He got up and disappeared in his library. I looked over to Nestor, but he only imitated my curious and, at the same time, suspicious facial expression. Soon after, the thinker returned with an object wrapped in a piece of cloth. With painstaking care he slowly unwrapped the object: it was a horn adorned with artistic carvings.

»This here,« he announced mysteriously, »is the ram's horn of the rush of the basic structure.« Nestor visibly suppressed a laugh.

»Nestor doesn't believe in the use of listening so much,« the thinker commented on Nestor's behavior. »That is so because his way is not so much associated with listening – actually he's not musical. So let's leave him alone. But I tell you: whoever is able to correctly blow this horn will produce a sound with it that will raise the intensity and thus the rushing sound in the picture.«

I didn't have a chance to question the effectiveness of that horn – my body reacted before my mind did. Simply knowing that a seer wanted to raise the intensity of my state of being made me search for excuses. Because I knew what this would mean: a higher pressure in my body, heart palpitation and faster breath. And these extreme physical states were always connected with the fear to lose myself.

»Tonight you'll find out what it means to listen to the rushing sound. What do you think?«

I could feel the strength in my legs waning. »Will I fall into a dream?« I asked concerned.

»You're already in a dream,« both replied as if with one voice.

It was about two o'clock at night when we left the house, equipped with blankets and flashlights. We had waited for so long because the thinker claimed that, in the deepest night, the sense of hearing was much more active than the sense of sight. And this was of utmost significance when it came to our plan.

The moon had just risen, but soon after it was covered by fields of clouds. We kept on hiking up the hill. Cool and humid air blew in our direction from above. In regular intervals, brief lightning flashes in the far distance brightened up the sky, but there was no roar of thunder that could be heard.

We didn't have to hike for long, perhaps a quarter of an hour, until we arrived at our destination near the foot of a rock face rising up steeply. The thinker led us to a deep recess in the rock in between low brushwood. It wasn't as deep as a cave but large enough to offer several people shelter from wind and rain. A fireplace in the center bore witness that people had actually taken a rest here.

While the wiry man cleaned the place, Nestor and I were searching for firewood. After we had sparked the fire, we kept silent because the thinker had demanded absolute silence once we were out here. Therefore we had discussed already in advance what had to be done.

After we had sat around the fire for a longer time, centering ourselves and our consciousness, the thinker suddenly got up and stood in front of us. Full of excitement, I watched each of his motions. Slowly and reverently, he took the horn that was hanging on a cord around his upper body. And with the same reverence he moistened the mouth part of the horn with his lips. He sipped on it three times, then he signaled me to close my eyes.

I listened attentively. For a sheer endless time I only could hear the crackle of the fire. Then the thinker seemed to inhale deeply. And indeed – shortly after, he vigorously blew into his instrument – but instead of the shrill sound I had expected, all that could be heard was how the air sort of »farted« through the horn. The sound was completely botched. Nestor and the thinker broke out in laughter.

Confused, I opened my eyes. Before I could react, the thinker made another attempt, but it was just as unsuccessful as before. Nestor got up, took the horn from the thinker and blew it several times as well – always with the same obscene sound. Both were laughing tears and quarreling like children over who was to blow the horn next. They engaged in an outright contest over who of them produced the most grotesque, »farting«, childish sounds with the horn.

It was totally clear that they did not have the intention to raise the level of intensity within me or to initiate me into something. Not a bit could be heard of that rushing sound of the basic structure – they had simply teased and fooled me.

I wanted to express my ill-humor but somehow I felt like being blocked. I didn't even know how I should feel about them: anger and resentment? They had certainly deserved it, but the situation was so ridiculous that I couldn't even become angry. Disappointment? Of course it hurt me that they were playing tricks on me, but because I knew that they were silly billies playing around, I couldn't and wouldn't take their tricks serious.

At a loss, I turned away from them. I had no clue how to react to something like that. I couldn't simply admit that they were right, but I couldn't object against them, either; I just had no recipe, and I believed that they were ridiculing me for that reason: because I was unable to show my colors in situations like these.

Right that moment I felt an enormous anger over my powerlessness and about myself. I was raging and had a hard time to keep my body calm. My heart rate increased so strongly that I had to breathe faster. Soon I started to sweat. Then I felt how the pressure in the upper part of my abdomen increased, which in turn caused that I could only breathe very shallowly. Filled with panic, I looked over to the two men who had taken a seat again in the meantime. They returned my look attentively.

»Close your eyes,« Nestor commanded me with such an authority that I obeyed in a reflex-like manner.

»Listen,« I could hear the thinker whisper.

Fear, triggered by the intense physical condition, had me firmly in its grips. I noticed how I constantly checked my physical state, how I contracted my muscles so as to sense myself. Most of all, I just would have liked to run around.

»Listen!« The wiry man yelled. His yell came totally unexpected, penetrated every cell of my body and caused a prickle on my legs and back. This prickle had a profound cathartic effect on my condition. From one moment to the other, I was calm and relaxed, and I was able now to hear the sounds of the environment clearly and distinctly.

Gradually my attention was absorbed by the dominating monotonous chirp of a grasshopper in our immediate vicinity. It was a consistent but not continuous sound: occasionally the grasshopper took a break for the fraction of a second, only to continue to chirp its presence out into the night.

The individual sounds the insect produced followed in rapid succession, but I didn't have a hard time to follow them. I was able to clearly perceive each individual sound the grasshopper made. I could feel that my heart rate had adapted to the pace and rhythm of these sounds: the number of chirp sounds between two heartbeats was always the same, subdividing the chirping into musical bars of equal length. In the same way, my breathing – deep and regular in the meantime – interacted with the subtle sounds. It even seemed as if the chirping sounds attuned to my breathing rhythm whenever I changed it. The realization that my body was somehow harmonizing with this animal brought about a profound indescribable joy within me. I felt as if I was able to directly understand the grasshopper.

Suddenly the frequency of chirping sounds increased in an unnatural way, and the pitch rose as well. Before I could awake to what was happening, they had picked up in speed so much that they could be heard as an uninterrupted stinging sound, or rather a high-pitched rush or hiss. This particular sound produced a feeling of deep detachedness within me; it was as if I was flowing along in a steady river while all other perceptions seemed to be shut off.

After a sheer endless time I noticed that the rushing sound was not even but accentuated differently. The result was a constantly repeating rhythmic pattern that developed further and became richer in varieties. Soon after, the individual beats assumed the qualities of sound, and I was able to distinguish between various pitches of them. A melody ensued – at first simple but enchantingly beautiful, endlessly playing in my ears. I wasn't able to stop the advancement of this melody, even if I had wanted it: it was like an immense compulsion, an irresistible desire for these sounds to just continue. And then I believed to hear words emerging from the music – dull, unintelligible words. These also changed until I could hear a clear voice – a deep man's voice I had never heard before that didn't speak with a dialect or accent but in clear High German:

»*Gib dich hin* – abandon yourself.«

The perception of this voice caused a jerk in my body so that I opened my eyes, scared as I was, moving my head back and forth wildly and kicking with my arms and legs.

»What's the matter with you?« Nestor asked. I recollected myself. My pulse was still fast-paced. I listened: the rushing sound, the rhythmics and the melody were gone; I only heard the sounds of the night, the chirping of grasshoppers and the blaze of the fire. Nestor and the thinker were still sitting across from me, looking at me.

»I've heard a voice. It said: ›abandon yourself‹,« I told them.

The two of them exchanged a brief look, then Nestor announced that it was time to return. Of course I wanted to know what this voice was supposed to mean, but neither Nestor nor the thinker were willing to talk about it.

Day had already broken when we arrived at the thinker's house. Exhausted, I went up to the room above the stable, laid down on the straw and fell asleep immediately.

When I woke up a few hours later it was bright day. Nestor was in the kitchen and prepared himself a coffee with milk and honey. I did the same, and eventually I wanted to ask him about last night's events. But he pressed his index finger against his lips in a silencing gesture and pointed in the direction of the small library, the door of which stood open. I was surprised to see a young woman in there, sitting at the table and absorbed into a book. She rested her head on both hands and didn't move an inch.

»Come, let's go outside,« Nestor whispered. I tried to take another look at the woman, but Nestor placed himself right between me and the library, virtually driving me out the door.

We sat down in front of the house where the thinker had already placed himself.

»What's that woman doing here?« I asked straightforward.

»She's reading,« the thinker replied mischievously.

»I mean: why is she here? Is she practicing the perfect restoration?«

»She has returned a book she had borrowed. And now she's looking for a new one she wants to take along. She's a bookworm.«

I was all confused. The idea that she was a seeker learning from the seers the way I did – this idea filled me with the excitement. There was nothing I would have rather liked to do than talk to this woman about the seers, the perfect restoration and, of course, *mouches volantes*.

Before I could ask any further questions, the thinker tried to awaken my memory of last night's events. He had to ask me several times before I was able to recollect myself and answer.

I described to them that I first believed they just wanted to tease and fool me; obviously there had been no intention on their part at all to teach me listening to the rushing sound.

»We had to do that,« Nestor asserted. »After all, we couldn't just ask you nicely and politely to please raise your intensity.«

»So then it wasn't the horn at all that had triggered this particular state in me?« I asked.

»Well yes, of course it was the horn,« the thinker vetoed. »It was the ram's horn of the rush of the basic structure. Do you actually believe anything would have happened last night *without* the horn?«

Nestor laughed and said that the thinker was just joking. The horn had been important, but just as important was the staging, that is, the seers' energy. With this energy, any old horn would have turned into the horn of the rush of the basic structure. The thinker made an offended face.

Then Nestor asked me to describe to them in detail what I had experienced. They both listened attentively, Nestor rather more concentrated, the thinker with a friendly smile. When I had ended, the thinker rose to speak. He stated he found it funny that the whole thing had almost gone awry – because of my know-it-all attitude. According to him, I had closed myself to the intensity of my feelings in the belief that I could solve the situation with thinking. It was only due to the fact that the combined power of my feelings had eventually turned against me, that I finally had been able to experience that increased intensity. In my own peace and quiet, the thinker concluded, I obviously was able to let my hair down and be emotional.

Nestor agreed and added that it was precisely this inclination – wanting to keep everything for myself – that had prevented me from opening up my body, and it still did, over and over. And right there the thinker had to intervene so that I could release the energy from my feelings and use it for listening to the rushing sound.

»I've heard much more than just a rushing sound,« I tried to avert the uncomfortable subject. I started to rave about the melodies and, most of all, the voice I had been able to hear at last.

»That voice was so real,« I told them, deeply impressed. »It sounded as if someone in my immediate vicinity, or better, within me, had said: ›abandon yourself‹.«

Nestor knitted his eyebrows. »You drifted away from listening to the rushing sound,« he interpreted my perception, almost looking at me reproachfully.

»That was your fine small world,« the thinker added.

»That's how it is. If you drift away from listening to that sound in such a high state of intensity, you'll quickly lose your reference to the outer screen and start to hear nonsense.«

»But perhaps this voice has some kind of meaning?« I defended myself.

Nestor seemed annoyed. »Who cares about the voice you've heard? Last night it was all about utilizing the energy of your feelings to produce the rushing sound and suspend your stability in one specific layer. That's not easy, it requires your full attention. The yakety-yak from nowhere simply meant that your attention had already been waning considerably.«

»Yes, but hold it!« the wiry man called out. »Perhaps that voice does have some significance, after all? ›Abandon yourself‹ – the message is unmistakable, and I'd suggest we take it serious; so, Floco: abandon yourself.«

»Abandon yourself,« I repeated to myself, glad to have found an ally at last – and stopped short right away: »But *to what* am I supposed to abandon myself?«

»How about washing the dishes in my kitchen?« the thinker suggested.

»Your roof could definitely need some new shingles,« Nestor proposed.

»Right. And the stable needs to be mucked out as well.«

Both writhed with laughter and started to outdo each other with respect to tasks to which I should »abandon« myself. Then Nestor turned serious.

»You weren't able to remain attentive enough,« he pointed out. »You could have just as well seen pictures with no immediate reference to the outer screen – ›hallucinations‹, as you would call them. But when we raise our intensity and have expanded sensory perceptions, it's important not to lose the ground under our feet but to be able to maintain the connection to the outer screen – in order to recognize what our picture basically is.«

»What you hear depends on your consciousness,« the wiry man turned concrete. »People with too low a level of consciousness drift into daydreams and may even hear melodies or voices when their energy level is raised. Then they believe that divine beings, angels or demons have spoken to them. But when someone becomes more conscious, if he or she is able to let the energy flow through their body better, then they're listening to the rushing sound in the basic structure.«

Then the thinker explained that, with each advance I made, I could further refine the perception of that rushing sound. He, for example, was not just able to hear the rushing sound; rather, he could also distinguish between different pitches within that sound: there was one basic vibration and eight harmonic overtones, all with different intensities.

»And I'm not even able, by comparison, to listen to that one rushing sound for a longer period of time,« I sighed with resignation.

»Your abilities only play a marginal role in this,« the thinker answered back. »You refused to really listen because you were afraid of that rushing sound.«

»Afraid? But why should I be afraid of it?«

»Because it produces a sort of emptiness within you that stands in contrast to you as a person. You cannot pay attention to the rushing sound and yourself at the same time,« he replied. »So when you completely concentrate on the inner rushing sound, you'll stop to constantly ruminate your person and the world. And the more you abandon that, the more intense the rushing sound will become, and the larger becomes the all-devouring emptiness. Permanently listening to this rushing sound would mean to forget about one's own personality, to lose one's own identity.«

»Exactly,« Nestor agreed. »That's why you needed all those rhythms and melodies and ›abandon yourself‹ – as a protective shield against the void of the rushing sound.«

I held that, in this particular case, I had done the only correct thing to do. After all, I was in no way interested in falling into some empty void, forgetting myself in the process. Both were laughing loudly when they heard me saying that, and the wiry man kept wiggling his ears; obviously he had a sophisticated sense of perception in the back muscles of his head and neck that he was able to wiggle each ear independently.

Then, with an encouraging tone of voice, he told me that I didn't have to justify myself.

»Your reaction was only natural,« he gently said. »What you've tried yesterday is about the most difficult thing there is: you tried to forget yourself – now who wants something like that? Who would give himself up voluntarily?«

»But why would someone want that?« I asked back.

»It's the only possibility to resolve the fixation in the right half of consciousness and to become free,« Nestor replied. »It doesn't matter whether you do this by listening to the rushing sound or by practicing any other exercise of the perfect restoration: it's always about dissolving your small world, that is, forgetting who and what you believe to be – so as to recognize who and what you really are.«

After a small lunch Nestor left us and went into the forest. I myself helped the wiry man lead his nine sheep out on a pasture nearby. In doing so, he explained to me many things around sheep breeding and farming, correct animal husbandry, keeping livestock, their preferred fodder, their behavior as well as what the shepherd was able to do with milk and wool. On this occasion he also mentioned that animals were creatures bestowed with consciousness; they had preferences, antipathies and feelings, just like human beings.

Perhaps with a touch of romanticism I revealed to the thinker that I would wish for a world in which the ideal of equality was realized, where people would treat themselves and all other living beings equivalently.

This made the thinker laugh. »Animals will never be equal to human beings,« he answered back. »And there is no equality among human beings, either. To assume something like that would be naïve.«

His words startled me. I asked him if seers, of all human beings, didn't see the equality in all things existent and thus had to fight against artificially constructed hierarchies and social injustice. He confirmed to me that seers did see the equality of all things. Everything originated from consciousness, according to him, and was part of it, or in other words: from that last sphere – the goal and destination of all seers – other spheres would spring up in turn.

»But seeing also reveals that there are hierarchies,« he went on. »There's not just that one sphere but many; in order to arrive at that one sphere, you have to pass through the other spheres and strands. Hierarchy as such is therefore already laid out in our consciousness. A sheep is farther away from this one sphere than a human being; for this reason, in the hierarchy of the shining structure a sheep is positioned below a human being, just as an ordinary human being is positioned under a seer. Not every living being has the same level of consciousness, after all.«

I defended my viewpoint: hierarchies, I was convinced, could not contribute to peace in a community or society in the long run. Because where there were hierarchies, there was power unequally distributed – and the higher up one came in the hierarchy, both power and its abuse increased in number and frequency. Social inequalities were thus pre-programmed.

The thinker replied that I was talking about a hierarchy organized according to criteria such as money, wealth and property. Within such a hierarchy, only those could rise who drained their competitors of their energy in the form of money, wealth and property in order to become big, powerful and mighty themselves. In the hierarchy of consciousness, on the other hand, it was unthinkable to treat beings at a lower level bad or even exploit them so as to drain them of their energy. This stood in conflict with striving for a higher level of consciousness. Because rising up in the hierarchy of consciousness was only possible for human beings if they put their own energy into the picture. In comparison to a money, wealth and property hierarchy, it couldn't happen in a hierarchy of consciousness that the responsibility for man, beast and nature would lie in the hands of some idiots whose level of consciousness was hardly any higher than that of those sheep in front of us.

After we had led all sheep out on the pasture where they enjoyed the lush grass, we sat down in the shadow of a large linden tree from where we could easily overlook the entire herd.

I deemed this situation a good opportunity to ask the thinker several questions pertaining to the perfect restoration. I wanted to hear his viewpoints on the development of consciousness, the phenomenon of *mouches volantes* and the path in the basic structure. In the process, I hoped to find something like a common denominator or connective pattern in the most obvious agreements of Nestor's and his statements, which in turn could bring me closer to the actual tradition of the seers. I wanted to achieve this by presenting to the seer the most important points Nestor had taught me about seeing so that he could give his own comments and viewpoints on it. For that purpose I had prepared a paper summarizing the most important features and attributes of the perfect restoration.

Thus I described to the thinker the perfect restoration as a system of physical and mental exercises aiming at building up the inner pressure and dealing more effectively with a higher level of energy. This in turn led to an expanded perception of the picture and, in connection with that, a dissolution of the small world in the picture – including the suspension of stability in one specific layer of consciousness and the change from the right to the left half of consciousness. The excess energy released had to be put into the picture as a whole directly through the body with the accompanying prickle feeling. This led to an increasingly better perception of the dots and strands that were known as *mouches volantes* in ophthalmology. This perception was referred to as »seeing«. Seeing the dots and strands that gradually came closer and turned into large spheres and tubes was ultimately supposed to result in overcoming duality and realizing one's own consciousness, that is, seeing the picture as a whole. And this was the mystic goal of the people living here on the left side of the Emme who call themselves »seers«.

I myself thought that I had done a good job at this brief summary. The thinker, however, just smiled at my efforts.

»Don't take these terms and definitions so serious,« he urged me.

»Why not?«

»Well, because a person like you tends to fill out terms and words with emotional content that you either long for or curse – the more so with terms you're dealing with very intensely. But if you want to find out what feelings are you'll have to stop tying them to terms and words.«

»And what are feelings?«

The thinker pulled on one of his earlobes with ostentation and answered that I should have recognized that in my more intense state of being yesterday. »Feelings are energy,« he finally said, »energy interpreted by you and interwoven with your personality. They are part of your constructed small world. Yesterday you were capable of using the energy of your feelings for listening – at least for a while. But if you're successful in transforming your feelings completely, then you'll spread this energy directly and in its pure form to everyone and everything, and you'll light up the web of consciousness. The price for that is that, one of these days, you'll have to drop all these terms and systems of thought.«

»Are you also telling this the woman hitting the books in your library?«

»She's not like you,« he replied, »she has a totally different relationship to words and terms. See, you're an orderly man, and you feel more secure when you can put a label on the things happening to you. There-fore it's easier for you to advance the development of consciousness using a firm system with clear and unmistakable terms. Nestor has rec-ognized that and made you familiar with the seers' system of terms – at the risk of you getting hung up in it. And I think that, in your case, there's a certain probability for that.«

»I don't think that I hang on to these terms any more than Nestor does,« I defended myself.

»You're wrong,« the thinker answered back. »Nestor is a seer, and as such he doesn't care the least bit about any systems of thought. That only contradicts being present in the here and now, and it also contra-dicts seeing the web.«

I resisted the wiry man's claims. Emphatically I explained to him that Nestor consistently used these terms and this system of thought, and he obviously stood behind it with much determination and convic-tion. Therefore it was inconceivable to me that he would not care »the least bit« about it.

»That's what I mean,« the thinker said undeterred. »You start to fight when someone starts to attack the validity of your world of terms. That was the same with me before, by the way. But that's only so be-cause you've pumped so much energy in the form of feelings into these words, and because you now believe in these terms. You'll have to do what every seer has done, that is, dissolve the feelings out of the lan-guage. To me, for example, words have a certain mental content at best, but no more emotional one. I experience my feelings as ecstatic energy that makes me listen to my inner rushing sound and which lights up my web of consciousness. And this is precisely what the seers' system of thought aims at in the final analysis.«

Nestor and I spent the evening of this beautiful summer day alone on the pasture in front of the house. The woman in the library had disap-peared, and the thinker had left us for a hiking trip through the forest.

After we had practiced archery with the arrows and longbow from the thinker's library, I told Nestor about my conversation with him. I was of course particularly interested in finding out whether Nestor in-deed didn't think much of the seers' system of thought. Our conversa-tion on the subject positions went draggingly sluggish. Nestor didn't seem inclined to really tackle this subject. He just repeated what the thinker had said about the necessity of dissolving the feelings out of words and terms, and he held that the terms in this system were all completely interchangeable and therefore not so important. As an example, he referred to the thinker who called the basic structure a *web* or *web of consciousness* now and then.

I tried to get across to Nestor that different terms had different, more subtle meanings that resonated along with it in each case, and that one couldn't therefore exchange or replace certain terms just like that. After all, a »web« was not the same as a »structure«. Nestor laughed and held that I obviously was a little conservative already.

This claim that I was conservative made me assume a defensive attitude at once. Because I personally considered myself generous, forward-looking and open for new things – not just in political terms but human ones as well. With fervor I tried to convince Nestor that I was precisely not what he claimed I was. But with several of his typical quack sounds he made me shut up.

For a while none of us said a word. I was vexed. And because I wanted to let him feel my anger, I accused him of being indifferent – indifferent towards the feelings of others. He didn't even deny this but replied that everyone who wanted to advance on the path in the basic structure had to learn to assign the same significance to the contents in the picture. Or in other words: to see the picture as a whole. Seeing the same significance in all things was the ultimate goal.

»And if everything were insignificant and indifferent, nobody would any longer do anything or strive for anything,« I sneered embittered.

»Ceasing to do things will inevitably lead to being,« he countered. »But we have already talked about these things. You should adhere to the advice of the thinker by all means: dissolve your feelings out of the words and put the released energy into the whole picture. Then, and only then, will you be able to assign the same significance and validity to words like ›conservative‹ or ›indifference‹, and to see them for what they are: just words.«

I didn't know what to reply. Somehow I never was able to »catch« Nestor. It was as if he wasn't there at all – or rather: too much there, too present, faster and smarter than anyone else. And it was as if he, like a mirror, just reflected whatever someone put out in his direction – only in much more intense proportions, yet free from any emotions. I just wasn't able to cope with him, and that didn't just drive me almost crazy; it also made my heart palpitate and my hands tremble.

I was pondering over him and whether his attacks against me were justified. In doing so, I realized that there were several personalities hiding in the human being called Nestor – personalities that he obviously played off to his advantage in certain situations. With these fast and frequent changes of his personality he also changed my feelings for him.

An example: Nestor was able to find something funny and joyful in the most banal everyday objects and situations. At times I considered this enviably childlike, but often just incomprehensively childish. At the same time he always needed my attention and some confirmation on my part – something that provoked my resistance all too often. Even if he didn't behave childish, he was able to impart to me that life was beautiful and worth living – until I turned all melancholic in my yearning desire and unsuccessful attempts to emulate him. But he also could be quite bitchy and scathing. Then he exposed the ugly side of all man's doings and ridiculed all pursuits and aspirations. On the other hand, though, Nestor could turn very serious and explain complex, almost incomprehensible, exercises of the perfect restoration with the greatest conviction. And if I was slow on the uptake he didn't hesitate to convey his point of view in a calm way but virtually without any possibility for me to express my objections – precisely what he had done a little while ago.

My anger was festering. Clandestinely I looked at Nestor now and then. To me, he was disgusting the way he sat there in the grass with his legs spread out and his arms and hands hanging down slack. He was wiggling the toes of his grotesquely oversized naked feet, and his laughter sounded like a malicious grin; when he opened his mouth, a set of monstrous and abhorrent yellowish teeth showed up – I took offense at nearly everything. And the more I fell silent with bitterness, the more alive and disgusting he seemed to become, just as if my repelling attitude nurtured him.

When I looked at Nestor again I was petrified. The way he looked seemed to confirm my thoughts: after all, didn't he have extraordinarily hairy hands and feet? And his black erect hair: didn't it really have the length and density of a lion's mane? And his left ear whose upper part protruded through his hair – didn't it seem to taper off in a strange way, even if it was inconspicuous? Didn't his fingers rather resemble claws? Wasn't he the abhorrent creature playing with my feelings and feeding on them unashamedly?

As if numbed, I turned my eyes away from him. I knew that I wasn't quite here in my right mind, that I had let myself go beyond all measure in my rage.

It was already late evening. To our left, the sun stood closely above the forest on the hill across from us, and its last rays made the entire environment glow up in bright red.

Suddenly Nestor began to laugh and stood up. »Look,« he called out with the innocence of a small child, »flying mosquitoes.«

I thought he wanted to fool me with this prompt and believed he wanted to show me his dots and strands – something that of course couldn't work out. I didn't look in his direction on purpose. I felt disgust over his cheap attempt to draw my attention to himself. Nestor, however, tapped on my arm – something he had never done before.

»There are flying mosquitoes,« he insisted and pointed in the direction of the young maple tree that was growing right next to the thinker's house. Reluctantly I turned my head – and indeed I could see a swarm of tiny mosquitoes dancing in the sunset glow. They flew closely above the tree branches where they rose in endless circles and sank down again. The sight of these dancing insects was so peaceful and gracious – this was perfect beauty.

Right this moment, the full burden of my shortcomings collapsed on me: my inability to let words be words and, instead, enjoy the beauty of the picture; the shabbiness of my »trench wars« against Nestor and the seer's explanations; the ridiculousness and voidness of my small world and my personality that I had to defend over and over again – a burden so devastating that tears ran down my cheeks.

All the more it felt like a small release when I sensed the brief but relaxing prickle feeling that flowed through my body at this moment.

The Shining of the Basic Structure

On the next day we accompanied the thinker with his sheep to another pasture in this high valley. From there we wanted to return to Nestor's house. Nestor, however, was not in a hurry, and so we sat down some more time with the wiry man.

While talking to the thinker, I noticed again that he pulled up his ears now and then. I asked him whether he pulled energy up into his head in this way – just like Nestor had explained why he wiggled his ears. The thinker looked at me in surprise, then he started to laugh loudly.

»I don't pull up my ears, I prick'em up – so I can hear better. Just like everyone of us is constantly realigning his attention while seeing, I realign my hearing as well. Pricking up one's ears is like blinking with the eyes.«

Nestor laughed. The thinker came close up to me and lowered his voice: »If Nestor believes that he is pulling energy up into his head by wiggling his years, let him believe that. But in truth you're pricking your ears with it.«

»In any case, you are putting more consciousness into your head and ears – no matter if you call it ›pulling up the ears‹, ›wiggling the years‹ or ›pricking up the ears‹,« Nestor added.

»Once again, the shortcomings of language,« the thinker called out. »Language constantly labels the same things with different terms. So let's free ourselves from language.«

»Language certainly might have its shortcomings,« I replied, »still it's the most important means of communication at man's disposal.«

»But that communication is very limited,« the thinker insisted. »It enables us to exchange ideas only with a small part of the world, that is, human beings. In addition, linguistic expression is becoming more multifarious and complicated, following the development in our society. That's why a profound communication is not possible with all people but only a certain group of people. Language splits and divides. It embraces certain things and excludes others.«

I held that language could always bridge differences and bring about understanding because it was changeable and adaptable – to a certain degree it even allowed communication between man and beast. Nestor replied that this communication still was always and only possible with a part of the picture – no matter how many men and beasts and stones were able to understand us.

»There's a form of communication, though, allowing a complete exchange with and understanding of all the picture's contents,« he claimed. »That's the exchange of energy with the entire picture. If I put energy into the picture as a whole, I can see directly what's actually going on in it. In this way, seeing brings about direct knowledge.

The seers call these perceptions that are raising the level of consciousness *sensations*. Sensations are individually different because their intensity and duration depend on how strong your inner pressure and how open your body is.«

»The sensation – that's the sensation!« The thinker called out.

Nestor replied that it was indeed a sensation when a person recognized that he could exchange himself with the entire picture and thus understand it, just by means of sensations. But at the outset, he explained, sensations were very short-lived, perhaps connected with chilly shivers or tremblings – indicating that there was not enough energy that could be mustered up, or that the energy was still blocked inside the body.

»But when a person accumulates more energy by leading an appropriate lifestyle, it'll express itself to him with more and stronger sensations. He'll be able to perceive the sensations more and more as a prickle feeling causing all body hairs to stand on end. Over time, this prickle feeling will flow through larger and larger portions of the body, sometimes even through the entire body. If someone has enough energy at his disposal, he'll be able to feel the prickle for a longer period of time and sense it as pleasant and relaxing – the shivers and tremblings finally subside. So the sensations you can feel more strongly since a while are indicators that you are on the way to open your body completely.«

Nestor went on to explain that this direct way of releasing energy was something that regularly happens to a seer. In this context, he called the seer's sensations no longer »prickle feelings« but »ecstasies«. An ecstasy differed from a prickle feeling in that it was much longer and more intensive; furthermore it could be experienced all over the body, from head to toe.

I personally sensed the prickle feeling as a pleasant and refreshing experience, but in my case it had lasted only for a few seconds. The idea that it could be possible to experience this feeling for a much longer time had something intriguing to me.

»Will the prickle feeling really increase and last longer when I build up the inner pressure and open my body?« I asked.

»You can be sure of that,« Nestor replied. »The *ecstasy* is the seer's bliss.«

»An ecstasy is nothing less than awesome, just mind-blowing,« the wiry man was raving.

»Sensational,« Nestor added.

»Simply ecstatic,« the thinker called out.

»Infinitely more than just a mere prickle,« Nestor knew. »But there are people who hate this particular feeling. Those are the egoists who equip their house with alarm systems and barbwires; but more than that, they would even like to seal off their body hermetically so as to avoid giving away energy by any means. But that's exactly what happens with a prickle or ecstasy, and that's also what seers basically do: they put their emotionally released, excess energy into the picture as a whole, thus dissolving the small world in the picture and starting to illuminate the basic structure with it.«

»Sensations have a relaxing effect and bring about calmness,« the thinker said. »I can stay seated and regularly release my energy as ecstasy into the world. On the other hand, if you are not a seer and your body is ›shut off‹, then you'll always have to fight in order to release your energy. Then you have to run around, climb up and down mountains or do the ›doctor thing‹ – or do it altogether. You have to toil and sweat, you must be glad and upset. And you're making love with it. But those are all *petty little kicks*. Give your power away like that, and you'll always stay restless and agitated, never completely satisfied. Simply because you pin down your power to certain intentions, feelings, people and objects that will bleach out and become old and gray. And you yourself will also bleach out in the process, become old and gray and die – without having found out what it means to make the web of consciousness light up with your energy, and to get along better with everything.«

Nestor repeated that the state of ecstasy was actually the only true and comprehensive form of communication because it addressed the whole picture. Human language on the other hand, earmarked and emotionally tinged, was not sufficiently rich in energy and nothing but a distraction from this direct form of communication.

»So let's free ourselves from language,« the thinker called out again. »After all, what do we need a whole alphabet full of signs and symbols for, just to talk to each other? It's pure idiocy to have so many letters and still not be able to adequately express oneself. If we want to express our sensations and perceptions, it would suffice if we just used the vowels.«

His words made me laugh involuntarily. I told them that one couldn't begin to imagine the chaos that would break loose in an information society like ours if everyone would only communicate with vowels from now on. But the wiry man seemed to be serious about it.

»For example, if I'm appalled or disgusted at something,« he explained, »I simply say *iiih*.«

Nestor laughed and joined in: »And if I find something unpleasant or out of place, I say *eeeh*.«

»And when I'm relaxed and doing well, I let out a gentle *aaah*. But when I *yell aaah*, then it's because something hurts or I'm afraid of something,« the thinker added.

»If I want to express my admiration and sympathy, I say *oooh* with a rising pitch in my voice; on the other hand, I use *oooh* with a lowering pitch if I want to pity someone in an ironic way.«

»*Uuuh* means an unpleasant sensation like a malaise or nausea, but also a certain fear which I want to express in a funny way.«

Both chuckled and continued to communicate for a while in a childish way, using these vowels only. Then they turned towards me, but when they saw that I didn't want to take part in their foolish game, they let up on me with an uncomprehending *eeeh* and a pitying *oooh*.

»Why can't we just behave like normal civilized human beings?« I criticized their mannerisms, provoked as I was.

»Human beings?« the thinker finally finished the senseless game. Then he looked around in surprise. »But there are no human beings around here, only sheep and seers,« he replied and pointed towards the sheep and us.

I didn't let it show but I was secretly pleased by the fact that the thinker considered me one of the seers. I was convinced, though, that this was a pure gesture of friendship – undoubtedly he knew that I was not a seer. So, humbly I pointed out that I have not yet attained the awareness level of a seer.

»You haven't attained the awareness level of a human being, either,« the thinker added with a laugh. »*Du bisch o es Schaaf.*«[15]

»But how is it possible that I have not attained the level of a human being when in fact I am one?« I defended myself.

---

[15] Swiss German for "you are also a sheep".

»According to your body, you're a human being,« Nestor explained, »but according to your current awareness level, you're not. To be a fully conscious human being means to a seer that you have made certain advances in seeing. But your seeing capabilities are virtually undeveloped. And your knowledge is not derived from seeing but from what you have learned.«

»*Du bisch o es Schaaf*,« the thinker called out again. Obviously he considered it so funny that he had to repeat it over and over. I explained to them that their definition of a »human being« was very peculiar – and inappropriate as well, because according to that definition there were only sheep on this planet. They found this funny, and the wiry man continued to call me a sheep.

»*Du bisch o es Schaaf. Du bisch o es Schaaf*,« he sang. Nestor cheered.

Of course it was obvious that they wanted to provoke and annoy me, just like they had done the other day. But I decided not to get annoyed and simply ignored them.

»*Du bisch o es Schaaf*«, the thinker kept talking at me insistently.

Why did he do that? Did he want to test me? But what a crude, childish test it was ... Pictures from my childhood flashed by; pictures from a time period when I had to deal with unjustified and witless remarks of this kind so as to keep my integrity. But hadn't we outgrown such nonsense by now, as adults? I told Nestor and the thinker that their childish behavior was not at all compatible with their claim of having attained spiritual perfection. But they did not want to take note of me.

»*Du bisch o es Schaaf. Du bisch o es Schaaf*,« the thinker repeated over and over, each time a little more insistent. I was fuming by now. Did I have to put up with that? Had I deserved something like that? It was foreseeable that his persistence in repeating that nonsense would soon surpass my persistence in holding back my anger. The only solution I could come up with was to just get away. But right the moment when I wanted to get up and leave, my pulse quickened suddenly, as if I just had overstrained myself.

»*Du bisch o es Schaaf*.« Now I could hear the thinker's voice clearer; it was more distinct and louder than before, as if he was speaking directly into my ear. But now it seemed as if the sentence had lost its significance. In fact, the thinker's words sounded so strange that I wasn't able any longer to understand their meaning. Instead, my attention had shifted to the sound of the words that the thinker emphasized in different levels of pitch: after an initial lowering, he raised the pitch of the following syllables, and the final one closed the circle, having the same pitch as the first one.

Then the melody gradually started to even out. High and low pitches converged until the sequence sounded completely monotonous. But now the rhythmics stood out more; I paid attention to the pace and length of the words. But they too started to even out until, at length, I only heard long monotonous, almost hypnotic vowels that the thinker emphasized in a clean manner – unusual for the Swiss German dialect spoken around Bern.

»... *uuuh*[16] ... *iiih*[17] ... *oooh*[18] ... *eeeh*[19] ... *aaah*[20] ...« This seemingly unending stream of vowels penetrated me so deeply that I began to feel each of the vowels in different parts of my body: with the familiar sensation of a strong prickle, I could feel the U down in the lumbar region; the I vibrated in my head, hardly perceivable; the O vowel produced a distinct feeling in the abdomen, under the navel; the E triggered a mild sensation around the larynx; and finally, the A vowel vibrated in my chest.

These sensations felt comfortable and pleasant to me; they increased my attention in the corresponding parts of my body. This held good in particular for the O sound that gradually started to dominate all other vowels in terms of intensity until this O was the only sound I could hear and feel. However, with each new sound the vowel lost some of its linguistic quality; soon I didn't experience the sound as a sound wave anymore but as a tangible impulse producing a rushing noise that gradually came to the fore.

When this rushing noise had become permanent and even, having absorbed my attention for quite a while already, I realized that it had broken away from my abdomen and my body overall – and that *I* had also detached myself from my body along with this rushing sound: I could not sense any longer where I began and where I ended; I couldn't even determine whether I was still breathing at all. This notion triggered a panic seizure within me that caused me to jolt up with a sudden reflex and run off in the next best direction.

A little while later I arrived at the edge of a little forest where I sank into the soft moss, drained and exhausted. My familiar body sensation

---

[16] pronounced [uː] ("mood", "food").

[17] pronounced [ɪː] ("see", "feel").

[18] pronounced [oː] ("boat", "so" without second part of diphthong).

[19] pronounced [eː] (in between "egg" and "see").

[20] pronounced [aː] (in between "hut" and "calm").

slowly returned. The rushing noise disappeared and I was able to perceive the sounds of the environment again, as usual: the humming of insects, the bleating of sheep and the resounding laughter of two childish characters who called themselves »seers«. I was not able to gain a clear understanding of what had just taken place. My anger about Nestor and the seer was still too deep, as was my shame because I had run away like a coward.

Before I was able to settle down I noticed how Nestor got up and said something to the thinker who turned around towards me, waved at me and eventually laid down in the grass. Nestor walked down in my direction, and when he passed me by in some distance he said that we would return to his house. Visibly amused, he added that I obviously couldn't wait for it ...

I followed him but did not reply anything in protest. We didn't say a word on the entire way back. Nestor didn't seem to be disturbed by my defiance, though – quite the contrary: my impression was that he even enjoyed not having to talk to me.

In the evening I joined Nestor who sat in front of the house. I felt an impulse to clarify matters with him. First I described to him how heavily upset I had become about the thinker's »sheep« remark, and how, in the next moment, only the melody and rhythmics of the words, and finally the vowels, had penetrated my ears. In the end, all I could perceive was a rushing sound while the words had lost any significance long before.

»You had listened to the words without further thinking about it,« was Nestor's interpretation. »That's why they sounded totally different. The important point was that you've transformed the feelings associated with those words into energy – and this way the thinker's remark lost any sort of significance. You could have put this released energy into the picture as a whole. But again, you were not open enough to do so, and so you had to ›discharge‹ yourself by running around like a madman.«

Then I told Nestor about the different vowels that I had felt vibrating in different parts of my body.

Nestor put out a knowing smile. »The thinker had seized the opportunity and wanted to show you that each vowel produces a certain vibration that can be felt in a certain part of the body. But that's not all. These specific body parts also correspond to certain layers of consciousness. In other words: the thinker wants to motivate you to consciously generate these vibrations in your body, thus trying to stimulate the corresponding layers of your consciousness.«

It wasn't clear to me how one could associate certain body parts with layers of consciousness. Nestor answered this question by claiming that seers could perceive this particular association: when seeing, they felt the sensation of a tickle in the corresponding body parts, according to which spheres and strands they directed their attention to.

»You said that there were countless layers,« I objected, »but I could feel the vibrations of the vowels only in a few body parts.«

»There are countless layers indeed. But to simplify matters, the seers, due to their seeing, have summarized all layers to eight main layers that have to be penetrated in our consciousness. The thinker, however, imparted only five vowels to you today that correspond to five layers in your consciousness – he had skipped the umlauts Ä[21], Ü[22] and Ö[23]. These vowels can always be felt at little higher up in the body than their underlying pure vowel.

Now, each vowel can stimulate a certain layer with its vibration, and ideally illuminate it in its entirety. Aside from that, the vowel vibrations also remove energy blockades, they render your body more open and get the energy to flow. That's why you should practice this.«

I wanted to know from Nestor whether I was supposed to voice the vowels in the same sequence that the thinker had imparted them to me. He replied that the ideal sequence ran from the bottommost vowel, the U, up to the topmost, the I. He admired the thinker's ingenuity, though, he said, because the thinker had pointed towards something very elementary with his remark and the corresponding sequence of vowels: the thinker had first generated the vibrations of the two top- and bottommost, the »extreme«, vowels in my body, then the two in between, and finally the one in the center near the heart.

»As a result of his seeing, the thinker knows that all our aspirations come down to our own center, our heart,« Nestor explained. »But only those who know the extremes are able to reach the center. For the act of seeing, this means to penetrate the layers of consciousness and perceive the objects in the picture in their extremes, that is, very large and very small. And on the path in the basic structure it means the experience of both the deepest abysses and the highest highs of consciousness. Then, and only then, will the seer find peace of mind in the center of his heart.«

---

[21] pronounced [æ:] ("had", "bad").
[22] pronounced [y:] (no English equivalent).
[23] pronounced [ø:], also [œ] (no English equivalent).

During the summer I kept on trying to restore the damaged inlay work on the bottom right-hand drawer of the secretaire, but the work was frustrating: even though I frequently worked on it, I couldn't get one single step ahead. Just like before, the secretaire exerted an undue influence on me, despite my regular experiments with different exercises I had learned from Nestor. But neither the perception of the afterimage nor looking at the dots and strands, nor generating vibrations by articulating or singing the vowels, nor trying to combine all of these, brought about the success hoped for. And just as stubborn as the secretaire that thwarted my attempts to continue the restoration, Nestor encouraged me not to give up.

During this time my dreams were unusually vivid. Each time that I became aware of my dreaming and the fact that I could exert some influence on my dreams was of particular interest. Typically, these dreams were nightmares at first in which I was conscious enough not to allow the usual weakening feelings of powerlessness. Whenever I succeeded in mustering up sufficient strength and staying calm in the face of perceived dangers, my emotional body became more awake.

Eventually it also was a special dream that gave me a clue about the further proceedings of the restoration on the bottom right-hand drawer. The dream started with me becoming aware of being stuck in some kind of cave complex – a dream that repeated itself from time to time. This time, however, the cave had lost its claustrophobic horrors: the passage I found myself in didn't seem to be as tight and narrow anymore as it used to be in previous dreams. The walls were not so close up any longer, and the ceiling was higher than usual – I was almost able to stand upright in the cave.

Slightly bent over, I began to follow the passage into the cave. I could move easily and realized that the cave, which used to be rather cool and moist, gradually became more dry and warmer – something I sensed as pleasant and comfortable. For the first time I also realized that there were no offshoots from the passage but only other passages merging into mine.

Soon I arrived in a spot where a wall blocked the access to the farther passage. On closer inspection I recognized that this wall was slightly brighter than the walls of the passage surrounding me. And the longer I looked at it, the brighter it turned. Startled, I turned my eyes away from it, only to provoke the fascinating phenomenon again a little later. Actually, this time the wall seemed to glow up brightly: I was looking into a yellowish light radiating more and more heat.

After I had stared into this light for an indefinite period of time, it suddenly lost its intensity and uniformity and condensed to an irregular structure. This structure was shimmering with a yellowish hue that became darker and turned green on one side; on the other, the yellow hue changed into orange and then red.

When I tilted my head slightly, the colors changed at once: now the structure adopted a reddish hue. Looking at it more closely, I recognized that this red was not just a static surface; rather, it was comprised of countless tiny spots smoothly moving along in the tracks of the structure. When I turned my head upright again I saw that the yellow hue also consisted of these tiny flowing spots that reminded me of insect-like creatures. But here, in the yellow hue, they seemed to move faster. I observed the same with other colors that showed up the moment I turned my head farther towards the left: the tiny green spots chased each other even faster, and the blue and violet ones rushed by so fast that I could perceive them only superficially.

What was irritating to me, in fact almost driving me to despair, were the transitions from one color to the next: they didn't blend harmonically one into the other; rather, there was a sort of borderline, a narrow black strip separating the colors from each other. In this way, the tracks of one color were not connected to those of the others. The tiny spots rushing by on both sides simply disappeared into the void the moment they reached these borderlines, instead of fluently blending into the other color.

I objected to this, and this urge I felt that everything should blend harmoniously into each other was as strong as the urge to breathe. This went so far that I woke up the next moment, actually gasping for air – only to realize that I was staring at the wooden ceiling of my room in Nestor's house, having dreamed with open eyes all that time.

Overheated and dehydrated, I got out of bed. It was a bright day outside, and the morning sun was shining through the window into the room. When I wanted to kick back my blanket I became aware of a beam of light on the pillow, broken down into its spectral colors, that seemed to come from the window. When I checked up on it I realized that it came from the rock crystal the stout farmer had given to me as a gift, and that I had placed on the commode in front of the window: the sunlight shining onto the crystal was broken down into its spectral colors and projected precisely onto my pillow.

It seemed as if the spectral colors had affected me while I had been dreaming with open eyes. The realization that the dream as such had only been possible with the interaction of the crystal – perhaps even being the cause of it – made me think of the farmer's words: after all, he had claimed that the clarity of the rock crystal would help me to gain clarity for myself – something I had dismissed as esoteric gobbledygook back then.

During breakfast I told Nestor of this dream. He interpreted the fact that I was able to move more freely in the cave as an advancement on the path in the basic structure, the advancement being the circumstance that I had become smaller in the dream – an interpretation he seemed to attach quite some value to. Because he resolutely opposed my objection that the cave might have become larger instead of me smaller.

»If you dream of having much space in a room, or more space than before, then this means that you're not so large any longer,« he explained. »This in turn means that you don't consider yourself as important as you used to in earlier times. The more we dissolve our small world, which includes our personality as well, in the picture, the smaller we become. And when we are small we don't collide with and bump into so many obstacles anymore – and this can directly express itself in our dreams.«

Nestor then showed strong interest in the tiny colored spots in motion and asked me about their precise movements and size. Finally he interpreted the phenomenon as the *dynamic effect* of seeing – only that, in my case, it had been superimposed by a dream.

»You already know the *static effect* of seeing,« he pointed out. »This one has to do with the spheres and strands, that is, the basic structure. The dynamic effect, on the other hand, only shows up in extreme situations – moments in which there is a high level of intensity within you, when the amount of energy is extraordinarily large in comparison to what you are able to stand up to. Then we start to perceive tiny luminous spheres moving fast in all directions. Basically this dynamic effect is nothing else than energy forming the tracks of the basic structure.«

What Nestor explained as the »dynamic effect« of seeing was something I knew from personal experience as well as through my research efforts with respect to *mouches volantes*.

From a medical point of view, it is a phenomenon related to white blood cells flowing in the capillaries of the retina but only becoming visible well in situations with extreme physical challenges. As such, shocks, dizzy spells and imminent blackouts, in combination with insufficient blood circulation in the optic nerve and the rear eye wall, can lead to the phenomenon of »flying corpuscles« or »luminous spots«, that is, the perception of those tiny luminous spheres moving along in wound tracks. An overstimulation of the retina, for example through a punch on the eye, can also cause these »spots« to show up – something commonly illustrated in cartoons and comics as stars circulating around the head of a person knocked out during a fight or an accident.

I informed Nestor of the medical explanation for the dynamic effect. As I could have expected, he didn't attach any importance to this explanation. Instead he assured me that this particular effect, even though rarely perceivable, could show up more frequently in a person being on the path in the basic structure. So whenever those luminous spheres in motion were showing up, I was supposed to observe them as closely as possible. The more my inner sense would develop, Nestor added, the larger they would become: seers were sometimes able to see them as gigantic glowing and rotating balls.

Nestor didn't want to comment in any way on the significance of my dream. Instead he advised me to visit the farmer and ask him about it. According to him, the farmer pursued a very concrete intention with this rock crystal – something that obviously had taken place now.

In the early afternoon I arrived at the stone terrace. The stout farmer had placed himself behind his house from where he had an optimum view over the valley and the mountain on the other side. When I came closer I could see that he was neither looking down the valley nor up the mountain but staring into the blue, increasingly cloudy sky.

His welcome was friendly but brief. We engaged in some casual chat, then I told him of my difficulties with the restoration of the inlay work on Mari Egli's secretaire. He didn't seem to be willing to tackle this subject with me, so I finally mentioned the *mouches volantes* and tried to talk to him about the seers and the basic structure for the first time. The farmer, however, didn't want to reveal anything; he ended the conversation with the remark that I had to *see* the structure in order to find out and learn something about it. His repellent attitude was irritating to me, and an embarrassing silence between us ensued.

»Why are you here?« the farmer brought our conversation to the point.

»The rock crystal you gave me has caused its effect,« I told him in Nestor's sense. He looked at me in surprise as if he could hardly believe it.

»And what effect did it have?«

I replied that I couldn't really judge it and told him of my dream. The farmer listened but seemed to waver somehow, not really knowing what to do with my story. For several minutes he kept silent.

Then, as if following a sudden spontaneous intuition, he got up and went into the house. I followed him and found him standing next to the stove. He lifted the lid of a pot in which he was cooking something, gave the contents a critical look and put the lid back onto the pot. Finally he sat down in the upholstered leather chair. I sat down across from him at the table, waiting until he would say something.

»What do you want to hear from me?« he asked after a while.

»I would like to know whether the rock crystal has some sort of connection to my dream.«

»You already know that. For sure it had some connection to it. Obviously the colors you saw in your dream were brought about by that crystal.«

»Does this dream have anything to do with my restoration of Mari Egli's secretaire?«

The farmer laughed quietly. »How am I supposed to know? I concentrate on that which is in front of my eyes.«

»But can't you tell me anything about the meaning or significance of the dream?« I kept asking.

»No. It is none of my business to assign any meaning or significance to your dream.« He explained that it was not the task of seers anyway to fill the world with meaning and significance. The seer's task, according to him, consisted of dissolving the world into light. To assign any meaning or significance to a dream would mean to draw light from the structure of consciousness – that is, to dim and darken the world.

»So, according to you, I'm not supposed to search for a meaning or significance?« I concluded.

»You're not a seer,« he replied, got up and walked up to the stove again. »No, you are not a seer. That's why you are looking for meanings and significances in the first place. But you'll never find them outside of yourself.«

The wiry man took the pot off the stove and started to stir the contents. Absorbed into his activities, he said that I had to derive the meanings and significances from *me*, just like he derived the essence of herbs by boiling them out and obtaining the concentrated liquid, the »brew«.

Impatiently I informed the farmer that I hadn't come to visit him on my own initiative but on Nestor's advice. So there must be some concrete information he, the farmer, should have for me.

»I don't have any idea what Nestor is up to,« I added. »I have to trust him completely.«

»I don't have any idea, either, what Nestor is up to. I also trust him completely.« The wiry man made a grimace and smiled almost imperceptibly. Obviously he had noticed my disheartenment and asked me whether I would like to stay for lunch, because after a good meal things usually looked quite different. As I still hadn't forgotten the farmer's »culinary skills« even after this long period of time, I declined his offer in a friendly but determined way.

I had to return to Nestor's house without the answers I hoped for. Nestor listened to my account of what had been said between me and the farmer but couldn't make any sense out of his responses. Still he was convinced that the farmer had given me instructions on how to deal with my dream. For that reason, he had me repeat everything that had happened between me and the farmer. I was supposed to recall any and all details, no matter how small or insignificant. After I had told Nestor everything for the third time, he suddenly grinned. He opened up to me that he now knew what the farmer actually wanted to tell me. And to him, it was funny that I had interpreted the farmer's profound words as useless chitchat, not mentioned by me until recalling the events for the third time. He sparked my curiosity with this, but I couldn't worm anything out of him – except for the announcement that we would go into the forest as soon as possible.

It took another week until it was dry and sunny enough to go for a hiking trip. We were already on our way for quite some time, but Nestor still kept silent about the farmer's words and their deeper meaning. The single-mindedness with which he kept walking ahead, however, showed me that he had a certain place for us in mind.

Finally we arrived at a small, relatively flat spot on the edge of the forest, close to a steep abyss. Somehow the place seemed familiar to me. I looked over to Nestor who sat down on an overturned tree trunk. Precisely this picture triggered an unpleasant memory in me: somewhere around here was that hole which Nestor macabrely called the »Emmental Cooking Pot«.

»I won't step down into this thing one more time,« I immediately clarified matters.

»It's the farmer's advice. And we'll have to follow it, because it was the farmer who had started it all: just like he derives the essence of his herbs, you'll derive the meaning of your dream – in the same way, that is, by boiling it out. And what better way to do this than by using the Emmental Cooking Pot?«

I started to argue that the farmer didn't refer to me but to the herbs when he used the word »boil out«; moreover he had used this term in a metaphoric and not at all in a concrete sense; and aside from all this, I was sufficiently familiar with the cooking pot and its effect.

»So that's your final answer?« he laughed. The fact that he didn't take me serious made me even more upset. I kept answering »No« and justified my decision with the fact that Nestor had the nerve to lead me to this place without obtaining my agreement in the first place – just as if I was someone underage.

When I didn't know what to say any longer, Nestor spoke up. »Interpreting dreams is not an easy thing,« he said, »because dreaming takes place in the emotional world, therefore in a layer in which you are not tied to material conditions. In dreams, your level of intensity can be much higher, and you can do astounding things with your emotional body. But when you wake up and return to the layer of your daily consciousness, you're missing that intensity required to understand the dream.«

Nestor went on to explain that I had the choice to either resort to dream interpretation systems already in existence or to try to find, by myself, a plausible correlation between this dream and my everyday life events. Such an approach was not wrong but merely lead to interpreted knowledge. Because to a seer, interpreting dreams was not a question of intellect and the more or less inventive correlations of experiences on the outer and inner screen; rather, what I needed was just the same level of intensity as in the dream, that is, shifting my consciousness into the emotional world, but without losing reference to the outer screen.

»When you act in your emotional body, and when you're able to cope with this level of intensity, then it is possible to obtain a much more direct and comprehensive knowledge of things you're dealing with. Today the cooking pot will help you bring about the level of intensity required.«

»I'm familiar with that level of ›intensity‹,« I defended myself. »The last time I crept out of the pot I felt depressive for several days after.«

»Today it will be different,« he assured me. »Today the fire will vaporize the water in the kettle because the fire will be sparked in the space below. In this way, the effect of the Emmental Cooking Pot will be reversed, and you'll find out how transforming sexual energy over a longer period of time will bring about an additional increase in the inner pressure. You yourself will reach a higher state of intensity in the course of that, and you'll vitalize your picture. And that will also bring about the intuition you need, for example, to interpret your dreams.«

I didn't know what to say. Nestor had managed, once again, to convince me of the necessity of an inconvenience. Perhaps it was the bitter aftertaste of the defeat that made me object halfheartedly that this particular dream was actually too unimportant to even engage in an interpretation of it.

Nestor laughed loudly and called me a shirker. It was his heartiness that made me relent eventually. Together we prepared the Emmental Cooking Pot for its use: we pushed aside the wooden lid of the hole; then I began to clear the channel feeding the water into the pot of all twigs, branches, leaves and debris while Nestor sparked a fire in the copper cone located in the small space under the glass pane. Soon after, I could see smoke rising from four openings around the hole. These inconspicuous openings were equipped with fine metal grids, similar to the channel feeding the water, to prevent leaves and soil from falling into the pot. Our preparations went smooth and fast; the silly idea popped up in my mind that we had already acquired some »routine expertise« in handling the cooking pot.

Finally I stepped down into the cooking pot, and Nestor covered the opening with the wooden lid. Then he began to open the floodgate. I waited, hemmed into this cool, moist and dark hole. It struck me that I could virtually smell nothing of the smoke rising from the fire. Whoever had rigged up this gadget – he understood his handicraft very well.

Soon after, I heard the water gurgle through the stone furrows. It surrounded me and flowed down into the copper kettle under me where it soon started to boil. The steam arising didn't only mist up the glass pane but also penetrated the space I was in. When the temperature rose and I started to sweat, it dawned on me how fitting the name »cooking pot« was for this device.

After some time I felt a pressure bloating my belly, adding to my nervousness. I had the strong urge to move my limbs, to fully stretch my arms and legs. But that was hardly possible in this narrow hole. In order to cool down and distract myself, I splashed some of the cold water flowing down in the stone furrows into my face several times. The pressure increased further and extended from my belly over the entire body. Soon after, my heart rate picked up more and more, and I felt as if each cell in my body had been inflated, short of and close to bursting due to the immense pressure.

In the next moment I felt a strong prickle on my back that finally extended to my arms and legs. This sensation of release lasted longer than any other I had experienced up to that point. Right after this, I realized that my sensations had changed: all of a sudden, the heat seemed to have disappeared, and the pressure in my body was gone as well. The prickle sensation repeated itself several times and enabled me to relax and feel comfortable in my skin. I wasn't disturbed any longer by being hemmed into this muggy hole; it didn't matter anymore that my clothes were uncomfortably moist and sticking to my skin. And right the moment when I thought that I could easily spend some more time down here, Nestor removed the wooden lid above me.

With deft movements I climbed out of the Emmental Cooking Pot, and when I stood up there next to Nestor I felt so refreshed and strong that I was in the mood to laugh and celebrate.

»And what are we going to do now?« Nestor asked.

I was slaphappy and full of zest for action. Many things that I would have liked to do popped up in my mind at once. I started to count them off, but while I was speaking I thought of even more possibilities I immediately picked up. Consequently, my proposals ended in unintelligible yakety-yak. Nestor laughed, but now his laughter – that I used to fear because it had often snubbed me – didn't affect me in any way, quite the contrary: I laughed along with him.

Nestor then took the initiative and went ahead. I followed him and was surprised about the adept movements of my body. I walked on the forest soil with playful, almost dance-like movements, cleverly sidestepping obstacles. Moving my body was something I had great fun with now. Still we were hardly getting ahead, because time and again, something caught my attention that I had to look at for quite some time. Many little but fascinating things struck me – animals, plants or stones I would have ignored or overlooked before now caught my eye.

I also realized that the environment had changed somewhat. Whereas the usual green colors, mixed with gray-brown hues typical for these surroundings, had dominated before my stepping into the cooking pot, now the most diverse colors were shimmering in my picture. For example, a pasture we came by didn't show only the usual brighter and darker green but strong red, yellow and brown hues in the individual blades of grass and at the tips of some leaves. Moss, shining in a deep green and golden yellow, was growing in between the grass, and together with the withering fern displaying colors from green, yellow and orange all the way to red and brown, the pasture looked like straight out of a fairytale. The light, the sunlight, glittering in countless little drops of water and shining on the long blades of wild grass; or the lichen sprawling on the branches of older fir trees, giving them a mysterious bluish hue; or the leaves with their brown-reddish warm color crowning the treetops and heralding the upcoming fall – all these impressions revealed the un-dreamed-of splendor of the picture.

We went on, passing by large roots of overturned trees seemingly lurking with their »tentacles« for anything coming into their closer vicinity. We came by deep all-devouring ditches and wild all-penetrating water, fantastic flowers, bizarre mushrooms, fascinating insects – there was so much to see, so much to discover. For a moment I was a little sad that I was missing the time to take a closer look at the beauty of all these things, but then my attention was caught again by the extraordinary clarity, sharpness and fascination the picture displayed.

Something was happening within my body. All that time I could feel a rumble in my belly. My stomach started to bloat, and I had to get rid of wind several times. Likewise, I had to burp now and then. This obviously hadn't escaped Nestor who now walked behind me, and he told me to stop for a moment.

»Farting and burping,« he explained with the voice of a teacher, »is a good thing. It means that your body is cleansing itself. And it also means that you are shrinking in the process: then you're not so ›bloated‹ any longer as you were before.« I had to laugh about his ambiguous remark, but Nestor wrinkled his nose and announced that he would walk in front again from now on.

After a while we arrived in a bright spot from where we had a nice view over the valley, and we sat down under the deciduous trees. Nestor knew that this particular place was ideal for seeing the basic structure around this time of day. Indeed, a large portion of the sky was visible here, and the sunlight didn't blind us as it was blocked out by the trees.

It was easy for me to see the dots and strands, and I could literally feel that I was much more alert and attentive than usual. Without effort I could focus on my structure and hold it in suspension over a longer period of time. And several times I discovered new forms and shapes: I suddenly looked at dots and strands I had never really noticed before, simply because they were not the usual ones I had focused on before. I also became aware of my behavior towards strands I was familiar with:

often enough I used to enforce the perception of strands at the periphery of my field of vision by mechanically flinging them into the center, time and again. But now I consciously directed my attention to dots and strands closer to the center. There was far less effort involved in looking at these objects: they didn't flow away to the left or right but only downwards.

I fixed my gaze on a strand familiar to me. For quite some time I played with it, holding it in suspension in the center of the picture or shifting it horizontally across the misty but bright sky. The longer I did this, though, the more it changed: to my surprise, the strand, in fact transparent, didn't only turn smaller and become more sharply focused – it also started to light up.

I quickly realized that looking at the strand in this luminous condition was something that didn't last for very long: one wrong movement of the eyes – too strong or too lax – or one look at the environment was enough to make the strand assume its original size again and lose its luminosity. Several times I focused on this, and each time the strand lit up again after some time. Concentrating on it for a longer period made the strand light up more intensely, even brighter than the environment; at the same time, however, I also noticed the same luminosity in the dots and strands immediately surrounding the one I focused on.

All excited, I told Nestor of my perception.

»What you've seen is the *light of consciousness*,« he said as if it were self-evident. »You can see it because you have compressed and condensed the layers of consciousness – but this time you did so without moving your body.«

I asked him what that meant. Instead of answering, Nestor pointed to a large bright stone to our right and asked me to superimpose my strand over this particular stone. When I had managed to do so he instructed me to walk up to the stone without taking my eyes off the strand. It took quite a few attempts but then I managed to hold the strand in suspension and, at the same time, move up so close to the stone that I almost touched it with the tip of my nose. In amazement, I realized that the strand turned smaller and started to light up when I approached the stone, just like I had observed it before when looking at the sky.

Then Nestor asked me to stretch out my arm and superimpose the strand over the palm of my hand. Now I was supposed to hold the palm of my hand close up to my face while still looking at the strand. The same thing happened here as well: the closer I held my hand in front of my face, the smaller and more luminous the strand became.

»That is concentration,« Nestor finally explained. »The light of consciousness becomes better visible due to your concentration. When seeing, you can experience directly and firsthand what concentration actually is: it's scaling down the section of the picture you look at. In the process, the space you spread the light on is smaller. Or in other words: you are compressing the layers of consciousness.

If you walk up to an object, or if you pull it towards you, it means on the outer screen that you can look at a smaller section of the object magnified, richer in detail and more sharply focused. You did the same when we were talking about the layers of consciousness, when you pressed your cup against your forehead – but back then you couldn't see what was happening simultaneously on the inner screen with your basic structure. Now you can see directly that the dots and strands become smaller but at the same time more focused, intense and luminous – and that's concentration.«

Nestor considered it a progress that, from now on, I wouldn't have to look at the outer screen any longer in order to concentrate myself. Concentration, according to him, came about by seeing the basic structure, independent from the material world. I pointed out that I was able to also concentrate on things such as thoughts, ideas and memories without having to directly perceive the material world, either.

»That's no real concentration,« Nestor replied determinedly. »People believe it's concentration when they ponder over something. But what is their attention actually doing in the process? It is constantly being realigned. People in thoughts relax time and again when they don't fix anything with the eyes and hold the picture in suspension. Full concentration, on the other hand, means that you can hold your dots and strands in suspension so adroitly that they don't flow away any longer.

Today you've seen that shining light for the first time. And starting today, you should, when looking at your dots and strands, apply enough attention and concentration each time so that your basic structure starts to light up. Therefore, the way your dots and strands appear when looking at them will show you your actual level of concentration.«

In the late afternoon we returned to Nestor's house. As I was still full of energy and optimism, I directed my attention to Mari Egli's secretaire. It was about time to finish up the job on the bottom right-hand drawer.

Ritually, I first sat down in front of the secretaire and spread out the wooden leaves I intended to glue into the prepared hole in front of me. Then I directed my eyes to the center of the object, with the intention to perceive the afterimage, in order to be prepared for the restoration.

After a few attempts, however, I realized that I wasn't able to concentrate. My thoughts kept circling around the light in the basic structure. A thought-provoking aspect to me was the fact that I was capable of exerting an influence on my structure that went beyond mechanically moving the dots and strands: whereas I could draw a relationship between my moving these objects and my physical eyes, bringing about this light phenomenon was a much more subtle issue. I took into consideration that there actually was a form of exchange, detectable in the basic structure, between me and the picture, and correspondingly, Nestor's demand for an open body, freed from blockades, made complete sense to me.

These thoughts revived my memory of the dream I had about the dynamic effect of seeing. I believed to understand directly now how important, even vital, the unimpeded flow of energy was in order to maintain an exchange with the entire picture or with individual people and objects within it. I had to admit to myself, though, that those moments of free-flowing energy and exchange were quite rare in my case. Undoubtedly I could have done more to remove blockades and obstacles in my body. I still preferred to seal myself off, thus impeding the free flow of energy between me and my picture – this didn't only show up in my everyday feelings but in that dream about those interrupted energy channels as well.

And this also showed me what was happening right in front of my eyes: in a moment of absolute certainty I recognized the wavy grain pattern of the inlay work as being identical with those tracks and channels ensuring a free flow of energy. The »energy channels« were uninterrupted – except for a few holes in the inlay work, among them the one on the bottom right-hand drawer. As a test, I held the small wooden leaves I had prepared on the corresponding spots in the hole – and found out that the grain pattern of these leaves did not align with the rest of the inlay work as they did not harmonically blend into each other on the borderlines. Now it dawned on me that I had attempted to enforce something on the secretaire that tainted its structure, thus impeding the flow of energy.

But when I pondered over having to find matching wooden leaves that would perfectly align with their grain pattern to the inlay at work as a whole, it was as if I woke up from a dream: how should it be possible at all to align the grain pattern of two different sorts of wood one hundred percent? The grain pattern of a piece of wood was so unique that there was no way around some sort of borderline interrupting or impeding a smooth blend of wood pieces with different cuts. At best, the different pieces of wood could be aligned in such a way that their grain patterns would match somewhat harmoniously. The search for a *perfectly* matching piece of wood would have been silly; it would have taken more than lifetime.

Still I felt inclined to disprove this realization, and I began searching for spots on the secretaire where the grain pattern was simply interrupted because different kinds of wood were in juxtaposition. But it turned out that the confounded pattern was actually like one single net spanning over the entire secretaire: it continued in all directions without interruptions, over all drawers and inlaid lines and rings – the secretaire was nothing less than perfect. At this moment there was no doubt on my part that its creator must have been vested with superhuman powers.

Contrary to all logic and reason, I began searching for spots on the wooden leaves I wanted to use as replacements that might have precisely fitted in the hole. But that search was utterly hopeless and futile. A grain pattern was like a fingerprint: unique due to its composition, the wood species as well as the location and direction of cut. To me there was no doubt that this was the end of the perfect restoration.

In the evening I talked to Nestor about this problem. He was pleased about the way I still had been able to wrest a meaning, favorable to the perfect restoration, from my dream. A higher level of intensity might not yet bestow me with the direct knowledge of a seer, he pointed out, but with the intuitive insights that would advance me on the path in the basic structure.

But when I pointed out to him that it was impossible to continue the restoration, he turned sour. He impressed upon me that I should jump over my shadow and not back down whenever some difficulties arose. According to him, I could only find matching pieces of wood if I searched for it – unfailing and unfatiguing until I had found it.

»Take this little bug here, for example,« he said and pointed to a small beetle that sat on the base of the only lamp in the room, lighting it up sparsely. The bug tried to creep up the base to get as close to the light of the bulb as possible but appeared somewhat awkward in its attempts. Because, no matter how much it tried – after having made some headway it always slipped back down to the bottom of the base because its surface was too smooth and even.

»Now here we have a little bug,« Nestor commented the ongoing events. »It does not have the consciousness of a human being. But still it tries harder to reach the light than most human beings do.«

I pointed out that the crazy search for a fitting piece of wood seemed to be more futile than the search for the light of consciousness, but Nestor replied that actually there was no real difference between these two: in the final analysis, we didn't search for anything else than this light, no matter what we believed to strive for. Because all things and objects – and this was something a seer could see – were formed and brought into existence by the light of consciousness. What the people basically did was trying to get hold of as much of this light as possible with each of their activities – of course in accordance with their respective layer of consciousness. For most people, this meant striving for the light in its condensed forms: striving for the right thoughts, desired feelings and shiny objects.

»A seer sees where the light comes from, how it splits up countless times and how it condenses until we can recognize it as small world,« he went on. »A seer therefore is not clinging to these condensations of light, contrary to ordinary people who get into arguments over the meanings of words, over feelings and over matter – like flies around shit.«

He laughed, then he looked at me and continued: »As you are not a seer, and because your light of consciousness is only lighting up sparsely so far, the outer screen is still the main field of activity you have to work in. So find the fitting pieces for the perfect restoration. But in doing so, you should not forget that you're actually searching for the light of consciousness.«

Nestor said this with such authority that I didn't dare counter him. But on the other hand, I couldn't agree with him, either. Clearly, his demand was presumptuous and unrealistic. I believed, even hoped, that this was some sort of test or joke he cracked, and that he would cease to do so any second. Nestor, however, kept quiet, and an unpleasant silence ensued.

In order to fill up this silence, I changed the subject and speculated loudly about a conceivable scientific explanation for the alleged »light of consciousness« in the basic structure. I speculated about luminescent matter in the vitreous that could cause perceivable light emissions by means of mechanics, biochemical processes or high-energy radiation.

Nestor didn't go into this. »If a human being develops his consciousness it is indeed possible that his eyes or even his entire body is undergoing a change,« he said. »Perhaps the body suddenly produces more of certain substances, while the production of other substances is reduced or even arrested. Perhaps a scientist could even determine when a seer experiences the condition of ecstasy, and he even might be able to describe the processes in the body causing an ecstasy.

But what's the point? We have to advance to the stage where we are able to experience ecstasies and see how the basic structure is lighting up in the process. Everything else is neither liberating, direct knowledge nor fun in any way – in other words, just blah blah.«

According to Nestor, it was good that I was now able to see the shining of the structure. And with a laugh he added that, from now on, I wouldn't have to hold books close up to my nose any longer in order to »see the light«.

His words directed my attention to something that seemed contradictory to me. I pointed out to Nestor that a book became larger subjectively, the closer I pulled it towards me. At the same time, however, as I could convince myself, the dots and strands in the structure turned *smaller*. According to Nestor, both cases had to do with concentration.

I asked him how it was possible that, in the one case, concentration magnified the object viewed, and scaled it down in the other.

»In the case of the material object it's not concentration all by itself having an effect here,« he answered. »If you want to take a detailed look at a material object you'll have to walk up to it or pull it towards you so as to make it larger and more distinct – in other words, you'll have to invest physical energy in addition to concentration. If you, on the other hand, sit down and concentrate on the basic structure, you don't put any additional energy into the picture. You compress the layers of consciousness and condense the same amount of energy in a smaller space. Consequently, the dots and strands appear more intense, that is, they start to light up – but they just become smaller, not larger.

To a seer, though, it's actually all about seeing the dots and strands on the inner screen larger and more closely, and in order to do so he puts additional energy into his shining structure – not physical energy but consciousness energy. That particular energy is comprised of transformed sexual energies, the energy resulting from physical exercises, released feelings and thoughts, and it flows as ecstasy into the entire picture. In this way, the dots and strands of his shining structure turn larger.«

I objected that I had never come across the like in the case of my sensations. Nestor smiled and intimated that, in the case of a slight prickle feeling the way I currently experienced it, so little energy flowed into the picture that I wasn't able to detect the difference. In order to experience this at all, he explained, I would have to put huge amounts of energy into the picture as a whole.

»Now this is exactly what I'm trying to get across to you,« he finally said. »A seer moves the picture with his excess energy. He puts it through his open body into the picture as a whole, that is, the basic structure. In doing so, he penetrates the layers of consciousness and is able to see directly what's happening, time and again, during such an ecstatic experience: the dots and strands of the structure, and with them the objects of our sensual material world, light up, come closer and become larger. At the same time, the seer obtains direct knowledge. This is the reason why I speak of the *shining structure of consciousness*.«

4

The Right Side of Consciousness

The Bridge with the Double Arch

For a long time, Bern and the upper Emmental were two radically different worlds for me, completely incompatible with one another. I responded to this conflict by adapting to the circumstances and developing contrasting behavior patterns or roles: in Bern I was a person with certain views, preferences, joys and worries. In the Emmental I was a learner who tried to expose these views, preferences, joys and worries as small world and thus arrive at an expanded perception of the picture – not least in order to restore Mari Egli's secretaire.

In the beginning I played the apprentice, knowing that I could return to Bern, back to »reality«, at any time. Over time, however, the change of roles and ideals, meanwhile taking place almost every week, resulted in me getting to know both convictions and ways of thought better, and I learned to accept them. And at some point I had to admit to myself that the idea of me as a solid, unchanging personality with very specific views and ideals was but an illusion.

With this, however, the borderline I had drawn from the beginning between Bern and the Emmental started to become vague and indifferent. For example, during my visits of the upper Emmental I regularly caught myself, more than at the outset, agreeing to the values and ideals of our society and trying to defend them stubbornly against the views of Nestor and the seers. And in Bern, vice versa, I started to criticize more and more loudly any erroneous self-complacency and »ideal world« behind which far too many people were hiding in order to consistently evade any and all efforts required for a targeted individual development of their consciousness – no matter whether they did it knowingly or not.

These two worlds, totally separate at first, started to merge more and more deeply – eventually to such an extreme degree that I even had to experience it on and in my own body. It was the time shortly before fall in which I unexpectedly suffered, time and again, from unpleasant symptoms such as nervous trembling, dizzy spells and heart palpitation. They showed up as a sort of attacks – sudden increases in the energy metabolism rate of my body. They lasted only briefly but were so extreme that I panicked every time they flared up. But as soon as these unpleasant episodes ceased, two things could happen: sometimes I experienced a prickle feeling on my legs, arms or back, and a pleasant exhilarating body feeling ensued. In that case I felt more relaxed for the remainder of the day, but I also had an easier time to be more alert and present. In most cases, though, the prickle feeling was only quite short-lived and accompanied by a nervous chilly shiver.

I realized that these were the same physical symptoms I had some-times experienced in the Emmental. Long ago, the area around Nestor's house turned out to be a place where things of that nature could happen at any time – a place that I therefore learned to fear and respect. What was calming me down, though, was that I knew the left side of the Emme to be a geographically limited area, and I also believed to know the causes of these symptoms: the work on the secretaire and the seers' »stagings«.

But now it happened that I was seized by these symptoms in Bern as well – in totally different situations so that I wasn't able to trace back the attacks to specific circumstances as source point or origin. Places that I so far had considered safe, that is, not causing unexpected in-creases in levels of intensity, suddenly became a physical and mental challenge. And I could see no way for me to influence events taking place. I decided to ask Nestor for advice.

I visited him at the end of October. Right after my arrival I told him of my unpleasant physical changes. Nestor, however, didn't really seem to be willing to talk about the subject right away. Instead, I was supposed to help him jar and preserve a portion of the mirabelles, apples and pears he had gathered.

In the evening, after that work was done, Nestor picked up the subject and started to talk about these sudden increases in intensity. He said that I had transformed enough energy by now so as to loosen and suspend my stability within one layer of consciousness.

»For years now, you're making your way on the path in the shining structure,« he explained. »And this means that you have slowly advanced through the layers of the right side – so slowly that you're not able to judge your advancements with your immediate seeing but only by look-ing into your past. The reason why your advancement on the path in the basic structure had been so slow and hesitant had to do with the fact that you were situated very stably in your layers. But now you're able to loosen your stability in one certain layer in one fell swoop. And that's what's causing these sudden increases in intensity. Obviously you're creating the according circumstances for yourself over and over so that this can take place.«

»I'm not creating anything,« I protested. »These attacks happen all by themselves.«

»It only seems that way. Of course you don't have a direct influence on these increases in intensity, just like a seer cannot directly bring about his states of ecstasy. But we are eliciting them by consciously working on ourselves and bringing about the according circumstances with our activities.«

Then I told him how frightening the moments of these attacks were for me because each time it felt as if I was about to dissolve and go to pieces.

»It's a part of your small world that's dissolving and going to pieces every time that happens. And of course you're defending yourself against it. Because your small world provides you with security. It's your yardstick for judging people, objects or views in the picture. And that, of course, you don't want to give up.

But it's precisely there where you're blocking yourself. And these blockades prevent you from being able to put the energy into the picture as a whole right at the instant of the attack, to release your fixation in the right half of consciousness and to enjoy the sensation of ecstasy in the process. What's happening instead is that your heart rate, your pulse and your breathing rate are still picking up.«

»So what am I supposed to do now?« I asked him.

»Precisely what you should do in all of these cases: open your body,« he replied. »I've shown you how you have to lead your life in order to remove blockades in your body and get the energy to flow.«

After a longer pause Nestor began to tell me of a unique and extreme experience brought about by endeavors aiming at opening the body. He called his experience the *leap into the left side of consciousness*. This leap inevitably occurred to people advancing on the path in the shining structure with all of their heart. When the energy level reached a maximum, according to him, the body suddenly opened up, and all the energy was discharged explosively into the picture. This initial state of ecstasy released the fixation in the right half of consciousness and made the energy flow upward in the body.

»What does that mean: the energy flows upward?« I asked.

»Your energy that you receive from the picture can either flow upward or downward; I could also say: the energy flows inward or outward – it's both the same. If it flows downward or inward, this means that you're binding most of the energy in the picture, meaning that you need it to structure your picture, make it material and build up your personality. If, on the other hand, the energy flows upward or outward, you're putting most of the energy as light of consciousness directly into the picture as a whole. In which direction your energy flows in the majority of cases depends on your state of consciousness.

With right-sided people, the energy usually flows downward – only when they fall asleep deeply, that is, when they fall deep into the left side, their energy flows upward. In the course of that, they cannot stay conscious, though. The same happens the moment a person dies: death is a reversal of the energy flow and a violent opening of the body. In the course of that, all energy is discharged at once, and the person dying falls into the left side, into the one sphere. But when a person has not completely developed his consciousness so that a very large amount of energy can flow through the body unimpeded, then that person cannot stand up to it: he drops into visions or hallucinations, goes unconscious and dies.

The seer, on the other hand, has already taken that leap into the left side of consciousness while still alive – without having lost his consciousness in the process. Basically, this means nothing else than that his daily consciousness corresponds to normal persons' state of deep sleep. Therefore, the energy of a seer flows upward more often than downward.« Nestor ended his remarks with the note that the only decision left to us as human beings was whether we wanted to prefer and consciously experience a reversal of the energy flow and thus the opening of our body, or whether we didn't want that.

It made immediate sense to me that the opening of the body and the release of energy were connected to death, but still it had something very frightening to me.

»According to that, every pleasant prickle feeling on the body would be a form of dying,« I concluded.

»Your small world is dying,« Nestor replied. »You yourself become more conscious and alive. It's this way: at the moment of death, everyone of us will have to release and surrender everything. A seer, however, who has already released and surrendered everything, that is, transformed everything into the light of consciousness during his lifetime, can enter into the picture as a whole in a fully conscious state of being. In this way, his consciousness is overcoming physical death. This is what the seers are striving for.«

On the next day Nestor announced that he wanted to talk to me about the leap into the left side of consciousness. For a while he remained silent, then he obviously had changed his mind: he asked me how I got along with my search for those wooden leaves for the inlay work on the bottom right-hand drawer. I had to admit to him that I hadn't even started the search yet. The task to find three different wooden leaves, the grain patterns of which would precisely fit in the hole on the drawer, seemed too hopeless, too senseless to me. And in addition I believed that continuing the restoration work wasn't necessary any longer as the secretaire had fulfilled its purpose.

»See, I've changed,« I opened up my thoughts to him. »The work on Mari Egli's secretaire certainly had been necessary because it had prompted me to see the shining structure. But meanwhile I've made further progress: you yourself said that my stability in the layers of the right half of consciousness is gradually suspending. I don't think that I have any further need for that piece of furniture. I want to arrive at the left side of consciousness and see for myself if things are the way you say.«

Nestor lifted his eyebrows in surprise. »Yes, yes, that's all still to come,« he promised. »You've got the willpower for sure but: the most adamant willpower won't help you when your knees are shivering in fear as soon as more energy is flowing.«

His words reminded me of all those situations where my body hadn't been open enough, where the energy flow had been blocked, with me panicking over it. Just the memory of these »borderline experiences« caused me to become nervous and made my heart pound hard.

»Mari Egli's secretaire is still a challenge to you,« Nestor continued our conversation after I had remained silent. »You've invested a lot into that piece of furniture, you have grown with it – but you haven't outgrown it yet. For you, the path through the structure to the left side is inseparably connected to this secretaire.«

On Nestor's request we went into the stable to take a look at the secretaire. Nestor pointed to the bottom right-hand drawer and said that this was precisely the place where I was hung up – both in the restoration and in seeing the shining structure.

»You always wanted to know what exactly it is that makes Mari Egli's secretaire so very special,« he explained. »Today I can tell you what it is: the secretaire is a depiction of the path in the shining structure. Whoever built this piece of furniture – he or she was a seer who had taken the path in the structure all the way to its end.«

»How can you be so sure of that?« I asked surprised.

»I know this as a result of my own seeing. With the buildup and composition of this piece of furniture, the artist has precisely expressed the course the path is taking within the structure, after all: from the bottom up, from right to left and from the front to the far back. And most of all, with the inlay work the artist has portrayed those important strands and sphere constellations that I myself can see on the path in the shining structure.«

Now the scales fell from my eyes. Indeed, at this moment I could identify the circular images in the inlay work as *mouches volantes* that the artist had replicated. It was so obvious that it struck me how I could have overlooked this.

Nestor repeated that, when it came to my seeing, my position was on the bottom right-hand drawer – precisely the point where the handle was missing and where I had to fight with the hole in the inlay work. Then he pointed to the inlaid zigzag strand spanning over the two bottommost drawers.

»This is a strand in the shining structure as well,« he explained. »A very special and important strand. It connects the right side of consciousness with the left. Therefore it's a kind of *bridge*.«

»Does that mean that I should be able to see this strand in my structure now?«

»Yes.«

»But isn't it so that we all see our own individual images of spheres and strands?« I asked in surprise.

»No, it's not that simple,« he answered back. »Indeed, every person illuminates the spheres and strands in this structure in his own individual way, and every person has his own sphere he ultimately enters into. But there's only one overall structure, and we all share the perception of the spheres and strands within it – just like we all share the perception of objects in the sensual-material world, even though each person has his own distinct viewpoint of things. Also, we all share the principle according to which the path in the shining structure is built up: for every person, this path will lead from the bottom front right to the top back left; it will begin with the perception of many small dots and strands and finally end in a single, all-encompassing sphere – and in between there are certain constellations of spheres and strands in the individual layers that are so formative and characteristic for a seer that he recognizes them as *landmarks*. This particular bridge is such a landmark – it represents the layer of human beings.«

All of this came as quite a surprise to me. Nestor's claims were dicey because he called for something like uniformity and commonality – in short: objective validity – for a phenomenon that was in itself the epitome of subjectivity. The question whether it actually was one and the same shining structure we illuminated and fathomed out with our seeing was something that, in my view, could not be answered at all. But I was certain that the seers had »agreed upon« their seeing of the shining structure and the interpretations associated with it, in just the same way as we, as human beings, are »agreeing«, time and again, on the perception and interpretation of our everyday environment.

I confronted Nestor with these considerations, but he kept insisting on his viewpoints. He said that, ultimately, there was only one single consciousness. And this consciousness formed one single structure that was the source point of all diversity. Consciousness was split up into light and matter via this shining structure, bringing into existence the small world and arranging the picture in such a way that we could recognize it as something meaningful and sensible. We, as human beings, were part of this one structure, just like the fruits of a tree were part of that tree. The buildup of the structure, Nestor repeated, followed a specific principle. This principle that a seer could see in the structure was always the same and determined our life in the world known to us down to the most minute details. I remained silent. Nestor mimicked my helpless shoulder shrug.

»For a seer this is all direct knowledge coming about by the act of seeing,« he confirmed. »At the moment of seeing, no further explanations are needed. Only in the diversity of the small world does the search for the principle of life become so damn complicated that people need computers, calculators and particle accelerators consuming huge amounts of energy, in order to slowly feel their way ahead, like blind people, to the source point of existence.«

I didn't say anything, but I could feel how I defended myself against the idea of a shining structure that all living beings shared. Because, somehow I had gotten used to the idea that my dots and strands were something of an individual nature, unique in their forms, dimensions and constellations.

»So then I have to reckon,« I concluded soberly, »that the dots in my picture are the same that, let's say, my room neighbor in Bern is seeing?«

Nestor laughed, confirmed this and added jokingly that, on that occasion, I should render my room neighbor a service by illuminating her dots in the process. Then he turned towards the secretaire again and began to explain the specific properties of the »bridge«.

»You'll find this strand on the right side of consciousness. You can see that it consists of two tips or arches, but they are not totally symmetric. When you can see the strand and keep it in suspension with your concentration, it means that you are situated in the layer of human beings.«

Then he pointed to the right end of the connecting strand. »The bridge is fastened down at the right end only – the left end is free floating. So when you want to get to the left side of consciousness it won't be enough to just walk the bridge – you'll have to fly.« Nestor laughed. Finally he directed my attention to the vertical strand that spanned between the drawers over the entire front side of the secretaire, dividing it into a left and right half.

»This particular strand you'll also learn to see in the context of the bridge. It's the Emme,« he said with a smirk, »the energy flow running from top to bottom that is reversed by the seers when they take the leap from the right over into left side. On the path in the basic structure you'll wander alongside this strand until you arrive at the bridge and change over to the other side.«

I didn't want to join Nestor's symbolism; to me, it was arbitrary and meaningless. Nestor, however, was confident that I would understand the inlay work on the secretaire better once I had seen and experienced all this for myself.

»Find the bridge with the double arch in your structure,« he encouraged me. »It is the most important orientation strand for right-sided people who want to change over into the left half of consciousness.«

On the same day I tried to find this bridge in my structure. From memory alone I wouldn't have been able to tell whether a strand of this kind actually existed or not. But due to my focused searching, I soon after saw a multitude of these kinds of strands that at least somewhat approximated a bridge in terms of their shape. There was not a single one among them, though, that exhibited all the properties of the bridge as described by Nestor. Soon the search seemed to be a senseless undertaking, but Nestor encouraged me to keep searching. But as that search was unsuccessful on the following day as well, I started to doubt the existence of the bridge.

Before I returned to Bern in the evening, I talked to Nestor about it. He kept insisting on the unique importance of the connecting strand.

»And what if I'm not yet able to see this strand? Perhaps it's not illuminated yet in my structure,« I speculated.

»Perhaps you can't recognize it because it's dancing right in front of your nose all the time. Perhaps you don't see this strand for all those *mouches volantes*,« he joked. Then he assured me with provoking certainty that I already saw and illuminated the bridge in my structure. »The bridge is there. It's the strand that you concentrate on most often.«

The fall of that year was unusually warm and mild, but eventually temperatures dropped so deeply that I refrained, as in previous years, from longer visits to the Emmental. The search for the bridge strand in my shining structure had long since become irrelevant to me; if there was such a bridge among my dots and strands, I just couldn't identify it as such.

Near the end of the year, when the shopping windows in Bern were flashing and glittering, heralding the upcoming season of »peace and reflection«, I had several encounters that, as it should turn out later, were crucial with respect to the perfect restoration.

While I was in town I was addressed by a young foreign lady. In broken German she told me of her escape from war, her expulsion and the rape committed on her. Here in Bern, according to her, she worked for a ridiculously low pay in a restaurant. She informed me that her boss had gone for a journey without paying her the three monthly wages he was still owing her. The woman – living together with her two small kids in a two-room apartment – needed money desperately to pay the outstanding rent; otherwise she risked getting kicked out right away.

Perhaps out of a naïve belief in the goodness of man, or out of a silent protest against the neglect, indifference and lack of trust in this society, I didn't want to assume that this lady was a fraud or trickster. Rather, I indulged in boundless sympathy, and what was more: I couldn't deny that this woman exuded a certain attractiveness. I was willing to borrow her a larger sum of money so that she was able to pay the rent in time. Both happy, we went our own ways: she walked away with my money, I left with her address and the proud feeling of having done a good deed.

After one week the case was clear: the address was wrong, the woman was a trickster, and my money was gone. I felt miserable. But shortly after I found out that this fraud was an organized issue: I was again addressed by a woman that supposedly came from the same region, wearing the same clothes, begging me whiningly for money in the same broken German. Her story differed somewhat from that of the other lady, but undoubtedly it was the same old »number«. I couldn't hold back my anger and berated the woman out on the open street until she ran away in tears – which caused me to feel miserable again.

Nestor, who I told about these encounters during a visit in November, held that I had wasted two chances to practice dealing with *kobolds*. I asked him what he meant with that, and he explained that people on the right side of consciousness liked to live on the emotional energies of others. He called such people »kobolds«.

»The things that happened between you and that woman were sheer koboldry,« he explained. »You had to buy off your guilty conscience that the beggar woman had instilled in you. And in the second encounter you acted just as hastily, only with emotions to the contrary. Instead, you could have accepted the encounter with these kobolds as a challenge.«

The way Nestor exposed my behavior, devoid of all ideals in all of its sobriety and ugliness, made me feel quite uncomfortable. I tried to justify myself and told him that I hadn't wanted to take the women as practice objects; rather, my intention had been to help them.

»You cannot help people when you allow yourself to get lulled by their emotional energies,« he replied sharply. »You'll have to notice the moment when the kobold becomes active. When it's all about sucking other people's energy, kobolds shift to a condition with a higher energy level – in this case, the beggar woman got all worked up about her misery, and in the end she probably believed her own words when she told you how bad off she was.«

Nestor advised me to watch out for different kinds of kobolds and the individual strategies they pursued. For example, there was the kobold that was able to impress others with his opinions, thoughts and systems. Nestor called him the *teacher*. He derived his power from the attention and respect of others, or he caused skepticism, anger and disgust about his teachings and took pleasure in that.

The second kind of kobold, according to Nestor, was the *cynic*. This character aroused emotions with his sarcasm and scathing ridicule over anything that touched people somehow. The cynic could evoke enthusiasm or resentment and consternation in others – either way he had a field day with it.

Then Nestor mentioned another kobold that he characterized as always being buoyant and in a good mood. This *happy-go-lucky* character, as he called him, was successful at everything, always optimistic, motivated and confident of victory. Many people liked to be together with him, and he elicited their admiration. In other people who avoided him he elicited envy.

And finally, the *child* surpassed all other kobolds in terms of cleverness. Its innocence, clumsiness and helplessness could evoke strong feelings of sympathy and mother-like feelings, that is, helpfulness. On the other hand, its defiant childish temper strained other people's patience to the extreme.

»The teacher is the one that has most of his energy bound in his system; that's why he has to hustle and push the hardest so as to drain others of their energy,« Nestor went on. »The child, on the other hand, has most of its energy unbound in the picture. It is capable of evoking strong feelings with a minimum of effort.

To us, the important point is to notice that this kobold game is being played in certain situations. If we are able to consciously pause during such a flush of feelings and observe what's really going on, then we'll find out that energy is actually flowing at a higher level. This energy is earmarked and personality-tinged, though, at that moment, and it creates dependencies. But when we're alert enough and our body is open, we can manage to uncouple this high-level energy from the exterior circumstances in moments like those and put it into the picture as a whole in form of a prickle feeling – thus canceling our role and kobold games.«

»Are all people kobolds?« I asked.

»In one or the other way, everybody tries to snatch energy away from other people around him over and over. And everybody becomes the victim, time and again, that has to give off his energy. Ultimately, there are no winners in this game.«

»Then seers are kobolds as well?«

»Seers are no longer kobolds,« he replied. »They no longer need the personality-tinged and earmarked energy of others. Seers have turned into a source themselves. They illuminate the entire picture with their transformed emotional energy.«

»Seers are lucky fellows,« I murmured, slightly envious. »I also want to belong to the left side of consciousness; then I wouldn't have to behave like a kobold and fall prey to other kobolds.«

»Stop behaving like a kobold,« Nestor replied and smiled. »Then you'll make the leap over to the left side.«

As it turned out, I was to get my chance soon after when I met a third woman that unmistakably was begging for money with the same »techniques«. The encounter took place in a handicraft shop in Bern that I regularly visited at that time in order to search for suitable wooden leaves for the drawer of the secretaire. My decision to still search for the »needle in a haystack« didn't only result from Nestor's persuasions but also from the fact that, the longer the restoration of the secretaire took, the more I felt challenged by the artist who created it. After all, the secretaire itself bore witness that it was possible to harmoniously align the grain pattern of the different wood species with each other.

I was in the basement of that shop where I had several large-surfaced wooden leaves spread out in front of me when that young woman attracted my attention. She had spotted me at the same time and headed right in my direction – slowly but surely.

While she was strolling towards me I started to become nervous and trembled slightly. When she stood in front of me she looked at me with big sad eyes and started to beg. She also told me despondently of blows of fate, miseries and money problems. Then she showed me pictures of her small child and the ring of her husband who, as she claimed, had deceased. She laid one of her hands on mine; with the other she played with one of three small pieces of transparent foil I had brought along, and on which I had drawn the specific grain pattern I was looking for while systematically searching for suitable wooden leaves.

While the woman was talking to me I became increasingly nervous until finally my body started trembling and my heart pounding strongly. I felt an increased pressure in my chest that forced me to take deeper breaths. I had the strange impression that her story became increasingly spectacular, and she more and more convinced of and going into despair over it, the more the pressure increased within me.

My inner tension suddenly ceased with a strong prickle feeling on my legs which immediately calmed me down. At the same moment the young woman became visibly nervous and started to fidget around. I myself began to sense the situation this woman was in; I could feel that she was living in surroundings causing her fear and uncertainty, where she had to lie to people in order to be able to survive. I offered her my support if she, in return, would show me her flat, her child and her financial situation.

She looked at me surprised, tried to make excuses that her landlady was a difficult person and started to beg for money again. When I kept insisting on my viewpoint, she made a derogatory gesture, threw my foil on the ground and left the shop in anger.

The foil had fallen onto a large wooden leaf that I had already inspected and put beside the table. When I wanted to pick it up, it struck me that it had fallen onto a spot where the grain pattern was almost identical with the marks on the foil. And I was more than surprised that I could, by slightly adjusting the foil, discover that there was a perfect match of the grain pattern with the marks.

On the next weekend, the first one during the Christmas holidays, I went up the Emmental with the fitting wooden leaf. I had a few days that I wanted to spend at Nestor's place.

When I arrived at his house – covered with a thick layer of snow – in the afternoon, Nestor called me into his living room where it was comfortably warm. He pointed out to me a natural spectacle that had just started: the sun was just about to disappear behind the western peak of the Hohgant, only to reappear behind the sloping hillside ten minutes later. Nestor explained that the time of winter solstice had begun, and that the duration of shadowing increased and decreased within a time span of twelve days.

To me, this was a nice natural phenomenon, but for Nestor it was more. He knew that times of transition, in which cycles were completed and tendencies reversed, were times of special forces and power. According to him, I should avail myself of that time and search for the bridge in my structure. And he was confident that I would be able to find it in this time period – after all, the bridge itself was a transition as well.

On the same night I was able to glue the wooden leaf I had brought along in the corresponding spot on the drawer without any problem – it was a part of the bridge strand. The following, mostly sunny days I spent with searching for the bridge in my structure again. Each day in the afternoon I sat in Nestor's living room and looked through the large window into the sky above the Hohgant. This time of day was particularly suitable for seeing because the glare of the sun was blocked out by the western peak of the mountain. Still the brightness made the dots and strands stand out clearly from the picture.

Following Nestor's instructions, I made drawings of the strands in my field of vision. Sometimes he asked me, after having inspected my drawings, to take another closer look at a certain strand and, if possible, also draw it in its other forms it appeared.

The strand that Nestor eventually took into consideration as the bridge was indeed one of those in my shining structure that I was most familiar with. The only point was: this strand was extremely movable, changing its form with virtually every single movement of the eye – so it needed a lot of goodwill to describe it as »bridge«.

At first, I had the impression that the symmetry of the strand was not distinctive enough: the right part was a little longer and flatter. This part of the strand came quickly into focus and started to light up; it had substance. The left part – thicker and not as bright – was shorter but went higher up. This difference in shape also corresponded with a difference in their respective movability: when I moved the bridge with my eyes, the right arch showed hardly any change; it was quite solid. The left arch behaved completely different. It was so flexible that it was flung back and forth with each movement of the eye. In addition, this strand was not horizontal, as could be expected of a bridge; at best, it pointed towards the lower left, but due to the movability of the left half it frequently pointed towards the lower right or, in the third spatial dimension, towards me. Only in rare cases they turned in such a way that the strand actually assumed the look of a bridge.

I talked to Nestor about these contradictions, but he just advised me to take an even closer look at this strand and observe its behavior.

Following his advice and taking a closer look at the strand, I found that its bridge-like shape didn't come about by coincidence; rather, the strand always assumed the form of a bridge whenever I could look at it long enough and with a high level of concentration – in other words, when it was small and luminous.

All these observations confirmed Nestor in his view that I had found the bridge in this strand. In doing so, he emphasized the conformities with the bridge he himself could see: the asymmetry, particularly with respect to the longer right and the shorter left part, as well as its belonging to the right half of consciousness.

»But this strand points downward more often than showing a horizontal position,« I objected.

»That's also correct,« Nestor answered. »The direction in which it turns depends on your inner pressure. In that way it shows you in what direction your energy is flowing. At first it points downward; it points in your direction and looks like a reversed ›3‹. So your energy is flowing downward which means that you draw more off the structure than you put in.

After the leap, however, when there is sufficient pressure within you, your energy flow will reverse in direction – and with it the direction of your bridge. It then points to the upper left, in the direction where you'll eventually find your own sphere. In this way, the further path in the left half of consciousness will become visible.«

Due to my frequent dealing with the bridge strand, I gradually began to see familiar forms in it. Depending on its alignment, it could take on the form of a snake, a fetus in the womb or an eagle's eye and beak. When I started to characterize the strand accordingly in my following conversations with Nestor, he asked me to refrain from doing so.

»You can recognize innumerous things in this strand,« he said. »It's only natural that we want to discover familiar forms of the outer screen in the basic structure. In the final analysis, though, that's just gimmickry. When we make the dots and strands light up, it means a resolution and reduction of our daydreams, ideas and thoughts. So it's not about entering new concepts into the shining structure.«

I called his attention to the fact that he had done the same when he called this strand »the bridge«. Nestor just shrugged. Seers, he admitted, assigned symbolic terms to the landmarks in the structure. These were very simple everyday images fittingly reflecting the form of the landmarks. Simple associations of that nature could help other people make personal advances, he was convinced. Still this didn't make less of the fact that all ideas that we entered into the shining structure were ultimately nothing else than the small world on the brims of the structure that we had to transform, sooner or later, into the consciousness of light.

On the last day that I wanted to stay at Nestor's place it struck me while looking at the bridge again that the old drawer handle on Mari Egli's secretaire was very similar in shape. This delicate brass handle also showed two arches of different length and was fixed to the drawer with its upper right end. Right that moment it dawned on me what was hanging on this drawer: it wasn't just some fancy handle but the bridge the way the builder of the secretaire had seen it.

Now I realized what I had done three years ago when I had tried to forge the handle according to the model of the old one: I had imitated the artist's act of seeing without me myself being able to see. Now I had no more doubts that this unconscious imitation was the reason why I hadn't been able to fix the handle to the drawer. To me this clearly meant: I had to form the handle according to my own seeing. I made a precise drawing of my bridge, namely in the position in which it was almost horizontal and I could hold it in suspension a long time.

Instead of returning to Bern on the next day as I had planned originally, I saw the farmer about my findings. The excitement and curiosity I felt caused such a vigor in me that I didn't even back off from fighting my way through the snow for twice as long as usual – with skis from Nestor's attic.

In the early evening, before dusk fell, I returned with the newly forged handle. Convinced and full of confidence, I mounted the handle on Mari Egli's secretaire in Nestor's presence. Everything went smooth and fast – not even my pulse rate picked up. Instead, I was in an extraordinarily euphoric state of mind.

After this work was done, I placed myself in front of the secretaire and reached for the new double-arched handle in order to pull on it. My success had made me a little slaphappy and I believed that I could be successful at everything, including opening the drawer. With determination I pulled on the handle but the drawer couldn't be opened. Sobered, I pulled again and again but to no avail.

»Let it go at that,« Nestor advised me gently. »It's enough that you've found out about the meaning of this bridge today. It'll play a major role on your further path in the shining structure. One day you'll have to cross it. Then, and only then, when you've opened yourself up completely, this drawer can be opened as well.«

I let go of the secretaire and sat across from Nestor. »You say I'm supposed to cross the bridge in my structure?« I asked.

»To cross the bridge means to overcome the two arches. In your case, the right larger arch is solid and luminous when you concentrate. That means that you're able to put your energy in there, that you're familiar with this arch. It stands for the outer screen, and by crossing the right part of the bridge you'll find that matter will exert less attractive force on you accordingly. A person that wants to overcome this first part won't have a particularly hard time with that: he'll be able to walk this stretch.

When it comes to the end of the second arch, though, you'll have to fly over it. This arch, which is not yet luminous in your case, symbolizes the emotional world. When you reach the other end of the bridge, you've shifted your daily consciousness deeply into the emotional world and completely developed your emotional body. Then you'll be able to put your transformed feelings directly into the picture as untinged energy, as ecstasy.«

»I still don't understand how that crossing of the bridge is supposed to take place in a concrete sense; the way you describe it, it seems to be a physical thing.«

»That's right, it's actually a physical thing: when the time is ripe for it, you will cross the bridge in all three bodies,« he replied cryptically.

Perhaps it was the sobering disillusion still having an effect on me that had followed on my euphoria; perhaps it also was my reluctance to Nestor's incomprehensible and »absolutizing« predetermination of my alleged way – in any case, I suddenly doubted that I could ever advance far enough to be able to »cross« that bridge.

Nestor answered that I shouldn't worry about that. He reminded me that I hadn't been able to see the dots and strands when I came over to this side of the Emme for the first time. But now I could see the bridge. And at some point that bridge would lead me over into the left half of consciousness, just like it had done with him many years ago.

I didn't want to be captured by his encouragements and pondered loudly that perhaps only certain people were able to become seers, and other people weren't; that it perhaps required a certain character, specific talents, a special fate or whatever.

»Stop it,« Nestor called out and laughed. »Are you searching for justifications to explain away your idleness and phlegm? Crossing the bridge is not a question of character, let alone fate. It is a decision. It is a decision that every person walking the path in the basic structure has to make. It is the point when a human being has to decide whether he or she wants to remain a human being that wants to continue to experience the small joys and woes of this world. Or if he or she wants to fly over into the left side so as to outgrow themselves in an ecstatic way, and to see the world with the eyes of a seer from then on.«

Iris the Seer

When I visited Nestor on a warm and sunny day in May, I didn't come from Bern but from Langnau were I had attended a seminar in the morning. On this route I made a stopover in a small village, not far away from the valley of the Emme but on the north side of the Schrattenfluh mountain range. There I sat down on the terrace of an inn and had a lunch meal.

On this occasion I could watch people who, time and again, stopped in front of a stone column with a small wooden roof on the other side of the street. They looked it over attentively before they followed the narrow street up into the wooded hills. The waitress told me that this was the first station of a Way of the Cross leading to a place of pilgrimage nearby. As I wasn't in a hurry I decided to take a look at that place.

Once I had left all fourteen shrines behind me, I arrived at the lovely sanctuary in the forest, on the bank of a creek. It was a relatively small paved square at the foot of a high rock overgrown with ivy and with a grotto hollowed out at the bottom. The access to the grotto and the altar inside was barred by a solid iron fence. In the rock niches above the altar adorned with fresh flowers, two large statues were enthroned: the Virgin Mother and a female saint after whom the sanctuary was named.

The wooden benches in the square, aligned to face the altar, and the slightly elevated stone pulpit on the right side indicated that Masses were held here now and then. In the hindmost part of the square, a considerable number of pictures of the Virgin Mary was hanging, as well as prayers of intercession and expressions of thanks in several languages; next to it there were images of Jesus, prayer beads and crucifixes made of plaster, wood and metal.

I sat down on one of the benches in the back and watched the few, mostly older, visitors. Suddenly, the wind blew so hard and persistently in the left half of my face that I turned towards the right and put up my jacket collar. When the wind ceased I noticed that someone had taken a seat right next to me. I avoided to look at the person but felt annoyed about the intrusiveness because there were enough free benches around. But when I was addressed with »Floco« and turned towards the person, I recognized the young seer lady beside me.

Her green eyes were glowing. Her young face, strewn with freckles, was shining in the sunlight. Her curly red hair fitted perfectly to the dark blue of her jeans jacket, and I noticed that she wore her hair shorter than the last time we had met. She simply looked stunning.

Surprised as I was, I fell silent and she began to speak. She asked me what I did in this place. I told her of my seminar and said that I actually was on my way to visit Nestor. Then I asked her for her name, but she just smiled and didn't answer anything. Instead, she pointed to the pictures of the Virgin Mary and explained that she was here as paintress; she wanted to study facial expressions, gestures and postures of a person venerated as holy. If I liked to, she said, we could take a look at the pictures together. I liked to, considered it a great idea.

The young woman led me from one picture to the next and lectured on the artists' concepts of terms such as »holy«, »devout« and »humble« as they understood and depicted it as ideal in their respective day and age. She took particular pleasure in certain symbols, especially in drawings of the heart in Jesus' chest that was beating in the middle of a crown of thorns and blazing on fire, with the cross enthroned at the top.

Finally we sat down again and kept talking about painting, saints and other things. I enjoyed being together with her. Just when I felt like forgetting everything around us, the seer lady called my attention to an older pilgrim woman who had kneeled down in front of a statue of the Virgin Mary. With a whining voice she mumbled unintelligible prayer formulas to herself. I could see that the face of the woman was drowned in tears.

»I could never understand how someone can generate so many emotions just by facing a cheesy plaster statue,« I commented mockingly on the events.

»Her heart is wide, and she is capable of deep feelings,« the seer lady replied. »But her love is an emotional love, restricted to individual objects, persons or ideas she is trying to attract. If she were a seer, her own attractive force would be so strong that she would attract everything in the picture in equal measure.«

I wondered about her use of the term »attractive force«. With this term, Nestor always used to refer to a force affecting us in a negative sense that we had to fight against.

The seer lady explained to me that the attractive force was nothing else than love that had a different effect in each layer of consciousness.

Someone living far away from his one sphere, according to her, was strongly attracted to matter – his love was restricted to material things. People who were already living closer to their sphere paid more attention to a love coming from the heart, but that love was still fervid and passionate; for that reason, it could still change into opposite emotions like resentment, hatred and jealousy. But when Nestor said that I had to overcome the attractive force, it meant that I should pay attention to not any longer being attracted to the material objects of this world.

Instead, I myself had to become so loving that everything around me, including the shining structure, was attracted by me.

»This pilgrim lady has never learned to see,« she repeated, »otherwise she would make the structure light up with her love and attract it – and she would be able to find her own heart within it and make it glow.«

When I asked her how one could make one's own heart glow, the young lady described a special strand in the basic structure to me that sooner or later became visible for every person and that lit up during concentration. According to her description, it was the same strand that Nestor had called the »connecting strand« and the »bridge«.

»This strand can be many things,« she replied. »It could be a scythe, a longbow, a bridge. What you recognize in it depends on your character – and on the way you enter into the left side of consciousness. To me, this strand is a heart.«

I recalled Nestor's viewpoint according to which the connecting strand was best to be described by symbolic images from our everyday world that reflected its form as simple and, at the same time, as precise as possible. The image of the heart, however – I confronted her with Nestor's words now – did not fulfill these criteria; that strand could at best picture the upper part of a heart but not one in its entirety.

She replied that perhaps I was too correct in order to recognize a heart in it. »Overly correct people are tied too strongly to their precise ideas; they are lacking fantasy to bestow the picture with life and inner sense. Such people have a harder time to walk the path in the shining structure.« Then she turned towards me and gave me a challenging look with her big green eyes.

Hit by her look, I asked her, slightly sobered, if she really believed that I was overly correct. The young woman started to laugh in a child-like manner and gave me a friendly pat on the knee. This caused an immediate electrifying feeling in my entire body and triggered a pleasant prickle feeling on my legs.

She told me that I shouldn't be concerned about developing my consciousness. I should accept, however, that my path would consume more time because I was a man. With these words she had put a stop to my musing and pondering at one blow.

»Men,« she claimed in response to my question, »have to fight and struggle much more until they can open their body completely and attract all things in the picture in equal measure with the energy released. Women, on the other hand, are more open by nature of their character, and they have an easier time to relax than men, even if they are not seers. That's why they experience that prickle feeling much more often than men. And accordingly, they also have an easier time learning to see.«

»But that certainly does not apply to every man and every woman, does it?« I tried to qualify her statement.

»Yes, it does,« she answered back boldly, came closer to me and lowered her voice. »Just taking a look at the bodies of women and men confirms this. For example, let's take male and female germ cells: the female body produces only a few ovules, and those are large, round like a sphere and resting in a certain place most of the time. When it comes to the male body, the energy is split up into countless sperms that are tiny in size and in constant‹ motion. That's why men are ›split‹ much more, and that's why they always have to compete with one another, driving each other forward all the time. These poor devils have to run around much longer until they are finally able to relax – and as soon as they do, they fall asleep most of the time.«

Her comparison of the sexes made us both laugh. I had to admit that my last relationship with a woman had more or less followed that principle: my girlfriend had been the one with a calming influence and an enviable charisma that I could only make up for with activity and performance.

Somehow I felt the urge to tell the young seer lady of that relationship in more detail: how it had started out, how much my girlfriend and me had enjoyed being together, but also where the problems lied. I described to her how the relationship eventually went by the boards because I had become virtually obsessed with having to prove my value to my girlfriend. This, I found, had been unavoidable because she was such a distinguished, sociable and popular woman that she was never lacking male company – and she visibly enjoyed that. I, in contrast, was degraded more and more to a mere »appendage« over time that could be exchanged on request – whenever some new »Romeo« entered the stage. I concluded my sentences with the remark that my current lifestyle – refraining from sexual pleasures – was far superior to the koboldry of a love relationship.

»If we want to develop our love to higher levels and give it away to everyone else directly through the body, then we'll have to do without the physical orgasm for as long as possible – no matter whether man or woman,« she consented with a serious tone of voice. »But this way should not be an escape from one-on-one relationships. We're doing without the small sexual pleasures so as to develop the inner sense, to vitalize our picture and to make it shine – not because we're afraid of contacts with the other sex.«

My first reaction was to defend myself against her admonitions and justify myself. After all, I said, the reason for my endeavors to live a life at a high energy level in the sense of the seers was not a rejection of the other sex but the fascination associated with being able to perceive the picture in a completely different way.

I had to admit, though, that my judgment of one-on-one relationships had changed considerably since I had started to practice the perfect restoration. Whereas a love coming from the heart and sexual pleasures once had been the highest feelings worth striving for to me, I now tended to devaluate that idea, most probably as a result of my doing without sexual relationships since some time. Now I viewed love between two people from the perspective of an investment:

one puts intentional energy in the form of interest, attention, rhetoric art and targeted activities into a person of one's choice. If this promotional campaign happens to be successful with that particular person, and the investment is returned with interest and compound interest, then the investment was worthwhile.

Of course, from that moment on a portion of the energy capital has to be used for the maintenance of the relationship, but over time this can be reduced to a minimum, thanks to write-downs and experiences gained. Only in crisis situations, additional investments have to be made; that's why it's always advisable to set up accruals. There will always be crises when the balance sheet isn't correct, that is, when the return doesn't justify the effort, or when both partners are living too much on the capital of just one of them – something that happens relatively often because: what prospective loving couple is willing to conduct a significant cost-benefit analysis prior to the investment?

»But isn't there a contradiction between a relationship and the path in the basic structure?« I wanted to know from the seer lady.

»Of course not. If the loving relationship between two people is complete, it will lead the couple into the left side of consciousness just the same.«

»With ›complete‹ you probably mean a platonic love,« I sneered.

»No,« she replied. »The physicalness has its place in a complete love relationship just like everything else.«

»But you yourself said a little while ago that we have to do without the sexual act if we want to walk the path in the shining structure.«

»We don't have to do without making love as such; the point is that we have to hold back the physical orgasm as much as we can, to transform the energy and channel it upwards.«

»You mean sex without fun,« it escaped me. The young seer lady laughed heartily. Then she replied that we wouldn't lose anything in the process, quite the contrary: we would transform the little pleasures of the sexual climax into the high joy of the prickle feeling and, ultimately, into ecstasy.

The seer lady then began to explain this ideal relationship that she called the *erotic unification*. With that she referred to a loving relationship between a man and a woman that is lived out physically as well – but always with regard to building up the energy in one's own body and opening it.

The young lady had just begun to talk about the erotic unification when several families showed up with their kids and arranged themselves with quite some noise. Soon after, everyone took pleasure in the sandwiches, candies and drinks they had brought along. The kids played soccer, the babies were screaming, the adults were chattering and laughing loudly.

The seer lady found that it was time to leave. At the entrance to the sanctuary I asked her where she lived and if I could drive her home. She answered that she would get along fine and pointed in the direction of the rising hill slope.

»If you walk beyond the Way of the Cross, up the street all the way to its end, you'll find my house,« she explained and assured me that we would meet again. On this occasion I asked her for her name once more.

»Individual personalities have names,« she replied. »A seer does not have a certain personality any longer, so she doesn't need a certain name, either.«

She smiled and her green eyes were glowing.

Even though I considered the seers' secretiveness about names childish, the way she said it made me feel deeply connected to her. Spontaneously, my body felt relaxed and a prickle feeling flowed through my chest. I was just about to tell her that I liked her, but she forestalled me by wishing me all the best and asking me to say »Hi« to »Nestorius«. Then she turned around and walked up the street.

Nestorius! This name accompanied me the entire way up to Nestor's house. Aside from the fact that Nestor pushed himself in between us at the most unfavorable moments even without being physically present, the seer lady's variant of his first name was a head scratcher for me. She spoke out this name with so much admiration that I tended to see more in it than just a play of words. Suddenly I was convinced that it could give me a clue to Nestor's position, how he was regarded in the circle of seers and what his function was. Another aspect that spoke in favor of a prominent position Nestor had among the seers was the fact that he was the only one whose name I knew. If nothing what the seers did here was coincidence, it was imperative to clarify the significance of this issue.

Before I crossed the bridge over to the left side of the Emme, I stopped in front of the inn because I wanted to take another look at the seer lady's pictures, particularly the initials. If the woman wasn't willing to reveal her name to me, I would just go for a guess.

When I came down the hallway to the restrooms, there were four color pencil drawings of boring flower motives – daisies, violas and the like – hanging on the wall, nicely arranged side by side. But there was no single trace of the seer lady's paintings – neither in the hallway nor in the other rooms and spaces of the inn.

Upset and confused, I asked the waitress at the bar about their whereabouts. Of course, the stout lady had no clue and referred me to the stout boss. Even though I described to him twice what the paintings had looked like, he could not remember having seen them. He explained to me that he sometimes bought pictures directly from artists or at the flea market. At any rate, they all eventually came *uf d'Gant*[24] or directly into the garbage bin.

I tried to recall what the initials of the seer lady had been. The first of the two letters on all her pictures, I could remember, was a small »i«. I was able to remember this »i« because it was drawn quite long and also a little curvy so that it rendered the impression of a stream of water flow-

---

[24] Swiss German for "up for auction".

ing from a spring – the dot above the »i«. The second letter, however, just wouldn't come back to my mind. I chose the sonorous and fitting name »Iris« for the seer lady.

Nestor, whom I told of my encounter with Iris, was full of praise for the young woman. With tender affection he called her *the hearty one*.

»She's a fascinating woman, isn't she?« he asked with a smirk.

I agreed and told him that, while being together with her, I had felt a prickle feeling on my body several times – something that I had never experienced so often and intensively when being together with other people.

»That's her specialty,« Nestor said . »She's radiating so much energy that you can only hope to be open enough so as to return this energy. Otherwise you'll soon feel your heart flutter and your knees tremble.« With a fitting gesture, Nestor mimicked a love-crazed but physically weak admirer shaking and gasping for air at the stunning look of his adored one. We both laughed.

»It's good that you were open enough,« Nestor went on. »When you're open enough and your energy flows into the entire picture, it means that you are able to love – and that's what the hearty one wanted to get across to you. And she's right when she calls the energy flowing out »love«. Because a sensation always means that you don't use your energy any longer to magnify or expose yourself; rather, you magnify the contents in the picture with it and render them more alive, colorful and peaceful. This energy flow produces a feeling of deep fulfilling affinity – and that's love.«

Nestor's words evoked a feeling of desire for Iris within me. I started to rave about her, but Nestor reminded me not to relate this beautiful prickle feeling only to certain people or objects in the picture. Indeed, it was the circumstances causing a prickle feeling, but in the final analysis, my ability to reach states of ecstasy came about through the efforts undertaken in the perfect restoration. Accordingly, the love of a male or female seer was an impersonal love – a love not restricted to individual persons only.

What Nestor told me sounded in my ears as if he wanted to keep me away from Iris. I protested against his insinuations and told him that it had been she herself that warmly recommended a love relationship to me that, by nature of an erotic unification, would lead over into the left side of consciousness. Having a seer as partner, I held, must be of great advantage.

»You had a good time with the hearty one, and now you've got a heartache.« He smiled. »You have to be aware of the fact that her love does reach you indeed, but it surpasses you by far. And when she recommends an erotic unification to you, she has the relationship to a woman in mind for you. The hearty one is a seer. She's not what you imagine a woman to be.«

»So then male and female seers do not have any preferences or wishes any longer with regard to people? I mean, if they love everything, they could love a certain person that much more, couldn't they?«

Nestor remained silent for a while. »As long as a seer has not overcome duality, he or she is not totally free of desires and wishes,« he finally explained. »Still the love of a seer is rather more impersonal than personal. He or she puts the largest portion of their energy into the picture as a whole – and thus he or she cannot approach a single person with all of their energy and attention. To do so, he or she would have to let their energy flow downward again, that is, tie up their energy in many individual things.

But what seer would do something like that voluntarily? A seer has taken great efforts to reverse his energy flow and open his body so as to experience the state of ecstasy. It just doesn't make sense to do without this deep joy and love for everything, only to grant that energy to one single person.«

On this evening I had a hard time to concentrate on anything. Iris had left such a vivid impression that I just couldn't help but recapitulate what had happened between us: conversations, situations, my feelings in these moments – I played through whole scenes in my mind once more, but not without altering them according to my ideal conceptions. And when I sat down to concentrate on the connecting strand in my shining structure, I tried to see the double arch of the heart.

Finally, however, the thought of the name »Nestorius« yanked me out of my daydreams. I wanted to clarify, once and for all, what was behind this name. For that purpose, I consulted the encyclopedia I had in my notebook computer that I had taken along for the seminar in the morning.

The only entry of the name »Nestorius« was the Patriarch of Constantinople that had lived in the 5th century A.D. He was involved in the debate of the Early Christian church circling around the question whether Jesus was God and man at the same time, or whether the divine and human nature within him were separate from each other, with separate effects. As Nestorius and his followers assumed the latter viewpoint – which caused the Orthodox Church to turn sour and against them – they were eventually accused as heretics and persecuted. Despite that, the Nestorian Church has been able to maintain its existence until today, particularly in parts of Asia.

Under »Nestor« itself I found several other entries. For example, Nestor was the name of a hero in Greek mythology. He was a king and a great warrior who had fought against the Centaurs, participated in the search for the legendary Golden Fleece and eventually went to war against Troy – where he served the Greeks as clever adviser. An interesting aspect was also that, in Greek, »Nestor« meant »the one who returns« or »the reborn one«.

Then there was a monk in Kiev by the name of Nestor; he was the one that the so-called Nestor Chronicles were attributed to. These chronicles, originated at the beginning of the 12th century A.D., tell the story of the Empire of Kiev from the early times of the Slavic tribes until the advent of Nestor. They are the main source for the reconstruction of Russia's early history.

»Nestor« was not just a name, though, but the term for the head or spokesman of a group. The authority of a Nestor is derived from his experience and his outstanding qualities. In this sense, we talk about a »Nestor of Physics« or a »Nestor of Literature« and so on.

Finally there was a parrot species in New Zealand with the scientific name *Nestor*, better known under the Maori names *Kea* and *Kaka*, that I added to the list for the sake of completeness.

Now several possibilities to view the issue offered themselves: either the seers considered Nestor the actual incarnation of one of these Nestor heroes, but that seemed rather improbable to me. In my view, the name »Nestor« had a symbolic connotation, with character traits such as bravery, heroism and fortitude attributed to it. But at the same time it was possible that the name »Nestor« was simply used for the head or »spokesman« of the seers on the left side of the Emme. In my guesses I tended towards that last option. What spoke in favor of it was the fact that all the other seers did not have a name but were rather called according to their activities; to me, this underscored the special role Nestor had among them. And second, the geographical location of Nestor's house – according to the map his house was right in the middle of all other seers' houses – suggested that he literally assumed the role of a mediator or facilitator.

314

After dinner I tried to talk to Nestor about it. I told him that Iris had asked me to say »Hello« to »Nestorius«. He smiled but didn't say anything.

»Why does she call you Nestorius?« I asked.

»Why not? Sounds good, too,« he found.

»Do you know at all who Nestorius was?«

Nestor shrugged defensively with one shoulder.

»He was a great church patriarch,« I informed him.

Nestor shrugged with the other shoulder. »What are you aiming at?« he asked.

»I want to find out why everyone is calling you ›Nestor‹ while they themselves don't have a real name. I suspect that you're somewhat of a leader to them. The name ›Nestor‹ is frequently associated with outstanding personalities, after all.«

I gave him my list. He glanced over it briefly.

»You think that we seers all have the feeling that I was the reincarnation of one of these Nestor guys here?«

»Are you?«

Nestor studied the list and replied, to my utter surprise, that he actually had been one of these Nestors.

»And which of these have you been?« I carefully asked. »Nestorius the Patriarch?«

»You mean, seriously engaging in heated debates over whether the two natures of Jesus were separate or one? I just couldn't have done that – in the midst of all that arguing, I probably would've had to laugh suddenly. Besides, the name is not even correct.«

»So then you were Nestor the Greek hero?«

»Going to war? Not my thing at all. Then I'd rather stare into the blue.«

»Nestor the monk?«

»Writing down the history of Russia? I would have been bored to death.«

I looked at Nestor questioningly.

»Nestor, Nestor, Nestor,« he mimicked a parrot and gave me back my notes. »I was the parrot,« he said and smirked. »In my last lifetime I had parroted too much, and that's why I hadn't become a seer back then.« Embarrassed, I shook my head. Nestor had lured me into a trap like a complete newbie.

»So there is nothing such like reincarnation for seers?« I concluded.

»The only reincarnation there is for seers comes about through the leap over onto the left side. When you fly over the bridge, you release your fixation in the right half of consciousness, and with that your individual personality dies. Because, being a person means to be fixated. Once your fixation is resolved, you'll be reincarnated as a seer on the left side of consciousness – as a free being that puts its energy via ecstasy into the picture as a whole from then on. On this left side, the seer sees the way to absolute being – consequently, any question about reincarnation becomes redundant and unnecessary to him.«

On the next day I went out to pay a visit to Iris. According to the map, her house was located two ditches farther and a little above the house of the thinker – more in the direction of the spring of the Emme. But in order to get to her house for sure, I drove to the sanctuary and from there up the street.

Her home was at the end of that street, just like Iris had described it. She lived in a two-story wooden house with a veranda. The view of the small hearts that were cut out in the middle of the window shutters – standing wide open and painted green – made my own heart leap for joy.

Just when I wanted to knock on the door I heard Iris' voice. She was standing in front of a building a little further above her own house. She waved me to her, and I headed for the building on a small path lined with hollies. Iris walked up to me and said that she hadn't expected to see me that soon again. Then she let me into the wooden building with large window panes that she called her »workshop«.

I took a look around. The seer lady had accumulated quite a bit of natural materials here. At first glance, they looked like ordinary tree bark, twigs, leaves and the like. But on closer inspection, the materials revealed peculiar features: the edges of the dried and pressed green leaves were shimmering with a violet hue; the tree bark, lying around in heaps, showed distinct bark beetle patterns; there were large black bird feathers, probably from birds of prey, as well as smaller colored feathers, in a mass of modeling clay; on her gigantic worktable I could see curly roots, crooked and tangled tree branches as well as fir cones and lichens in all colors and sizes.

Iris explained that, in her artistic work, she drew inspiration from the buildup of the shining structure. Either she directly took the shining structure as template or she found its principle out in nature, in the natural patterns and structures of plants and stones. This was also the reason, she found, that natural patterns had the strongest appeal to man's sense of sight.

When we stepped out of the workshop and walked down to her house, Iris asked me why I had come to visit her. I asked her to tell me about the erotic unification. Because, I explained, if there is a possibility to reach the left side of consciousness via the physical unification of man and woman, I wanted to become acquainted with it at any rate.

Iris was just about to answer, but right that moment a younger man left her house. He was wearing hiking boots, a black leather jacket and a backpack. It seemed as if he was going for a trip. Iris walked up to him. Both had a brief conversation, then they embraced each other – a little long, for my taste. Seeing them in that position not only produced quite some heat in my body; it also reduced my interest in having Iris explain the erotic unification to me. Doubts came up in my mind: was it actually possible that sexual contact could contribute to a development of our consciousness? Was Iris really able to give a correct judgment on that question? And: was she even a seer at all?

Both called me to come over to them. With each step towards the house the heat in my body increased. The young man introduced himself as – Romeo! His face was radiating and he chattered frankly and in a broken German with Romand[25] accent about himself, for example, that he often returned to this place to enjoy the »beauties« of this country-side. I thought I had seen how he, when he uttered the word »beauties«, had looked at Iris from the corner of his eye.

Finally, at last, he said goodbye and, whistling cheerfully, walked down the path in the direction from where I had come. I took a look at him for a while: he was taller than me and slim but athletic. But his face just looked like a dented car door. And his eyes stood apart so far that I asked myself whether he was capable of seeing a three-dimensional picture at all. And he didn't seem to be particularly musical, either: I could see how the birds flew off and took refuge on trees farther away in response to his off-key whistling.

Iris yanked me out of my musings and asked me to enter her house.

»Is he a seer?« I asked her when we took a seat in the living room.

» He's a wanderer on the path in the shining structure – just like you.«

---

[25] Romand: a Swiss citizen from the French-speaking western part of Switzerland.

»Does he see the double arch of the heart in his structure?« I also wanted to know so as to be able to judge him better.

»As I told you yesterday,« she replied coolly, »men have to fight more than women on their path in the shining structure.«

For a while we sat across from each other, not saying anything. Iris had made herself comfortable on the soft sofa, with her legs angled.

In order to fill the uncomfortable silence, I told her of my research with regard to the name »Nestor«, and how I had once again fallen flat on my face when I confronted Nestor with my findings. She, however, didn't seem to warm to that theme. I could feel the same uncomfortable distance to her that I had sensed when we met at the inn. Acting against my better knowledge, I tried to develop a prickle feeling within me and to give Iris some energy of mine, but I couldn't make it.

Finally the seer lady responded to my wish and started to talk about the erotic unification. She repeated that this was a way that could lead over into the left side of consciousness. But at the same time it was a way requiring a great deal of discipline as it was all about preventing the relaxing orgasm – because, according to her, a huge amount of energy was materially tied up in an orgasm. Instead, the lovers were supposed to engage in an interchange in increasingly higher layers of consciousness with that energy until relaxation ensued as ecstasy that permanently opened the body, attracting everything in the picture in equal measure and making it shine.

I expressed my astonishment over this possibility. »Nestor had told me of the leap over into the left side of consciousness and the ecstasy,« I said, »but he had never mentioned the erotic unification. Before I met you, I didn't know that a person could become a seer via a love relationship.«

»To walk the path in the shining structure means to increase the energy within you,« Iris answered. »In order to obtain this energy, and with this energy, you have worked, danced, become acquainted with your feelings and pondered over you and the world. The erotic unification is but another possibility. In order to carry it out, though, it requires strong willpower and much energy. Nestor thought that you should, first of all, curtail your sexual activities so as to transform sexual energy and accumulate more strength. He has given you the exercises that a man or a woman can practice by themselves for that purpose.«

Then Iris began to explain the practice of the erotic unification in further detail. »The embrace or even the close proximity of two people loving each other increases their inner pressure,« she said. »This holds good even more for the erotic unification: it will massively increase the energy, in this case the sexual energy, within you and your partner. This energy is stormy and furious, so you and your partner have to feel and learn to channel it so as to utilize it for the development of your consciousness. The basic principle is simple: during the unification, both of you pull up the sexual energy – at first by using the corresponding muscles, later by pure feeling – from the genitals through the spine into the head. While your partner is relaxing and exhaling slowly, letting her energy flow over to you, you take a deep breath and pull up the sexual energy. Then it's your turn: you relax and let your energy flow over to her while she takes a deep breath and pulls up her energy.«

Both partners, according to Iris, benefited from this exchange of energy, not least because of the qualitative differences in the sexual energy of man and woman: female energy felt cooler, male energy hotter. That's why the woman could cool off the man with her energy while the man was able to warm up the woman with his. In addition, the exchange of energy helped to level out imbalances, release blockades in the body and relax deeply.

»This kind of energy exchange is practiced until you and your partner consider it enough, or until your bodies open up and the energies flow directly into the whole picture as love in its highest state of expression – as a prickle feeling or ecstasy,« she explained. »As I said: the erotic unification requires a high level of discipline and strong willpower. Orgasms have to be avoided, first by muscle contractions in the genital area, later by pure ›feeling up‹ the sexual energy through the spine into the head. Metaphorically speaking, the goal of the erotic unification is about not letting the sexual energy drain away like water but pulling it up and vaporizing it with the surplus of fiery energy brought about in your bodies in this way. The wind resulting from that will eventually vitalize the picture.«

Iris continued to talk for a while but suddenly she fell silent and took a longer pause. Perhaps she had noticed that I didn't listen to her attentively any longer. Actually the subject felt uncomfortable to me, even though I myself had asked Iris about it. What's more, I couldn't get this Romeo guy out of my head. I wondered about the naïvety of his naming; who would show up next here? Don Juan or Casanova?

Iris leaned back and talked about the change of body sensations resulting from the transformation of sexual energy: people practicing this became more present, alert, aware and also more elegant in their body movements. This in turn had an influence on the erotic unification: the higher the energy level and the more open the bodies of two loving partners were, the less physical movements they needed to feel each other. Mechanics were replaced by tenderness, and instead of orgasmic moans they experienced a calm and fulfilling ecstasy. She laughed.

»It's a pity that many young people don't know of this possibility to make love with each other,« she regretted. »Even though they had the energy to do so, they rarely know about this. And even if they knew, they are lacking insight or willpower. When they become older they sometimes feel the wish to further develop their consciousness in a targeted way. And even though they still had enough energy at their disposal, they are entangled in their social role play so inextricably that they just don't find the time for it. Then, with advanced age, they had the time but in most cases not the energy any longer.«

Iris interrupted her explanations once more. I felt a deep desire within me and wanted to reexperience a prickle feeling by all means, as I had felt it the day before in her presence. I tried to take deeper breaths and relax – but the prickle feeling failed to set in. In order to fill the uncomfortable silence, I repeated that I had a hard time believing that the leap over into the left side of consciousness could be brought about by the erotic unification alone.

»Of course not by that alone,« she replied and smiled as if I had just voiced something foolish or absurd. »Of course it also needs a healthy lifestyle and all those practical exercises you're already familiar with. But in my case, the leap took place during the erotic unification with my longtime friend.«

»Did your friend also practice the erotic unification?« I asked.

»He did,« she beamed. »He has supported me as best as he could. He's a wonderful being.« She recalled how she had always made stronger efforts to love her friend in a higher, more spiritual, way. Both had practiced exercises to develop their consciousness. And that had also been the reason why they had searched for solutions so as to harmonize the physical love with a spiritual one. In the course of that, they came across these sexual practices that Iris now called the »erotic unification».

After years of practicing, as Iris frankly continued her account, she had suddenly become enormously big during a very intense erotic unification. She had felt like an all-devouring monster and experienced her partner as a pitiful little manikin. But right the next moment her entire energy flowed into the picture abruptly, and her partner had turned into a giant right after – that had startled her so much that she jumped out of bed and avoided her friend for several days. Then, during another erotic unification, the same thing happened again, but at that time she had taken a leap over into the left side of consciousness instead.

»What happened during that leap?« I wanted to know.

»I experienced the ecstatic energy all over my body for the first time – that was the feeling of fulfillment I had been yearning for. In the beginning I experienced this feeling only when I was together with my partner. But soon I noticed that this energy can flow into the picture anytime and everywhere. But the wildest thing is that, during each ecstasy, the objects in the picture start to light up and are attracted by me – and with them these floating dots and strands that Nestor later explained to me as the shining structure of consciousness.

With this, my love had turned into an impersonal one, and this of course changed the relationship to my friend. I had an increasingly harder time to view the love of my life, the one, in his person exclusively. And he wasn't able to comprehend and deal with this ecstatic energy flowing out in his direction. Consequently, we drifted apart until it made no more sense to stay together. We broke up and I moved to this place.«

»What ever happened to your friend?«

»For a long time he just couldn't understand what had happened with me. He went through a time period that was very difficult for him. He didn't see any sense or reason any longer to live for the development of his consciousness – after all, precisely that had taken away from him what he loved most. Instead, he was making plans ...« Suddenly she fell silent, as if she didn't want to talk about it any longer. »He bethought himself again,« she then said. »Today he tries to get over into the left side by doing unselfish work. This wonderful being comes to visit me from time to time.«

I felt a strong urge to ask Iris whether Romeo was this oh so wonderful being. Instead, I asked her about the way she had recapitulated that episode in her life: even though she had to give up her love to an individual being, her story sounded as if something amusing had occurred to her. She replied that she had found what she had been looking for, even though things had eventually taken a different direction, compared to her own ideas and visions.

»Now it's your turn,« she said with a smile and gave me a wink. »If you practice the erotic unification with your partner, she'll be the first one that you make light up and shine.«

I liked the idea that I could make someone light up and shine. And as if she had known about my feelings, Iris said that this was not just a nice thought but something I could see directly.

»You are the one that makes the world light up and shine with your strength and energy,« she explained. »And when you make the world light up and shine, you'll be bestowed with a natural glow and shine in your face and eyes as well – it's your transformed sexual energy that brings this about.«

She continued to talk about that glow and shine; even though most people gradually lost that shining glow due to their lack of knowledge because they bound their energy in material objects and social role plays, thus dimming and clouding their picture, they still knew instinctively about the significance of that glow: having that glow meant to have a strong charisma – and everybody wanted to present themselves in that way, the young seer lady held.

»So the people try to mimic that shine in the material world: they wear shiny jewelry, put on shiny sunglasses, wash their hair with extra shine shampoo and apply extra shine crème to their face,« – she gave me a mischievous look – »because they feel it's in their own best interest. But the people do not only polish up themselves; they also try to keep their material surroundings brightly polished: their apartments, their shoes, their cars.

These poor fellows!« Iris called out. »Seers know that a genuine shine cannot be brought about by artificially polishing up material belongings; rather, it's the result of constant work on themselves. They have transformed their individual personality into light and, like a mirror, reflect everything others are putting into them.«

She lowered her voice and looked out the window thoughtfully. »The world could be a fantastic place,« she went on, »but we have to learn to *see* it that way. Instead of investing energy into making our outer appearance beautiful and shiny, we should practice to put more energy into the picture as a whole. In this way, everything around us becomes beautiful and shiny, and not just the objects individually preferred. What else do the people want than to live in a beautiful and shiny world?«

Iris paused in her explanations. Her silence made me want to say something to let her know that I admired her and that I wanted to spend more time with her. But there was still this oppressive tenseness in my body that prevented an open conversation. In desperation, I was frantically looking for something brilliant or quick-witted I could say, but all my pondering eventually came down to Romeo that I wanted to blame several times for my tough stubbornness. Once more I tried to be open, relax and feel a prickle in my chest so as to give Iris some energy – in vain.

I finally told her that I really took to her and liked her.

She laughed. Obviously she found this funny. »Don't waste your energy,« she urged me. »Accumulate and transform it. Then you'll be able to put it into the entire picture with your states of ecstasy. As a result, your picture will turn bright and clear, and you'll understand what it is that you see and admire.« And with a level of conviction I knew from Nestor she added that, at some point, I would find the right female partner with whom an erotic unification would become reality.

Iris got up and went into the kitchen to put on some water for a tea.

When I sat alone in the living room – kind of lost and feeling uncomfortable – I could hear the front door opening. My mood dropped immediately because I believed that Romeo had returned to take another look at the »belles« of the countryside. In my sudden nervousness I got up, perhaps to avoid the appearance of being idle. But when I turned around, the old danseuse stood in front of me. Her sudden showing-up was so unexpected to me that I was scared out of my wits – but the scare opened my body and was discharged in a strong prickle feeling.

»Uh, the boy!« the old lady called out, walked over to the table and put her cloth bag on it. Then she gave me a scrutinizing look. »What's he standing around there for, so lost and lonely?« she asked and mimicked my stumped posture.

My natural reaction would have been to become annoyed and upset. But that prickle feeling had such a relaxing effect on me that the danseuse's innuendos didn't bother me any longer.

»You've startled me,« I told her.

»That's quite right,« I heard a voice from the hallway. It was Nestor who entered the living room. »In moments of fright, the intensity increases. Those are precisely the moments in which people learn the most.«

»The way it looks, the boy seems to believe that he can do without an increased energy flow – probably because he thinks he's Mr. Know-It-All,« she added with a cynical tone of voice. »That'll make him turn old and senile in no time.« Then she looked at me with an expression of distrust. »What's he doing here at the young lady's place, anyway, hey?«

I seized the chance to parry her sneering remarks: I was here to become even wiser, I explained. Iris, I told her, informed me about the erotic unification.

»Uh, the erotic unification,« she giggled. »Yes, yes, it's a hell of a difference whether the dickie is attached to the boy, or the boy attached to the dickie.« Nestor and the danseuse laughed loudly.

Iris brought the tea into the living room. Each of us had a cup and we exchanged random trivialities. But the three seers soon came to discuss a special sphere in the left side of the shining structure that Nestor allegedly had discovered not too long ago. He called it the *source* or the *origin*, and with that he assigned it a central place in the shining structure. And this had obviously led to a reinterpretation of another landmark in the structure: in this context, the old lady kept talking about a *last hurdle* that, thanks to the new discovery, had now been put into proper perspective.

When Nestor noticed my questioning look, he suggested to the women to show me that »last and biggest hurdle« for a seer. I had the impression that Nestor wanted to act up in front of the women at my cost; as the »last hurdle« was a landmark in the left side of the structure, it was impossible for him to show it to me. But the seers got up and obviously prepared themselves, in complete unity, for a trip.

We left the house and hiked up the hill nearby. On top of it we sat down on an overturned tree trunk, facing the mountain rising up on the left side of the Emme.

For a short while no one said a word. The three seers looked towards the mountain; perhaps they saw their shining structure. I also tried to concentrate on the structure, but my attention was captured by the bizarre washed out stones and canyon-like rock sections characteristic of the immediate surroundings that were still partly covered with snow.

»The wind is coming,« Iris suddenly announced. The others agreed. Nestor asked me to pay good attention to the wind. And indeed, the next moment there was a slight breeze.

»Just a while ago, when we were moving, it was calm and windless,« he explained. »But now that we have sat down and were settled and relaxed, the wind came up to us.«

I shrugged my shoulders. I couldn't confirm what Nestor said because I hadn't paid attention to the wind before.

Nestor suggested that we should try it another time. So we got up and walked back the way we had come for about ten minutes; then we turned around, walked back up to the overturned tree trunk and sat down again. All that time it was relatively windless. Expectantly I waited what would happen now. The three seers squinted their eyes and looked around attentively.

»The wind will soon come to us,« the danseuse assured me. »Can he see? Now it's already down there in the trees.« I could see the wind blow through the leaves of that group of trees.

»Now ...,« Iris said with a low voice. Right that moment a slight breeze caressed my body.

The seers laughed and considered this a confirmation of their claims. I myself couldn't assign any particular significance to that play of winds – that's just the way it was: sometimes the wind blew stronger and sometimes less.

»If seers sit down and relax, thus putting their energy into the picture as a whole,« Iris explained, »then they change the picture. They render it more intensive and move everything within it. To the degree that the objects come closer and turn larger, the elements are moved as well. There's either going to be more rain, or the fire is blazing up more, or the wind is blowing more strongly. At the same time, the seers move the elements in people with their energy and provoke movements, feelings and thoughts in them.«

With this, Iris claimed the same that I had already heard from Nestor: with their release of energy, the seers had a direct influence on the physical, measurable world – both on nature and man. Nestor, who had commented on that now and then, had always created the impression that he wanted to get across to me that I only felt, thought or acted in a certain way because his energy had triggered that within me. So at that moment all my being was supposed to originate from his energy. Time and again, I had resisted utterances of that nature and defended my autonomy.

»Perhaps it is so that only seers experience the elements in the picture more intensely but others don't,« I suggested. »If a seer sees more rain coming down, then that's probably the case only for the seer.«

»If a seer sees more rain coming down, it is raining more indeed,« Iris answered back with determination, but I believed that, from the corner of my eye, I saw how she refrained from laughing.

»What I mean is: does there actually, and measurably, fall more water from the sky?« I asked.

»Well, if it's raining more, then yes, there is actually more water falling from the sky,« she mimicked my sober objectivity. Nestor and the danseuse were giggling.

»So what you claim is that the seers are something similar to wizards or magicians, and all they had to do was to perform their raindance – and *voilà*, it's raining?«

»Seers don't conjure up rain out of thin air,« Nestor answered, »but they strengthen the tendencies in the picture. When there's a tendency towards rain in the picture, it will be strengthened by the seer – but the seer doesn't do this by jumping around and dancing; rather, he does it by relaxing and giving away his energy into the picture as ecstasy.«

I was joking that, if that was the case, we should examine the issue with corresponding statistics techniques in order to arrive at reliable results when it came to the actual »magic« the seers could produce in the picture.

Iris smiled and shook her head. The old danseuse gave me a piercing look. Nestor knitted his eyebrows and replied that this way to acquire knowledge was the way of people who believed to be disconnected from their picture.

»It's the egoists that believe that they don't have a direct influence on the picture, that they ›can't do anything about it‹,« he pointed out. »In that way they try to seal themselves off and shirk their responsibility for their own picture. These poor morons don't want to understand that they are directly interconnected with the picture.«

»Only if the boy knows about the nature of the picture will he be able to arrive at the last hurdle,« the old lady added, reminding me of the reason for our trip.

»So what is that last hurdle?« I wanted to know. She pointed to the mountain in front of us.

»This mountain is the last hurdle?« I asked surprised.

»It's the last hurdle for the seers,« she replied. »What the seers are doing here is, they wait; they wait until they have accumulated enough strength so as to be able to climb that mountain and get to the source. It's the seers' last journey.«

»What's the problem with this mountain?« I objected. »With the right equipment ...«

»The danseuse cannot show you the last hurdle in her shining structure,« Iris explained. »That's why she talks about the mountain as the last hurdle: on the left side of the Emme, which is corresponding with the left side of the structure, this mountain symbolizes the last big hurdle.«

»The last hurdle in the shining structure is a special sphere,« Nestor went on. »You're attached to this sphere like you were to your umbilical cord before it got cut. If you put your energy into the picture in an unselfish way, that is, into this sphere, then it'll come closer and become larger – until you become one with it.«

»To climb the mountain, seers will have to give everything, *all of their confounded small world*,« the danseuse went on. »Those who are not willing to surrender it will never be able to overcome the last hurdle.«

»But are human beings capable at all of overcoming this last hurdle?« I asked.

»The boy can bet his life on that,« the old lady assured me. »Mari Egli has done precisely that. When she had finished building her secretaire, she had taken to her heels, climbed the mountain and thus overcame the last hurdle. Now she's *über e Bärg*, ›over the hump‹.«

4

The Left Side of Consciousness

On the Bridge

»Floco,« I heard a voice, full of expectation.

Then I started to move through the passage of the cave, easy going and with high speed, accompanied by a prickle feeling on my body. This feeling didn't only give me a deep fulfilling calmness; it also seemed to change the walls of the cave. Everything around me became brighter and more transparent – until I recognized that I was moving through a kind of glassy tube. I could see through the transparent walls how far this glass structure branched out and how dense it was: it was a gigantic structure filling the entire room, as far as my eye could see.

Not far away in front of me, a gigantic tube was floating, the two unequal arches of which spanned horizontally across my entire field of vision. With a glance of my eyes, this majestic formation could be made to move slowly and flexibly, and soon after it was ablaze with bright light. The view of this illuminated tube was so overwhelming and euphoriant that I almost forgot myself – were it not for the strong prickle feeling in my head that made me calm and collected.

When this sensation ceased I experienced some resistance, some pressure from the front reducing the speed with which I was moving along. At the same time the inner walls of the tube changed: to the left and right it solidified, with stone formations from which water was seeping down in many places into a deep canyon. A small river was flowing down there, and I was moving against its current.

In some distance I could finally see the temporary end of this canyon: a massive rock prevented any forward motion. And the closer I came to it, the stronger the pressure became affecting me. With a last effort I reached the rock and came to a standstill.

I found myself in the middle of a natural rock bridge leading across the narrow canyon. The bridge didn't run straight over to the left bank but was wound in two horizontal arches over the water so that everyone who wanted to cross it had to walk a half circle directed to the right twice. But I was neither able to recognize the other bank nor the end of the bridge: the second arch right in front of me disappeared somewhere in the void.

I took a step forward in the direction of the second arch and became aware of my lying body. The next moment I woke up.

Later on the same day I sat down next to Nestor in front of the house because I wanted to talk to him about that dream; he had encouraged me already before to tell him about these constantly repeating cave dreams.

Nestor said that I had dreamed an important dream. The fact that I could perceive the cave as a transparent shining structure was an indicator of the advancing dissolution of my small world in the picture. When I then told him of the rock bridge he kept silent for a moment. I thought that he had recognized the similarities with the bridge strand in the shining structure: a bridge with two arches and a free floating left end. I myself had interpreted the bridge in the dream as a projection of the connecting strand in the shining structure. But to my surprise, Nestor opened up to me that my dream was a hint at a natural bridge with that form in actual existence.

»This bridge does actually exist?« I asked.

»It doesn't only exist in the structure but also in the three worlds,« he explained. »It exists in the thoughts as a concept of the transition over into the left side, as a dream bridge in the emotional world and as a natural bridge in the sensual-material world.«

»And where is that natural bridge?« I wanted to know.

»It's where the young Emme flows through a deep and narrow canyon for the first time. We can get to it if we hike upstream alongside the river, farther then we have done so far.«

»Will we go there?«

Nestor kept silent for several minutes; obviously he was undetermined. I asked him once more and he answered that this was a decision he would leave up to me.

»Ever since you have started with the perfect restoration,« he pointed out, »you have traveled a double path: you've taken the path in your shining structure that has led you to this connecting strand, and during our hiking trips you've taken the path upstream alongside the Emme, almost all the way up to this bridge – it's both the same, there is no difference between inside and outside: whatever you do on the outer screen corresponds to your inner development; and on the inner screen you can only see that which you have already transformed into the light of consciousness.«

I looked at him questioningly.

»The moment we go to the bridge,« he explained, »there will be no turning back for you. You'll have to change over onto the other side.«

»Why? Is it dangerous to walk the bridge over to the left side?«

»I told you already that it won't be enough to walk the bridge,« he replied seriously. »You'll have to fly. When you make this change, your fixation in the right half of consciousness will be released. In doing so, an enormous amount of energy will also be released that will literally make you lose the ground under your feet. Everything else depends on your openness: if you're open enough you will fly over into the left side; otherwise you will fall into the left side.«

I told Nestor that this didn't sound particularly encouraging. He replied that my doubts were justified: indeed I could see the bridge in my shining structure and I had pondered over it and dreamed of it. These were good prerequisites for going to the bridge in the Emme Canyon. On the other hand, I was still in an incomplete state in the right half of consciousness. According to Nestor, I still distinguished too sharply between outside and inside, between that which I could perceive with my outer senses and therefore considered real, and that where my »orderly arrangements« failed so that I constantly tried to shut myself off from it. And this conflict kept me from consciously releasing all of my energy.

I thought that Nestor was exaggerating, that he was simply imputing things to me. But he reminded me that I could read my condition and my conflict directly off of Mari Egli's secretaire: there was still an unfinished spot on the bottom right-hand drawer; there were still two parts missing to finish the restoration on the hole of the inlay work.

»The moment you decide to go to the bridge there must not be any doubts, uncertainties or reluctances in you,« he said. »You must be determined to go to extremes and recognize, what the picture basically is.«

During that summer I had this dream several times. But Nestor refused any further conversation around the natural bridge. He drove home to me that talking about it was useless unless I was firmly determined to take the hiking trip to the bridge. Nestor didn't push me to make this decision, though; he didn't take the initiative to talk about it, either. This and the constant doubts of my willingness and determination finally resulted in me relativizing the alleged far-reaching significance of this dream. And that I interpreted it according to circumstances I was most concerned with at that time: for example my illusory relationship to Iris.

No matter how often I visited the young seer lady and how close I was to her, she remained as unrecognizable and inaccessible as the other bank in my dream. The bridge that would have led there disintegrated before reaching the destination – and in the same way my hopes and ideas that Iris could be more for me than a seer lady pointing the way disintegrated – the more so the closer I wanted to come to her.

Her hearty girlishness, but at the same time her immense willpower and her confounded perfection, regularly had the effect that I felt stupid about my, by comparison, primitive and naïve intentions. All my efforts to prove my value to her failed. They had to fail because, in the final analysis, I tried to get across to a seer lady that I, and only I, was the one she was searching for – a seer lady claiming of herself that she had already found the one: her own shining sphere that she could see wherever she turned her look to.

The love I felt for her gradually changed into disappointment, resentment and contempt – with just the same intensity. As I was ashamed of such feelings in her presence, I decided to stay away from her for a while. My only comfort: Iris didn't show any interest in Romeo either, that romantic rose-smelling Romand, beyond a teacher-student relationship – which obviously didn't impress him very much. Perhaps the guy had sincere intentions, after all? Or was he just too stupid to understand that she was harder than granite?

At any rate, my embitterment made me bitch about those two over and over – and I was startled what an easy time I had at that, and how much energy I could put into cynical excesses of that nature. In moments like that I had to think of Nestor's words and admonitions, that is, that a person on the path in the shining structure had, over time, quite an amount of energy at his or her disposal, and that, accordingly, they had to become more careful of what they did with that energy. Because as long as a person belonged to the right side of consciousness, it was alluringly easy to get carried away by emotional outbreaks and live out the energy as a kobold.

Of course I couldn't hide my broken heart from Nestor. Empathetically but unambiguously he made me understand that my bad feelings arose from an attempt that was bound to fail from the outset.

»You're trying to fit the hearty one into your own ideas and ideals and attempt to hold on to her in this way,« he said on this occasion. »That doesn't work. The hearty one is a seer and that means that she lives from moment to moment and doesn't care about any concepts of herself. She won't confirm any of the ideal images you're addressing her with. She is free from ideals and intentions; her only actions are for the sake of seeing.«

Nestor's reminder that Iris and I were worlds apart had something painful to me. I wanted to change the subject of our conversation but

Nestor wasn't deterred that easily. He pointed out my despondency and drove home to me that I was supposed to put the energy bound in these feelings into the whole picture so as to free myself from it. And if that didn't work, I should dance with it or do something else creative with it.

»And if that doesn't work either, I guess I have to be put in the pot«, I was griping, alluding to the Emmental Cooking Pot.

But what I originally intended as polemics made immediate sense to me the next moment: indeed I could have needed the »cooking pot« right now – in the combination fire below, water above – so as to be able to perceive the world in a fantastic way, free from all worries and depressions. When I suggested this to Nestor he laughed and replied that this was completely out of question; otherwise, I perhaps even wanted to dwell in the cooking pot in the long run. His humor was so soothing and liberating that I had to laugh, after all.

»What's happening to you is happening to all passionate people,« Nestor went on. »For these people it goes without saying that they're trying to hold on to objects, kind persons and emotional experiences. But that's a delusion because it is the attempt to hold on to things, and making them timeless thereby, that are undergoing constant change.«

»Do you think it's possible to completely refrain from this attempt?«

»Of course not. Man's nature is such that he wants to hold on to things he is concerned with. It's not about no longer wanting to hold on to anything – such a person would be just like a leaf in the wind. Rather, the solution is to hold on to that which is not subject to change, and that's the spheres and strands of the shining structure.«

»But the shining structure is also undergoing changes,« I argued and told him how the picture of my structure had changed up to this point in time: I saw new strands and dots that had formed on the periphery of my field of vision as well as around the bridge – in part only dimly illuminated but clearly perceivable.

»Your shining structure changes to the degree that you change,« he answered. »You either render it clear and luminous or blurred and dim. But a seer who is able to hold on to his last sphere in full experiences the moment: because he's not realigning his attention any longer, he's consciously extending the moment to eternity, into timelessness. And there is no change in timelessness.«

The hiking trip to the bridge was to take place a few weeks later. Before I drove up to Nestor's place on that bright sunny summer day, a Thursday, in the early morning, I stopped in front of the small grocery store in the village and bought some food.

In the store I met a friendly medium-aged man who I got into a conversation with. For a while we talked informally about the weather and the Emmental. It soon turned out that the man had remarkable knowledge of local tales and legends and mythical places in the region. According to him, magical practices had been the order of the day here, at a time when the people still paid reverence to Celtic deities like Lug, Belenus and Teutates.

The man, who wanted to be called Esus, eventually sparked my interest because he maintained that he studied the techniques of the old Celtic seers and druids – practices that eventually boiled down to astral projections, that is, a shift in their consciousness. He invited me to his house and offered me to enlighten me about these things. I agreed and came along.

His house was located outside the village, in a strikingly shadowy place on the right bank of the Emme, hidden between trees. Obviously it was a new building: the bright wood and the shining red roof tiles bore witness of that. A colorful collection of different religious, mythical and esoteric objects and symbols surrounded the house: Tibetan prayer flags had their place here just like stone towers, miniature labyrinths, hedges with bizarre forms and a huge copper kettle adorned with runes, hanging down from a wooden beam, as well as a number of sculptures with human and animal forms. Esus proudly declared that he had designed the house himself, and that it was located in a spot with particularly high energy: a former meeting place of Helvetic druids.

The rooms inside the house rendered a well-tended impression. Brass statues of Greek and Roman gods and heroes stood in line neatly and cleanly. There were glass bowls, small golden pyramids and a large amount of shimmering gemstones on the table. The walls were decorated with shadowboxes filled with all kinds of little figures, amulets, rag dolls and other things.

Esus had prepared some Ayurvedic tea for us, then he took a little chest with a golden lock out of a glass cabinet. He opened it with a key that he had hidden in a small babushka doll. Then he took a deck of playing cards out of the chest – cards with strange motives, unknown to me.

Esus declared that I – if I wanted to become a druid – had to bring my positive and negative astral energies into balance. These cards would help me do so – if one knew how to interpret them correctly.

I started to become nervous. Obviously, Esus was inclined to a naïve streak of esotericism, and my relationship to such people was quite ambivalent: my experiences on the left side of the Emme made me agree to their beliefs in general: that the world amounted to more than just the sensual-material and rational plane we could perceive with our outer senses; rather, there were secrets in hiding, and we as human beings were capable of revealing and understanding these. On the other hand, the search for enlightenment along the esoteric way often boiled down to frequent visits of weekend seminars as well as hocus-pocus with objects that were supposed to contain certain energetic qualities.

Without hesitating, the man asked me for my name. Then he took a piece of paper, did some calculation based on an attribution of the letters in my name to certain numbers and arrived at some figure. Then he summed up the digits to the cross total and took a corresponding number of cards off the deck. All this he did with the greatest of solemnity. Then he put the resulting card face down on the table, mixed the remaining ones and spread them nicely and evenly on his table. Finally he asked me to slowly sweep my »lucky hand« over the spread-out cards and select the one I could »feel«.

I told him that I wasn't really interested in things like that. But he kept insisting that I should do it so that my destiny could fulfill itself. I did him the favor.

Finally he took these two cards – the one he had counted off the deck and the one »felt« by me – and put them into my hands face up. One card showed a sort of mythical creature, an animal with disgusting claws, horns and a salivating mouth. The other card showed a small delicate plant growing in an enclosure.

Esus behaved as if he had expected something like that. According to his interpretation, I indeed had the same forces within me that were also active within him, but I still would have to develop them. He offered to teach me these things as I fulfilled the requirements to do so.

I put down the cards and tried once more to explain my viewpoint, namely that I did not see any use or benefit in practices of that kind. I tried to stay polite but the man kept talking to me insistently and wanted to persuade me by all means. In the end he even threatened with bad luck and evil if I kept resisting his instructions. To confirm this, he pointed to my hand, took it and followed the lines in my palm with one of his fingers. His »reading« resulted in the conclusion that I would never be able to live a happy life.

Meanwhile I could feel the resentment that had built up within me. At the moment I was just about to cut him down to size, I felt a liberating prickle feeling in my head.

I was surprised how simple and easy it suddenly was for me to explain him my view of things, and how calmly, but at the same time how insistently and determinedly, I went about doing it. I explained to him that, to me, a genuine development of consciousness was neither brought about by adding up numbers and letters nor by interpreting cards. The only way to really develop one's consciousness was by constantly working on one's own body, feelings and thoughts.

Esus gaped at me, stunned and speechless. Then he looked down and remained silent. He was playing nervously with his hands. When I realized what I had done I almost felt sympathy for him. Esus put the cards back into the chest and mumbled something of the sort that everybody had to go his own way. I got up, said goodbye and left him behind – I knew that I had no more place in his house.

A little while later I arrived at Nestor's place. I sat down next to him in front of the house and told him of my encounter with Esus. Nestor listened attentively to my story and laughed at the same time, as if my experience had been a complete joke.

Then he said that people on the right side of consciousness of course also established their teaching systems and passed them on to their students. In most cases, however, these teachers and masters did not intend to lead their students to autonomy and an awareness of their self, thus showing them the way to freedom; rather, they held the students in dependence of them and their teachings.

»That sounds very pessimistic,« I found. »Every teacher or master, no matter in which field, is after all convinced that he is conveying correct and useful beliefs and views of the world, isn't he?«

»Of course they are convinced of themselves,« Nestor replied, »but in most cases they are not aware of what they are doing with their students: they snatch away their bound energy, namely with the respect and admiration they demand of their students – so they are kobolds. And that's exactly what you had defended yourself against today when you felt that prickle feeling in your head.«

I looked at him questioningly.

»The prickle feeling you felt in your head was transformed aggression,« he explained. »This aggression came to the surface in a positive way: not as emotion any longer but as a sensation, a prickle feeling.

Thanks to that prickle, you didn't have to act aggressively; rather, you could stay calm and get across your viewpoint with insistence.

It's precisely through those kinds of sensations that seers are successful in putting their emotional energy into the entire picture without getting entangled in it. If you were a seer, you would have been able to enjoy the beautiful feeling of ecstasy, and you would have seen how the shining structure and the picture light up in the process.«

Today I had experienced, Nestor went on, that certain emotional states that were very intense could trigger sensations in and on specific spots of the body. Now I knew that a prickle feeling in the head meant that one's own aggression or anger was transformed in this way, and that, in addition, it could bring other people to a point where they could gain insights. A sensation in or on the torso, by comparison, indicated the energy flow of emotions such as love, joy and peace. If, on the other hand, I felt the sensation only in the lower part of the body, then the adjustment of the balance was directed to the lower planes, that is, material and sexual aspects and feelings like greed, envy, lust and jealousy.

»Due to these locally restricted sensations you will be able to understand directly why people associate love with the heart and the heart region, and why an embrace can be so hearty. And you will make the experience over and over that aggression, volition and instruction take effect through the head, and you will understand why angry people's heads turn red.«

Nestor considered this very characteristic of our existence as human beings, and with a laugh he added that, obviously, good spirits dwelled in the heart and bad ones in the brain. Then he went on to explain that the ecstasies a seer could feel in the individual regions of his body allowed him to detect energy deficits of people. According to the locality of the ecstasy, a conversation partner either had a need for material and sexual energy, for energy in the form of passionate feelings and love of the heart, or for energy in the form of mental insights and new ideas so as to advance in one's own individual development.

»So then one could, based on the locality of the ecstasies, establish a tenet of the different types of human personality,« I concluded with interest.

»That would be taking it too far,« Nestor answered. »Seers are not interested in tenets or teachings of that nature. It's enough for us to release our energy as ecstasy, obtaining direct knowledge in the process and lighting up the structure — this all by itself will bring about the state of conscious existence all people are ultimately yearning for.«

We both fell silent. When Nestor got up and went into the house I began to concentrate on my dots and strands.

The bridge strand showed virtually no motion at all, and that was something happening only very rarely. It didn't take long until I saw it light up in a horizontal position – and it struck me that it was floating just as slowly and graciously as the gigantic tube in my dream.

The thought of the dream immediately woke the memory of the prickle feeling in my head: I hadn't only felt it in my dream but in my daily consciousness for the first time when I had the argument with Esus.

From that moment on all my thoughts were circling around that natural bridge only: somehow I had the inkling that the floating of the connecting strand and the prickle feeling in my head were indicators of the time being right for the hiking trip to the bridge in the Emme Canyon.

»Floco,« Nestor called out from inside the house before I could engage in more thoughts. I believed to have heard the same sound of expectancy in his voice that I knew from my dream.

Nestor asked me something but I didn't listen to him. Now I knew that these hints pointing to my dream were no coincidence. I got up and went into the house to Nestor.

»We'll go to that bridge,« I said with a rock-firm voice.

For a while that seemed like an eternity, Nestor looked at me scrutinizingly. Immediately, his hesitation triggered a feeling of doubt in me, and I was just about to cancel the undertaking when he finally nodded in agreement. From that moment on everything went very fast and without many words: Nestor gave me some things I was supposed to pack – blankets, supplies, foodstuff for several meals, paper and empty garbage bags. Once we had packed our bags we left the house.

It was almost lunchtime when we arrived at the shallow bed of the Emme. Nestor asked me from the beginning to walk bare feet. Walking on stones did not pose a problem to me any longer as my feet had gotten used to the rough ground around Nestor's house and the stones on the banks of the Emme over the years.

Soon the hills were rising to the left and right, and the Emme became narrower and deeper. We came to a spot where the river occupied the entire space between two narrow rock faces. Here the water was too deep for us to wade through it. We packed our stuff into the watertight garbage bags and swam against the current for several minutes.

After I had gotten out of the pleasingly cool water I felt strong and refreshed. For a moment I stood there to dry off when all of a sudden I could hear a loud bang. Startled, my body reacted with a leap to the left, and in the next moment I saw what had happened: a piece of rock, the size of a football, had broken out of the rock face and hit the ground close to my right. Shocked, I looked over to Nestor, but he just laughed and found that I should save up all my flying activities for the bridge.

When we went on I frequently looked up, to be on the safe side. But soon my attention was impaired by the heat: by now, the sun stood so high up in the sky that its rays fell directly into the canyon, turning the latter into one big baking oven. I was looking in vain for shadows, and the stones were so burning hot that I had to walk in the water. But the heat impaired my concentration so much that I had an increasingly harder time to walk over the skiddy stones, covered with algae, without slipping and falling now and then.

In the afternoon we finally arrived in the place immediately in front of the bridge. Here the steep rock faces rose up perhaps seventy or eighty feet. Alongside the left face, the Emme flowed gently from a cave, narrow but high up, in the front rock face positioned crossways to the canyon. This massive rock face showed recesses to the left and right, whereas the center was bulging out in our direction, towering up to a sort of natural bridge connecting the right bank to the left.

In the meantime, Nestor had taken a seat on one of the stones. I sat down next to him and told him how surprised I was about the similarities between this natural bridge and the one in my dream.

»It is a very special bridge in a very special place,« he replied. »This place is a landmark on the path in the shining structure; it's a place of transition and reversal of the energy flow. Only very few people find their way to this place, because only very few people know of it, and even fewer make any efforts to develop their consciousness to that degree.«

Shortly after, we heard loud voices yelling. Several young adults stepped out of the darkness of the cave the Emme is flowing through. Three women and three men, who obviously had swum through this cave from the other side, were dressed in full gear and with backpacks – and they were soaking wet. They took a rest a little further away from us. When they saw us they gave us a wink and laughed. They were in a boisterous mood when they poured the water out of their backpacks and wrung out their wet clothes. Then they enjoyed their sandwiches that were just as soaking wet as their clothes. One of them blew up a beach ball, and then all of them had a blast playing with it, chasing after each other with loud screams. After a while they packed up their stuff and hiked on in the direction we had come from.

Nestor and I had silently witnessed the events and had to laugh: a special, untouched and unknown place? Not at all. Nestor wasn't impressed by this at all but pointed out that these people followed the river »down the consciousness«. Only people who let themselves get carried away by the inert mass could afford to be loaded that heavily, he found. But when I wanted to swim against the current and fly over the bridge, I had to be light and flexible.

I didn't reply anything in response to his words; instead, I looked around for an ascent to the bridge but I couldn't find any.

»How do I get up onto the bridge, at all?« I asked.

»For that problem you'll have to find a solution yourself.«

»Is there something like a hidden path?«

Nestor kept silent and made me understand that I was supposed to get up and do the search.

I took a look around. There wasn't much to see in this narrow canyon. If there was a secret path up to the bridge, I would have certainly found it soon. First I inspected the right rock face, then the left, but there were no signs of steps, caves or passages leading upward.

Then, when I turned towards the front rock face, I believed to have found the solution to the riddle: in the right recess I discovered an opening in the face, hidden behind low bushes. Obviously it was some kind of passageway. I squeezed myself through the narrow opening, but the passage narrowed down further after a few feet, making any advance impossible.

The only remaining option, in my view, was to climb up one of the two rock faces, but this was only an option for an experienced and trained climber – and certainly not for me.

I told Nestor my findings. »There must be another way leading up to the bridge,« I speculated. »Perhaps we'll have to hike back downstream alongside the Emme and look for an access around there.«

»There is no other way. You'll have to find a way right here to get up onto the bridge,« he repeated.

»Then tell me where the access is. After all, you must have experienced the same, haven't you?«

»My leap over into the left side didn't take place here – and even if it had: when taking that leap, you'll be completely on your own.«

»Goodness, am I supposed to climb up a rock face?« I called out in despair.

Nestor reminded me to pay attention to my feelings. Doubts were something I couldn't afford. Then he got up and began to build a fireplace by moving some of the stones around us into position. From a tree, probably uprooted by a strong storm and collapsed into the canyon, he picked up enough wood for the fire.

When he returned and saw me still sitting in the same place, he gave me a stern look and said I had better go and search for the ascent. Because, he explained, we would stay in this place until I had crossed the bridge.

I jumped up and searched the place once more for any steps or passages, but there was nothing of the sort. In my despair I seriously thought of climbing up one of the two rock faces. The left side was out of question because it was wet and slippery. I turned towards the right side. The round rubble stones protruding from the sandstone mass offered themselves as steps and handholds. I tried to use these stones to climb up the face but didn't get very far; when I wanted to step on the second stone, it broke out of the mass, confirming my doubts about the stability of these steps.

Nestor laughed about my awkward attempts which in turn made me angry. I blamed him of confronting me with an unsolvable task, only to make fun of me right after. I told him that I shouldn't have taken the whole thing serious from the outset, and that I would return to the house now – something that made him laugh even more.

»Sit down and relax,« he finally prompted me. »You can't afford to indulge in feelings like that.«

I sat down but the anger within me grew and heated up my entire body. Merely following his instructions already caused a feeling of strong reluctance in me. I was in a condition of powerlessness that made me escape into my thoughts: I pictured how it would be to simply take off and undermine Nestor's authority in this way. All I had to do was just pack my stuff and split.

Nestor quacked as if he wanted to calm me down with it.

»Your kobold is waking up,« he explained his quacking. »Don't let the kobold within you get the upper hand.«

»Cut out the kobolds, Nestor. This here isn't about kobolds, you know that.«

He quacked another time. I ignored him, but then he asked me to quack just like him in order to drive out the kobold, as he said.

That was the proverbial last straw that broke the camel's back. I snapped at him to stop the nonsense.

»There are no kobolds, and I'm certainly not going to quack,« I hissed.

»What's your problem?« he replied in the same harsh tone of voice. »Just a few quacks can't be that difficult.« He quacked a few times as a sort of prompt.

I was raging with anger. I didn't dare yell at Nestor, but I wanted him to feel how upset I was. If he wanted me to quack, he should now get my quack for sure: I mustered up all my anger and produced one single quack sound – but it was completely botched: my quacking rather sounded like a choked crow.

Nestor laughed loudly. He laughed so hard that he had to hold his belly. Indeed, the situation was so funny that I just couldn't help but join in his laughter. It took a while until we recovered. Time and again, one of us tried to imitate my quack sound – without success, of course, but to the repeated amusement of both of us.

The new confidence I gained from this humorous »intermezzo« kept me from giving up but made me search for options again how to get up onto the bridge. After we had a meal, I went from one end of the place to the other once again; I sat down in different spots and took a scrutinizing look at everything in the picture. In between, I practiced some physical and breathing exercises.

When dusk fell, I knew every single corner, every stone and every confounded plant in this joint – but I still hadn't found a way up. Nestor said that I shouldn't allow myself to be discouraged. Apart from that, he kept silent. It seemed as if I would have to continue my search on the next day.

It became dark, cool and damp quickly. Nestor had laid down to rest, and I couldn't see whether he was asleep or not. I had wrapped myself in a blanket and sat down facing the Emme, still trying to perceive everything in the picture.

It was a clear summer night. The Emme flowed calmly; the weak rushing sound that could be heard came from further downward. The only sounds that could be heard here were the gurgle of a small waterfall nearby and the dribble of water drops falling from the left rock face into the Emme. The individual drops produced different sounds that echoed distinctly in the narrow canyon.

I felt the tiredness in my limbs, but my thoughts were crystal clear. The longer I thought about my task, the more I arrived at the conclusion that there was no concrete solution to it. There was no way up – I would have found it long ago. There must have been a deeper reason for the purpose of the exercise: was the fact that the task was unsolvable supposed to point to something unpromising or hopeless in my life? But what could that have been? Or was it Nestor's intention that I had an encounter with my own powerlessness? That I, against my better judgment, did not give up and kept searching? Or, to the contrary, that I hadn't given up enough yet?

Gradually, the place in front of the bridge became brighter. The moon – I noticed it was full moon – rose up above the canyon and lit up its left rock face, the wet one, first, then the Emme itself as well.

I began pondering over the circumstances that led me into this absurd situation. With a slight touch of narcism, I was surprised about my courage to shoulder the ungrateful fate of one's own development of consciousness; and I admired the resoluteness with which I had pursued that goal. I speculated whether it rather was the love for my fellow man or the commitment to a higher power that prompted me and made me endure even the most hopeless situations.

»Why am I doing this?« I sighed out into the starry night.

»Because you want to be good,« Nestor replied from near the fireplace. He rolled over onto his belly and rested on his elbows. His eyes looked attentively. It was as if he had waited all the time for this precise moment.

His answer came unexpected to me, and the criticism I could hear between the lines embittered me. I voiced my disagreement.

»Why are you defending yourself against it?« he asked. »After all, that's the way it is: you want to be good – no: basically you want to be the best – and earn yourself some tender loving care in that way.«

I felt the resentment growing within me, and I wanted to make some kind of objection to it, but somehow I felt blocked.

»That's also the reason why it wasn't difficult to convince you of the perfect restoration and to motivate you, time and again, to keep practicing,« he went on. »All I had to do was spark your ambition – and you've got more than enough of that. I just had to convince you that seers were really awesome guys, and that was already enough to excite your vanity.«

My heart started pounding. I just couldn't believe what Nestor had just told me.

»You have manipulated me?« I asked stunned.

»You've got an incredible drive within you,« he answered. »You just want to be awesome. You would go pretty far in order to maintain the image of your perfect ideal personality. And I have taken care that you gain access to precisely this power. I haven't manipulated you; I have set new standards for your vanity: the perfect restoration. And in doing so, the message I got across to you was: practice the perfect restoration, and you're really awesome.«

Nestor smiled. His words were completely free of polemics or know-best. He explained all this as if he would explain a mathematical task to someone.

»And you've got the ambition and aspiration to be awesome,« he went on. »The problem with you is that, basically, it's not so important to you what exactly it means to be awesome; it's not so important to you what you have to do to be that way. Main thing is that it will be recognized and accepted by those you want to reach and get an edge over. I think with your ambition and aspiration you could have just as well become a politician or manager or colonel or professor. So now you just become a seer.« He laughed heartily.

I knew at once what he was talking about. With incredible marksmanship he had exposed a weak point within me that I now became perfectly aware of: the actual reason for my efforts and endeavors to walk the path in the shining structure.

Of course, the secretaire had long ago ceased to be the real reason for my regular visits to Nestor. I was fascinated by his knowledge and lifestyle. And I wanted to walk the path in the shining structure by all means and gain the insights and power Nestor had at his disposal. And that was what the perfect restoration ultimately aimed at.

But what it actually was that prompted me to walk the path in the shining structure was something I had always pondered over only superficially. I justified my efforts to live a life in the sense of the seers with my deep disappointment over this perverted world causing so much suffering: hypocrisy and war-mongering; famine and unrestrained gluttony; bitter poverty and unbound shopping frenzy; species extinction, global warming and arrogant carelessness; in addition, my own powerlessness that I felt when facing this crazy hustle and bustle – by no means did I want to contribute to the continuation of such a world.

But when I was honest to myself now, I had to admit that I played my role as a little cogwheel in the world's gear just the same – not out of conviction but out of a naïve craving for recognition and admiration:

indeed, fulfilling duties and adhering to rules were the reasons for my efforts and the source of my gratification. I was like a soldier: as such, I went through great pains to satisfy higher-ranking soldiers and received praise for that. This made up my sense of self-esteem. I always associated acts like these with values such as discipline, loyalty, reliability and modesty, and of course I considered it a personal strength.

It was precisely this craving for recognition and admiration that became an end in itself – showing up in the fact that I uncritically took part in many things just because it was valued by those at the top of the hierarchy determining rules and laws – and that played a crucial role when it came to my acts and decisions, as Nestor had correctly pointed out. It was an irony that it had been, of all things, my vanity, my naivety and my uncritical attitude that had made me find the path in the shining structure – a course that, in order to advance on it, I had to radically question and challenge myself, the world and its values. In other words: thanks to my idiocy, always »resolutely applied«, I was stumbling towards freedom today.

»Basically it doesn't matter at all why someone comes to walk the path in the basic structure,« Nestor went on, and undoubtedly he knew how I felt. »Some of us have been hit so hard by fate that they try to put an end to their suffering, or at least feel some alleviation, by walking this way. Others are driven by their thirst for knowledge and can't rest until they exactly know how the world ticks. You in turn belong to those who want to reach for the ultimate simply because it *is* the ultimate, and because you believe that, by attaining the ultimate, you'll become the best and the greatest.«

It wasn't important, Nestor repeated, what motives and intentions made us walk the path in the shining structure. The only important point was that we did it, and that we invested all of our energy in that. Because on the way over into the left side of consciousness, all previous motives, reasons and intentions were transformed into energy anyway, lighting up the basic structure in the process.

»By the way: do you know why seers are such awesome guys?« Nestor looked at me with glowing eyes. »Because they don't have to be awesome by all means any longer.«

I understood his humor but wasn't able any longer to relax and laugh along with him. The shame that Nestor knew me better than I myself, that he had seen me through and that he once again destroyed the illusion of a perfect and impeccable personality – all that caused my body to heat up and my heart to pound, blocking me right then and there.

But then the force of my feelings captured my body completely: the heart palpitations increased and turned into a heart race, and my body began to tremble and twitch. I tried to stay calm and not let it show, but soon the immense inner pressure forced me to uncontrolled, seemingly senseless actions: I was constantly tapping spots on my body, played nervously with my hair and made hasty gestures and movements. When I was afraid to completely lose control over my body, I jolted up and started to move around.

Driven by panic, I leaped from one foot onto the other, flailing around with my arms. I couldn't manage to concentrate until I started to breathe deeply, following the spur of the moment. This had a tremendous effect: my body awareness increased markedly, and the trembling subsided.

Now I was able to put all my attention on the body movements. Soon these became very powerful and so well coordinated that my body was moving along in perfect harmony and complete balance. I was full of activity and deeply calm at the same time. I perceived this as spontaneous dancing producing a state of delightful exhilaration.

My movements became faster but not less powerful. Completely effortless and with absolute certainty I was gliding over the stones on the bank, from one end of the place to the other and back again. I noticed how I could overcome these larger distances without further ado, how I covered a larger distance with each step – because I was so big and turned even bigger.

In contrast, the place under me became smaller and smaller – and seemed farther away as well. Whatever I looked at seemed to lengthen more and more. And as if looking through a tunnel, I now saw the place in front of the bridge in a far distance. I looked down and noticed that I moved backward alongside the Emme. The small narrow river, the small trees and the tiny stones made me laugh. Everything in the picture was ridiculously small, and I was kind of reigning over objects and laws, even the attractive force, that all had become meaningless.

Then I saw the spot where the river occupied the entire space between two narrow rock faces. After I had gotten out of the pleasingly cool water I felt strong and refreshed. For a moment I stood there to dry off when all of a sudden I could hear a loud bang. Within fractions of a second, the tunnel contracted and all objects shot in my direction with an incredible momentum. At the same time I had the feeling that I was pulled in a certain direction.

When the picture reassumed clear forms and the bang had faded away, I found myself in the middle of a natural rock bridge leading across the narrow canyon. The bridge didn't run straight over to the left bank but was wound in two horizontal arches over the water so that everyone who wanted to cross it had to walk a half circle directed to the right twice. But I was neither able to recognize the other bank nor the end of the bridge: the second arch right in front of me disappeared somewhere in the void.

I took a step forward in the direction of the second arch, and right that moment I could feel a gentle breeze stroking my face. I paused and listened. The wind ceased and it was silent again. I took another step and saw the wind blowing in the trees, and the next moment I could feel how it swirled vigorously around my body. I started to tremble and my heart was pounding.

I contained myself and stepped ahead rapidly. But each further step demanded more effort than the previous one: I had to muster up more and more strength to advance more and more slowly. And the wind became stronger and aggressive, relentlessly blowing in my direction from the other invisible end of the bridge and from above it.

When I came closer to the spot where the bridge dissolved, the pressure within me increased by leaps and bounds, soon reaching the limit of what I could bear. Here I was overwhelmed by the reality of the picture. What I perceived became the only thing existing here and now, and I understood that it was me creating this picture with each new moment: with each heartbeat new life flowed into it, and each look reinforced its reality.

Startled, I stopped in my tracks, but the reality of the picture became more immediate – and threatening: to the same degree it stretched into infinity and the eternity of here and now, it superseded my ideas and concepts of world and man. The overwhelming here and now reacted against my urge to connect up to past moments and keep up my identity. The picture left no room for my individual personality.

I felt how I began to lose control. I tensed my body at once and defended myself with all my strength against the claustrophobic containment of my self, against the merciless enforcement of the unbearable here and now, against the picture filling everything and assuming too much reality. But my panic reaction only added to the pressure in my body, and an overwhelming force began to pull me downward – I could feel that I was about to lose my consciousness. In a reflex-like response I wanted to turn around and run back to the other bank. But before I could start to move I heard a second ear-deafening bang.

The Navel

A strange couple stood on a hilltop at night in the bright full moon light. The man, wearing a long black nuns robe, a white shoulder scarf and a hood under a black headscarf, gave the woman a wild and determined look. She evaded his look and dreamily played with her hat feather. Her new shiny and clean outfit revealed that she was a huntress, equipped with hat, horn and polished shotgun.

Turned towards each other, they started to move, the man to the right, the woman to the left. She let her body glide over the mountain meadow, smoothly and elegantly, as if she didn't know about the burden of heavy boots, correctly fitting clothes and a heavy shotgun on her back. The man then answered this with precise and strong movements of his arms and legs.

For quite a while they moved about in this strange way, somewhere in between dancing and fighting. Both tried to gain the upper hand, neither acting hostile nor friendly towards each other, and without ever touching one another: because the moon, the large glowing sphere, separated man and woman: she was covered by the transparent moon; he, by contrast, was strutting in front of it. So it seemed as if none of them would carry off the victory; at best, they took turns at dominating each other. This, however, did neither keep the man in the bright nor the woman in the dark from trying to achieve that ultimate validation by engaging in more and more exceptional and fancy movements.

Soon there was an immense growth of strength within them. Time and again, the pressure built up within them, only to suddenly discharge a few moments later. The movements of the two dancers or fighters didn't appear fluent any longer but rather by jerks and jumps – until it became obvious that there wasn't only one man and one woman but several of them, moving one behind the other in transparent layers. In the back layers they appeared small and sharply focused, in the front layers larger and less focused. The actors were each only active within one layer whereas they were resting in all the others. And as if moved by an invisible hand, the lively hustle and bustle regularly jumped from one layer into the next.

The two multi-layer figures revealed all of their power now by starting to distort the picture which took on the form of two gigantic vortices: where the picture was circling counter-clockwise around the woman and threatening to disappear in a whirlpool like a black hole, the man pushed it far away from himself in the same manner but in a clockwise direction. The picture, it seemed, was directly connected to the two figures, or rather: it was created and obliterated by them. Who ever approached these two figures was attracted on the one side and repelled on the other, with an intensity like nowhere else.

When the man with his repellent forces and the woman with her attractive ones started to spin in opposite directions, and the two vortices started to move away from me, I recognized that the vortices turned out to be the two eyes of a face well known to me. These two eyes, spinning in opposite directions, produced a current that distorted the face into two halves. The right warming half repelled me; the left half attracted me and made me shiver with cold.

The face took on a life of its own and was pulled, together with the moon, to the upper left and deeper into space. From below, another face, similarly divided into two halves, moved into my field of vision, then another one and finally a last one. I could see how these faces, with their eyes spinning in opposite directions and their chins all directed towards the center, were grouping at even distances around the moon that had shrunk meanwhile. The rotations of the eyes generated four currents that now became more than clear. Two vertical currents flowed from the center upwards and downwards, and two horizontal ones moved from the left and right side towards the center with the moon disk: these impressive glowing currents produced the image of a gigantic cross.

Just as fast as this lively cross had come into existence it ceased glowing, cooled off, hardened and solidified. To the same extent, the picture darkened until I could only see the contours of what seemed to have been the cross. In reality, a human being, a man, was standing there with his feet firmly side by side and his arms stretched out horizontally.

As if petrified, he paused and remained in the middle of a large beach with two bays in half moon shape. His eyes were sweeping over the heartland in the far distance, past plain wooden buildings covered with palm leaves, past gigantic trees entwined by aerial roots, towards the untouched wooded hills. The full moon was reflected in the ocean and lit up the night. But it wasn't the moon illuminating the bright clothes of the young man but colored light.

When dull and vague sounds began to fill the still of the night, the young man released his cross position. He started to move all of his limbs, slowly, smoothly and steadily like flowing water. As such, he flowed in the midst of other dancing figures until all of a sudden the rhythmics of never-ending music started to sound. Now the dancers started to dance vividly over the white sand, strong and smooth at the same time, as if he was the music itself.

Then the fire seized him completely. Absent-minded he whirled and leaped around faster and higher, feeling ever lighter and buoyant. Putting a limit to limits, he became as light as the wind, stretched out his hand and flew above the heads of the other dancing figures down to the end of the beach, and from there back again. And always back and forth. He watched the people below him, the tiny toiling people.

But right the moment he ceased to fly and his movements calmed down, there was an ear-deafening bang. And two more. The dancer was confused. He thought of fireworks but couldn't see any colorful lights in the sky. Instead, he saw that the people around him had turned much larger with each single bang. At the same time the grown figures started to move, rave, scream wildly and laugh gleefully.

Of course he had resisted it, Nestor said. After all, he didn't want the others to be big and able to move rapidly and elegantly whereas he himself was small, with hardly any strength left. So he had started to dance again, thereby pulling the energy back into his body. Again he had turned big and the others small, and again he had been flying above the heads of the others. But when he calmed down he heard those three bangs for a second time: his energy had flown out of his body in three surges, making everyone else gigantic and him small and powerless by comparison.

»That night I left the place with mixed feelings. Yes, I had lost my size, but in turn I had vitalized the picture and the people surrounding me.« Nestor gave me a broad smile.

»What are you talking about?« I mumbled confused. »I don't understand a single word.«

He seemed uncertain of what to do with my remark.

»I'm telling you the story of my leap over into the left side,« he explained, »because you had asked me for it.«

I told him that I couldn't remember having asked him for that. I was in a lying position and wanted to sit up, but my head was hurting so that I abstained from any kind of effort.

»I rested for twelve days,«, Nestor went on. »On the thirteenth day I stepped onto the dance floor again. It happened in the same place, the *Om Beach* on the southwest coast of India; it was the sixth of January, more or less precisely twelve years ago. That night I was all filled up with the wish to fly once more. I started to move my body on the dance floor, full of energy and suspense. And it worked: I became bigger and floated above everyone else. And I overcame large distances in the wink of an eye, simply through my willpower alone.

Then I landed on the left end of the beach and stopped dancing, but there was no bang as I had expected. Instead, I experienced a wonderful feeling of energy flowing out of my body. This ecstatic experience was not limited to myself: in the course of this, trees and rocks around me became larger, more colorful, intense, and the entire environment leaped closer. I myself was shrinking like a balloon whose air was escaping.«

Nestor said that this had been the first time he had completely reversed his energy flow and put his energy as ecstasy into the picture as a whole. In doing so, his body had remained open. In return, however, he had to accept that, with each ecstasy, he had to trade his physical movements for the relaxation, and his own grandeur for the beauty of the picture.

»I permanently stayed in the left half of consciousness,« he added. »The openness of my body and the energy flowing upwards have the effect that I'm experiencing ecstasies everywhere, and that I obtain the direct knowledge about the buildup of the picture. Now I'm a seer, and I see what's happening when I put my energy into the picture as a whole: no longer do I fly towards the objects in the picture; rather, the objects, and with it the shining spheres, are being attracted by me. As such, I myself have become the center of affairs.«

He fell silent. I was still confused and tried to orient myself. It was early morning, cool and damp. I was freezing slightly, though the first rays of the sun were already shining through the trees.

Through the trees? I sat up, looked around – and realized that I wasn't down in the canyon of the Emme but on the bridge itself, in the immediate vicinity of the left bank!

In disbelief I looked over to Nestor who returned my look in a mischievous way. But then doubts crept up on me: was the dream over or was I still in the midst of it? And how could I judge this at all? I started to shake my head vigorously – something I had formed a habit of whenever I wanted to wake up from a dream by all means. My unwilling gesture made Nestor laugh.

»How did I get up on this bridge?« I called out.

Nestor looked at me in a way that seemed to signify that I myself should know the answer. I tried to recall my dream-like experiences, but I couldn't find any clues revealing to me how I had gotten up here.

»You've been flying,« he said as if it was self-evident.

I ignored his answer – if there was something I did not need at this moment, it was mystical transfigurations. Instead, I confronted Nestor with the most plausible explanation I could think of: in my extraordinary state of consciousness last night I had followed the Emme downstream to a spot where I was able to leave the riverbed on the right side behind and find a path through the woods all the way to the bridge.

Nestor knitted his eyebrows and dissented. »Leave your small world aside,« he asked me. »Last night you had very much energy at your disposal. You were capable of doing astounding things. You have overcome enormous distances – just like that.«

I paused. Nestor was indeed right that I had felt like having overcome extraordinarily large distances with just a few steps and floating high above all things. But this subjectively distorted perception still couldn't explain how I had overcome the vertical distance from the canyon bed all the way up to the bridge – which, after all, had actually taken place. I told Nestor this and gave him a dozen rational reasons why it was impossible for a human being to fly.

Nestor amused himself big time when he listened to my speculations: he had to admit that all of my objections were right, but in the end he kept claiming that I had been flying, after all.

»I'm really not in the mood for little games like that,« I told him, slightly testy.

»I know,« he answered, suddenly turning serious. »You don't have a reason, either, to be in a good mood. Look where you came round: still on the bridge. You haven't made the change over into the left side of consciousness. That's what you should think about, not about whether you've been flying or not.«

When I saw how ridiculously small the distance between me and the left bank was, I started to laugh with ostentation. »So I had no trouble flying up here, but then I couldn't make it to take the last four steps over to the other side,« I sneered. »What are you actually trying to tell me, Nestor?«

He kept silent. Finally he said it would be better to return to his house now. He gave me my backpack that he had taken along with him from down in the canyon and began to pack his things. I complained that he didn't take me serious. As I felt strong and right with my view of things, I tried to get an answer out of him.

Nestor answered my behavior with an admonishing look that hit me to the core. The façade of strength and self-righteousness disintegrated to dust from one second to the next, and both doubts and regret came up in me at once. I became aware that I had allowed myself to get carried away by my feelings in an extraordinarily strong way. To recover myself, I did what Nestor asked me to do. Silently we left the spot.

Around lunchtime we arrived at Nestor's house. I withheld my questions on the entire way back, and Nestor had remained silent as well. But now that I could have asked him, I felt so exhausted from the stresses and strains that I laid down at once and slept until the evening.

After I had gotten up I was looking for Nestor. I found him in the kitchen where he had prepared green beans and potatoes, scalloped with cheese, for us. After dinner he wanted to hear everything from me that I had experienced subsequent to my dancing. I described to him what I still could recall.

»You definitely were deep in the left side,« Nestor interpreted my visions. »You had the intensity of a seer but not the openness and awareness. Otherwise you wouldn't have seen people and crosses but some large shining spheres in specific constellations.«

»Then why did I see all these things?«

»Because you had lost reference to the outer screen, and your small world on the inner screen still has too strong an effect on you. It had led you to believe that you saw forms and colors in places where there were, in actuality, shining spheres.«

Seized by a sudden feeling of reluctance, I doubted Nestor's explanations. I asked him why, of all things, it had to be spheres, and why my perceptions were wrong. I wanted to know from him how he could assume the right at all to judge experiences of such a subjective nature as if he was the only authority far and wide capable of issuing and determining the truth.

»I'm a seer,« he replied calmly. »I can see every day how the picture looks in the left-sided consciousness: both inner and outer screen are intense and immediate but free from all kinds of visions and daydreams – on my way I had transformed those into the light of consciousness. And all that remained are these huge glowing spheres allowing a recognition of the principle of the shining structure, with the small world emerging and vanishing on its brims.

You, on the other hand, were only briefly over in the left side. You haven't seen the enormous energy over there as light of consciousness but interpreted them as objects and figures you know from your everyday life. That's why you didn't wake up on the left side of the Emme but still on the bridge.«

»Merely four steps away from the left bank,« I smiled at his stubborn attitude.

»This is about more than merely four steps,« he replied seriously. »You were not able to overcome yourself. You're not ready yet for the left side of consciousness.«

After we had kept silent for a while Nestor urged me to stay at his place for a few more days. Because, even if my leap had not been successful, I was still in a highly energetic state. That, according to him, was both a chance and a hazard.

»The left side of consciousness has never been closer than right now,« he said with a mysterious tone of voice. »If you can make it in the next few days to completely wake up in your emotional body, then you are, and you will, stay here on the left side. Watch out for everything you do with this energy: if you let yourself go, you're going to maul yourself as kobold.«

I spent two more days and nights at Nestor's place. He was right insofar as I was indeed in an extraordinarily energetic and clear state. And I managed to wake up as well – but not in the way Nestor expected it.

The »messed up« leap had demonstrated to me in all clarity that the promises of a left side, where everything supposedly was bright and beautiful, were nonsense. To me, Nestor's view that I should have seen glowing spheres instead of the visions I had was nothing else but a subterfuge so as to keep me at it.

I didn't even doubt that I had been in an extraordinary state of consciousness in that night – a state in which a person can have experiences that are difficult to grasp with the mind. Neither did I doubt that physical peak performances might be possible in states like that, like dancing for hours and making huge leaps. But I held that these abilities – improved yet in all cases limited by natural laws – and the visions that showed up subsequently, were the utmost a human being was capable of.

But what was the point of having such abilities? All these nicer and higher states ended as fast as they had begun. And at best, they led me to believe in a delusory wonderland with no permanent values to be found in it. Instead, they had a disintegrating effect on my personality and most probably a damaging one on my body as well.

With this newly gained clarity, and authorized by my own long-time experience, I began to cast doubts on the perfect restoration in its fundamentals. I didn't reject the possibility of developing one's consciousness as such, but I seriously questioned the approach of the perfect restoration that I considered precarious, even presumptuous.

Because in my view, developing one's consciousness had to do with letting go and surrender. The seers around Nestor, however, didn't leave it at calmly sitting down, switching off, meditating, closing the eyes and focusing on the inner world. Their way was precisely not about coming down and relaxing. Rather, Nestor tried to get across to me over and over that these aspects were the hard-won fruits of permanent work that had to be done beforehand. The first thing that had to be done was to raise the intensity, that is, the increase of energy metabolism and inner pressure. For that purpose, the person practicing had to assimilate much energy by ingesting high-quality food, doing breathing exercises and absorbing sunlight.

But here was exactly the point where the perfect restoration, in my eyes, didn't add up: because the pickup of energy was associated with wishes and egoistic motives; the person practicing had to draw the energy off the world and claim it for himself, for one's own body. Even though Nestor had emphasized more than once that seers did not use this energy in a selfish way but rather transformed it and lit up the picture and the basic structure with it, the fact remained that the individual person had to be moved into the center of focus first. In other words: one had to be downright selfish first of all in order to arrive at unselfish altruism at all.

And speaking about »unselfishness«: the ecstasy, as »unselfish« – because »freed of intentions« – release of energy into the picture as a whole, beautified and vitalized the individual picture of the seer at best – but what benefit were others supposed to have from that? How did society benefit from that? Society in turn had to supply the products capable of meeting the seers' high demands because they were no ascetics. They were choosy when it came to their food, their living environment and their material basis of life in general: they were ingesting high-quality food in sufficient amounts; they lived in nice wooden houses out in the green, far away from stress, noise and bad smells; and some of them even owned cars.

When it came to their »mental« demands, seers were again every-thing else but modest and frugal: they penetrated »layers of conscious-ness«, dissolved a host of »small worlds«, and with their immense will-power they developed »inner senses« that allowed them to directly rec-ognize, time and again, the »basic structure of the picture« and thus the »origin« of our everyday world in their »seeing«. So, all in all they as-sumed for themselves the position of having found the »truth« in and by themselves. What I was missing in the seers' attitude was a certain mod-est or frugal character as well as at least some concessions to reality.

Nestor, whom I confronted with my insights, wasn't willing to en-gage in a conversation about the approach of the perfect restoration. Instead, he pointed out to me that – with these values of restraint and modesty that I suddenly preferred over the perfect restoration – I had fallen back into the old pattern of my education: both my distinctive Christian education and my scientific training promoted such values – because both were systems setting limits to the independence and im-mediate cognitive faculties of an individual. So if I wanted to insist on the limits of human cognitive capabilities and adapt a modest, frugal and humble attitude, I should become an abbot or a professor.

The fact that he didn't accept my attempt to oppose the seers' pre-sumptuous claims, with regard to cognitive faculties, to an ideal of con-sciousness development closer to reality, was something that further estranged me from him and embittered me on top. In my opinion it was about time to put in some distance and turn my back on the Emmental for a while – or forever.

Therefore, on the third day I wanted to drive back to Bern, but I wanted to stop over at the natural bridge to take another look at it. My intention was to bring the events back to my mind in an unhurried way, and I hoped to get a more realistic picture of the »leap over into the left side«.

This time I didn't walk alongside the Emme but cut my way through the forest where I arrived at the natural bridge much faster. When I arrived there I sat down and enjoyed my triumph over Nestor who had claimed that there was no other, more direct, way to this place.

The pleasant feeling of satisfaction made me find other examples of situations and events that Nestor was mystifying in order to confirm his perfect restoration with it, but which didn't conform to real circum-stances. These were explanations and interpretations that no rational-minded person could take serious.

For example, Nestor had a way of correlating the inner and outer world in an imaginative manner: as such, the path in the shining structure was supposed to be analogous to the way alongside the Emme; or the intensity of afterimages was supposed to give information about the intensity of the object looked at; or the energy in one's own body raised the level of energy in the environment, and what's more, the seers' energy even moved the elements in the picture – all of them subjective sensations and assertions lacking precise derivations and explanations.

But what took the biscuit was that Nestor was bold enough to claim that the eye complaint *mouches volantes* was an object of meditation and an indicator for the degree of a person's development of consciousness. This didn't only contradict any and all medical studies on the subject of *mouches volantes* but plain common sense as well. In this way, Nestor outright negated material reality, but what was far more worse: he made fun of thousands of people concerned, even mocking and ridiculing them: the more opaque the vitreous was, according to him, the higher was the state of consciousness of that person. And following that line all the way: the more diseased and blind a human being was, the more enlightened and perfect he was supposed to be!

I enjoyed taking a realistic and critical look at the inconsistencies of Nestor's »perfect restoration«; I took pleasure in depriving his »shining structure« of its shine by rationally reflecting on the issue. And it felt good to not just dissolve the »small world« in the »picture« but to dissolve the »picture as a whole« in the fire of rationality at the same time. It was like a little release.

The more I did this, the stronger, more independent and mature I felt. Because I realized how much I had gotten used to Nestor's yakety-yak over the years, how much I had tolerated his explanations, eventually even making them my own. Actually he was nothing but a full-time esoteric. Obviously he could afford to deal with detached and otherworldly issues, far away from the real problems of our society, that at best inspired the utopian fantasies of a small minority of happy hunky-dory characters.

I was free. I didn't sit on a materialized mystical connecting strand linking up the two sides of consciousness; rather, I was sitting on a rock, a natural bridge, that had formed over thousands of years by the natural process of erosion. And I could cross this rock formation any time and in any way I wanted because there was no substantial difference at all between the right and the left bank.

With the goal in mind to walk the talk and take the last four steps to the other side, I got up and walked over to the left bank. But before I got there I suddenly became aware of the paradox of my intention: wasn't the active and compulsive attempt to rebut Nestor's myths already proof of how deeply immersed I was in these myths, after all? Didn't my behavior indicate an uncertainty, still considerable, about what I just had seen through with my mind? Wasn't I free, after all?

Full of doubt I stopped in my tracks. When I noticed that I had once again stopped another four steps away from the left bank, I was stunned and speechless. I tried to dismiss this fact as pure coincidence, but the attempt was overshadowed by the certainty that this other mystic reality I had cultivated in all these years still had a strong effect on me: it didn't only affect my thoughts and feelings but even my physical movements.

All the compulsions, restrictions and limitations I was stuck in entered my mind now with total clarity – not just those that I had imposed on myself so as to create a mystical world but also those everyday compulsions, restrictions and limitations that always prompted me to create that mystical world again in order to escape a too rational, too self-complacent and too callous world without a higher sense. I realized that I was nailed down on this bridge – precisely in the spot where I was standing now. It was impossible for me to simply turn around and walk back, back into that perverted mechanical world I tried to escape from. But neither was I able to take those last four steps towards the other side of the bridge because they were, like Nestor had said, more than I could overcome at this moment. I understood that I was on my way, and that I didn't have any other choice than to reach the left bank, that left side of consciousness.

This irony made me sneer: all that this striving for freedom could produce was bondage, constraint and powerlessness; all that the perfect restoration could offer was perfect restriction. I felt bitter mockery spreading as a sensation throughout my body, creating an unbearable tension within me. With an abstruse joy I was wallowing in this mockery, and the pressure increased further – until I noticed that it didn't only have an effect within my body but that it also reached me from the outside. In fact I was downright repelled by a force that seemed to come from above the bridge.

I looked upstream and could feel the pressure now hitting me from the front. It was so strong that I had to brace myself against it so as to not be thrown off the bridge. But right the moment when I felt how the inner pressure built up directly under my skin, stretching it to the point of pain, as if something was just about to break out of me, I was hit by an immense shock wave throwing me far backwards.

In those short moments when the momentum lifted me up, I could recognize the canyon of the Emme and the bridge in front of me as two huge glowing transparent tubes stretching vertically and horizontally across the entire field of vision. This sight was connected to a last vague notion of clarity and freedom.

Then, however, when I lost further altitude while still being thrown back, my skin ripped in a thousand spots, and hair was growing out of my body in tufts. My hands and feet crinkled up, my nails became pointed and razor sharp. My ears began to deform and started to hurt. My lips dried out and burst open. My tongue became coarse and sticky. In panic I wanted to yell but all I could get out were inapprehensible non-human sounds.

To the same degree that the pressure from the front ceased, the picture changed its appearance: the bright tubes solidified and turned opaque. I found myself in the passage of a cave, still being thrown back. The pressure ceased further and the passage became darker and narrower. When I finally came to a standstill I was cowering in a muggy cave, sparsely lit and quite low.

»Floco,« I heard an expectant voice, and at that moment I became aware of my body resting in a lying position.

»Floco«, Nestor said again. He stood next to my bed and looked at me questioningly.

»What?« I asked confused. I looked out the window and realized that it was already dawning.

»Everything okay with you?« he asked.

»Yes – why?«

»You've been quacking loudly all along. Just like a duck.« He suppressed a laugh and left my room.

Later on the same day I sat down next to Nestor in front of the house because I wanted to talk to him about that dream; he had encouraged me already before to tell him about these constantly repeating cave dreams.

Nestor said that I had dreamed an important dream. The fact that I could perceive the cave as a transparent shining structure was an indicator of the advancing dissolution of my small world in the picture. When I then told him of the rock bridge he kept silent for a moment. I thought that he had recognized the similarities with the bridge strand in the shining structure: a bridge with two arches and a free floating left end. I myself had interpreted the bridge in the dream as a projection of the connecting strand in the shining structure. But to my surprise, Nestor opened up to me that my dream was a hint at a natural bridge with that form in actual existence.

»This bridge does actually exist?« I asked.

»It doesn't only exist in the structure but also in the three worlds,« he explained. »It exists in the thoughts as a concept of the transition over into the left side, as a dream bridge in the emotional world and as a natural bridge in the sensual-material world.«

»And where is that natural bridge?« I wanted to know.

»It's where the young Emme flows through a deep and narrow canyon for the first time. We can get to it if we hike upstream alongside the river, farther then we have done so far.«

»Will we go there?«

Nestor laughed loudly so that I believed I had said something totally wrong.

»No,« he then replied. »We're not going to repeat that for now. You couldn't make it over to the left side. In addition, the bridge has repelled you and you have turned into a kobold at the same time. Those are clues telling us that you're not ready yet.«

His words confused me. I knew that he referred to my dream. But at this moment I thought he was talking about an event that had actually happened. He deprived me of the opportunity to get to the bottom of this feeling, because he started to talk about the significance of the bridge.

»Ever since you have started with the perfect restoration,« he pointed out, »you have traveled a double path: you've taken the path in your shining structure that has led you to this connecting strand, and during our hiking trips you've taken the path upstream alongside the Emme, almost all the way up to this bridge – it's both the same, there is no difference between inside and outside: whatever you do on the outer screen corresponds to your inner development; and on the inner screen you can only see that which you have already transformed into the light of consciousness.«

I looked at him questioningly.

»The moment we go to the bridge,« he explained, »there will be no turning back for you. You'll have to change over onto the other side.«

»Why? Is it dangerous to walk the bridge over to the left side?«

»I told you already that it won't be enough to walk the bridge,« he replied seriously. »You'll have to fly. When you make this change, your fixation in the right half of consciousness will be released. In doing so, an enormous amount of energy will also be released that will literally make you lose the ground under your feet. Everything else depends on your openness: if you're open enough you will fly over into the left side; otherwise you will fall into the left side.«

I told Nestor that this didn't sound particularly encouraging. He replied that my doubts were justified: the experiences had shown me that I was still situated too stably in my layer of consciousness. So when attempting to reach the left side of consciousness, all I experienced were merely visions instead of seeing that which was the only thing significant: a certain constellation of huge shining spheres.

When he looked into my sobered face he smiled. »Don't worry. You'll get your chance. Time and again.« Another time he engendered my distrust by laughing long and hard.

»What is it about these spheres in the left side?« I finally asked him.

»These spheres are located close to the source point of the shining structure. They produce a breakdown of the elementary power into four energy flows determining our thinking, feeling and our physical existence. Through them we are capable at all to recognize the picture and arrange the objects within it. To a seer, seeing these spheres directly means to obtain direct knowledge of the buildup, nature and essence of the picture.«

Nestor took off his old hat and stroke through his hair. »Above all, though, you'll find the *navel* of the shining structure deep in the left side of consciousness. It's the one sphere you're directly connected with. The danseuse has described it to you as *the last hurdle* – as a mountain you'll have to overcome so as to get to the spring of the Emme.«

He explained that the seers tried to overcome the last hurdle, that is, to become one with their navel while being fully conscious. To achieve that, our physical energy, our feelings and thoughts, to wit, our entire personality, had to be transformed into energy and put into the picture as a whole. In this process, spanning over years, we became smaller and smaller and the navel came closer and turned larger – so large that we had sufficient space in that sphere.

»What happens when we arrive at our navel?« I asked.

»Once you've become one with this sphere, there will be no more duality for you. You'll see the picture as a whole and experience the freedom of a seer: conscious being, the ecstasy and the direct knowledge connected to it.«

I told Nestor that this freedom did indeed sound very tempting, but the price to be paid for that was extremely high. If we had to trade ourselves, our own personality, for that navel and that freedom, then this way was a very unattractive one.

»It's not about attractive or unattractive,« Nestor replied. »The point is that we don't have any alternatives at all in this world. We are all being attracted by our navel like by a black hole. I can see that it is always the same sphere coming my way as soon as I relax and my energy flows into the picture. No matter how much I try to concentrate on other spheres – every time it is this sphere, my navel, moving into the center of my field of vision.«

Nestor pointed out that the navel was the ultimate goal of all human endeavor anyway. Because no matter in what direction we looked – it was always this sphere we had in front of our eyes. And when physicists were looking for their so-called »Theory of Everything«, or when love-crazed people were searching for their counterpart, and even when fashion conscious people were looking for the *dernier cri*, then these people were actually yearning for unification with their navel. Just the fact that right-sighted people lived in the diversity of the picture, keeping their navel at great distance, produced the illusion in them that they were chasing after objects and people.

»The navel is the gateway to eternity,« he went on. »Once we have reached this sphere, we'll see what it is that we fall into every time we go to sleep, but also when we die. But while ordinary people go unconscious when they fall asleep or die, the seers try to reach the navel already in their lifetime and enter into the picture as a whole from there with full consciousness. If a human being is successful at becoming one with his navel only once, and if he catches a glimpse of what's behind it, then he has, I would say, fulfilled his purpose in life.«

Nestor fell silent and began to play with his hat. I admired the matter-of-factness and calmness with which he was talking about the ultimate goal of the seers. His words had triggered a strong feeling of desire within me that prompted me to look at my small dots in the left side and search for the navel.

The day was perfectly suited for seeing: the sky was covered with a fine and even layer of mist that made the sunlight shine through diffusely. Only above the Hohgant the mist condensed to thick fog, reaching for the peak of the mountain. And dark thunderclouds, floating deep around the mountain ridge, started to pile up more and more. It seemed as if heaven and earth had approached each other so as to get in touch.

I, for my part, couldn't establish any connection between the worldly here and now and higher planes of existence: after I had let the dots and strands of the left side flow downward as far as possible, I could see the uppermost and hindmost dots in the left side. It was an accumulation of an indeterminable number of tiny spots floating in the picture without any recognizable order. They were hardly flowing anymore, but still they were difficult to see because minimal eye movements were already enough to fling them out of the field of vision. So with very careful movements I was able to keep them in my field of vision and renew their weak luminosity each time they were about to sink down and fade out. In the long run, though, my concentration on these tiny spots failed.

After a while Nestor began to speak. As if he had known about my troubles, he admitted that the attempt to become one with one's own navel was actually about the most difficult undertaking a human being could perform at all. Because, on the way there we would lose our fixation in the right half of consciousness and therefore our individual personality as well. On the one hand, we would be released into freedom so that we could project our picture onto different levels of consciousness, according to the intensity. But on the other hand, it also meant that there wouldn't be a solid and clearly defined world any longer that we could hold on to. It also meant that we would be seized by the most diverse and contradictory thoughts and feelings, but we had to watch out not to cling to them or get stuck with them. And the higher our intensity rose, that is, the closer we came to duality in our seeing, the more extreme the opposites in our thoughts, feelings and actions would become.

»The price for the absolute freedom of our consciousness is to live this self-inflicted duality with full awareness and keep it in balance. Only in this way can we hope to reach the navel of the shining structure. But when we have become one with this sphere and see the picture as a whole, then we have overcome duality in our consciousness. Then we'll go through the world and take joy in its diversity without being compulsively attached to it emotionally or mentally – because we can see that, in the final analysis, everything goes under the same hat. And that's exactly what seers basically do: they bring everything, the entire world, under one hat.«

He laughed and put on his hat with verve. But he pulled it down into his face so deeply that he had to lift his face so as to be able to look at me, radiating like a small child at the same time:

»Got the hat already.«

Lightning Source UK Ltd.
Milton Keynes UK
UKHW040725010421
381306UK00011B/17